The earth growled.

"RUN!" ELIAS'S SHOUT HIT HER A SPLIT SECOND BEFORE another noise rent the air, so loud she couldn't locate the source, could only feel the rumbling beneath her feet. A mix of thunder and heavy artillery and the world ripping open.

The ice. The ice was finally breaking, and she had nowhere left to run.

A series of pops like rapid gunfire sent her skidding to the side. In flashes, she took in sky, mist-wrapped trees, Elias's moving silhouette. Water, dark and churning, licked at the ice she'd been standing on seconds before. Faster than she could fathom, her body slithered down what was now a slide. With dizzying swiftness, the ice seesawed back, sent her careening up, then down again, tumbling toward the roiling water, at the mercy of the elements and fate, like a die being thrown over and over.

Everyone is talking about *Whiteout*

"Scorching hot and beautifully emotional. A pulse-pounding, edge-of-your-seat read."

—Lori Foster, *New York Times* bestselling author, for *Whiteout*

"Strong heroines, sizzling tension. Heart and heat abound! Do yourself a favor and start this book early—you won't be able to sleep until you finish."

—Molly O'Keefe, *USA Today* bestselling author, for *Whiteout*

"Sexy, smart, and tough characters in a beautifully ice-cold landscape will grab you from the first line and keep you along for a wild ride to the very end."

—Rebecca Zanetti, *New York Times* bestselling author, for *Whiteout*

"What a thrill ride! The action is nonstop—I don't think I took a breath until I finished."

—Katie Ruggle for *Whiteout*

"An exhilarating story of survival and love against all the odds. I couldn't put it down!"

—Katee Robert for *Whiteout*

"The gripping characters, fresh writing, unique setting, and a villain as cold as the Antarctic itself make this a fiercely enjoyable story."

—Toni Anderson, *New York Times* and *USA Today* bestselling author, for *Whiteout*

"A thrilling chase across the desolate and changeable beauty of Antarctica. Adriana Anders is a master."

—Maria Vale for *Whiteout*

"Anders launches a new series with a bang… Heart-pounding sexual, emotional, and physical tension keep the suspense high and the pages turning."

—*Kirkus Reviews* for *Whiteout*

"Anders strikes an impressive balance between romance and page-turning suspense. Readers who crave high-stakes action mixed in with their romance will be taken by this consistently surprising adventure."

—*Publishers Weekly* for *Whiteout*

"With suspenseful scenes and steamy moments that offer heart-warming relief to the story's tension, this book will entrance lovers of romantic suspense."

—*Library Journal* for *Whiteout*

Also by Adriana Anders

BLANK CANVAS
Under Her Skin
By Her Touch
In His Hands

SURVIVAL INSTINCTS
"Deep Blue" in the *Turn the Tide* anthology
Whiteout

UNCHARTED

ADRIANA ANDERS

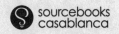
sourcebooks
casablanca

Published by Sourcebooks Casablanca, an imprint of Sourcebooks
P.O. Box 4410, Naperville, Illinois 60567-4410
(630) 961-3900
sourcebooks.com

Printed and bound in Canada.
MBP 10 9 8 7 6 5 4 3 2 1

To those who risk everything in the fight for justice.

CHAPTER 1

LEO OPENED HER DOOR TWO INCHES AND SQUINTED, BLINDED by daylight. She dropped her eyes, surprised to see a tiny, wizened old woman standing on her porch.

"We've got a problem," said the woman.

"You the one who's been bashing at my door?" Leo asked.

"Sure am."

"Then we *do* have a problem."

"Let me in there. I need to talk to you." The woman put a gnarled hand to the solid pine and pushed. "It's urgent."

Leo didn't give an inch, though she did let the hand holding her weapon at her side drop. Of all the days for the village elder to bust in on her privacy, it had to be today, when she was alone, without her teammates as backup, and exhausted from a night of vomiting. She cast a quick, helpless look outside. "Um, I don't think that's a—"

"I'll give you his location." The woman's voice was a low, raw whisper that sliced through Leo's nausea.

This time when she took in their surroundings, her gaze was razor-sharp, her weakness forgotten. She tightened her hand on the Glock. "Whose location?"

"The man's. The one you're out there looking for every day, you and your friends." The woman's eyes flicked to Leo's face before she shoved at the door again. "Let me in."

This conversation wasn't one they should have out in the open, even if Leo hadn't detected anyone lingering in the forest. She stepped back, opening her door wide and visually searching the woman for weapons as she entered. Everyone and her grandma was packing around here—she spotted the telltale bulge at the old woman's back—*literally*.

The stranger waddled into the small space, taking in the pine-clad interior as if she'd never seen the inside of the Schink's Station Lodge's cabins before. Uninvited, she walked over to the picture window and drew open the curtains, allowing too much light into the darkened room.

For a quiet moment, she stared at the view—sparkling lake ringed by evergreens, the crystal-tipped mountains beyond it as serene and surreal as a painted backdrop. The first time Leo had seen this place, she'd hummed "The Hills Are Alive" for so long, her teammates had threatened to jump out of the bush plane to shut her up.

"Cozy." The woman settled into the cabin's single armchair with a sigh. "Daisy did a good job in here."

"Oh, come on. Are we really gonna talk about interior desi—"

"You look like hell."

"Well, I was *sleeping* when you woke me up."

The nosy old lady looked at the empty trash can by the bed. "You pregnant or something?"

Leo shot her a glare. "Something." Probably food poisoning, maybe a stomach bug. Either way, it was none of her business.

"You sound stuffy; some yarrow steam'll unclog you right as—"

"I'm good, thanks." The woman had dropped her bomb and now she wanted to talk local remedies? "Let's get back to what you were saying." Leo couldn't help adding a "ma'am," to that. There were some habits she'd never lose.

"We know what you're doing here. You and your guys. We know who you're looking for."

Leo's pulse kicked into high gear. "I don't…" Forget it. After her night spent hugging the toilet, she was too weak to keep her reactions under wraps. And this was too important to play dumb. She had taken her teammates out on daily grid searches of the rough terrain surrounding Schink's Station, Alaska, for the past week and a half, and they hadn't located a damned thing. If this woman could tell her where to find Campbell Turner—and the virus he'd stolen from Chronos Corp—then she'd take it.

Instead of prevaricating, which was obviously irritating the woman anyway, Leo sank onto her unmade bed, set her shaking elbows on her shaking knees, set her heavy head in her hands, and gave the woman every ounce of her attention. "Tell me where to find him."

"Promise something first."

"Listen, lady, I *just* got to sleep after puking up my guts all night. I don't even know your name and you're already making demands."

"Amka. Everybody calls me Old Amka." The woman's prune face folded into what could have been a smile. Or a pained grimace. "For obvious reasons."

"Okay, Amka. Where can I find him? Where's Campbell Turner?"

"Turner." Amka blinked. "Right." The woman's lined lips worked for a few seconds, her skin folding and unfolding like an origami swan.

"What?"

"Need you to promise me something. If I give you his…uh, *Turner's* location, you've got to fly him out. Now. Before—"

"Fly? Now? I can't fly like this." Leo massaged her temple with one hand. "I can hardly see straight."

"You've got to." The woman looked out the window again, and Leo realized with a jolt that she wasn't admiring the view. She was looking for something, searching the cloudless sky, anxiety in every deeply etched line of her body. "Today." When their gazes met, the woman's dark eyes were so desperate, Leo couldn't look away. "Right now."

"The last aircraft took off for Anchorage this morning, with my teammates on board," Leo said, barely breathing. "No planes here."

"Might have one you can use." She leaned forward. So did Leo, caught up in this now—not just the excitement of finally catching a break, but the palpable apprehension that the woman exuded. Something was happening. Finally, a lead in their search for Campbell Turner and the virus. "Promise you'll pull my godson out. Promise me."

Leo pictured the fifty-three-year-old man she and her team were after, and wondered just how old this woman was. "Campbell Turner's your godson?"

Amka met her eyes head-on and held them. "He's the man you want."

"Why now? Why this very minute? What happened?"

And then, as if conjured by the question, a sound reached Leo's ears, so familiar and out of place in the wilds of Alaska that it sent shivers skittering across her overheated skin. She stopped abruptly, head tilted. "Hear that?"

Old Amka gave her a funny look before turning to eye the mountains in search of whatever it was she'd heard. A few seconds later, she nodded slowly. "Doesn't sound like a plane."

"It's not. That's a helicopter," said Leo, her voice hard, sure. "Thought they weren't allowed in the park."

"*It's them.*"

Another wave of chills racked her body. "Who? It's *who*?"

"People comin' for him." Shaking her head, Old Amka stood and hobbled to the window, where her fingers gripped the sill so hard, her umber skin went white at the knuckles. "My cousin called me from Juneau. Now, Janet's nosy, so she—"

"Cut to the chase."

Her shoulders slumped. "We're too late."

"Too late for what?" Those were twin turboshaft engines approaching. Leo would know that sound anywhere, no matter how out of place. There weren't all that many reasons for that type of equipment to visit these particular sticks. The only ones allowed were Search and Rescue aircraft, but she doubted that was what headed their way.

Only one entity would send this kind of airpower here right now: Chronos Corporation. One of the biggest pharmaceutical companies in the world.

Earlier in the year, she and her teammates had just barely survived a confrontation with a Chronos-funded team of scientists and mercenaries tasked with stealing and testing a deadly virus found under the ice in Antarctica. What they still didn't know was what Chronos wanted with the virus, or why the clinical vaccine trials they'd planned to run had been kept secret.

Today, there were but two known samples of that virus—the one that she and her team had rescued from Antarctica and the one stolen a decade earlier by Campbell Turner.

The only certainty in this whole affair was that Chronos would stop at nothing to get ahold of the virus. Now, it was up to her team to get to Turner before the other guys.

"What happened, Amka? I want details."

From the west, the twin engines droned closer, louder, overwhelming in their intensity, the rhythmic thump of rotors thrumming through Leo's bones like the vibrating call of a tuning fork. It sent her blood pumping one way and her brain spinning another.

She knew helicopters the way she knew her family, complete with all the love and guilt and dread of those intimate relationships. Right now, her belly flipped with a confusing mix of craving and disquiet.

"A team stopped to refuel at the airfield in Juneau. Janet said they're clearly paramilitary. Got top-level clearance to fly here. My cousin overheard them talking about coordinates. Exactly where El—" She snapped her mouth shut. "They'll hunt him down." Shaking her head, she sank back into the chair, shoulders bowed. "It's too late. I got here too late."

Never too late, Leo thought. *Not while there's breath in my body.* She hadn't come all the way to Alaska to give up her search the second the opposition arrived. Her team had worked too hard to stop now. They had a job to do—a virus to retrieve, a corporation to stop. People had already died for this. It had to end.

Leo wouldn't admit defeat until she'd done everything in her power to keep Chronos Corp from getting its clutches on Campbell Turner and the virus.

But that aircraft sounded awfully close. "Wait. Is he here, in Schink's Station?" Wouldn't it be ironic if Turner had been hiding in town this whole time, right under their noses? Instead of wasting days looking for the guy, she and her teammates could be back at base, questioning the man and safeguarding the sample. Leo's pulse picked up at the possibility.

"No. Why?"

"They're headed this way." Letting the excitement in, Leo cocked her head and closed her eyes. "They have to fly over town to get to him?"

"Not at all. No, he's east of here." Like a flash, Amka was up and back at the window. "Think they're landing at the airfield?"

There was no denying it. The helicopters weren't carrying on to some far-off location. They were *here*. In Schink's Station. "Affirmative." A thrilling shot of adrenaline blasted through Leo, pushing the exhaustion and lightheadedness right out of her system. *Too late, my ass.* She'd fly to Turner and get him out, right under the Chronos team's noses. Just like she'd done in Antarctica. It was what she did best after all.

And with enemies as ruthless as Chronos, there was no time to lose.

She yanked her pajamas off and started getting dressed, uncaring that she was naked in front of a stranger.

Amka eyed her. "Gonna need more clothes than that."

Without hesitating, Leo grabbed extra base layers and wiggled her way into the underwear. "Why's that?"

"You'll see."

"I'll see." She snorted. "Great. Just great. Famous last words, right?" Once she'd strapped on her weapons and put on every layer of clothing she could come up with, including her thick parka, she grabbed her flight bag, shoved water and some painkillers inside, and went to the door. "Think I can reach him before they catch up to me?"

"No." The woman's smile wasn't exactly heartening. "But you can try."

———

It was time to get a taste of civilization, Elias Thorne finally acknowledged as he poured boiling water over the coffee grounds he'd scraped from the bottom of the can.

Clicking his tongue, he set Bo's bowl on the rough log floor and watched her attack her dried salmon as if she hadn't eaten the very same thing every evening for the past nine months. If only he could drum up that amount of gusto. For anything. How long had it been since he'd felt real excitement?

Contentment, maybe, but actual enthusiasm? Not just months. Years.

Once the coffee finished dripping, he grabbed the steaming cup and headed out onto the bare-bones front porch, where the simple railing, roof, steps, and chair had all been made with his own two hands.

Admiring his work no longer stirred up so much as a spark of pride. He felt nothing.

With a sigh, he leaned against the railing, sucked in a deep coffee-laced breath, and warmed his hands on the thick, chipped enamel, eyes on the stream far below. The ice had started its spring symphony—a precursor to the massive breakup that would hit any day now—its low, musical crackling as intricate and varied as an orchestra tuning up for the big show.

The sound plucked its way up his vertebrae to sing along every one of his nerves until he thought he'd lose it. He should go down and check the lake, make sure he could cross it before breakup started and he got stuck here for another week at least. He could go around the lake, of course, but that trek took days.

He exhaled and slugged back more of his too-weak, too-hot coffee, craving the burn. Craving *anything* to interrupt the rhythm of the hours. Months. Years.

Eleven years of this eternal cycle.

The ice popped again, so loud that it echoed off the cliff face. He hadn't planned on leaving for Schink's Station today, but with breakup coming earlier every year, he might have to.

Maybe he could go for just a few days. Enough time to grab the supplies he couldn't make, hunt, trap, gather, or grow. Give him a chance to make sure the world hadn't blown up, and, if the stars magically aligned, find himself a woman to scratch the itch he couldn't take care of on his own.

As usual, he ignored that other thing—the thing that was too deep to reach. So deep he barely recognized it as a basic human need.

With a low woof, Bo took off on her usual rounds, sniffing out all kinds of interesting creatures—a couple of ground squirrels that skittered off with angry hisses, an osprey, which rose to higher ground to watch Bo with a dark, fixed eye; and finally, the female northern goshawk he'd been watching for the past few days, her wingspan impressive as she took off with three hard beats, then glided low in search of early spring prey.

No sign of the grizzly whose scat he'd spotted early that morning in the quickly melting snow. Good. He was bone tired. Didn't feel like dealing with the bear. Or anything else.

The heaviness in his limbs decided him. It was either go now or go nuts on his own.

If he wasn't already there.

Leo leaned against the worn clapboard of the boathouse, keeping an eye out for pursuers while Amka fiddled with the lock. "You sure run fast."

"For a fat old lady, you mean?" The woman glanced Leo's way, eyes narrowing on her face. "Lived here my whole life. I know every pothole in Schink's Station." She shoved hard, sending the rickety wood door flying open. "Besides, I'm not the one who spent the night upchucking in my room."

Leo followed her inside, caught sight of the plane, and came to a dead stop. "No freaking way."

"Shush. Don't talk like that in front of Dolores." Amka rushed forward. "She'll take it personally."

"Dolores?" Leo eyed the little Piper Cub with distrust. "She's... beautiful," *for an antique.* "But I pictured something a little more substantial than this." Had they truly just raced to this side of the lake for this? No way could she outpace a helicopter in this aircraft. It would be like trying to beat a Maserati on a tricycle.

"Yeah, well, she's all we got." Amka patted the bright yellow fuselage. "I'd go myself if I could see worth a damn." Leo bet that was true. Though she covered it well, anxiety rolled off Amka in waves. "Airfield's due west. If you taxi all the way out to the eastern part of the lake, they won't see you take off. Maybe won't even hear you."

Leo was banking on that. She'd need the head start or she and this little tricycle were fried.

Shoving back a wave of residual dizziness, Leo closed the boathouse door. "Could you at least have put the door back on? Or put in some windows?" She took in the floats. "Maybe some tires?"

"Door hinges are rusted. I was gonna fix that, but then I didn't figure Dolores would be flying anytime soon. And I'm still waiting on the windows I ordered." Even if she had the parts, there'd be no time to replace them now. Old Amka didn't have to say it. If Leo didn't get there before the helicopter, Campbell Turner was a dead man, and the virus would fall into Chronos Corporation's clutches—again. Amka ran her hands over the plane for a quick last-minute check. "Least there's a windshield. And hell, if she had tires, we'd have to take off from the airfield." Which would be a problem. That she and Amka had managed to get down here unseen was a miracle. Getting in the air without attracting notice would be another. "Don't worry, taking off from water's a breeze. All you gotta do is take care of my girl and she'll take care of you."

"I will," Leo promised as she threw her bag into the cockpit and jogged to open the boathouse door, revealing the kind of view people lost their heads over. A landscape that made women quit their jobs, leave their lives, and become Wilderness Wives. Perish the thought. She was about as far from a poet as a person could be, but even in her current rush, Alaska stole her breath.

Nestled beside the enormous lake, this tiny settlement was nothing but a lodge and guest cabins, along with a handful of blocky wooden structures that belonged to the few year-round residents, and an airstrip, where the massive Sikorsky S-92 helicopter had touched down less than ten minutes ago. Not a single paved road came within eighty miles of the place. The nearest highway was a hundred and fifty miles away, and it took even the fastest aircraft at least an hour to get to the nearest town—which, like Schink's Station, was the kind of dot she'd tried to flick off the map before realizing it wasn't a piece of fly poop.

The newly unfrozen lake's diamond-smooth center was marred only by the occasional ripple, while the edges were jagged with piled-up remnants of what the locals called breakup. Jagged shards of ice, dark and grimy, rimmed the entire thing, creating a wall along the shore. Around it, the brown and green and white forest appeared deceptively sparse.

Crowning it all were the mountains, bathed in light so bright, it was like a filter had been removed. People lived out there, alone in the wilderness. In the time she'd been here, she'd heard of a handful of men—some with families—who'd claimed a homestead a few decades ago. Others hadn't even gone the legal route. They'd just…gone. She squinted. How many of them were out there now? Mountain men who'd lost their taste for civilization? She shivered at the idea. Nope.

"Oil and gas are good," Amka called. "Inspected her a couple days ago, so we just need to warm her up and push her onto the lake."

Not checking every detail herself made Leo nervous. She cast the woman a look. "You sure? Last thing I need is for one of these cables to give out while I'm up there."

Amka's expression told her just how stupid a question that was. "I need you, remember? This is life or death."

"Right." Leo stepped onto a float and leaned into the cockpit. "Walk me through start-up."

Amka pointed and talked and Leo nodded. A bird cawed overhead and while the sound was loud enough to startle her pulse into overdrive, Leo didn't otherwise react. If the sound wasn't man-made, she'd ignore it.

In the distance, a low *boom* signaled a hunk of ice calving from the glacier and smashing into the lake a fraction of a second later. Some aspects of Alaska were painfully slow, inching forward like that glacier cutting through the landscape. Other things, though, moved quicker than blinking. Weather changes, for example, could be as treacherous as an avalanche, as devastating as one of those mudslides that obliterated everything in its path. If the weather turned tonight, she'd be stuck out there. If it turned while she was in the air, it could be much, much worse.

A cold breeze ruffled her collar, making her glad she'd layered up. Hell, even with all these clothes on, flying this thing in the cold would be a trial.

Focus. She was a mess after last night—no sleep, no food in her system. She was weak as a freaking kitten. She sucked in a deep, bracing breath of Alaskan air. There was a freshness to it that dug deep into her lungs, cleaned them out, and made room for more. Beneath the woody, outdoor scent that air freshener companies would never figure out was the comfortingly familiar smell of fuel.

A scan of the horizon showed not a single cloud in the sky. "Clear as a bell out there."

Old Amka snorted. "Don't you believe it. Storm's coming in. Better hurry."

As if the odds weren't stacked against her already.

"Get Eli—" Amka coughed and shook her head. "Get my godson out and keep going east. Refuel, then head into Canada."

Leo narrowed her eyes. Something was off about this—beyond the obvious. "He know I'm on my way?"

"Daisy's working on it."

Daisy, her hostess at the Lodge. Geez, was the whole town involved? Had they all been sitting there laughing every time Leo'd flown Von and Ans out to search for Turner?

Shoving back the doubt, she leaned over. "Get in touch with my guys. Don't stop calling them. Tell 'em to turn around and get right back here, soon as they land."

"Yep. Like I promised."

Even with the reassurance, Leo had to make one final attempt herself. She pulled out her sat phone and dialed. Still not working. Had to assume the newcomers were jamming the signal. She typed out a quick message to her teammates—Ans and Von, who'd left for Anchorage that morning, and Eric, Zoe, and Ford, back in San Diego. Only Von was set to return, since Ans had gone to check out a lead in Colorado, but she figured this was big enough to warrant bringing the whole team in.

Got trouble. Second team arrived in SS, target's coordinates in hand.

She hit send.

Too bad *she* didn't have the coordinates. She cast the old woman a dirty look. Nope. Around here, they flew by Visual Flight Rules—especially in the old aircraft. The old lady's directions ran through her mind on a loop: fly up the river 'bout an hour, take the left fork. Not the little fork. The big one. Wait for the big one. When you get to the big kidney bean lake, you land.

> Heading out in borrowed aircraft to grab target. Due east.
> Will report coordinates asap.

They'd hate that, but she didn't have more to give them.

Anxious to leave, she stuffed the phone in her bag and nodded to Amka, who pulled on the propeller once, twice… Leo hit the starter and the engine coughed before catching. A flock of birds took off.

So much for stealth.

"Hang on!" Amka climbed over to the open door and poked her head inside. "Promise me, you'll get my godson out, no matter what you…"

"What?"

"No matter what you find when you get there."

No matter what I find? Leo's insides did a little flip. She'd mistake it for another bout of nausea if she didn't recognize it for what it was: foreboding. "What are you talking about, Amka? What haven't you told me?"

"I should also mention: you can land on ice with floats, but you need real clean, flat ice. The lake up there'll do…" Amka's eyes shifted to the side. "Long as it hasn't started breaking up yet."

"And if it has?"

"We're all screwed." Without another word, Amka dropped off the float onto the dock and shoved the plane out into the water.

CHAPTER 2

"LET'S DO THIS, BABY," LEO MUTTERED, APPLYING SLOW pressure to the stick in order to increase the speed and push the little plane straight into the headwind. Five hundred yards. Four.

While taking off this far east was the only option, it put Leo closer to the opposite shore than she'd like. "Come on, Dolores. Come on, old girl. You've got this."

Her eyes shot up to the evergreen wall before her, then down to the controls and back up again. She'd seen aircraft eviscerated by just the tip of a pine tree. She had to get over them. *Come on, Dolores!*

Another dozen feet and she was airborne. Up, level, hanging just off the water, so low she could still jump without dying. She let the stick slide forward into neutral to get her flying speed up, eyeing that mass of death up ahead. Oh, come *on*.

Man, was she bad at this patience business. The waiting and teasing and more waiting that an aircraft like this needed were totally out of her comfort zone. Especially now, when she wanted to yank at the stick and *make* this little lady rise.

Back to climbing position. And climbing. Gaining on the trees... Three hundred yards, two hundred.

Never make it.

The adrenaline was wild. A drug, coursing through her, turning everything bright, technicolor, alive—like there were three of her inside this one skin suit. Three *thousand* of her. As with every risk, every painful near miss she'd been through, she loved it, lived for it, ate it up. Shivers, heat, and the blood-pumping reality of being alive assailed her the way they did every time she dared the world to end her.

Bring it! she taunted, as if she hadn't experienced the stench and pain of death, hadn't soaked in its slow, inexorable ooze, hadn't tried to stop it with her bare hands—stuffing guts back inside of friends as if their souls weren't already gone.

"Okay, Dolores. We've got this, sweetheart. Come on." The plane took on a touch more altitude. Not enough yet, but getting there. All she could do was hope that the Chronos team hadn't caught wind of her departure.

But, oh man, did she love this. This daredevilry, this thirst for risk didn't come from her; it came from out there—from the elements, maybe, the universe, or possibly even from death itself.

Ten yards, eight… Closer…closer…

"Come on, baby. Come on," she muttered, firm in her belief that an aircraft had a soul.

A final pull on the stick and the left float grazed the very tip of a pine as she soared into the sky, tilting wildly before finally straightening out.

She turned, craning her neck to see if anybody was in pursuit.

Nothing but mountains and river and the quickly setting sun. Had she truly made it out unseen? The chances seemed pretty slim. How long would it take them to head out after her? With no intel on what they'd been doing back in Schink's Station, she couldn't say. Were they five minutes behind her? Thirty? She'd never flown this blind.

Anything could happen.

She let out a long sigh—the only outward sign that her brain and body were buzzing like a million live wires—gave the stick an affectionate little rub, and turned into the mountains to save Campbell Turner and keep that darned virus out of the wrong hands. Again.

It wasn't until a half hour into the flight—without any sign of the other aircraft—that she truly understood Amka's final warning about ice.

Parts of the river she followed into the higher mountains looked way too close to breaking up. If the lake was melting too, she'd have nothing to land on.

And even adrenaline junkies wanted to live.

━━━━━━━━

Elias's phone rang in his hands. He almost dropped it, then caught it at the last minute. It was Daisy, calling from the lodge. *Finally*. He shoved it to his ear.

"Oh man, am I glad to—"

"Don't talk." Daisy didn't sound like herself. Gone was her easy drawl. Instead, she was crisp, curt, all business.

He closed his mouth. The background noise—though light— hit him hard. Music. Probably a song he'd never heard of, from some band so young they'd been barely out of diapers when he'd left. The low murmur of people talking, the loud hiss of steaming milk.

The hum of civilization.

"Hey, Frank!" Daisy said in an artificially happy voice.

Frank? Why the hell was she calling him Frank?

Something shuffled and heavy footsteps sounded. He could picture those feet tromping over worn wooden floorboards, could see the ancient rugs, and when the door toward the restrooms creaked, he envisioned the quiet, dark back hall. "Hang on, let me grab the order from the kitchen!"

Was that yelling in the background?

Unease tickled at the nape of his neck.

"Thank God," she whispered. "Tried calling you a million times. This is the first time it's gone through."

Another shiver, this one deeper. "What's up?" He had more questions—like *Why'd you leave the bar to take this call? Why'd you pretend I'm someone else? And why are you whispering now?* He didn't take the time to ask them. Something was wrong. Something that sent disquiet slithering through him, while the trapped feeling welled up and moved him to the front door. Caution made him scan the landscape twice before exiting. Bo bounded happily up the steps and nudged her face against his leg. He automatically dug his fingers into her fur. It was cold on the surface, hot close to her skin. When she yipped and did her happy little pony jump, trying to get him to play, he tightened his hold, told her this was important.

"Got trouble."

"Go ahead." Adrenaline spiked through his chest. It sped up his breathing and made his gaze jump at every little sound.

"They're here."

His innards plummeted. Last year, someone had nosed around asking questions. He'd wanted to leave then, but as Daisy and Amka had pointed out, there was no point in going if he hadn't been found.

The muted sound of voices coming through the phone now told him that by *here*, she probably meant *right there*. "Okay. I'm out."

"Wait!" Her voice was a stage whisper. "Hold on." The phone shifted. "Be right there!" she yelled. Then quietly, "They're…"

"What? I can't hear you."

"They know… Helicopter landed…overheard and—"

"You're breaking up, Daisy." He was yelling now, though it wouldn't make a damn difference. "Slow down."

"She's on her way to get you. Thinks you're—*Shit!*" Someone screamed in the background. Daisy's words and the scream were cut off so abruptly, he wondered if he'd somehow squeezed the life out of the phone.

"On her way?" he yelled, staring at the dead instrument. "*Dammit!*" *Who* was on her way? And what did that mean, *get him*? Help him or kill him?

No response but the high, alarmed *kak kak* of a gyrfalcon, displeased at being interrupted midhunt. And then, right on time, as if he'd conjured it, came the buzz of an approaching engine—faint but there.

He turned toward it, breathing hard, eyes wide-open, every muscle in his body ready. He should have been scared, should have worried that he'd been found, that everything would come to a bloody head, that it was over and the bad guys had won.

But God help his messed-up soul, he felt nothing but relief.

And, if he was honest, a guilty hint of excitement.

CHAPTER 3

LEO HAD BEEN IN THE AIR FOR OVER AN HOUR WHEN SHE spotted the other aircraft.

"Took you long enough."

The helicopter swooped over the western ridge behind her, blotting out what sunlight remained as it gained on her with frightening speed. There went her chances of carrying out a quick and easy evacuation.

"I've seen worse," she muttered, reassuring the plane, maybe, or herself. "Walk in the park for an old girl like you, Dolores. Just a walk in the park."

No way could she escape the power behind those engines. Just wasn't possible in the tiny, ancient Cub. Oh, Dolores was quaint with her fabric-covered fuselage and top speed of eighty-seven miles per hour. She'd no doubt been a wild ride back in 1947, but she left a whole lot to be desired when it came to evasive flight maneuvers.

Leo considered her options.

Lead them away.

Pure suicide. And pointless. Especially if they already knew where to find Campbell Turner. Amka's cousin had heard them mention precise coordinates. If she headed in the wrong direction, they could grab Turner and then come after her.

And where would she go? There was nothing but mountains on three sides, chunks of rock deadlier than the approaching bird. Even if she could contort the aircraft into physics-defying evasive maneuvers, they'd follow. With absurd ease.

She craned left, trying to get a better look at them.

No dice.

At least the dizziness was gone, so that was good. Nothing like a race and a chase to get rid of food poisoning. Not the recommended remedy, but it would do in a pinch. And, hey, since she was looking at the bright side, nobody was shooting at her, which was—

Ping.

A hole appeared in the windshield.

Oh crap.

Another bullet punched through the fuselage behind her. Her instincts told her to duck, but that wouldn't help. She might as well be flying a hot air balloon for all the protection the Cub provided.

Leo banked right, trying to make herself as small as possible.

She wasn't going out this way. Wouldn't allow it. She forced her breathing to slow and shook her head, rolling her eyes. "*Nobody shooting,*" she muttered, as if talking to a copilot. "*No stupid shooting.* What kind of idiot jinxes herself by thinking that?" A bullet hit one of the wings, followed by another.

Talk about well and truly screwed.

No. Not screwed. Thrown slightly off course.

At least she'd been obliged to pilot the two-seater from the back seat. If she'd been in front, she'd be dead. And how lucky was she that the bullets hadn't smashed through glass?

Because there's nothing to smash through.

She'd been miffed about that earlier, but suddenly it seemed like one hell of a silver lining. On many levels. For example, not having a door or windows had forced her to put on every single item of cold weather gear she had. Now when she'd have to land out here in the middle of Nowheresville, Alaska, she wouldn't die of hypothermia. Not immediately, at least.

Okay. There was a decision to be made. Fast as lightning, she took in the scenery, eyes flicking left and right, mind calculating.

She had to land. The question was, did she have time to do it on the lake? And would the stupid ice even hold?

Squinting against the blasting winds, with the lowering sun and the approaching helicopter at her back, Leo eyed the glacier-fed waterway slithering between the peaks, reflecting sunlight like some holy fire serpent. Mountains, pines, a slender river, too curved to take head-on.

The ice looked almost cracked.

So, no sweat. No sweat at all. Of course, her body belied that statement by sending a cold, wet rush of perspiration to her armpits.

Another look back. They were close. Their next shot wouldn't miss.

The sun was just starting to melt into the horizon behind her, a candle sputtering out before dying, leaving the world without detail or depth—the sky nothing but the flat outline of sharp black mountains, silhouetted against the day's last gasp. Clouds stained the sky, dark as inkblots. Each one was like a drop on the wind-shield, drawn toward the next and the next, gathering to form a low, roiling ceiling. Was that the storm coming in?

Are you freaking kidding me?

One more problem she could add to the quickly growing heap.

Something connected with her plane, so hard it shook. Another bullet? She couldn't see where she'd been hit this time.

Leo took another lungful of crystal-cold air to brace her, clear her mind.

Concentrate. Land. She could put this thing down on that ice. Looked okay—in parts. Sure, she could do it. Piece of cake.

One step at a time. One breath after another.

"Baby steps," she told Dolores. Or herself, or whatever.

The lake's kidney-bean shape nestled among steep, jagged mountains boiling up from the earth like lava from Mordor. It was close enough now to make out details. They hit her in quick, split-second bursts. The bluish-gray surface, mottled with little puffs of white, as if eddies of bubbles had flash frozen beneath the ice crust. Islands of pines floated like dark castles caught in a spider-web sky. Near to the edge, the ice turned into reptile skin, chunks pulling apart into individual scales.

Oh man, it was definitely breaking up. Or about to. The aircraft would sink. No question about it. If it didn't flip first and crush her to the ground.

She took another frantic look over her shoulder.

The helo was breathing down her neck, so near she could feel the thrum of its blades, could picture a sniper taking aim, could feel the hot metal piercing her.

No. Not happening.

Following an instinct she'd been born with, she swooped right, put her nose straight into the wind, and catalogued all the challenges she'd have to beat in order to stay alive.

She could do this, even if she was shaking and so nervous she was almost seeing double.

Obstacles? Meant to be overcome.

Like landing straight into the blinding sun, with night and a storm hot on her heels, avoiding those islands covered in ever-greens and putting this thing down on a surface that looked smooth but would fall apart any second, full of bumps and breaks and ridges. Each one of those was capable of flipping a plane like this—especially since the landing gear consisted of big metal floats made for water landings, not slush.

"*Yay!*" The word sounded like a sob, no matter how much happy she tried to inject.

Another shot hit the plane, rocking it like unexpected turbulence.

She did her best to ignore it, squinting hard at the strange honeycomb pattern that gave the lake's frosted surface a fishing net appearance. The complex swirls reminded her of an illustration of synapses lighting up the brain. And cracks, all over. Or… Could they be animal tracks? Maybe an odd freezing pattern, if she squinted really hard.

She flicked her eyes back. Shit. Shit. They were right there. Close enough so she could count the ship's individual occupants. *Many* occupants.

All that manpower for little ole me?

Ignore them. They don't matter. Concentrate.

So, best-case scenario, if breakup hadn't truly started here, the ice on that lake would hold the Cub's weight, which was what— eight hundred pounds, with her on board? Nine hundred? What about the helicopter's fifteen thousand pounds? Would it hold up to that?

No. Definitely not.

That was one advantage. She took in a shaky breath. It was a start.

The bird swooped closer.

She had to do it. A short ice landing on floats with enemy air- craft in hot pursuit. The close proximity of the mountains and trees turned this from a daring attempt into a stupid one.

Coming in at this angle, there was a single, ridiculously tight area in which she could land. To one side, a glacier overhung the lake, eating at it like a frozen set of sky-blue fangs. To the other lay a teardrop-shaped, pine-studded island, as treacherous as a cluster of metal spikes rising into the air. And straight ahead, the shore.

Maybe shore was the wrong word. What lay ahead was a wall of pure, solid granite.

She sucked in a deep, freezing cold breath and said a little prayer to her mom.

Then they shot out the fuel tank.

─────────────

He took off, slipping and sliding in the direction of the lake, which was still a good fifteen minutes away. And then, because he was worked up but he wasn't stupid, he took a detour toward the overlook. From there, if he liked what he saw, he could continue on his way, head into the deeper woods, or take the more treacherous path leading to the river. The one thing he'd understood from his conversation with Daisy was that he needed to get back to Schink's Station. Now. No more deaths. Nobody else should die for this cause. He knew the people searching for him. They'd stop at nothing.

He leapt over one of the many tiny streams cutting through the area—frozen solid, though that would change any day now—and plunged into the last stretch of pine and spruce. There, he skidded to a stop, his boots leaving two deep, obvious furrows in a patch of snow.

"What the hell?" On instinct, he retreated into the shadows to watch.

Bo responded with a happy little yip.

Was that Old Amka's Piper Cub? When Daisy'd said someone was coming, he'd pictured one of the tour company's bush planes, not this rarely used antique.

It was coming in way too fast. Tail draggers like that needed to ease their way down, not force a landing. He squinted. And what the hell was she doing flying with floats when the water was still frozen?

That had better not be Old Amka or he'd…kill her, he'd been about to think, but he nipped that thought in the bud. No more killing, even in figures of speech. But, hell, everyone knew Amka wasn't allowed to take the Cub out. She was half-blind, for God's sake. What was she—

That was when the low *whomp* of helicopter blades hit him, and he understood just how completely the shit had hit the fan. They were here.

Where was it coming from? He searched the visible slice of sky. Nothing.

Fueled by alarm and anger at himself for recklessly craving this kind of excitement just a few hours earlier, he turned and made his way over the mud- and snow-covered ground, no longer keeping to broken branches and rocks. Not leaving a trace didn't seem nearly as important right now. What mattered was hurrying the hell up.

The engines grew louder, warring with the thump of his pulse in his ears. He broke into a flat-out run, his attention divided between the ground and occasional flashes of darkening blue.

There, between two lodgepole pines, a glimpse of empty sky, then a shot of the little plane, small and slow as a bumblebee, careening toward disaster. Seconds later, through the branches, a flash of the helicopter, massive and malevolent, closing in like a wasp or a bird of prey. Fast, strong, with a razor-edged precision.

He took in the scene: the Cub dipping toward the lake at breakneck speed, close enough for him to see that only the back seat was occupied—one person. The helicopter, swooping behind it, looked almost close enough to touch.

His eyes darted down to where the Cub was headed. Nothing but glacier and the mountain's sheer face. A kamikaze flight unless it could land on the frozen surface before then, but that wouldn't do either. The damn lake was on the cusp of breakup. It was a slushy, uneven mess. He'd risk walking across it, but he wouldn't drive. And he certainly wouldn't trust it to hold up the weight of a plane.

It plummeted. The chopper plunged. Beside him, Bo's frantic barking added to the mayhem. In her short life, she'd only seen aircraft a handful of times and had certainly never witnessed anything like this. Frankly, he hadn't either, and for a few harrowing seconds, he had no clue what to do.

When the helicopter swung to the side, he blinked in disbelief at what he was seeing. A person was hanging out the open door, holding…a weapon?

He raised his rifle, sighted through the scope. Too far, too fast.

He'd never get a decent shot. His arms dropped. What was it Daisy had said exactly? She was coming for him? Who? Who the hell was in that plane? Was this suicide mission meant to save him or were there two groups after him this time? Either way, the pilot was one more person to add to the list of deaths since he'd first heard of the virus over a decade ago.

In the next split second, something cracked—a gunshot, splitting the air—the helicopter lifted and the plane angled dizzyingly to the side before dropping from view.

Whoever was flying was one hell of a pilot. Amka had been decent before her vision got bad, but this person was on a whole other level. They had nerves of steel and the reaction time of a mosquito.

Better hurry up and establish whether they were friend or foe. He released Bo's fur and sprinted down the mountain.

The fuel leaking from the tank changed Leo's plans drastically. Instead of the straight landing she'd planned—stopping right before the cliff face—she swung to the right, angling harder than the little plane liked, forcing it down, which was exactly what she shouldn't do in an aircraft like this one.

And then—*yes. Oh, hallelujah, yes!*—the cliff opened up to reveal a frozen tributary, feeding into the lake. Narrow as the gate to hell, maybe forty feet wide, if she was lucky. On her left, the glacier-veined mountain shot straight up from the river. The tree-lined incline on the other side was gentler, but just as impassable.

"Not yet. Right, Dolores?" Leo muttered, angling herself straight into the tight opening. "Haven't killed us yet." The Cub barely fit inside, which meant the helo would never make it.

And then, slow as dripping butter, the plane floated in, while

Leo's heart and eyes and hands worked quick as lightning, keeping pace with the rotors of the beast she'd left in her dust.

Immediately, the river wound left, leaving just enough room to maneuver before shifting right, barely widening, providing an extra few feet on either side.

She'd flown places like this in small helicopters, back in the day. But they'd skittered and dropped, risen and flitted like an extension of her body, whereas this one sailed at its own pace, as unwieldy and slow as a big fat kite.

If they would just come after her, the terrain would do the dirty work.

When the river flared out on both sides, giving her another foot or two to work with—yet still not wide enough for the helicopter's nearly sixty-foot wingspan—she let out a sigh. At the last second, she lifted its tail and slapped the ice with an ungraceful scrape.

The sound was ugly, but it was the best thing she'd ever heard.

Her muscles had just gone weak with relief when a rock came out of nowhere, a dark stain rising from the still water, barely a blip the size of a baby's head. Around it, the ice had melted entirely.

Against the float, it might as well have been a boulder. By the time she'd spotted it, it was too late to do a thing. The float caught, spinning the plane to the side—ironically fast, considering the snaillike landing—tipping the right wing down and sending the cockpit up into the air before seesawing in the opposite direction.

Leo braced for the other impact that was sure to come—wing tip to ice.

"I'm so sorry," she whispered to her team, her dad, Old Amka, the world.

A final sickening flip spun the old Cub a slow ninety degrees and boomeranged her toward the cliff face. She barely had time to cover her head before metal ground against rock and the world went dark.

CHAPTER 4

BO DISAPPEARED AHEAD, BARKING OUT OF CONTROL.

There was no room for hope as he rushed down the steep, muddy slope to where the plane had gone down. No prayer, no wishes.

He'd hoped, prayed, and wished enough for a lifetime, and God—or whatever the hell was out there—had ignored him.

Because there's nothing there.

Right. No God, nothing divine to balance the scales, no justice to make things right. The world was what it was. Nothing but life and death. And more often than not, those things weren't pretty.

So, while he raced in the direction in which the plane had gone down, he didn't expect the outcome to be a good one. In fact, he didn't expect a thing. The only way to live a life like his was without expectations.

He jumped from an eight-foot ledge, landed hard on his heels, and sprinted the last twenty yards to the edge of the woods, where his body stuttered like a cartoon runner hitting a wall.

One bright yellow wing lay across the ice, its tip blown apart like a burst paper bag.

Bo barked again, the sound coming from the right, around the bend, where the glacier overhung the river. He figured that was where he'd find the rest of the plane. On the ice or, more likely, under it. He whistled in response, letting her know he was on his way, and sped on, sliding across the river where the boulders jutted out, past the curve, and through the invisible wall of denial his mind threw up when he saw it.

No. No, God, no.

The nose was gone—flattened against the glacier like a crushed soda can—the cockpit crumpled, as if a cardboard box had been mashed up and straightened again. The other wing was quickly sinking into the water.

As he fought his way over the slick, crackling ice, his mind fed him the weirdest kaleidoscope of images. God, the one people prayed to all the time, was nothing but a spoiled toddler, smashing airplanes into the earth for the hell of it.

Then a vague memory from his parents' living room, back when he was little and his dad played the classics on repeat: a black-and-white King Kong swatting at model airplanes, which bizarrely morphed into the scene in that movie he couldn't get enough of even as a kid, where Fay Wray's breast fell out of her ripped dress and she was left, helpless, struggling against the giant. He'd never been able to look away, for so many reasons. The boob, first of all, 'cause even back then, he'd been a boob man—but also her helplessness, flailing in that enormous ape hand, had done things to him.

Yeah, well, today, he wasn't panting from excitement as he touched the plane's perfectly intact, shiny tail, but from his own powerlessness.

If the pilot was dead in there, he'd—

Shit, he had no idea what he'd do, but whatever it was, it would be big. Huge. So cataclysmic that God would feel the aftershocks, wherever the hell he was.

He thought of the secrets he harbored, thought of his sacrifices in the line of duty, to his country, to humankind itself, and then he thought about how maybe humans weren't worth it after all.

Sucking in a breath that hurt his lungs, he ignored the roar of the nearing helicopter and stepped onto the float, holding on tight as the plane sank another foot into the water.

What he saw through the Cub's open window stopped him dead in his tracks.

"Don't move." Leo's voice was miraculously steady. So was her gun.

With her hands occupied, she blinked in an effort to get rid of the blood dripping in her eyes. It coated her lids, clogged her vision, made breathing difficult.

Everything wavered so much, she couldn't focus on the bulky creature. *Please, God, don't be a bear.* The ground shifted. *Or a yeti.* "S-said stop."

"Didn't move." Okay, so not a bear, unless they talked around here. She wasn't entirely prepared to rule out yetis. She could, however, say with absolute certainty that this massive man was not the one she was after. Sure, they were both white, but that was about where the similarities ended. Campbell Turner topped out at five nine. This guy was well over six feet tall.

Great—then who the hell was this? Had her landing somehow attracted the attention of one of those wilderness freaks? Seemed unlikely that one of her pursuers had already reached her, but then again, her head wasn't on straight. For all she knew, she'd blacked out for an hour. No. No, it was still light out. She squinted at the man. Mountain man seemed about right. He didn't look like he'd seen civilization in a while.

He raised massive, gloved hands to wide shoulders and wiggled his fingers, as if they itched to reach out, like one of those Wild West characters just dying to unholster their weapon. Though he didn't, technically, have a holster, since he wore his rifle strapped across his chest. "You, uh, okay?" Like an afterthought, he added a "ma'am."

"Step back," she panted. Why was it so hard to speak? To breathe? There was too much pressure on her chest.

Her unfocused gaze skimmed over a thick beard and wild hair, managing to home in on bright eyes that narrowed, picked her apart from the top of her head to wherever her blood flowed, and finally disappeared when he stepped off the float. Whoever this person was, he did not fit Campbell Turner's description.

Without his weight to anchor it, the plane lurched for a few nausea-inducing seconds before settling again.

Belly heaving, she tried to release the harness and wound up sinking into her seat again, blinded by the pain as much as the blood.

"I'm coming back up," growled the man.

Her stomach swam. "I can manage."

"Gotta get you out. Fast. Or you'll wind up drowning."

Drowning? What the hell was he talking about? And why would he care?

His weight made everything lurch again. Something fell from her hands with a metallic clunk, her eyes shut out the painful light. She concentrated on sounds and smells and textures. Her stomach settled, thank God. Now if her head would stop throbbing, maybe she could figure this mess out.

If this guy wasn't Campbell Turner and he wasn't part of the Chronos team, could he really be a random mountain man who just happened to be strolling by when she crash-landed in the location Amka had given her? Leo didn't believe in coincidences. At all.

Somewhere not too far off, a helicopter's blades beat the air, dull but present. Way too close.

"Climb to the front." Quick as a flash, the man undid her harness and backed out of the cockpit. "Now, dammit! You're sinking!"

Sinking?

"Put your hand here."

She started to shake her head and stopped. "Trying not to vomit."

"No time for that," barked the angry bass and, hell, the man was right. "Come on."

It took every bit of willpower she had to set her distrust aside and let him help her onto the float and then to solid ground.

Her feet slipped out from under her and she careened painfully to the ice. Not solid ground at all.

Something wet touched her face. Leo's eyes opened. She grunted in surprise at the sight of a dog or a wolf, maybe, with those weird, colorless eyes.

"Back up, Bo," the man said, then leaned down to offer his hands. After a second's hesitation, she clasped them and let him haul her back up to standing.

"Let's move."

Concentrating hard, she slid beside him. After a few slippery steps, the vise tightened around her skull and her stomach convulsed. Dropping to hands and knees on the pocked ice, she gagged. The effort twisted her insides, but didn't bring up a thing.

The stranger squatted beside her. "You okay?"

Hell if I know. She'd be damned if she'd let him see the self-doubt. With every bit of strength she could muster, she pushed back up to her feet, where she swayed for a few queasy seconds. "I'm fine."

He rose and flicked a narrow-eyed look over her face. "Who *are* you?"

"Who are *you*?"

With an annoyed grimace, he turned toward the darkening forest. "We need to run. Can you do that?"

"Yes," she lied.

The yeti didn't look like he believed her either. He opened his mouth as if to protest, and then shut it. Good. She didn't have the energy to argue at the moment. And she'd like to know just who this guy was before she decided what to do about him.

Was he a friend of Campbell Turner's? Did he plan to lead her to the other man?

"You can't keep up." The yeti leaned down and put his face close to hers. "I'll have to carry you. Or leave you behind."

"I'm good," she deadpanned. No way in hell was she letting this man carry her, no matter whose side he was on. "Lead the way."

Though every instinct told her not to trust a stranger, Leo had neither the equipment nor the stamina she'd need to survive on her own. Paul Bunyan here, however, seemed to be doing just fine out in the wilderness.

So, she'd follow him, at least until she figured out what the hell was going on here.

And then she'd do whatever it took to get Campbell Turner and the virus out before the other team reached him.

What a day.

CHAPTER 5

BEHIND THEM, THE HELICOPTER WENT LOW FOR A FEW minutes and then took off again in the direction of Schink's Station.

Elias pictured reinforcements swooping in, armies descending.

And here he was leading a stranger straight to his place. *She's coming to get you,* Daisy had said. He still didn't know if that was a good thing.

He knew absolutely zilch about this woman, aside from what he'd gleaned from a few quick glances. She was a good deal shorter than him—maybe five six—with dark brown skin and closely-shorn hair. Even bleary-eyed and injured, there was an efficiency to her movements, a calculation in the way she took everything in, that made him think she was not to be underestimated, whoever the hell she was.

And then there was the question of what she was doing crash-landing Old Amka's plane less than a mile from his cabin.

He looked over to see her stumble again. When would she give in and let him carry her? The blood from her lacerated scalp had left a glaring trail of breadcrumbs behind them.

Whoever'd just rappelled from that helicopter would be able to catch up with them in no time at this rate. The dying light didn't bother him so much, but she didn't know the area the way he did. If only the ice had already broken up, he could have used the water to hide signs of their passage.

Yeah, and frozen to death in the process.

He stopped and listened.

Nothing out of the ordinary. Not yet.

If they were being followed, at least he had the home advantage. *My woods, assholes.* If they chased them, they'd do it in unknown territory, whereas he'd spent the last decade right here.

Night fell faster than usual, the clouds skittering in to block out the stars and moon, making the darkness dense as a lead-lined blanket. *Good.* His neck prickling at the woman's presence behind him, he humped his way up the steep slope toward the cabin, content to let Bo's quiet, sure-footed silhouette lead the way. *Home-turf advantage.*

The temperature plummeted, which was fine for his warm, steadily moving limbs, but when the woman's chattering teeth reached him, he knew he had to hurry. Between the shock and the blood loss, she'd be close to hypothermic by the time the sun fully disappeared.

Less than a quarter mile from his cabin, Bo went stock-still, one foot lifted, nose in the air. Without missing a beat, he froze, shut his eyes, and listened. The woman surprised him by following suit.

One…two…three… He counted out the seconds, scanning the forest's usual sounds for something off. A scuffling in the underbrush, leaves scraping above. Below, the river cracked and shifted. The woman's breathing evened out and went quiet. He'd bet anything she was straining her ears, too. Whoever she was, she'd had training. Not many people could leave a crash like the one she'd just survived and hike straight into a frozen wilderness. She looked like she'd stepped straight out of a horror movie, as constant as the Terminator, staggering up the mountain behind him. Grim, determined, driven by something he didn't yet understand.

Time ticked away while they listened. They'd been waiting for close to thirty seconds when he heard it: a scraping that ended abruptly. It wasn't close. If he weren't so attuned to everything right now, so on edge with expectation, he'd think it was a normal noise—ice shifting and falling, maybe a waterlogged branch hitting the ground. Could be. Could be something else, too. Like the downed plane seesawing under the weight of a person straining to look inside.

He torqued his head back and squinted at the woman. It almost felt like they exchanged a look, though he couldn't be sure in this light.

After a few more seconds, Bo let out a hushed *woof*, dropped her paw, and dipped her head to sniff the mud at her feet before moving on. Cautiously, he followed, turning his head from one side to the other as he went.

A few hundred yards from the cabin, he armed the first perimeter trap and half buried it under the snow, pointing it out to the woman before leading her west, arming more, leaving only subtle tracks as he went. She was doing better with that, he noted—no more blood drops in the snow, and her prints mostly stuck to his. Good. They'd left just enough to ensure they were followed, without making it so obvious the others would feel they were being led.

He made the final approach with his usual caution, leaving as little trace as possible. He'd never figured out how to make sure Bo didn't leave footprints on the ground, but he'd taught her to cut away in order to enter the protective rock circle from above, through a hole that most people couldn't see, much less access.

Once within the sheltered area, he eyed the unlit structure warily, sniffed the air, and listened. No unusual scents. No sound but the wind singing through the black spruces' top branches. Storm moving in. He caught its high, electric smell, the underlying sweetness that could only mean snow. As if that weren't enough proof, he could feel its approach thrumming deep in his bones, lighting him up with expectation.

Once he was sure the coast was clear, he made his way to his cabin, assessing the situation as he went.

Weather was on its way, which would limit movement. While he knew the lay of the land, knew how to escape and where to hunker down safely for tonight at least, the others did not. And there *were* others around. That scrape had just confirmed what his instincts told him.

So, right now, he'd just assume there was an army after him and take things from there. Assuming the worst was how he'd survived this long after all.

Which meant he had to assume that this woman was the enemy.

———

Leo plodded up the slope, her feet slipping on ice and sinking into snow. She reached out a hand and wiggled her fingers, surprised at how hard they were to see in the eerie, bluish light.

A few feet ahead, the steady crunch of the man's footsteps came to a stop. She did the same, waiting for him to move again, to lead the way or take off running or, with the way things were going, just turn around and shoot her point-blank.

It took a few seconds for her eyes to pick out a strange irregularity in the scenery up ahead. Trees, boulders, a rock face, natural shapes formed by wind and water and then—there: a dark rectangle. Another. She tried to focus, but her vision felt wrong.

Swiping a hand over her eyes to clear them, she stared until the shapes became a structure, built up against the stones or, actually, into them.

She cast the man a quick a look and blinked, her lashes sticking together. "What is that?"

"Cabin."

"I'm not going in there."

"It's the only way."

She scanned the area. From what she could tell it was a dead end. "We'll be trapped."

He shook his head. "Got a way out."

A way out of a cabin built into a mountain? What earthly reason could he have for leading her here, with people after them? Understanding dawned. "Is *he* in there?"

She couldn't see his face in the dark, but she pictured those big brows lowering. "Who?"

"The man I came to find."

"Nobody in there." With an annoyed noise, he took off for the cabin, leaving her standing in the middle of the clearing. "Your choice," he said over his shoulder. "I'm going in."

She looked around. There was nothing but woods in every direction, with a dip that appeared to be a creek to one side. The cabin was built into what looked like solid rock. No way out.

Something snapped in the woods behind them and Leo jumped.

Decision made, she followed him up and into the dark cabin. As soon as the door closed behind her, the man lit an oil lamp, then opened cupboards, emptying things into a pack. "Take off your wet clothes," he said without even glancing her way.

"No."

"Here." He threw a cloth. A towel? She caught it, blinking in the near dark. "It's clean. Put pressure on your head."

She shut her eyes, pressed the towel to her injury, and bit back a groan. A fresh bout of pain sent the room spinning. Slowly, carefully, she shuffled to the bed and sat.

"Let me see that." The man's voice was deep and rough, the words slow and strangely precise, as if he had only just recently learned English, though his accent was perfect. She scooted away when he sat beside her and let out a frustrated *puh* sound, pulling the towel away to get a look. "Need to clean this up." He cast a look at the door. "No time right now. Got to move."

Move? Grimacing, she took in the small, smoke-scented space. "Move where?" She coughed, which made her head pound so hard, everything but the pain receded for a few seconds. When she came out of it, all she could hear was her own raspy breathing.

He got up and came back. When he pressed something cold and wet to the side of her face, she couldn't drum up the energy to push him away.

"Your eye's stuck." He bent close. "Lashes glued. Wipe the blood away."

He shoved the washrag into her hand and went back to packing. Slowly at first, she scrubbed at her eye, then worked harder to remove the last bit of blood. Finally, she got her eye all the way open, relieved that she could see. "What's the plan?"

"How about first you tell me how you got that plane?"

"What?"

"Where'd you get the Cub?"

Who was this guy to be questioning her about this? She didn't trust him, his questions, or his dead-end cabin. "Someone loaned it to me."

Grunting, he returned to the front door and rammed a board into brackets on both sides, effectively barring it. And locking them inside.

Was this some suicide thing? Had he brought her here to die? Or to wait for the others and hand her over? No, that made no sense. If he was with them, he wouldn't have drawn her away first. Unless he planned to barter his life for hers.

And where the hell was Campbell Turner?

She squeezed her eyes shut, trying to figure it out. "Freaking Amka," she muttered.

"*I'd* be scared."

"What?"

Even through his dark beard, she could see how tightly the guy pressed his lips together. "You crashed Amka's plane. She's gonna kill you."

"If you don't kill me first."

"If I was gonna kill you, I'd have done it on the river." That was probably true. But who the hell was he?

"How do you know Amka?" she asked.

"Everybody knows Amka. You say she *loaned* you the plane?" He scoffed. "Nobody flies that plane."

The old woman's anxious, crinkled face flashed in her mind. "I didn't steal it, if that's what you're insinuating." Trying for some kind of rapport, she forced a half-assed smirk to her face. If she could just get him talking, maybe she could figure this situation out. "Amka's *scary*."

He watched her closely. His eyes narrowed into dark, suspicious slits. "Who the hell are you?"

"Didn't we already have this talk? How about you show me yours, I'll show you mine." Or some of it. No way was she divulging anything important until she knew who the hell he was.

Ignoring her, he moved to the front wall, swung a big, roughly made shutter over one window, and locked it into place, then did the other. Leo looked around. The cabin was rustic but clean, made of rough-hewn logs and furnished mostly with what appeared to be homemade pieces. The quintessential woodsman's retreat. Automatically, her eyes scanned for weapons. A rifle hung above the door. An axe leaned against the wall by a fireplace. And while someone more relaxed might have taken it off upon entering, the yeti still wore his rifle strapped across his body. Which again begged the question—was this guy a random mountain man or was he somehow linked to Campbell Turner?

As she watched, he dropped his pack and grabbed another bag.

She blinked. "That's my flight bag!"

He opened the pockets, upended it on a thick wooden table, and pawed through the contents—Mylar blanket, matches, first aid kit, personal locator beacon. He picked that up and removed the batteries, which ratcheted her fear up a few notches.

"I need that. My team can't find me without—"

He stopped, slowly turned just his head toward her, and stared. "Your team?"

Every hair on her body stood up. "I'm not alone."

Another movement from him, just as slow but more theatrical, as he took in the room, then faced her again with the grim, flat expression that appeared to be his baseline. "Look pretty alone to me."

"I need that gear." And what about her sat phone? Had he found that? She tried to remember. Did she have it with her when she crashed? No. She'd tucked it into the plane's storage pocket. Gone. She could *kick* herself right now. Food poisoning or not, she'd gotten herself into quite the bind here.

"Making sure we don't double up." He was all business now, returning items to her pack and discarding others—like her bright orange vest, which would be useful if her guys, indeed, came looking for her.

Had he taken her weapons? There was no sign of her Glock 20. She'd had it in the Cub. She knew that. She shut her eyes and tried to remember. Nothing. No idea what had happened to her firearm. This was bad. Slowly, she rubbed one leg against the other, knocking her shin bone into the knife strapped to her ankle. Good. She wasn't entirely unarmed.

Her eyes followed his movements as he repacked her bag along with his and set them both against the back wall beside the wood stove.

"They coming?" He turned.

The dog woofed from its place by the front door, dragging Leo's gaze back in that direction. It was one of those fuzzy white-and-gray animals that looked like it was made for Alaska. Made *by* Alaska. Right now, it stared at the door, its big, pointy ears standing at attention.

"Time to get up."

That wasn't happening. If she sat here unmoving, the pain in her head was bearable. Almost.

The man—whose bulk took up most of the space—grabbed a pile of clothing and set it on the bed beside her. "Clothes are a mess. Put these on."

"I'm not getting undressed."

"Bad idea to be—"

A sound echoed, outside the house. It sounded like a scream.

Leo pictured the scene—cabin, woods, harsh screams in the night. *What Alaska Chainsaw Massacre nightmare have I fallen into?*

"Forget it. Time to go. Got two choices right now, lady." He glanced at the dog, who'd stood and started a low, ominous growling. "Now's the time to tell me who you are and why you're here, or I send you out there." He pointed at the front door. "To the wolves."

With effort, she pushed herself to standing, knowing as well as he did that the biggest threat in this wilderness—in *any* wilderness—wasn't wolves or bears or even the goddamn cold.

It was humans.

———

A scream pierced the night's subtle cacophony.

Lightly poised on the balls of his feet, Ashwin Benton went very still and listened. The agonized sound went on for a few seconds before cutting off abruptly.

Whoever had let out that godawful shriek was in terrible pain. A foothold trap, perhaps, with tightly sprung steel jaws. The kind that sliced through flesh and crushed bone. He'd seen two in the last few minutes. They had told him a few things. First: the traps had just been sprung. This was clear because very fresh tracks led to it and the greenery hiding it had been put there quite recently. Which confirmed that the traps weren't meant to kill animals. They were meant to slow humans down. Second: the man expected pursuit. And he was well prepared. Interesting.

There would be no emergency medical evacuation tonight. The poor bastard who'd been caught in their quarry's trap would never walk the same again. This job wasn't starting well. At all. Already, the complex plan had been thwarted. By someone in an antique aeroplane, no less.

Oh, Deegan—the one in charge of this venture—hadn't liked

that at all. Ash, however, had found it rather charming. The irony of it was rather poetic.

He went on as before, slowly and carefully, studying the soggy, half-frozen ground. He took another silent step, paused, took another. Another. *He* wouldn't be stepping in any traps tonight. But then he didn't rush into things the way other operatives did—impatient Americans with their high-tech gadgets and thirst for violence.

He thought back to the crash site—a treasure trove of information that the others had glanced at before taking off in hot pursuit. Ash knew, for example, that the pilot was injured—likely a head wound, given the splash patterns in the cockpit, and the volume of blood. He also knew that the pilot was a woman and that the person she'd met with was a large male who left very little sign of his passage, accompanied by a canine. Neither was Campbell Turner.

Patting the handgun he'd slid into his pocket, Ash pulled in a satisfied breath.

Movement up ahead made him freeze again, this time watching as the people he was purportedly working with forged on, utterly insensitive to the destruction they wrought. Thankfully, their heavy, steel-toed footprints were easily identifiable. They were also at least an inch shorter than the ones belonging to the man he was stalking, whose feet were a size sixteen American, he'd venture to guess. There had been no mention of either a woman or a bigfoot in their briefing. Their target—Campbell Turner—was a midsized fifty-three-year-old man.

Curiouser and curiouser.

Eyes hitching on an irregular shape, he paused. There, hidden alongside a fallen branch, was another trap. He squatted to get a closer look. It was clean, not marred by a single speck of blood, as if it had never been used before. This little monster would do significant damage.

Up ahead, the injured operative groaned deeply. Someone else spoke—a woman. So much for stealth.

Ash watched as the woman helped the man up. Once Ash was close, he cleared his throat. They both jumped and reached for weapons, searching the dark in vain.

"All right, mate?" Ash asked, letting them know where he stood.

It took them a few seconds to spot him. "Uh, yeah," whispered the injured American—a tall Black man whose name Ash hadn't bothered getting. This wasn't a team he'd get to know. Or trust. Or, hopefully, spend any significant time with.

Ash moved closer and nodded toward the bloke's foot. "Looks fucked." He didn't keep his voice down. No point after all the yelling, was there?

"Be fine," the man replied with admirable bravado, given the sad state of his appendage. He was breathing quickly, though. Close to hyperventilating.

"Shelter's not far." Ash sniffed the air.

The other two exchanged a look. "You smell something?" the woman asked, nose raised as if trying to locate the odor.

Silly question. There was always *something* to smell. Blood and sour sweat just now, from the injured man. On the frozen river, the air had been greasy with the stench of fuel and, again, blood. With a little distance from the wreckage came the soggy newspaper scent of a boreal forest rising from hibernation, a heady cocktail of sweet conifers, moist bark, iron-rich mud, and bear. Now above it all came a sharp high note that his animal mind had picked up before his conscious brain.

An extinguished wood fire.

They were close to the giant's lair.

"Have you got what you need to care for that?" Ash asked the woman. At her nod, he set off without looking back. Something much more intriguing drew him forward. Something he'd always had a hard time resisting: a mystery.

Yes, the identity of the big man piqued his curiosity, of course, but that wasn't what made him as eager. No, what he really wanted to know was why the giant had led this team of hunters straight to his home instead of away from it.

———————

Elias grabbed a few plastic water bags and canteens, stuffed some more dried fish into the pack, and made sure he had a supply of watertight wet bags.

The woman swayed on her feet, doing her damnedest to stare him down, her eyes dark, shimmering daggers in her sculpted, brown face. If she weren't in such bad shape, she'd attack, of that he had no doubt. He'd bet anything the bulge at her ankle was a blade. Bound to be more knives hidden on her.

Who the hell was this woman? She was stubborn and strong. Unwilling to back down against some pretty tough odds, and a pilot who'd handled her aircraft with precision, finesse, and great big fiery balls of steel.

Despite the head wound and the blood and everything else, he noticed, she was attractive. In a dangerous, bristling-with-weapons kind of way. Black, tightly shorn hair hugged her skull, as if to show off a fine, delicate bone structure that needed no added ornaments. Below it, her brown skin looked soft and warm.

Dammit, if he'd gone to town and gotten laid already, he wouldn't be letting this distract him.

Liar. He'd like her looks and her prickly attitude no matter what. Everything about her was tightly wound, as if she weren't made of flesh and bones but of pure energy, barely contained in what looked like a muscular body, although that was hard to tell with all those layers on. Her expression was in no way inviting. More like calculating the exact moment she'd put her knife through his jugular.

Whoever she was, her presence here didn't make any sense.

She wasn't with the helicopter people. But what was to stop more than one group from coming after him? Though the world thought he was dead, he'd always suspected the authorities had doubts. For all he knew, the entire National Guard could be hot on his trail, along with an army of mercenaries and bounty hunters from the lower forty-eight.

What was it Daisy had said on the phone? *On her way to get you.* Right. Well, *get you* could mean any number of things. No way could he trust this woman. But no way could he leave her to die, either.

Bo growled again. Time to go. His cabin would come under fire any minute now and in here, they had a stalemate. He needed to make a move.

"You don't want to talk to me? Fine. Talk to them." He stalked to the door, reached for the bar he'd installed as a barricade, and started to slide it up in what he hoped wasn't an obvious bluff.

"Wait!"

He let out a long, silent exhale. When he turned back, he caught her eyes racing around the room. Looking for something to say? Trying to buy time until that team of hers showed up? Searching the corners for a weapon or a way out?

"Listen, lady. I don't know who you are and I don't know who you're looking for, but I'm not it. I don't have time for this bullsh—"

"Leo."

"What?"

Something thumped outside and Elias dropped the barricade back in its slots.

"My name. It's Leo."

"That's a start. What're you doing here?"

"Look." Her attention shifted from him to the door and back. "Maybe we want the same thing, you and I."

A cold beer? A warm bath? His eyes flicked over her body before returning to meet hers. "Doubt that." Bo stood, the hair on the ridge of her spine tufted straight up. Elias swallowed back a curse. He couldn't leave the woman behind to die, but he couldn't take her with him until he knew more—namely whether she'd been sent by Amka to help him, or whether she'd stolen the plane after all and was here to stab him in the back the minute he turned around. There were too many people who wanted him dead to give anyone the benefit of the doubt. "Who sent you?" Elias demanded. Bo growled in warning. This was cutting it close. Too damned close. "What do you want with me?"

"With *you*? Nothing."

"Lady, you don't give me something worthwhile, I'll throw you out there."

She looked at him for five seconds—which was four seconds too long—and appeared to come to some sort of decision. "Will you? Then open the door." She folded her arms over her chest, her expression clearly saying *I dare you.*

If he opened that door, all three of them were dead, with at least one of them being tortured first. Bo's growl turned urgent. She backed away from the door, hackles raised higher than he'd ever seen them. "Dammit."

The woman half smiled.

In that moment, three things happened: a foot landed carefully on his booby-trapped porch step, setting off literal alarm bells; someone yelled; and Bo started barking, out of control.

There wasn't time for more questions. He'd have to take her or leave her here. To die.

Elias grabbed a gas can and uncapped it. Bo went wild. Heavy footsteps shook the floor beneath their feet. The people out there weren't even trying to be stealthy. Bad news. Very bad news.

He slung his pack on his shoulder and soaked everything with gas. "Let's go!"

As if she'd done her own quick math and decided she liked her odds better with him than with the operatives who'd shot down her plane, Leo grabbed her bag and followed him to the back of the cabin.

"Campbell Turner!" a voice yelled from out front. The name barely threw a hitch in Elias's stride, though something broke inside him every time he heard it. His gaze connected with the woman's, whose eyes narrowed on him. Whatever her role here today, this woman was well aware that Elias was not Campbell Turner. "We're here to discuss a peaceful surrender. We know you're in there."

Yeah? he thought, though he kept his mouth firmly shut. *You don't know the first damn thing.*

With that, he squatted, pulled the rug back, and pried out the panel he'd created for just such an occasion.

"Hop in, Leo." *Whoever the hell you are.* When she appeared to balk, he bared his teeth—half snarl, half smile. "Sorry, lady. But this is it. Do or die."

CHAPTER 6

THE DOG JUMPED INTO THE HOLE AND THE MAN SHOVED HIS pack inside, followed by Leo's.

More aggressive pounding on the door made her jump and, though it hurt to bend and crawl, that was exactly what she did, cursing under her breath as she went.

"Go. *Go*." There was no arguing with the urgency in his voice. "The passage is flat, then it dips. Push the bags ahead, if you can. Be right behind you."

As fast as she could, she slithered through the stone crawlspace, shoving at the packs. She wouldn't let herself imagine what kinds of creatures lived in the cave beneath the cabin.

After what felt like an eternity of crawling, one of the packs tipped over the edge ahead of her and fell to land somewhere below. She pushed the other down, almost entirely blind now. One outstretched hand encountered nothing but cold air.

A glance back showed only the smallest hint of light seeping down from above. What was he up to? Was he coming or had this been some creepy ruse to get her under his house? Crap. She could be trapped here.

"Hey! Are you—"

"*Go!*"

He doesn't want to kill me. He doesn't want to wear my skin. Bolder now, she waved her arm out and down, expecting a sharp drop. Instead, she slapped canvas a foot or so down—his backpack. She shimmied to the edge. Impossible to tell how big the space was, but it felt cramped and damp.

Sounds came from behind—banging, more fuel splashing. It stank even this far. The place would go up in seconds.

"Keep going! Don't stop!" He didn't bother whispering now, as if the urgency had amped up. As if he were barely holding the enemy back, waiting for her to advance before he could leave.

Faster than she'd meant to, she pulled forward until she dropped onto the pack, glad for the cushioning, though the fall sent a wave of nausea through her. She barely held in a shriek when something cold and wet touched her cheek.

It was the dog. Just the dog. "Geez, you scared me."

For a precious second or two, she let herself sink to the cold, damp earth, leaned against the animal's soft fur, and breathed, willing her head to clear. Up was down in this darkness. Down was up. Were her eyes even open?

The sounds behind her were muffled by distance and, she figured, tons of rock. Were they battering through the door? Had they made it in? She scrabbled for something to guide her, connected with rough stone, and pushed slowly to standing.

"Grab your pack and go! Far as you can get!" he ordered, his voice low and terse, closer now. She'd made it maybe a dozen stumbling steps when a red light infused the cave. She turned in time to see what looked like a handful of flares disappear before something slammed shut, leaving them in the dark. Then, judging from the quick, frantic sound of fabric scuffing against the ground, she guessed that he was army-crawling through that tight tunnel—fast.

Carefully, hand to the stone wall, rough even with gloves on, she felt her way forward. Something crashed so hard it resonated through her feet. The front door? Were they in?

Time's up.

Light suddenly blinded her. She raised her hand to shield her eyes. After a few dull seconds, she realized that the man was moving toward her, wearing a forehead lamp.

"Run." He hefted his bag. "*Now.*"

She moved, pushing her body as fast as it would go, and focused on the narrow illumination he provided. After they'd advanced maybe ten, twenty, or infinity feet, something, he grabbed her hand. Though she didn't like it, she didn't pull away. He knew where they were going, clearly, while she was running half-blind into... What was this place?

The space felt huge, though she couldn't see enough to tell how big. Was there an echo to their steps? The dog's glowing body was the only thing to focus on in this black hole.

Suddenly, her view narrowed and the man's hand loosened. "Duck," he said before nudging her slightly ahead of him. "Once you're out, crawl up the rocks, then through the opening at the top. Follow Bo. Keep moving." He shoved a flashlight at her. "Don't wait for me. Just go."

Gritting her teeth, she ignored the inner voice screaming *Don't leave me here alone!* and scrabbled up a pile of boulders to a tiny, dark opening, barely big enough to fit through. Every movement hurt her body, but she used it, focused beyond the pain, and stuffed herself into the hole, wondering what fresh trick this incredibly well-prepared stranger had up his sleeve.

He listened to the far-off thump of metal to wood, satisfied that they'd finally breached the cabin. They'd be fighting the flames right about now. *Good.* He crossed the cave, focused on the head-lamp's glow, and climbed. *If they made it down here, then he didn't deserve to survive their attack anyway.*

As if *merit* had anything to do with life or death. He knew for a fact that it didn't.

No more death, he'd promised himself. Of course, that was a lot easier to uphold when you didn't have a team hunting you down. He didn't want them to die, dammit, even if they'd picked the wrong side. Most of them were probably contractors, here doing a job. Just like he'd been when this whole thing started.

And what about the woman, Leo? Just another contractor, doing her job? Something inside him panged at the idea of her dying, even though he truly didn't know her at all. He wanted her to be on the right side. On his side.

At the top, he peered through the hole to see her at the end of the low passage with one hand gripping the flashlight, the other sunk into the fur on Bo's back.

"Good girl," he whispered, and Bo's tail thumped once in response.

After crawling through, he turned and worked to roll a few large stones across the opening. It wasn't a perfect fit, but if those assholes somehow managed to survive and then find their way through his first couple of blockades, this would hide their tracks for a while at least. "Gonna be harder from here on out," he said. "Single file for now." He emerged, pointing at the next section they'd have to maneuver.

Muttering something under her breath, she turned and followed Bo over more massive stones.

The woman had grit. Which was fortunate, because at some point, things were sure to go from dangerous to worse.

If only he knew who the hell she was.

———————

The explosion made Leo drop the flashlight, hunker hard into the rock she was perched on, and cover her head.

For a few eternal heartbeats, she stayed suspended, every nerve in her body expectantly awaiting the searing burn of carbonization or the bone-breaking collapse of stone.

It didn't come.

Aside from the dull blast and the brief shuddering of the boulder beneath her, a sprinkling of dust was the only indication that the ceiling could possibly collapse. After a few more seconds, she caught her breath, pushed herself to sitting, and turned to catch a grimace on the man's shadowed face.

"You actually blew the place up."

"I did."

"That's…" She snapped her mouth shut.

"Cold?" His dismissive huff expressed more than words. It told her exactly what he thought of the people chasing them. And wasn't he right after all? If this group was anything like the others she'd encountered, they'd stop at nothing to get what they wanted.

"Well executed."

"You think?" He sucked in a deep, audible breath. "Well, we're not out yet."

She peered around, blind until the dog shot ahead, blazing a pale trail through the murkiness. With her first step, she banged her shin into a rock and swore.

"Here." The man put his gloved hand out, palm up. "Take it."

She paused, staring for a few seconds before letting her eyes rise to meet his in the dark. "Okay," she said, surprised at how certain her own voice sounded. Then again, she had no other choice.

———

Ash watched from the shadows as what had once been a homey, rustic wooden cabin lit up the night like a torch. *Mystery solved.*

Well, part of it. He knew now why the giant had led them to his home.

To blow us all straight to hell.

An excellent play. Ash had caught the scent of an accelerant the moment the cabin's front door had swung open. Most of the others hadn't been so lucky.

Guilt scratched at him. His warning shout had come too late.

Then again, these operatives should have known better. A man like their team leader, Deegan, who according to Ash's intel had led missions in hot spots around the world, should have known better. He should have protected his people, taken the time to scout out the situation rather than blundering in like that and risking lives.

Ash looked around, glad that he didn't have to answer to that man.

In the meantime, their quarry had just grown more interesting.

The wind shifted, bringing with it the scent of an approaching storm.

Not a good start to the mission. They'd just arrived and most of the Titan Security team were either injured, dead, or dying. The real bugger was that as of this moment, rescue was impossible. Too dark and, with the imminent weather change, too dangerous.

Ash made his slow, careful way around the perimeter, following the paw prints he'd first spotted near to the crash site. The canine, he reckoned, would be what gave his quarry away. Eventually.

He sighed, regretting the devastation, not just to human lives and nature, but to what had been a lovely little home in the wild. This place—the cabin, the scenery, the absolute isolation—spoke to him. He felt something like kinship for the man. And respect.

But he had a job to do.

He catalogued each and every paw and boot print as he returned to the front and approached the team leader. "Deegan," he said, with a hint of petty satisfaction at the big, square-jawed American's startled response.

"Shit, man. How'd you get there?"

"Walked," Ash replied, not showing a hint of humor.

A snowflake curled to the ground between them.

"Lost four good people tonight." Deegan couldn't, for the life of him, speak quietly. Even his whisper boomed. "Now you're a fuckin' comedi—"

"Target's gone."

"Yeah, I know they're—" Deegan's hand dropped from where he worked a gloved palm over his shaven skull. "You saying they survived this?"

"You won't find their remains in there." Ash put out a hand, watching as a few more flakes settled on the worn leather of his glove only to disappear, as fleeting as life itself. "It was a trap."

"No shit, Sherlock."

Ash blew the remaining tiny, playful crystals from his hand, then focused back on the flames. A spot of cheer in this colorless setting. "They're *in* the mountain."

Deegan blinked and slowly turned to take in the ridge rising behind them. "How the hell'd they get in there?" he asked, doubt lacing every word.

"You ever hear of the troglodytes?"

The narrow-eyed look Deegan threw Ash's way told him he wasn't thrilled at the prospect of an onsite history lesson.

"Cave dwellers, Deegan. In parts of France, even today, you'll find homes carved from—" He broke into a smirk, leaned forward and gave the man a light smack to the shoulder, like a cat taunting a big, angry dog. "Don't worry. I'm not about to *actually* give you a history lesson. Taking the piss, mate. No time to chat." With a wink, he hooked a thumb over his shoulder. "While you care for your wounded, I shall find an alternate way in." He considered the numerous ins and outs of the rock face, every one of which could be an entrance—or merely an indentation. "If I play my cards right, I'll trap them inside and let you lot get home to your families."

CHAPTER 7

IT TOOK TWO AND A HALF HOURS TO GET TO HIS HIDEOUT—twice as long as it normally did. By the time they arrived, it was close to midnight and the woman—Leo—was having trouble. As far as he could tell, only the walls kept her standing.

"What's this?" she mumbled, squinting at the tight, low space he'd prepared for just this type of event.

"My getaway cache."

"Cash?" She collapsed onto a stone ledge and leaned back against the wall, eyes closed. "Oh. Oh, supplies. Right."

He went to a natural shelf in the corner and pulled things out—first, the oil lamp, which he lit, then first aid supplies, rations, water.

"Sh…sh…" The woman's eyes slowly opened, no doubt in response to the unexpected glow.

"What?"

"Shouldn't…stop. Keep…going."

"Not sure you're in any shape to go on."

"I'm fine." Clearly a lie.

"Lemme check your head."

"Mmm."

She watched, eyes dull, as he set his supplies on the ledge beside her.

"Prepper," she said, blinking slowly.

He huffed out a humorless sound. "Comes with the territory."

Her brows rose, though even that effort looked extreme. "Territory's that?"

The question wasn't worth answering. Instead, he dragged out the bedroll he kept here and set it up in a corner of the cave. "Lie down." Cozy it wasn't, but they were a long way from comfort at this point.

From this point on, really.

She opened her mouth as if to refuse, apparently recognized how desperate her situation was, and shut it again. Slowly, as if her bones hurt, she pushed off the wall.

In two steps, he was at her side. She sagged against him, dropped her head to his chest, and moaned, long and low. Not a pleasant sound. Bo whined, clearly in agreement.

He put a hand to her back, hesitated, and when she didn't react, wrapped his other arm around her. Just supporting her. "Here. Lie down." Gently, he helped her onto the pallet. "Drink." He held out a water bottle.

She accepted, managing a sip or two before she dropped her head in her arms.

"Let me see your eyes."

"What?"

"Your pupils. Got to check 'em."

"Oh, right. Right. Sure."

A look with the light of his headlamp showed two quickly contracting pinpoints. He let out a relieved sigh. "Okay. Your eyes look okay. Rest for a bit while I…" He stopped short.

"While you what?"

"Nothing." He looked at the narrow gap that would take them to the outside world and all the problems it could possibly throw their way.

"Where is he?"

"Who?"

"Campbell Turner. They called you—" She blinked, a frustrated breath puffing from her mouth. "If my head didn't hurt so much, I could figure this out." She shut her eyes tight, looking for all the world like her brain hurt. Which it probably did. Her unfocused gaze landed on him. "Wanna tell me who you are?"

"No," he said, pausing in the nearly invisible crack in the wall. "Wouldn't do too much wandering, if I were you, Leo. Place is dangerous." He took off.

"You coming back, whatever your name is?" A pause. "Hey, yeti! You coming back?"

"Wait and see!" he responded, calling Bo to join him outside.

———————

The moment the tiny plane disappeared on the horizon, Amka had shuffled back to her home for some painkillers and a nip of moonshine. She'd watched the helicopter take off, a good hour later, pleased, until she'd understood the reason for the delay.

While she'd been sending Leo off on her rescue mission, the guys from the helicopter had taken over her town. Every man, woman, and child had been rounded up at gunpoint. As far as Amka could tell, she was the only straggler.

Daisy—her partner and the love of her life—was being held at the lodge, with the other adults. The kids had all been rounded up at Marion's house. The bastards had taken every last person Amka cared about prisoner, aside from Elias. She hoped.

It was up to her to remedy the situation.

Now she eyed her ATV mournfully before heading up the hill to the overlook. Like the Piper Cub, she'd been eighty-sixed from driving land vehicles. As if she couldn't navigate this place blindfolded.

Too old to drive. Too old to fly. Too old to shoot. But she could tell you when a storm was headed this way.

And she knew some wild shit was going down right here, in her little corner of Alaska.

The place was eerily dark. Only a couple of lights shone. Hadn't seen it this dark since…maybe twenty years ago now. Or was it thirty? Before the lodge was built and equipped with panels and backup generators.

Somewhere not too far off, a dog howled, the call as mournful as a wolf's. More joined in from kennels and houses all around town until the whole damn thing was like a chorus. Somebody'd have to feed them or they'd get riled up.

Maybe riled up was good. She'd have to think on how she could use that to her advantage.

She shifted her scope to the right. Two people guarded the exterior of the lodge. Couldn't get a clear view of the airfield from here, but since the helicopter had returned for the night, she assumed there'd be at least one watching over it. She'd counted another at Marion's house, though there might be more inside. She doubted it. People underestimated kids the way they did old people.

Good thing they'd forgotten all about her—or had no idea she existed—cause she planned to haunt Schink's Station like the ghost of caribou past. Like every tourist trophy kill she'd ever seen. She pictured their heads waking up on walls all over the lower forty-eight and attacking the hunters who'd killed them. These people thought they could waltz into her town and terrorize its residents without consequence? Nope. Every person she loved was here—all but one, and she'd done what she could for Elias. The boy was strong and smart. With the help of that Leo woman, he'd be just fine.

Speaking of which. She pulled out the sat phone. Still jammed. Son of a bitch. How far out of town would she have to go to be able to call Leo's team again? Not that it would make a lick of difference tonight, with the storm coming in.

With a grunt of discomfort, she stood, hefted her rifle, and patted the holster at her belt to make sure her skinning knife was still there. She squinted into the darkness, wishing she knew what those shots had been. They'd come from the lodge. *Please don't be Daisy*, she prayed for the first time in years. If they'd done something to Daisy, she wasn't sure she'd survive this.

Jaw hard, she set off shuffling down the back path to Marion's, humming "These Boots Are Made for Walking" under her breath. Time to wreak some old-lady havoc on these motherfuckers.

CHAPTER 8

LEO PLANTED A HAND ON THE ROCK WALL AND SHIFTED, THEN slowly made her way to standing. *Whoa.* Okay. Okay, she had this. It just might take a little longer than she was used to. Between the stomach bug last night, the lack of sleep, and the crash, she was running on fumes.

She looked at the two exits, each only a few feet from where she stood. Although *stood* was a kind word for the way her body depended on the rocks. Drunk leaned was more like it.

So far, the man seemed like an ally, but Leo hadn't survived this far by counting on the kindness of strangers.

Go! her inner voice screamed. *Grab whatever supplies you can and get out of here.* It was the voice that had saved her time and again on deployment. The voice that told her when to head in for her guys and when it was too hot to try. She listened.

Not trusting herself to walk, she sank back to the ground and crawled to his pack, tore at the zipper, and dug inside. Military-grade rations, energy bars, a plastic bag of stuff that looked like worn orange leather. She opened it, sniffed, and came close to barfing at the fish stink.

I'll go with the rations.

And that was saying something.

As fast as she could, she rifled through the contents. Clothes, batteries, flashlights, tools, water. Socks. Everything—literally every item—double wrapped in airtight bags. A tarp—or maybe a poncho?—and a couple Mylar blankets. There. A metal box, also bagged. With hands so weak they shook, she opened it, only to have her hopes dashed. A fire-starting kit. She shut it, slipped it into her coat pocket, and continued looking. A bag contained first aid supplies. She kept ahold of that, too. Socks, socks, socks. Farther down, a sleeping bag and more damned socks. Wet wipes, hand sanitizer, biodegradable soap. The man was clean, she'd give him that. Another sleeping bag, more socks. The outer pockets and straps weren't any better. Camp stove, sleeping pad. Snowshoes. Ski poles. More wipes. More socks.

"Okay, Sock Man," she muttered, shoving it all back in. "What else we got?"

Her own pack contained even less. Water, a couple of blankets, her extra set of clothes. One measly pair of socks. Her own wipes. She clearly hadn't packed for the occasion.

Her attempt to heft his pack was futile. The thing probably weighed a hundred pounds, and she was currently weak as a kitten.

What about her Glock? Had he taken it or left it behind? Had she dropped it in the plane? She turned. *Whoa.* Shutting her eyes hard on the spinning room, she waited out the dizzy spell.

Okay. He had to have a phone, right? Something to communicate with the outside world.

Must have taken it with him. His rifle too. He'd brought that, right? How had she not noted that kind of detail?

And who on earth *was* he?

Nothing made sense. She'd come here in search of Campbell Turner, a five-foot-eleven man in his fifties. This giant was maybe thirty, maybe forty. Hell, who could tell with the beard and hair and coat? The deep voice and long silences. Could he truly be just a wilderness freak in the wrong place at the wrong time?

That sure seemed fishy. She'd buy the random-hermit thing, but here? *Right here*, where Amka had sent her? No way. Besides, what Arctic wilderness guy had an emergency exit like his? None was the answer. He'd set fire to his own cabin, for God's sake. Blasted the thing to kingdom come and then dragged her through miles and miles of tunnels. No, the guy was definitely part of this whole mess somehow, but she didn't have time to play his games.

She needed to get ahold of her team, locate Campbell Turner, and get to the virus or more people would die. And that meant ditching the yeti.

Heavy as lead, she forced herself onto her knees and finally to standing. Determined, she stood, circled the cave, running her hands along the wall in search of any place he could have hidden a weapon or a phone.

I've got to warn Eric and Ford and the others. Get Von and Ans back to Schink's Station. Figure out what's going on.

The walls were surprisingly smooth, no cracks or fissures where he could have squirreled things away. She stretched, reaching as high as her five-foot-six frame would allow. Nothing.

There was only one place left to look—the hole he'd gone through on his way out.

She made her way over, ducked, and squinted down a short, narrow passage. It was cooler here and it smelled like...something. Like the outdoors, though she couldn't say just what that meant.

She went still. Were those footsteps approaching?

Impossible to tell down here, where noises echoed dully off stone walls and ceilings and floors. She cocked her head to the side. There was no sound but the steady drip of water.

Time to get out. No more waiting to see what the big mountain man had in store. No more hoping he was one of the good guys. She needed to locate Turner, who hopefully would have some means of reaching out to her team. Whoever this guy was, she'd figure it out later. Or maybe not. Maybe he'd forever remain the nameless, paranoid yeti guy whose bug-out bag she stole after he pulled her from her one and only crash.

Ignoring a pang of guilt, she staggered back into the cave, dug a few items from his pack, and threw them on the floor. She couldn't leave him with nothing after all. Then, using every ounce of effort she could drum up, she heaved his pack up, braced it and herself against the wall, and slid both arms through the straps. With a deep inhale, she pushed off, staggering under the load. The effort sent the pressure in her head skyrocketing.

Working hard, she shuffled forward, hunched, one hand skidding along the rock wall. The lamplight's yellow gave way so gradually to blue that she didn't notice the change until the ceiling went from claustrophobia-inducing to cathedral. Slowly, her gaze slid up, up, up. The space was tinged with a light, ethereal hue, as though someone had left a television on in a far corner. Except there weren't corners in this place—only curves, rippling in the lamplight. Layers upon layers, glowing as if from within. Some spots were dark as black holes, others bright, all of it frozen in time. In places, what looked like water bulged down into half-finished drips.

It was the most unearthly thing she'd ever seen. No, not seen—experienced. It felt like she'd stepped from the dark cave into another planet, like being submerged in the ocean, deep-sea diving without a mask or oxygen. Never in her life had a place made her feel this way: cold and lost and caught up in the wonder. She spun, shrinking back instinctively at the movement within the walls. Swelling, billowing, whitecaps rushing, like being caught beneath a wave about to crest, the tide sucking up, bright and shiny. Like galaxies in the sky, swirling, shifting, unending. Yet utterly still.

She released a lungful of metallic air, unaware of having held it in, and took a step.

Her boot hit something with a clang. She glanced down. Millimeters below her foot, a trap sat, armed, the two sets of sharp, gleaming teeth wide-open. With a gasp, she overcorrected and wobbled. Pendulum-heavy, the pack dragged her weight in the opposite direction, straight at the gaping jaws. Her instincts, though slow, told her to dive. Airborne for a few breathless seconds, she twisted in a pointless attempt to land on the pack, before ramming into cold, hard ice. The impact emptied her lungs in a single, painful burst.

Her skull exploded in white-hot pain.

The air outside stank of fuel and burned plastic and, if he wasn't mistaken, charred flesh. He didn't dare approach the ruined cabin to do a head count. It wasn't worth the risk, given that his tracks would lead them back here. Even this far, he could hear them taking over the woods around his home with the confidence and recklessness of men convinced they were on the right side of things.

Been there, done that. Got the scars to prove it.

Hopefully they assumed he'd died in the fire.

He swiped a gloved hand across his wet face. The stuff falling from the sky was somewhere between snow and ice. The kind of precipitation that slowed *everyone* down.

Him included.

He glanced at the entrance to the cave. Given the state of his unexpected guest—or prisoner, depending on who she was—a few hours rest probably wasn't a bad thing. The trick would be to time things right. If they left too early, they'd get stuck in this crap. If they waited too long, the other team had the numbers and equipment to catch up with them.

This time of year was treacherous for travel. Snow and ice melt meant floods and landslides and muddy, impossible terrain.

He stepped inside, automatically scanned the space, and went dead still. Bo yipped.

By the time his eyes adjusted, he'd figured out what he was looking at—sort of. The woman appeared to be struggling to sit up on the cave floor, right where he'd armed one of his traps. Filled with dread, he ran toward her. "Leo."

She made a sound that was half-grunt, half-gasp and fought harder to rise. By the time he made it to her side, he could see that the trap was still armed—thank God. Her head, on the other hand, was bleeding again.

"Hold on. Stay still." He squatted beside her. "You okay?"

As if finally giving up, she sank back to her butt and let her face fall into her gloved hands. "No."

"What'd you do?"

One dark eye peeked out from between her fingers. "Can't you put it together?"

He took in the trap, her arms still strapped into the backpack, which anchored her to the ice floor, a blood smear on the ice wall above her head. "Didn't make it far."

"I almost stepped in that thing." She threw him a dirty look. "You trying to maim me?"

"Trying to maim the guys who came after you."

"Well, it foiled my escape attempt."

"You're not a prisoner, Leo." At least he didn't think so. He hoped not. He didn't want her to be.

The impact of her gaze meeting his was visceral. There was something wild in the way she watched him. It reached deep inside him and tweaked a savage little chord of its own. *Recognition.*

"Why'd they call you Campbell Turner?" Her question wasn't what he expected. When he didn't immediately respond, she carefully leaned her head back on the pack as if it were a pillow and tracked him with her eyes. "That's what I can't figure out. Some random guy just minding his business might pull me from the crash. But you…" She swallowed with a grimace. More blood seeped from her scalp, down her forehead to the corner of her eye. She swiped it away and pointed that same gloved hand at him. "You hauled ass up to the cabin like you knew exactly what was about to happen." She started to shake her head and grimaced. "Shit, why can't I figure this out?"

"You cracked your head." He glanced up at the blood on the wall. "For the second time."

"Not feeling so hot."

"I can tell." He scooted closer. "I should clean it. Will you let me do that?"

The look they exchanged was long, searching. It hit him in that place again—too deep in his bones to identify. Her eyes flicked away. "Yeah. Just...just tell me one thing."

He lifted his brows, waiting.

"Are *you* her godson? Amka's?"

She must have seen the surprise and acknowledgment on his face because she laughed—or started to. Apparently, that hurt, too. After a long, low groan, something like a smile tilted her lips.

She was beautiful, even in her current state.

"Is he even here? Turner? She begged me to..." Her mouth went tight. "You know what? I don't think she once mentioned his name. The old biddy tricked me." There was admiration in her voice. "I fell for it hook, line, and sinker."

"What'd she say?"

"Told me these guys had his location." She snorted. "But she didn't say that, did she? She said..." Her brows lowered in concentration. "She said she could give me the location of the man we were looking for." Her eyes flew to his. "Not Turner's. Her godson's. *Your* location. Turner's not here, is he?" At his head shake, she grimaced. "Crap, my head hurts."

"I'm sorry."

"About my head or your godmother?"

"Both." A warmth worked its way through him.

"Well, thanks." She appeared to hesitate. "Can I count on you not killing me? For now at least?"

The feeling took hold—part relief, part something too painful to consider. "Guess so."

She looked up with a grimace. "I can't get up."

"Here." He squatted, loosened the pack's shoulder straps one at a time, and helped her to slide out. "Sorry about the trap."

"Want to make it up to me by explaining what's going on here?" He couldn't bring himself to respond. "Didn't think so." She stood with one hand balanced against the wall. "We heading out?"

"No. Squalling out there, which is a complication."

She looked around, eyes wide, as if she'd just noticed where they were.

"You all right?"

"What *is* this place?"

"Glacier cave." He'd forgotten what it was like to see it for the first time.

"So, we're inside a glacier?"

He nodded and surveyed their surroundings, trying to picture it through her eyes.

"It's like…" Sounding out of breath, she stared up at the slick shapes curled above them. "Like the ocean just…flash froze or something. Like a rogue wave that'll never crash."

He cleared his throat. "Should see it in daylight. Blue's electric."

She opened and shut her mouth a couple of times and, despite the blood crusted along her hairline and the smudge of something dark on that sharply carved cheekbone, there was a softness to her face that he hadn't noticed before. Not that he'd had the opportunity to look—running for their lives wasn't conducive to rubbernecking. Now that he'd taken a second to look, though, he couldn't stop seeing the velvet plumpness of her lips. He liked the symmetry of her perfectly sculpted head, the crown round and high, while her chin came to a tiny, sweet point.

"I always figured people messed with photos to make stuff like this more impressive."

"Some things don't need to be messed with." He had to drag his attention from her mouth and the blue-black sheen of her skin in the glacier's light. He wiped a hand over his face. *The hell's wrong with me?* "I'm a… I've got to, uh…" He stood, reached for the wall for balance, and lost his footing. His arms pinwheeled as he slid ungracefully onto his ass at her feet.

He'd just opened his mouth to cuss when a sound like choking hit him. No, not choking. Suppressed laughter, which bubbled up and out of Leo's mouth. "Ow." She moaned, grimaced as if in pain, and got the laugh under control before giving him a sheepish look. "I'm so sorry. I don't usually laugh at other people falling. Are you okay?"

He worked his way back to standing. "Fine."

"I'm…sorry. It wasn't even that funny, except you're just so…" Her eyes made a trip up and down his body. The kind of look that would speak of appreciation, under better circumstances. Or maybe that was wishful thinking.

"So what?" The question just popped out.

"I don't know. Sure-footed? Able-bodied?" Christ, he knew that wasn't meant to be a come-on line, but it hit him low and hard. She squinted at him. "Sure you're not hurt?"

"Only my pride," he responded, realizing with a little shock that his mouth had tightened at the corners in the start of a return smile. The ache in his chest lessened.

Beside him, Bo whined, probably unsure of why her person looked less grim than usual.

He turned to hush her and spun back just in time to catch Leo's arm as she took her own unsteady step and started to go down. For a second, they stood there, tense and ready to drop, holding on to each other for dear life.

"Crap."

"Room spinning?"

"Pretty much. I'm not sure I can take another hit to the head."

His body finally found its equilibrium. "True. That lump gets any bigger, it'll look like you've got two heads."

"Ew." She wrinkled up her nose, still grinning. Still crushingly beautiful. Their gazes caught and held. His pulse picked up. "Thanks," she finally said in a whisper.

"For what?"

"For helping me out here."

He tightened his hold on her arm. "Let's patch you up. Get some rest."

"Okay." She inhaled shakily and gave him the sort of smile that had probably left a pile of broken hearts the size of Denali in her wake. "But I'm scooting across this ice on my butt."

She put up a hand when Elias tried to help her down, so he stepped back and watched her slide toward the rock cave on her ass.

Ah hell, Amka, he thought as he scooped up the backpack and followed her, hopeful in a way he hadn't been in forever. Which scared the crap out of him. *What were you thinking?*

CHAPTER 9

BACK IN THE CAVE, HE THREW THE PACK DOWN WITH A *THUNK* and bent to find the first aid supplies.

"How long will we stay here?"

"They're out there. Storm's coming. Nobody's moving tonight. Beyond that, got no idea." He rifled through the pack—noting that she'd turned it inside out—pulled out the first aid kit and then snagged a few of the energy bars he'd stocked for an occasion like this. "Hungry?"

"I could eat."

He handed Leo a bar, a water bottle, and a couple pain pills, all of which she accepted with a nod, then set food out for Bo.

The cave was tight, maybe fifteen square feet total. The low ceiling hemmed them in even further, making the space small, though not warm and nowhere near as cozy as the cabin he'd been forced to destroy.

Without the blue tint of the glacier cave, Leo's skin had taken on a wan, gray cast. But the stubbornness to her jaw said that it would take more than a couple bumps on the head to stop this woman. "So, where is Campbell Turner?"

He sank to the floor beside her and let his head thunk back against the stone wall, cushioned by the thick fabric and fur of his hood. "How'd you know I wasn't him?"

He didn't have to see her features to hear the *Oh, please* in the air between them.

"The man's last driver's license—which he got sixteen years ago—says he's five eleven." She handed him the water, eyes closed, and breathed for a few beats, then leaned her head back and gave him an exaggerated up and down. Though he didn't think it was meant to be sexual, the attention licked at his nerves. "I don't need a tape measure to see that you're well over six feet." She let out a humorless laugh. "And even in my current state, I know you're not fifty-three years old. Or blond." She arched one fine eyebrow. "Natural or otherwise."

He thought about making a stupid crack and reconsidered. Instead, he gave her silence.

"Do you know him?"

For the first time since this whole thing broke open, he was tempted to spill it all. But what if Amka had made a bad call and Leo wasn't one of the good guys? What if Amka hadn't sent her at all? That possibility pricked at his spine, alongside the pull of hope he couldn't quite tamp down.

"What's Amka call that plane you were flying?"

She didn't hesitate. "Dolores."

Relief flooded in. No way would she know that if Amka hadn't sent her. "I knew Campbell," he finally conceded. "Good man. Got caught up in something way beyond his control." He leaned forward so she could see his face and lifted his eyebrows, nodding to indicate her head. "Can I..." Their eyes met for a long moment; hers flicked down to his mouth and back up. It sent a bolt of pure heat through him. He blinked and focused anywhere but on her lips.

At her nod, he examined her scalp, breath coming in fast and light. "I'm no expert, but this doesn't look good."

"We talking stitches?"

"Might be able to manage with butterfly bandages." He grabbed his flashlight. "Let me check your pupils again."

Both pupils contracted, so that was good. He set to work cleaning her wound, noting the way her body shifted, not moving, per se, but sort of sinking into itself, as if gravity and fatigue were finally taking their toll.

The silence between them had lulled him too, he realized, when she broke it. "What about you?"

"What about me?" He pressed a butterfly bandage to her head, moving on to the next one when it appeared to be holding.

"You get caught up too?" Her voice was low and rough.

He went still but didn't respond. If she heard the shakiness of his breathing—and she had to, given how quiet it was—she'd know she hit a nerve.

"In something beyond your control?"

A dozen seconds went by in silence while his brain fought an internal tug-of-war. How good would it feel to share the burden?

No. Not now. She was injured. She needed to sleep. There'd be time to rehash it all later. If he decided to.

The secret, kept too close for too long, felt as impossible to let go of as an addiction.

Who would he be without it?

Didn't matter. Who he'd been, who he could have become. This kind of *what if* conjecture served no purpose but to stir up regret. And he'd had enough of that for a lifetime.

Ignoring her question, he stuck another bandage to the cut on her head, then another, each press as gentle as he could make it. The laceration wasn't what bothered him—it was the bump. Add to that her exhaustion and the dry heaving near the crash site and there was a good chance Leo whatever her last name was had a concussion.

He bit back a yawn, recognizing his own exhaustion for the first time—aching muscles, gritty eyes, heavy head. He worked hard to concentrate as he covered her injury with a clean white bandage. Yeah, so maybe she wasn't the only one who was close to passing out.

"This'll have to do for now." He fought the urge to let his hand linger around her ear and shoved himself back, then up to standing. "Let's rest."

Her only response was a long, low hum. He unpacked a few more items and grabbed a bedroll, spread it beside the first, and caught a glance from her. "Not much room."

"It's fine."

"You can go up the hall if you need to use the, uh…"

She shook her head.

And then, because he had the feeling she wouldn't settle in until he did, he zipped himself up, careful to face away from her, definitely not touching but, by necessity, close.

Once she'd done the same, he doused the oil lamp. The silence that followed lasted so long he was convinced that she'd fallen asleep. Then: "What's your name?"

He swallowed, considered pretending he hadn't heard, and changed his mind. A first name couldn't hurt, could it? "Elias."

"Huh."

"What?"

"Suits you."

Eyes wide-open, he stared into complete darkness, breath held. Would she put the name with the face and figure out who he was? He hoped not. After her smiles, disapproval would kill him.

"Pretty sure you saved my life back there, Elias," she finally whispered. "Thank you."

He released a long breath. "Anytime."

She snuffled and shifted, as if getting comfortable—not exactly easy on the hard ground. Though he couldn't see, he pictured her snuggling deeper into the bag. He listened to the short, shallow sound of her breathing, layered with Bo's slower cadence.

When maybe ten minutes later it deepened into a more restful rhythm, he considered waking her to check her eyes again. Or had they decided you didn't have to do that for concussions anymore?

Waking her up wouldn't help at this point. What could he do out here if there was brain swelling? If they were going to survive this at all, it would be by taking their time and being smart. Not acting stupid. If she didn't sleep, she wouldn't make it. *They* wouldn't make it.

They. Not *him.*

And that, right there, freaked him out more than any of the day's events.

A part of him—the feral loner that had kept him alive all these years—shouted at him to get up and get the hell out of there. Company, he'd learned, wasn't an asset when running for his life. It was a ball and chain.

But leaving her right now would likely sign her death warrant, and that wasn't something he was willing to be responsible for. One more life.

She shivered and he shifted closer, sharing his warmth and whatever comfort he could provide in this bare-bones setting.

They'd be safe here, he hoped, for now. But there was always the slight chance their pursuers would find these caves, in which case they were screwed.

He clicked tongue to teeth and nudged Bo to the woman's other side. Unlike the humans, his canine companion had no trouble giving in to slumber. As usual, it took about three point two seconds for her to pass out, happily unaware of the danger surrounding them. Bo was probably enjoying this.

Hell, *he* was almost enjoying this woman's presence. With a happy sleepy sound, he let himself fall deeper into slumber, let his body heat mingle with hers, let himself come as close as he ever did to relaxing.

He was warm, floating somewhere in that place between sleep and consciousness, when he awakened to the ball-shriveling sensation of a blade piercing his neck.

———————

"Leo," an unfamiliar voice rasped as the speaker's chest rose and fell, moving her with it.

Leo shook her head, trying to clear it, trying to see or understand something—anything—in this absolute pitch-black, dark so thick it coated her tongue. Or was that blood?

"You okay?"

She pressed the blade deeper. "'s going on?" Her slurred whisper sounded frantic to her own ears. She couldn't calm her breathing, couldn't manage the wild beating of her heart.

The man between her legs barely moved, his only reaction the slow expansion and contraction of his rib cage. She tightened her thighs around him and dug her toes into the ground, wondering for a handful of seconds if her brain had somehow shorted out and turned a one-night stand into a nightmare.

Not that she did one-night affairs, but she couldn't remember. Not who this was or how she'd gotten here or even where *here* was.

"You forgot." A statement said in a gruff, strained voice.

Her head hurt like hell. Had she been drugged?

She took a second to get her bearings. The place gave her nothing at all. Just dank darkness and quiet. She cocked her head. Not absolute quiet, though. Something dripped not too far off. "Where're we?"

"Cave."

A cave. Definitely not a one-night stand. Unless it had gone very, very badly. Or unless this guy had some interesting kinks. Her tongue was thick and dry and took up too much of her mouth. She screwed up her face in concentration. A deep sniff gave her the smell of earth, along with the unmistakable scent of blood. Fuel too. But that made no sense.

Think! Figure this out!

Where was she *supposed* to be right now? Which deployment? Had she been captured outside the wire? He sounded American, so if this was a prisoner situation, he was probably in the same position. Confusion swamped her, turned even the dark hazy, unsteady as a wave of seasickness, which she'd never had in her life.

"Trying to kill me, Leo?"

Her name in that low, hoarse voice gave her pause.

"I know you," she whispered. Not a question.

"Yeah."

"Why can't I remember?"

"Bumped your head. Couple of times."

"There a light?"

"Gonna reach for it, okay? Don't cut my throat out in the dark."

Right. Much better to do that in the cold light of day.

"Easy," she finally conceded. What choice did she have? She could only assume they were trapped here together. Who the hell had she wrapped her thighs around? "Any fast moves and I do it."

The shape beneath her shifted, something scuffled at their side, and a light came on, blinding her. In the split second before her eyes slammed shut, she recognized him—not who he was, exactly, but that she knew him.

And she liked him.

She released the pressure on her push knife, let herself feel the width of him, hot and thick between her legs. Before she'd finished inhaling, he'd rolled them and she was trapped.

CHAPTER 10

In a perfect turnabout, the man's bulk weighed her down, anchoring her in her body, though she wouldn't have minded leaving it and succumbing to blessed oblivion right about now.

"Remember me, Leo?" Before she got her hand out from between their bodies, he grasped it and disarmed her, chucking the knife to the side, where it landed with a clang.

The sound of her name on his lips was familiar. Not unpleasant.

Slowly, as if approaching a bull elk in the wild, she put her hand on his shoulder, ran her fingers over the tight muscle, trying to extricate the memory from a skull that felt like Humpty Dumpty after the big fall.

Her gaze stuttered on her hand. *Why do I have gloves on?*

She shut her eyes for a few seconds, trying to figure this whole thing out. All she saw on the back of her eyelids was that intense, shadowed gaze and—oddly—the skin of the man's neck where she'd just touched it. Pale and warm looking.

Alaska. The crash. The virus.

"Campbell Turner." She mumbled the name before she'd consciously thought it. That was wrong, though.

"Shit, you forget everything?" She grunted in surprise and tried to bat him off when he pried open first one eyelid, then the other, blinding her with his flashlight. "You were hit on the head. Pretty sure memory loss means concussion." His big hand probed at her head, then moved to her face, cradled it for a few seconds, and finally released her. "You okay?"

"Yes, *Elias.*"

"You remember my name."

She groaned, shielding her eyes. "Turn those off."

"Those what?"

"The lights. All the lights." She nudged at him until he rolled off her, then she turned over and hung her head, wobbling on all fours as she waited for the wave of nausea to pass.

"Only one light, Leo." The man's voice was a rumble, each sound purling out measured and slow.

Slowly, she pulled in a deep breath, finally allowing herself to notice that it wasn't just her brain that hurt. Her chest, arms, back, neck—everything she flexed ached.

"Okay." She did her best to parse out the memories her brain threw at her—the little plane, being shot at by a helicopter. Relief flooded her, loosening her limbs. "Okay. Okay, it's coming back."

His response was a rumble, low in his chest. She guessed that passed as an affirmative in his book.

"Could you put the light back on?" She slowly lowered herself to her butt. "Just…don't shine it in my face this time."

He clicked a flashlight on. It shot through the space between them, the single beam precise as a bat signal, offering up next to no information on their surroundings.

"Shine it on you…please. The light."

He hesitated before complying.

She grimaced when he chose the worst possible angle—from straight below. "Geez, man."

"What?" His shadowed brows dipped, carving him into a horror movie nightmare.

"You look like a demented yeti. Give me that."

He handed her the light and remained still through her long, slow scrutiny, which only confirmed that the guy didn't need spooky effects to look like something straight out of a sleepover ghost story. His beard was maybe five inches long, bushy, and blended with the dark brown hair curling over the nape of his neck, showing no signs of grooming—ever. What she could see of his mouth was a thin line, grim, without the slightest potential for softness. Above it was a long, hard nose, possibly straight at some point but clearly battered by whatever life had sent his way.

Bear fights, her rattled brain threw out as an idea, complete with images of this massive, thick brute of a man engaging in shirtless, bare-knuckled combat against a grizzly, like some vintage Russian circus act. Hand-to-hand. Or would that be hand-to-claw?

For reasons she could not fathom, her eyes went to the curve of his neck again. As if that spot held some secret she needed to unwrap.

She'd just lifted her hand—to touch him, maybe—when something moved against her side, making her jump and pulling her from whatever head-trauma-induced reverie had taken hold.

"*Hell.*" With a hand flattened to her chest, she blinked at the wolf dog. "I'm delirious," she whispered, shoving her alarm, along with her messed-up imagination, far, far back. She examined the man again and let her eyes work their way down, over his thick, worn, fur-lined parka, then immediately back to the dark area below the beard. "You're bleeding."

"It's fine," he replied, covering his neck with one gloved hand.

"Did I do that?" She strained to look at her knife lying in the corner of the cave and pointed the flashlight at its shiny crimson tip. She had. She had nearly cut out his throat. "Oh no. I'm sorry. I didn't want to—"

He put up a hand. "'s fine."

She didn't even remember sliding the small blade from her boot. Couldn't figure out what had awakened her in the first place. And now she'd injured him—the only man who might have some clue as to what was going on around here.

"Hey." He scooted closer, putting them face to face, Leo up on her knees—another position she didn't recall getting into—and him seated in front of her, legs spread wide. "Hey, Leo. Leo."

Calm down. Calm the hell down.

She never did this. Didn't lose it, ever. Not for years, at least. Decades. Not since Mom died.

"I'm fine, Leo. Throat doesn't hurt."

"You're bleeding. *Shit.*" She put her gloved palms to her eyeballs and pressed. "It was dark. I was hurting. I was blind and..." She couldn't catch a breath, couldn't get her nerves to settle. Had to get outside. Had to—

"Leo." One big hand grabbed ahold of her bicep and everything stopped spinning.

She stared at his hand, remembering. "Your arm." Her eyes flew to meet his, which sparkled in the ghost light.

"What?"

"Your arm. You had your arm on me. Around me. I thought you were..." She didn't finish. Didn't have to, judging from the way his expression hardened.

He opened his mouth, shut it, and then spoke. "Won't do it again." Unexpectedly, the lines around his eyes deepened with what might have been humor. "Unless you ask me to."

The memory lapse worried him, along with the other symptoms. He couldn't do anything about a concussion out here. There wasn't a hospital or clinic or even a doctor for hundreds of miles. He could get her to Schink's Station, but that trip took him days on his own. And who knew what would be waiting for them there? With snow on the ground, plus a storm, towing an injured person, he had no idea. Add to that the team of killers after them.

Might never make it.

Had to.

He knew these people—or the ones who'd hired them—and he knew exactly what their game was. They'd take over the entire town of Schink's Station and use its citizens as bait. He had to get back there before they started killing people. Under normal circumstances, the town's citizens could take care of themselves, but these attackers were relentless.

Damn it all. If only his phone hadn't died, he'd call in. Hell, he'd give himself up if it made a difference.

But even that wouldn't save lives. They'd kill them all in the end. Every man, woman, and child would be sacrificed to the greed of the people at the top. Greed or something darker. They'd never shared their motivation.

Worst of all, he'd sworn no more people would die on his watch, and yet here he was again, in the thick of violence and mayhem. The people back in town, the ones who'd attacked his cabin, this woman. Dead or dying or injured.

He stared at her, jaw hardened at what he had to do: get to Schink's Station—as fast as was humanly possible—and take back the town.

And keep Leo alive in the process.

He stood, decided. "Got to do something about that head." Bo's warm body pressed up against his leg, ready to move.

Leo, however, sank back onto her pallet and shut her eyes. "Gimme a sec."

"Be right back." He grabbed his ice axe and a plastic bag from his pack and made his way to the cave entrance before turning to look at her. "Don't do anything."

A thin layer of glacial silt a few feet into the glacier cave's entrance told him everything he needed to know about exterior conditions. It was worse than bad. He got down on hands and knees and crawled through the narrow opening, then stood outside.

If it were just sleet, they could risk moving, but that wasn't the worst of it. A thin layer of ice had formed on everything, from the snow that was already on the ground to the rock face behind him. Even in the dark it shone, slick and deadly.

The wind, though, was what scared the crap out of him. It danced around him, whipped the tall treetops into a frenzy and picked up whatever precipitation hadn't frozen to the nearest surface, blasting it back into his face like a sandstorm.

No way could he take Leo to get medical care in this weather. They'd have to stay here and give her a chance to rest, wait out the weather. If it cleared, they could take off in the morning.

He slid his way down to the frozen stream, squatted, and chopped at the water with his ice axe. It gave quickly, providing chunks for him to stuff in the bag.

Something cracked behind him.

He dropped the bag and swung around, rifle up and at the ready.

Nothing.

A quick search of the shadowed, ever-moving landscape showed no living creatures, but that didn't mean someone—or some*thing*—wasn't approaching. Rather than wait for a confrontation that couldn't end well, he snatched the bag of ice and his tool, fought his way back up the rise to the rock wall, and sheltered there, eyes scanning every inch of his surroundings. A shape finally materialized from the woods. He squinted.

Bo. It was Bo.

Relief poured through him like hot whiskey. "Come on, girl." The wind stole his whispered words and hurled them at the sky.

Still on edge, still wary, he made his slow, careful way along the rock face to the cave.

As he went back in, he stretched his near-frozen fingers against the cold. He was getting too old for this. To run, to hide, to fight the elements that would win out in the end, no matter what. How many times had he wished himself back at that crucial moment, when he'd been given the chance to choose between right and wrong, good or bad? Run or die.

In the cave, he dropped to his knees and eased Leo's hood back as far as he could, shoving it under her head in a way that should have woken her up. The fact that it didn't only underscored the seriousness of her condition.

She might not survive this.

Everything else evaporated.

With the kind of clarity that comes from a decade of living in near-complete isolation, he saw his mission in a way he hadn't in forever.

"Leo," he whispered. "You need to wake up."

He had no idea who she was or why she was here, but he needed to get her to safety. Save the woman, the town, the world. Shouldn't be too hard.

But first, she needed to wake the hell up.

CHAPTER 11

LEO OPENED HER EYES TO FIND THE BIG MAN BENT OVER HER, calling her name over and over. "You can stop yelling now," she croaked. "Elias."

He shut his eyes and mumbled a handful of unintelligible words, then pressed something to her head. Almost immediately, the cold seeped through.

"Bleeding again."

"You'll have to take that up with the guy who bandaged me."

"Doesn't look good."

"No? Think you'll…" She swallowed and fought to keep her eyes on him. "Have to cut it off, doc?"

With a low snuffle, he lifted the ice and leaned forward. "Better give you stitches."

"Yeah?" The fingers she touched to her scalp came back glistening red. She met his eyes. "Go for it. I figure, you haven't killed me yet…"

"Injury gets bad enough, won't have to."

A shocked laugh jolted her so hard she had to deep breathe for a few seconds. "No more grim jokes. Especially not about killing me." She finally managed to lift her head, opened her eyes, still smiling, and went very still.

He was watching her intently, almost hungrily, she'd say, though that was ridiculous, given the state she was in. But she couldn't deny this new thing filling the air—a third presence as unlikely as everything that had led to this moment: *attraction*. Ill-timed and absurd, but there.

Bullshit. She was delirious.

"Here, hold this." He handed her the ice pack and peeled back the rest of the bandage.

A low hum rose from her belly.

"Let's ice it for a while and I'll sew it up."

"I hate stitches." She grimaced.

"Had 'em before?"

"Yeah." She just kept her eyes from glancing down at her body. "Three times."

He grunted.

"Don't worry. I heal fast."

"That so?" His brow crinkled. "My mom always said the same about me."

"You get in a lot of scrapes?"

All humor left his eyes. "Could say that." With an awkward hand movement, he indicated the open bedroll. "Better if you, uh, lie back down."

She complied, settling onto her side with a sigh of relief. It felt remarkably good to let her muscles go, even if it meant putting herself at his mercy. *Back* at his mercy.

A shiver went through her—from the damp ground, obviously. Couldn't be from the feel of his bare hand at her nape, the whisper of fingers to earlobes and then—

She groaned when the ice pack settled back on her head. After a while—geez, who could tell how long—the pain receded.

"Okay. Hold on." He messed with something in his bag, then slid his long fingers beneath her head and gently lifted it just long enough to place a cloth under her face. "Gonna sting. Ready?"

"As ever."

No careful dabbing this time. Whatever he poured over the wound made her grit her teeth so hard, they should have cracked.

"Sure you trust me with a needle to your head?"

"You being...funny again?"

"Is it working?"

She opened her mouth to respond and then realized that his attempts at macabre humor *were* distracting her from the pain.

"Don't trust many people. Even fewer that I'd allow to hold a sharp instrument to my head. But…" Enigma though he was, he'd saved her life. And that meant something.

He was seated beside her, unmoving, one hand on her head. She couldn't imagine being in a more vulnerable position.

"Go on then, mystery man. Do your worst."

He cleared his throat. "Be right back." He got up to do some more gathering of supplies, including what appeared to be a sewing kit. Jesus, she hoped it was clean. "Go fast as I can."

She nodded, rubbing her cheek against the wet cotton.

"Ready?" The flashlight's glimmer hit the curved needle in his hand.

"You gonna disinfect that thing?"

"Nah, it's good. Few germs never hurt anyone, right?"

"Are you—"

"Ah, come on, Leo. You're tough. You telling me you can't handle a little bear blood?"

"You're not seriously—"

"Only ever used it to sew together hides for my hearth rug. You'll be fine."

"Ha-ha. Right." The smell of alcohol wafted over her, and she shut her eyes. "Sorry I doubted you."

"Understandable." After a quiet moment, he said, "Tell me when."

"I'm ready." Which was complete bull. The first stitch made her want to cry to her mother. And she'd been dead for three decades.

Forcing the tears back, she ground her teeth together through the prick and pull of two stitches before she fell into the breathing rhythm he'd adopted. Slow breath in, slow breath out while he pierced her scalp, then another in, and so forth. The tears receded, prickling her sinuses until she managed to squelch them, shoving them down to her throat and her chest before they settled as an ache in her belly. If she could ignore the weird pull at her scalp and maybe concentrate instead on the warmth of his other hand anchoring her in place, she'd make it through this.

After a few more minutes, he sat back. "Done. I'll clean, bandage. Leave you be."

"Thank you, Elias." Her eyes sought him out. "Whoever you are."

He opened his mouth, as if he'd tell her what his role was in all of this. Like he *wanted* to tell her. And then closed it, tight as a steel trap.

For some inexplicable reason, she felt something like hurt. "My last name's Eddowes," she gave him, maybe as a peace offering, maybe as a thanks.

His eyes flicked toward her before skittering away again. Was that guilt on his face?

She'd just opened her mouth to say that it didn't matter when he told her his last name.

And everything changed.

———

"Thorne." Elias said the name that had put a target on his back and turned him into a pariah. America's most wanted. "My name is Elias Thorne."

Everything was quiet.

There was relief in telling the truth, pressure releasing like a balloon popping in his chest.

Now he'd have to deal with the fallout.

Shock, disgust, fear. Maybe even anger. None of those would surprise him.

She blinked. From where she lay, her eyes dipped to take in his entire form, before rising again. "Bullshit."

He shrugged and her eyes narrowed in response. "You're serious?"

"Why would I make this up?"

"*The* Elias Thorne?" At his nod, she cocked her head, her expression wary. "You sure have changed."

No point responding to that, was there?

When she started to sit up, he shifted toward her, stopping at her quelling look. "Still got to bandage you."

Instead of responding, she turned slightly and watched him. It was a weird sort of standoff.

The mass murderer and the woman he'd saved.

"The Point Pleasant massacre." Her eyes pulled him apart. "That was you."

His only response was a grunt. Why bother arguing when he'd been judged and hanged before the damn thing was over? Well, shot anyway.

"I thought they killed you."

"That was the goal."

"To kill you or to make people think you were dead?"

"Yes."

She wheezed out a laugh, which quickly turned into a cough, leaving her teary-eyed and breathless.

He squatted, unmoving, as she considered him, pulled him apart with her big, intelligent eyes.

Finally, he gave in and broke the silence. "What do you want to know?"

"I'm just trying to understand."

"What?"

"What the hell *the* Elias Thorne is doing here, for one thing."

He gave her a minute. "Figure it out?"

"What's the link between you and Campbell Turner and the virus?"

He went still at those last words.

"You know about the virus, Elias?" Her chest moved up and down with each deep inhale.

"Can't talk about it."

"Can't, or won't?"

"Wanna go first?" he countered.

Distrust pinged through the air between them, as present as the scents of stone and blood and wet dog. After a second, he nodded toward her injury. "Gotta bandage you."

"Hold on." She tilted her head and narrowed her eyes. They were an awful lot clearer than they'd been half an hour ago. "No way you're with those guys. They're after *you*."

"You brought them here." He couldn't help the accusation in his tone.

"They had your coordinates."

"You know that for a fact?"

Tightening her mouth, she looked away. No. She clearly didn't. And maybe she had led them here, but Amka had been the one to send her.

Unless the whole story was a lie. Which seemed unlikely at this point.

Trust, he knew, was hard won, and neither of them had gained it yet.

It was so quiet that he heard her dry swallow, so close that he could almost feel her body heat. Funny how the distance felt insurmountable.

"They said you killed colleagues, witnesses. Whole families. Your own…"

Parents.

He opened his mouth and closed it. Defending himself, he'd proven back then, was not his strong suit. "You wanted my name." He stood. "You got it."

She inhaled audibly. "Elias Thorne." Was she unaffected by his prickly demeanor or just pretending? She set her forearms on her bent knees, looking almost casual despite the stained clothes and the beat-up look of her face. "You were, what…FBI? DEA or something?"

America's most wanted. "U.S. marshal." He kept his back to her, eyes unfocused while he cleaned the blood from his hands.

"Were you involved in his arrest?"

He didn't ask whose. Pointless to play innocent. He grunted an assent.

"I'm sorry, I don't speak Bigfoot. Was that a yes?"

"I was the deputy U.S. marshal responsible for apprehending Campbell Turner."

"After he stole the virus from Chronos Corp."

"From the Department of Defense."

She sucked in a breath, the sound like an unvoiced *oh.* "Huh. Okay. Why did you—"

"Done talking." He sat back down again and ripped open a bandage. "You gonna let me finish or not? Doesn't matter to me either way."

It took her a while to realize he meant her head. Her hand went halfway up and then stilled before returning slowly to her knee. "Oh." Her gaze shifted from her hand to her leg, where Bo had settled, then on to his pack, and beyond to the passage leading out. Though she didn't look satisfied with his response, by the time she came back to him, she'd apparently come to some kind of decision. "I'm Lieutenant Commander Leo Eddowes. Retired."

Right. She looked as retired as the guys who'd flown in on her tail. "Navy, huh?"

"Aviator first and foremost. The Navy was…" She shrugged and he still couldn't tell if her nonchalance was real or forced. "A means to an end."

"Leo your real name?"

She snorted, something approaching a smile hitting her eyes. "It's Leontyne. But only my dad's allowed to call me that."

He grunted.

"Thank you again. For…" Her hand fluttered toward her head. "For not leaving me back there."

This time, he responded with a slow nod. When she didn't go on, he ripped off a piece of tape and edged as close as he could without touching her, eyeing his handiwork, trying hard to calm his thoughts while something inside was going wild. His heart, maybe, flailing in his chest like a salmon on a line.

He glanced her way and went still. "There it is."

"What?"

"Way you're looking at me. I've gotten a lot of that."

"How am I looking at you?"

"Like you just found out you're sharing a cave with Osama bin Laden."

She opened her mouth to protest and then closed it, tilted her head, and stared at him for so long he started to itch. "You're right. I'm sorry."

"Understandable."

"No. I'm getting there. Recalibrating. Adjusting."

He wasn't convinced.

"What about Turner? Was he innocent?"

"Depends on what you mean by innocent."

"Okay." Her eyes on him were calculating, intelligent. He didn't see any fear there, but that could've been a trick of the light. "Let's see. Chronos Corporation was running clinical trials for the U.S. government? And, what? Turner went and stole the virus?"

"Something like that."

"No?" She squinted at him. "How did it really go down, then?"

Wishing he hadn't said a word, he applied the bandage, his fingers too big and awkward for such a delicate job.

"I'm trying to understand. You were a college football star, right? Turned U.S. marshal? How'd you go from arresting agent to so-called mass murderer? How'd you get embroiled in all this, Elias? How did Chronos get to you?" She watched him. "They did, didn't they? Chronos Corporation and whatever government entities are involved in this whole thing. I've seen the kinds of things they're willing to do. Did they kill those people to set you up?"

He stilled, hands hovering above her head like a crown or a halo, then smoothed the tape to her shorn hair, one careful finger at a time. Finally, he pulled away and stood. "Hungry?"

"That's it? You're seriously cutting off all discussion? Just like that?" When he didn't react, she shook her head, clearly unhappy. "No. Thanks."

The air in the cave managed to be both chilly and close. A not very pleasant sensation.

"Here." He handed her water, returned to his pack, and came back with his own, then hovered, too agitated to sit. "You want to know my story? Who is Elias *fucking* Thorne?"

"Yeah. Who are you?"

"Then?" He sank to the ground, not sure what he was feeling. "Or now?"

"Now. Who are you now?"

"Now?" An empty husk? A shadow in the woods? A guy who'd become more animal than man in order to survive? He shut his eyes for a sec, working through it in his head. "You got any bad habits?"

She threw him a quick side-eye. "We talking nose picking or, like, mainlining heroin?"

"Shouldn't have said 'bad.' You have any habits—just things you do that are a part of your life? Who you are?"

She half shrugged and wiped a few drops of water from her mouth. "Sure."

He waited.

"This the part where we share personal stuff?"

He put a hand up, started to turn away. "No. It was stu—"

"I'm addicted to potato chips. That work? I really love those light, kettle-cooked ones. So thin they're see-through, like lace. But I'll take whatever I can get. I eat 'em constantly. That's a habit, right? A bad one."

He grimaced. "Nothing else?"

"Okay. I found out pretty early in life that if I didn't *move*—and move fast—I'd go bananas." She shut her eyes for a few seconds. "Or drive my parents bananas, actually. So I run. Every day."

"What happens if you miss a day?"

"I *don't*. Unless I'm in a…" Her words fizzled out, her hand gingerly explored her head, and she gave him a quick, easy look, filled with unexpected humor. "In a situation like this."

"Running for your life?"

"Sitting for my life right now, but yeah."

"So, that feeling? Where you've gotta move, get your legs—what's the word?—*pumping*, or else… What? What happens?"

She turned her body more fully now, her eyes knowing when they landed on him. One fist went to her chest. "All hell breaks loose."

"*That*. That's what happens if I let this out." He leaned in, needing her to understand. "Sharing the burden of this particular secret *kills* people." He stood again, tired and wired and buzzing. "So, forgive my hesitation." He wiped his brow, surprised to see sweat shining on his glove. "It's the only thing I am. Only thing that's kept me alive."

He headed to the cave's entrance, dipped his head, and paused. Without turning, he spoke. "Only thing that's kept *anyone* alive."

Old Amka waited for one of the operatives to leave Marion's house before making her move. The kids and Marion were inside—safe but scared, from what she'd been able to see through the back windows—and a single guard stood watch on the front porch. As good a time as any.

Part of her wanted to siphon all the gas in town, lay some big-ass trap, and blow these bastards sky-high, but that wasn't practical for a number of reasons—primarily collateral damage. She'd opted instead for a stealth operation. Baby steps, she figured, were better than shock and awe. Now, after three hours of watching and waiting and hunkering down outside the cabin's windows, her joints were suffering, but it would be well worth the trouble.

Bent low, with one hand on her back, she hobbled up to the front steps. "'scuse me," she said in her quaveriest old-lady voice.

The toy soldier on the porch turned and pointed her weapon, tracked Amka's slow progress up the steps, and then dropped it. Apparently, she deemed Amka no threat at all.

The woman—dressed all in black from her coat to her big boots, with a communication device in her ear—had the hollowed-out cheeks and square RoboCop jaw of someone who spent most of her time in the gym. Which wasn't something Amka could relate to. Or respect, really.

Especially when she'd so easily dismissed her—for being old and small and fat. As if she really were RoboCop, with one of those screens in her head beeping green at the sight of an old lady.

Of course, if she did have a screen, she'd have known Amka carried a knife in her hand and a gun in her holster. The woman would have known that Daisy's hunting rifle was leaning on the porch rail beside her. Out of view but not out of mind. Much like Daisy herself.

She smiled now, thinking of the woman she loved more than anything in the world.

And the Robo-woman smiled back.

Good Lord, these people were simple.

"They sent me here to give you this." She held out the plate of cookies she'd gone back to her place to get. On her best china, too. Part of the set Daisy had inherited from her family.

"Oh." The woman put out her hand and pulled it back, with a slight shake of her head. "I can't…"

Amka shoved them forward, taking a couple of limping steps

closer, even though she risked revealing how well-armed she was. "They're diet."

The deep-sunk eyes went to the plate and stayed there. "Diet cookies? You mean like, no—"

She didn't get another word in. By the time Robo-lady realized the knife was at her throat, Amka'd already pressed it close enough to the skin to keep her from finishing. With her other hand, she set the plate down and yanked the communication device from the woman's ear. "One sound," she whispered, "and I skin you like a bear." The woman stiffened and Amka put more pressure on the blade. "I've killed bigger creatures than you. Don't for a second think I'd hesitate."

When she nodded, Amka let up, just enough to wrap one of those big-ass twist ties around her wrists and pull it tight. Nudging the woman along in front of her, she stepped to the side of the door and threw it open. "Marion!" she stage-whispered. "It's Amka. I'm coming in there to untie you and the kids. Don't attack me or anything. I brought cookies." She threw the woman a wicked smile. "And we got ourselves a prisoner."

CHAPTER 12

ELIAS STOMPED BACK INTO THE CAVE, FOLLOWED BY HIS DOG, and went straight to his sleeping bag, not once looking Leo's way. Which was disappointing, because now that she knew who he was, she was riveted. Okay, a little weirded out, because *Elias freaking Thorne*. But also undeniably fascinated. Here she was, stuck in a cave with a dead man. A man who'd turned against his own government, his own people, who'd stolen and killed before being shot to death in the biggest massacre America had seen since 9/11. The media had gone wild, she remembered, the conjecture had been over-the-top. Spy theories, terrorism, even some cult thing. Wait, hadn't his girlfriend written a book?

Except none of it was true.

She opened her mouth and shut it, reminding herself that she wasn't here to get to know the real Elias Thorne—even if the man was intriguing as hell. She was here to stop the bad guys from getting the virus and maybe figure out what exactly they planned to do with it.

"Will you answer one question? Just one." Her voice came out louder than she'd intended, echoing from one side of their den to another. "Do you have it?" When he didn't respond, she forged on. "The virus. Do you have it with you?"

Without acknowledging her, he slid into his sleeping bag, zipped himself up, and turned on his side, away from her.

"You freezing me out?"

"We need to sleep."

"You don't get to do that."

He glanced a question her way.

"You don't get to decide when I sleep or eat or—"

"*I* need sleep. You do what you want."

Deflated, she sank back into her own bag, suddenly aware of all the tension in her back, the tightness in her shoulders. She did her best to relax, though every part of her wanted to *move*.

Andante, Leontyne, Papa would say. Drove her bananas when she was a kid and needed to run, run, run, but in this place, it had a weird way of working. If she closed her eyes and concentrated, she heard the metronome slowing, felt her pulse ease off, the air sailing in and out instead of churning, constricted. By the time she'd settled back into a normal rhythm, she was half-asleep, her body finally catching up with the day's—and night's—events.

"I'm sorry, Elias. I get…worked up about things. I didn't intend to harass you."

After a few seconds, he grunted, which seemed to be his fall-back response to pretty much everything.

It was the last sound she heard before passing out.

Leo knew where she was this time before she opened her eyes. Even before she was fully awake. It wasn't the cold bedrock beneath her body or the slow drip of water somewhere above that told her. It wasn't even the soft nap of fur against her cheek, redolent of dog. It was Elias Thorne's solid body against hers.

She couldn't even be mad about it, because as promised, his arm was nowhere near her. *She* was the one who'd wrapped herself around him. No doubt in search of heat, because the man put it out like a radiator. Her hand was so tightly pressed to his chest that it pulsed with the light, constant beat of his heart.

Or maybe she just imagined that last bit. You couldn't really feel a person's heartbeat through ribs and muscle and flesh, could you? Not to mention coats and sweaters, base layers, and gloves.

She should roll back or something, because sleeping in close—or even overlapped—quarters with a stranger was definitely not a good idea. This particular stranger—accused murderer, spy, and who knew what else—should be especially scary, and yet she'd bet every piece of survival equipment they had that he was as innocent as he claimed. She remembered his expression when he'd told her about keeping his secret. This man wasn't a murderer. She didn't *want* him to be a murderer. And she knew enough about how Chronos worked by now to feel confident he *had* been set up to take that fall.

Besides, throwing him off right now would be like losing a heavyweight feather comforter on a lazy Sunday morning…in the dead of winter.

Well, worse than that, because his heat was actually helping to keep her alive at this point.

Ignoring all her embarrassment, along with a few misgivings, she forced her breath to stay slow and even, so as not to give away the truth of what she was doing—even to herself—and scooted forward just the slightest bit, put her face to his back, and inhaled. Good God, he felt good; smelled good, like a toasty—

He groaned, the sound twisting deep and warm in a place she'd rather not acknowledge at a time like this.

She stilled.

When he didn't budge, she slowly let her breath out through her open mouth and inhaled quietly through her nose. Another slow inhale/exhale and she relaxed her shoulders.

He was out. She should be, too. Forcing her eyes shut, she tried to find sleep—not easy now that her body had felt that *zing* of attraction.

"Know you're awake." His voice vibrated from his chest.

"Crap." She stiffened and rolled fully away, bumping the dog, whose comfortable bulk disappeared with a snuffle, leaving the cold to seep in at both the front and back. "I'm sorry. I know I said you shouldn't—"

"Don't mind." He yawned, the sound sending her into a jaw-cracking yawn of her own.

Shivering, she wrapped the sleeping bag tighter around her shoulders and hunkered down—a foot from him.

The air shifted when he rose, his body whispering through the absolute darkness, which finally relented when he lit the oil lamp. Even its tepid glow was blinding after so much nothing.

For a few long moments, he stood, wide back to her, as if waking and gathering himself or gearing up to do something unpleasant. Finally, what felt like ages later, although it was maybe just a minute, he turned to her. "Not used to human company." The massive shoulders rose and fell almost apologetically. She pictured herself wrapping her arms around them, giving him comfort. "It almost—I don't know—*hurts* to have someone around." Each slow, considered word struck her with the impact of a tiny dart. Simple, clean, and piercing in the way of deep, personal truths.

She opened her mouth and shut it—why add noise to a silence already rife with emotion?

When she didn't speak—and for some reason she got the impression he expected her to—he grabbed the headlamp and took off into the long passage that led to their temporary restrooms.

Just as discombobulated by her reaction to the man as the bumps on her head, she sat up slowly and leaned against the wall. Gingerly, she lifted one heavy arm, pushed her hood back, and investigated her scalp.

It was numb. Why couldn't she feel anything?

A few panicked seconds passed before it occurred to her to remove her glove. Right. She yanked it off and tried again, this time relieved to touch fingertips to hair—matted though it was—and to finally find the tender bits, covered with a bandage.

Her gaze caught the front of what had once been her gray coat, now mostly brown with blood.

The reality of her near miss smacked her with a wave of dizziness and she eased her way back onto her sleeping bag. She could have lost an eye in that crash. Could have died. Instead, she'd come out with a cut head and a hangover.

Would she have gotten out if Elias hadn't shown up? No. She'd have bled out or wandered around, eventually freezing to death, or—more likely—been murdered.

What was probably delayed shock made her shiver, even after she'd slid back into her sleeping bag, wishing he were here to warm her.

She owed her life to Elias Thorne. Whoever he was, whatever he'd done, there was no doubt about that. Now, she needed to repay him.

———————

Say nothing.

Trust no one.

Two rules to live by.

So, what now? He watched the woman as she slept, thinking he too should get more rest before the weather changed, turning this brief respite into a race for their lives.

But he was way too antsy for that. Like Bo, whose eyeballs flicked back and forth from him to the entrance, as if to say *Come on! Let's hunt!* he wanted to get out there, put some distance between them and the enemy.

And he'd do it if it were just the two of them. But this woman changed things.

I could leave her.

The thought lodged in his chest like a blood clot.

Rather than dwell on what an absolute prick he was for even considering it, he got up and led Bo outside, where she braved the elements with glee. As a malamute-husky mix she was pretty much made for this place.

He stopped just inside the glacier cave's camouflaged opening and watched her bound over the thick layer of ice, completely unheeding the nasty crap falling from the sky. How much longer would this last?

With daybreak, what had started as ice could turn into rain too damn quickly. And rain meant snowmelt. A bad time to be out there, running for their lives.

When Bo returned, he took a final look at the sky and followed her inside, eager to slide back into his bag. Not to be close to Leo, he assured himself. But to get warm and rest before the long haul out of here.

He and Bo had just settled down as far from Leo as possible when they heard something—and this time it wasn't outside.

———————

"Gotta move, Leo."

A light burned, so bright it hurt her eyeballs. Hands grabbed, nudged her. She slapped them away.

"Leo. Get up. Now." Another nudge made her hunker down and try to cover her head. "Come on."

She batted at the relentless hands, mumbling for them to stop.

"Leontyne." The voice was quiet, deep, in her head.

Once Leo got her sandpaper lids unstuck, her eyeballs were the only part of her she could move. The rest was a dead weight. The *Yeah?* she tried to say came out all wrong.

"Got to go."

"Time is it?"

"Time to move."

Her eyes focused, took in the big, human shape above her, darkness all around. Within a split second, adrenaline flushed into her veins. "Ready," she lied.

Elias and the dog both stared at the cave entrance, sending her instincts into overdrive.

She stood too fast and leaned against the wall, waiting for the wave of sickness to pass. "What is it?"

"Something's wrong."

"Beyond the obvious?"

He ignored her attempt at humor and eyed the passage back up into the tunnels. "Someone's close. Gotta go."

The little hairs on her body pricked up.

"Right now." He went to work rolling up the sleeping bags.

"Where?" She reached for her boots.

"Where do you need to go?"

"To Campbell Turner. To the virus." She slid him a look. "Unless you have it."

His "Let's go" wasn't exactly a response, but she didn't push. There wasn't time to chat.

"Or Canada. Amka made me promise I'd take you to Canada."

"Made you promise, huh?" He shook his head, before his eyes narrowed in on her. "What you got on under those?"

She stopped struggling with her boot. "You mean besides underwear?"

"Base layers. You got any base layers?"

"One."

He muttered an obscenity and threw another look at the doorway. "Put these on. Fast."

She caught the tights he flung her way—two pairs—and a thin, synthetic pair of socks. As fast as she could manage, she stripped off her trousers and pulled the oversized layers on top of her base layer—loose wasn't ideal in the cold, but better than nothing. While she struggled to get dressed, Elias remained occupied, his back to her.

"Happen to find a fire kit when you searched my bag?" he asked, still not looking her way.

"Oops." She pulled it from her coat pocket. "Sorry."

He looked down at her hand and back up. "Keep it."

"But you—"

"We're in this together. Keep it."

She nodded and continued getting ready. The next couple of

minutes were a jumbled sequence, performed in almost absolute silence. Dressing, finally shoving her feet into boots and her head into a ski mask that Elias handed her, spinning to take a last look at the space, before following him into the glacier cave.

No time to stop and marvel at the brighter blues, the shocking swirls. No time to get down on her ass and slide across like a toddler. She put her arms out for balance and slipped along, grateful when he snaked an arm around her back.

"What'd you hear?"

"Don't know. But it was something."

"Close?"

"Hard to tell in the tunnels." He stalked carefully around clear stalactites—or stalagmites, or whatever these structures were called.

Leo didn't think she'd ever felt so small. Elias was fast, keeping pace with his dog, who looked for all the world like she was about to embark on an easy stroll at the dog park.

In flashes, she was again struck by the eerie beauty of the place.

Frozen, as if by God's hand, only God wasn't some bearded white dude up in heaven. He—they, it—was these endless, jaw-dropping, swirling layers of ice. Millions of tons of it, soaring up with such absolute majesty, such surreal extravagance that it literally took her breath away. Or maybe that was the cold, gusting in from outside.

"Think it was a person?"

He stared at her.

"What you heard, back there. Was it a person? People?"

"Yes." His voice held a grim sort of certainty. At a narrow fissure in the ice wall, he stopped and looked down at her, his eyes glittering hard in the strange light. "Gotta move fast, make sure they don't catch up to us." He leaned in and even through the ski mask, his breath heated her cheek. "Not gonna be easy with what's out there."

"The storm that bad?"

He shook his head before shoving their packs out through the tight opening. "Worse."

CHAPTER 13

SHE FOLLOWED CLOSE BEHIND, HER BREATH SNATCHED straight from her mouth when she emerged into an icy, wind-blown wilderness like nothing she'd ever experienced. And she'd been to Antarctica.

Snow and ice pelted everything. Yesterday's brown-and-green-flecked landscape was coated in white, washed with the angry, tumultuous gray of a storm that wasn't close to letting up.

She reached for her bag. When he didn't immediately release it, she moved in. "We get separated, I'll need my gear." Maybe they should have split the fire kit in two. Or maybe they'd just need to stick together.

"Sure you can handle it?"

"Yes," she lied.

There was no shift in his expression when he handed the thing over, no change to features that were already mysterious behind all that hair, not to mention the screen of ice and snow separating them, but she felt his hesitation.

Without wasting words, she hefted the bag onto her shoulder, nodded once, and blindly followed him into the thick of the storm.

Five minutes in, Leo was already reevaluating her physical fitness. No, more than that, she was reevaluating her entire life. Survival, Evasion, Resistance, and Escape training, also known as SERE, had nothing on this. And she'd suffered back then. But this, trudging through more than a foot of hard-crusted snow, without snowshoes, the wind slicing through her, precipitation making visibility essentially nil, was the hardest thing she'd ever done. And she was somewhat protected in Elias's wake, his bulk serving as a windbreak for her. She had no idea how he plowed on, but he did. Unerringly.

It wasn't even light yet. How could he tell where they were? Much less where they were headed?

At some point, they grabbed hands—no way of knowing who reached first, but it helped balance her as they plowed a path forward.

She turned, squinting through the nasty precipitation at the clear tracks they'd left. A path their pursuers couldn't fail to follow.

They walked forever, her hands and feet not even feeling like parts of her body after a while.

When she listed to one side, he scooped his arm beneath her shoulders, her armpits. Leaning in, he said something in her ear. She couldn't hear it, didn't know what words he'd used, but the heat of his breath against her face melted her a little.

"Hold on," he said, setting her to lean against a wall that turned out to be a tree. He disappeared, muttering unintelligibly.

Alone, she felt the fear that his presence had staved off. And cold. God, it was freezing out here. Her teeth chattered, slapping together with a constant, wooden rhythm. She slid down the trunk to the cold earth, put her head to her knees, wrapped her arms around them, and waited.

Hands grabbed her. She couldn't say if they were his or someone else's.

Her hood fell back and a bare hand landed on her forehead. It felt good—warm and cold at the same time.

"You're burning up."

She huffed out a weird sound that felt like a laugh. "I mention I had a stomach thing? Food poisoning, I thought. Maybe it was a bug?"

He paused, eyes wide. "Kidding me?"

"No." She managed a woozy head shake. "Fun, huh?"

"Right." His eyes roved over her face. "If all else fails, maybe we can get them with a stomach flu."

No point mentioning that this whole thing revolved around a

virus. "Could work." She cocked her head. "If you don't catch it first."

"Guess we'd better hurry then. Here, I'm giving you meds." He rooted around in his pack and came out with little pills that she swallowed back without hesitating. Talk about trust.

She smiled, let her head thunk against the tree, and stared up at the whispering branches, blinking at the falling snow. "Thank you, yeti."

"You're welcome, Leo." He bent, grabbed her under the arm, and hauled her up. "Let's go."

———————

They trudged over slick, uneven ground for another half hour before Elias slowed, narrowing his eyes at the still-dark sky. What a night.

"I'm...fine. Don't...stop." Leo caught up to him, lagging and out of breath but apparently forged from steel.

He threw the pack against the thick trunk of a black spruce and just stopped himself from pushing her hood back. Asking permission wasn't something he did all that much anymore. If something needed doing, he just did it. "Uh, mind if I check that?" He indicated her head and hovered over her, feeling big and backward.

She pushed the hood away, lifted her ski mask, and wiped her sleeve across her snow-flecked eyes, then watched him work.

It didn't bother him at first, but after a few seconds, he glanced down. "What?"

She blinked fast. "Nothing."

"You're looking at me weird." He yanked off a glove and put his hand to her forehead. "Still feverish?"

"It's just...you don't look anything like..." She shut her mouth tight. "Never mind."

He grunted. Not much of a response, but he figured he knew what she was thinking. That he didn't look much like the golden boy whose photo the media had plastered everywhere back when it happened.

Well, he didn't. And he was fine with that. That guy was dead. Gone. He'd done the right thing instead of the smart thing. He'd trusted people he shouldn't have. And he'd lost his life because of it.

She shook her head. "If I had a camera right now."

Rage welled up. "What? You'd show the world what I've become? How far I've fallen from America's favorite college quarterback? You think I even give a—"

"No." She faced him head-on, not backing away, despite his obvious fury. "I was *gonna* say that I'd make a fortune by proving once and for all that Bigfoot's real."

When she reached up and brushed a mini avalanche from his beard, it was all he could do not to back away. Not because he was scared of her, but…

Shit. Was he scared of her?

Maybe, though he wouldn't delve into why right now. What he knew was that, even feverish and wounded, trudging through the roughest terrain in America, in some of the worst weather the place had to offer, she kept a sense of humor.

He liked that. A lot.

Self-consciously, he rubbed at his snow-crusted face, and then, because it was second nature, flicked a look at the wintry trees that clung to the side of the ridge.

His eyes narrowed. Had something moved up in the woods? They'd left tracks behind them, inevitably, but he'd assumed the sleet and wind would erase most signs of their passage. Had he been wrong? Were they blazing a mile-wide trail for whoever was after them? The storm slowing down was a relief—at least physically— but without its scouring effects, following them would be child's play.

"What? They catching up to us?" she asked, her body appearing as tense as his had suddenly gone.

"Not sure what I saw. Maybe nothing." Warily, he handed her

water. She drank, grimacing while he put his own canteen to his lips and took a long slug. It was achingly cold against his teeth.

His eyes scanned their surroundings, all the while investigating the forest for that extra presence.

It was hard to isolate a single movement with the flurries dancing around them. Though the storm seemed to be settling, motion was everywhere. "No, definitely something."

"Where?" she whispered.

There. He zeroed in on it. "Your five." He could have sworn something shifted.

Her nod was a slight dip of the chin, but she didn't otherwise move. Just her eyeballs, swiveling right.

Beside him, Bo had frozen into one of her poised and ready positions, body vibrating with so much energy he was surprised it didn't shake the snow from her fur.

The harder he stared, the more it just looked like another innocuous part of the forest—cloaked in night and snow and wind. "Just something off." He let the words slide from the corner of his barely moving mouth. "Movement in the shadows."

"You think they're that close behind us?"

"Hope not." He had no words to describe what it was that told him danger was near. No way of telling her it wasn't just sight and sound that guided him, but something else. Something not quite real. She'd probably laugh.

"Should we keep moving?"

"Yep." He picked up his pack and hefted it onto his back, sending one last uneasy look over his shoulder. "We'll stick to the river for this last mile. Cover more ground." Which would, unfortunately, make them easy targets. "Then comes the rough part." For maybe half a second, he let a smile tug at his lips.

The guarded way she watched him, you'd think he was some wild creature that needed taming, instead of the man who'd pulled her from a plane crash.

But then he realized with the same jolt of self-awareness he felt when he met his own eyes in the mirror—maybe he *was* the wild creature. Maybe those hunting them were the civilized ones.

If that was civilization, he wanted nothing to do with it.

"Rough part?" One sleek, dark brow disappeared under the bandage's stained, off-white edge, then lowered again. It was thick and smooth and perfectly arched. Which wasn't something he'd ever noticed on a woman before.

Shit. Now he was thinking intimate thoughts about eyebrows.

"You'll see," he muttered, his good humor gone the way of any refinement he'd once had—crushed to smithereens beneath the boots of those who'd spent the last decade hunting him.

"I'll see. Great. That bodes well."

She didn't shy away when he reached out and pulled her mask back over her face.

"Need more distance." He gave the woods a final probing stare before turning toward the river again. "This'll be hard. But it's the only way."

Yeah, it was the hard part. It was also the part that—if it worked, and that was a long shot—would buy them a little time.

———————

Got you.

Ash eyed the cave with satisfaction. Two people had slept here recently. Or rested, at the very least. The ground had been scuffed to hide signs of passage, and there, someone had splashed water along the rock. To wash something, perhaps?

He drew close and sniffed.

Blood. It would take a lot more than a little water to mask the iron-rich scent.

He took his time, searching every possible passage out of the cave, noting a temporary latrine and clear footprints in the dust.

Tufts of white hair clung to the corners. He'd bet his earnings that it belonged to a canine.

He followed the jumbled prints to a passage, ducked through it, stood, and went stock-still, his jaw hanging open.

A glacier cave—majestic and soaring and absolutely enchanted. Blimey, what a sight. He took a step, nearly fell, and righted himself. Then slowly slid around the space, running a gloved hand over curved ice, taking in the bumps and dips with the wonder of a child. He *felt* like a child here, younger than he had in ages, and utterly alive, which was sweet and tragic. Tears clouded his vision. It was beautiful, utterly still, frozen in time, like a wave at its apex.

He shut his eyes and fought the pain that tried to tear into the hard black diamond of his heart. After a few steadying breaths, he moved on.

Close to halfway round, he found a second way out—a low, tight tunnel, showing clear signs of passage. Outside, he stepped down, straight onto the frozen river, and took one last, longing look at the gem hidden just inside. The perfect juxtaposition of nature and mathematics, a wave, as symmetrical as a nautilus shell, hidden beneath the surface of this innocuous wash of ice. Not a crystal out of place. The most perfectly designed architecture on the planet.

With a sigh, he let his assessing gaze sweep the chilly scenery. It took a while, but eventually, he spotted what he was looking for through the hard-driving snow, which was lovely as confetti but as painful as tiny shards of glass. A series of peg holes, too even to be random. It could be another animal, of course. But a wolf would have to be absolutely daft to be out in this weather—and those tracks had been made in the last few hours. He *knew* he was onto them.

He put a gloved hand out and watched, transfixed, as a mix of flakes and ice settled on his palm, some rushing to land while others meandered as if they had all the time in the world, both covering the ground with mesmerizing efficiency.

With a single overloud slap of his hands, he sent so many little masterpieces puffing away to join the others on the smooth ground and followed the dog's prints west.

CHAPTER 14

LEO'S GAZE REMAINED FIXED ON ELIAS'S BACK AS THEY PICKED their way along the slippery boulders and geometric ice chunks lining the river. He'd given her one of his poles, which made walking marginally easier, and used the other to test the ground every few steps.

Though visibility was basically nil, Elias walked and climbed as easily as if this were a nice stroll in the woods instead of a constant battle against wind and snow, water and ice and rock formations clearly designed by the devil.

Elias Thorne. His name hit her like a surreal punch to the gut. The whole situation was so out of left field that she wondered if she'd lost her mind. Had she? Was this the fever talking? Was she actually tucked in bed back at Schink's Station, suffering through an epic flu? If that was the case, wouldn't her brain have made Bo a blue zebra? Or, hell, her reincarnated mom?

She watched Elias's sturdy silhouette for a few more minutes, mesmerized by the steadiness of him, his constant, unerring progress. No way she'd invent someone like him, who tromped through the storm with the easy confidence of the local wildlife, in well-used, top-of-the-line boots and a worn mud-colored, fur-lined parka that could have come from another century. His pace was almost mechanical in its constancy, as if he were barely human—or so at home here that neither the terrain nor the weather affected him. Only the occasional glance over his shoulder altered his pace. He was checking on her every hundred feet or so.

None of this was the erratic behavior of the mass-murdering psychopath the media had made him out to be back in the day.

She did a quick gut check and came up with nothing but

respect for the man. He'd saved her life after all. And even without that, hell, she kind of *liked* him.

Except not just kind of.

She took in the world around her. Nothing was visible aside from the flat line of the river to her left and the almost sheer vertical rise they'd spent the last half hour skirting. The storm turned everything, including the now nearly invisible shape of the man in front of her, into an almost uniform gray, flattening distances and tamping down sounds. There could be an army out there and she wouldn't know it.

She needed to hurry or he'd get swallowed up by the weather, a ghost fading into the landscape.

It wasn't a comfortable feeling—being entirely dependent on the man.

On they trudged for maybe another fifteen minutes, the snow-sleet mix turning so gradually to rain that Leo didn't notice the change until her clothes were soaked. Ironically, she shivered with cold now that the atmosphere had warmed. Beneath her feet, the ground was turning to soup, the surface of the river dangerously waterlogged in places and deadly slick. The light was so odd, it was hard to tell if it was day or night.

Stopping to catch her breath, she looked right, where the high rock wall they'd followed had tapered off. Left, as far as she could see, was nothing but flat snow. She squinted through the pelting rain.

Nope. That wasn't snow. It was ice.

"Hey," she stage-whispered. "Hang on."

He turned, his coat completely dark, what features she could see pinched, his eyebrows, nose, and beard dripping water.

Slipping and sliding, she caught up to him. "Isn't this dangerous?"

"What?" he deadpanned.

"Walking on the river in this downpour."

"Not a river."

She blinked. "What?"

"We're on the lake."

"But isn't that…" Whatever she was going to say frittered to nothing on the tip of her tongue as she spun in a slow, dizzying three sixty. Was it just yesterday that she'd considered landing on this lake? "There's got to be a better way."

"Fastest way to the other side is across. Going around would take at least two days. This, we can manage in a few hours." He threw a look back in the direction they'd just come from. "Need to get there before the pea soup clears and that helicopter catches us smack in the middle."

"But doesn't rain melt ice? Won't it accelerate breakup?"

"Yep." After taking a long, swooping look behind them, he turned, giving her his back again. "Better hurry."

It would take them hours to cross the lake, and even then, it could be too late. Because he'd felt that presence. He knew someone was on their tail, dogging the two of them every step of the way.

He didn't have to see them to know they were there, somewhere. Didn't have to smell their alien presence or hear the crunch of feet on ice. He felt it—in his bones, along his spine, his nerves, or wherever these things lived.

There were lessons he'd learned the hard way: not to trust strangers—sometimes even family and friends—not to depend on anyone else for survival, and to listen to that sixth sense that told him trouble was near.

Right now, every one of his internal warning bells was going off.

If nothing else, this woman who'd literally fallen from the sky had pushed the big red button in any number of ways, just by being here.

A little late, as far as warning signals went. And still not entirely to be trusted.

He huffed out a cynical sound.

Trust.

He couldn't remember how it felt anymore—to really trust a person. Aside from Amka and Daisy, there wasn't anyone alive who had his back.

One thing was damn sure—judging from the way Leo'd looked at him, she didn't entirely trust him either, despite what he'd told her. Or maybe because of it. And that was as it should be. Meant she was smart.

He remembered the way she'd sat there and let him work on her head. Okay, so maybe she trusted him a little. Enough to let him stitch her up. Enough to follow him out here.

Enough to sleep against him in the dark.

Up ahead, through the almost horizontal wind-whipped rain, a group of pines slowly appeared, dim and silent, a shadow army emerging from the gloom.

He walked past it, feet splashing through puddles now rather than crunching over freshly fallen snow. His jaw was clenched, teeth gritted against the shocking chill of water soaking through his socks.

Leo was fairly well equipped, but nowhere near ready for this. And with a concussion to boot.

To boot. He huffed out a humorless sound. Since when had he started thinking like an eighty-year-old pioneer man?

Suddenly it felt too close to the truth to be funny.

Had he ever been carefree? No. No, he didn't think so. Driven, yeah. Goal oriented. Even in college, he'd been hell-bent on success.

Another puddle engulfed his foot, this time with an audible *splash.*

"Hey," Leo called. "Is that land?"

"Island." The one word obviously dashed her hopes. But this was no time for hope. No place for it either. He could survive on his own, but unless this plan of his worked, the two of them, together, probably had about a five percent chance of making it out of this alive.

She drew up alongside him, her face turned away to look at the tiny, pine-spiked land mass. With longing, he imagined. And, sure, it would be good to stop and build a shelter. Get a fire going, warm up their toes.

"Nowhere near the other side yet." Better to crush the hope now. No point letting it linger. Like trust, hope was pointless bullshit that only led to disappointment.

And death.

Geez. Morose much?

He swiped a hand over his face to clear the water from his eyes. Had the rain slowed?

It had better not. It was too early. As long as it continued, keeping the helicopter from joining in the manhunt, he and Leo could outpace the enemy. He glanced back. Where there'd been nothing only a short while ago, the other bank now appeared as a dark, hazy mass, the mountain like something out of one of those Japanese pen-and-ink drawings. The weather was improving. Dammit. "Come on. Gotta hurry."

Instead of following his gaze and looking over her shoulder to confirm whatever he'd seen, she picked up her pace. As if she believed him. Trusted him.

He shivered and tried to shake off the extra weight on his shoulders. Damn word again.

"What is it?" She glanced up at him.

"Rain's slowing down."

After a few minutes fighting the headwind, bent almost double, she spoke again, her voice barely audible. "You're worried about the aircraft returning."

He nodded.

"So, what? You think they'll hunt us down across the ice? And when the sun comes out, pick us off from above like…"

"Alaskan wolves?"

Unless he was mistaken, they'd shoot her on sight. She was expendable. More collateral damage in a senseless war. He sped up. Pushed himself faster, harder.

He was a different story. They needed what he had.

Or they thought they did. Either way, they'd stop at nothing.

He knew this from experience.

"Guess we'd better hurry across, then, huh?"

"Yeah. And once we make it, pray the ice cracks." He forced a grim smirk to his lips. "With them on it."

She stumbled, righted herself, and nodded. "Will do."

Leo was not used to being the ball and chain in situations like this. She was used to speeding ahead, her body strong, her mind clear.

Right now, neither was true. But if she focused on a far-off object, she could keep up. The second she turned to the side or slowed or looked at the ground, she lost her steam.

Then again, even without the head injury and a body that felt beaten and broken, she would have had difficulty matching Elias's pace. It wasn't just that he was fast either. It was that he was fast in a place that wasn't meant for humans. It was made for wolves and bears. Leo eyed the man's wide back. *And yetis, oh my*.

Elias's hand lifted, the movement sharp and sudden, and Leo froze instantly, eyes wide-open in the drizzle, poised for whatever came next.

Her eyes dipped to take in what she could see of his solid, muscle-bound form. He had the sure, careful gait of a man who'd definitely seen action. *Of all kinds*, whispered a lascivious little inner voice.

She blinked. What the hell was that? Had the bump to her head damaged her brain?

No, she reasoned. The action, the fatigue, and the stress of this situation felt like being back on deployment, where shit-talking was the norm. Except here she was having dirty, trash-talking conversations in her head instead of with her guys.

She flicked a look around, searching for whatever had made him freeze, and instantly regretted it when the world spun out of control.

The protein bar he'd foisted on her burned its way out of her belly and up her throat as her knees tried to give out.

Oh, hell. Not again.

She straightened her knees, swallowed to keep from gagging, and blinked fast and hard to keep the world right side up. *Bile down. Air in. Bile down. Air out.*

Her vision blurred, darkened. She shut her eyes and waited for the wave to pass.

When she opened them, Elias squatted beside her and leaned in, hand outstretched.

Whoa. Had she fallen?

"I...I'm fine. I can get up." Maybe. If she concentrated really hard. Ignoring his hand—not to be a jerk, but because depending on him seemed like a long, slippery slope in a world of slippery slopes—she shifted back, steadied herself, and shoved up to standing, eyes screwed tight until the spins went away. Mostly. The ringing in her ears continued. Not a good sign.

"You walk?"

No. "Yes." Definitely maybe. She put as much certainty into the word as she could. Sometimes confidence was all a girl had.

He pulled away, then returned with a curse when she started another slow slide earthward. Iceward.

"It's fine," she tried, but the words slurred together to make a sibilant mess in her mouth. "I'm fine. Don't carry me. I can..."

He didn't release her. Didn't even look her way. Just trudged on, lugging her with him. The two of them a sodden, limping mass of humanity, with the happy dog leading.

Oh God. "Hang on." She managed to pull away and yank her ski mask up just before throwing up on the ice. The pressure made her head feel close to exploding. Once she caught her breath, she breathed deep.

"Sorry." Groaning, she put her hands to her streaming eyes. "I'm sorry."

He didn't respond.

When she looked up, it was to find him staring back in the direction from which they'd come.

"Let's go." The words were staccato quick. She grabbed the hand he offered this time and let him help her to standing just as a sharp bark burst through the quiet, so loud that she didn't know where it had come from at first. Then another and another, the echoes pinging from one side of the lake to the other until the dueling retorts sounded more like rolling thunder than individual gunshots.

Gunshots.

Adrenaline was already pouring into her system by the time she recognized the sound. And this guy, superhuman machine that he was, didn't even flinch when a bullet hit the ice inches from his foot—sending crystal in all directions, the shards sticking to his dog's fur like minuscule chunks of glass. Aside from a grunt, his only response was to grab Leo, throw her over his shoulder, and run.

CHAPTER 15

ASH SPUN, READY TO THROTTLE WHATEVER ABSOLUTE WANKER had fired a weapon. Were they idiots?

Deegan's team—or what was left of it—was behind this. He couldn't see them, but he knew they were there. The cretins had spent all morning thrashing through the woods, as if they were alone in the world. And now this.

He'd bet the shot hadn't connected.

And the next had bloody well not either, or he'd have to pick off his ostensible allies himself before going after his far more intelligent quarry. Nobody was supposed to be killing their target. That wasn't their mission. And it certainly wasn't his.

He made his way to the cliff's edge and put his thermal monocular to his eye just in time to catch a heat signature southwest of him. Almost in the very center of the ice. He could only assume it was the two he'd been following all along, with the dog, though it was difficult to tell from this distance.

He narrowed his eyes at the loping shape, almost sure that it was a running person.

It could be an elk, he supposed, or even a bear, though neither animal would venture onto ice that could be just hours from falling apart.

There! Another shape, low to the ground. That must be the dog. So, where was the second person?

He watched for a few moments before the truth hit him. *He's carrying her*, he thought, his stomach dancing. Who were these people?

Goose bumps spread out over his skin, with shivers of excitement rather than cold.

The edge of the lake, he could see, even through the mixed precipitation and even from this height, was beginning to get that mottled look that said the ice was close to breaking.

My God. They were doing it, weren't they? Ballsy bastard, whoever he was.

He swung the monocular left, toward Deegan and his team who, like Ash, were too far above the lake to reach it in good time.

Assuming that he was right and that was his target racing across the kilometers-wide lake, then the man had taken the risk of heading out onto the ice knowing full well that whomever followed would likely get caught in the breakup.

Quite the gamble, wasn't it?

Unpredictable. Another long, slow shiver went through Ash. His quarry was not to be underestimated. He didn't know yet if this was good or bad, but it stirred him. He hadn't felt this energetic in forever.

After a final look at where the man and woman and dog made their way across treacherously thin ice toward the other side of the lake, followed by a deep breath, he set off again, rounding the lake to the other side. It might take him longer than Deegan's team, but at least he'd get there with his life. He couldn't say the same for them. Then again, if the lake took those fools, that would be one less problem to solve.

Spurred on by the excitement of the chase, he started off again, slow and sure and steady, the way he'd always stalked his prey—human or otherwise.

———

Elias jogged through a frosted mist, so thin it was more cloud than rain. Beneath his feet, the lake was a soggy ice rink, wet and frozen and melting all at once. One misstep and they'd go down. Except smashing to the ground at this point could be a whole lot worse than a broken coccyx or a twisted ankle. It could shoot the three of them straight through the quickly weakening crust into the treacherous water beneath.

A death sentence.

"They've stopped shooting," Leo called, her head hanging at waist level. "I'll walk." When he didn't respond, she smacked him on the ass. "Elias! Put me down. Please."

"I've got you," he huffed out, tightening his hold, adjusting her weight. "I got you."

"Come on, Elias, we've outrun them. Put me down."

He wanted to set her down—he meant to. He just couldn't.

"Too dangerous," he muttered.

Driven by something stronger than him, he humped on, listening for more shots, voices, and below it all, like the rumbling of a volcano about to blow, the telltale crackle of ice pulling apart. A glance at Bo showed her scraggly wet fur tufted along the spine. "Away," he whispered to his dog, hoping that dispersing their weight would lessen the chances of falling in. Because breakup was coming. And if this rain continued, it could happen today.

"Put. Me. Down." She smacked his hip with each word. "I swear I'll vomit on you."

The threat didn't bother him, but he slowed anyway. She was right. He couldn't keep going for long like this. He squatted, let her slide to her feet, and studied her from below, ready to intervene if she passed out or anything. "You gonna throw up?" He kept his hands wrapped around her legs at the knee. To help her, not because he needed steadying.

"I should. Just to get back at you for ignoring me." She glared at him before turning to Bo. "He do this to you too?" Bo cocked her head, ears pricked, listening. "Or is it just females of the human persuasion?"

Bo yapped a reply and a grin pulled at Elias's mouth. Which would have been strange under normal circumstances. Out here, in pain and running for his life, stranded in the middle of a body of water as dangerous as a minefield, it was completely bizarre.

Dropping the smile, he rose. "Come on."

"Wait. I didn't clock them. Where were they? On the ice? They gonna shoot at us again?"

He turned to scan the horizon. "Doubtful."

"Why?"

With a nod, he pointed out a rock shelf high above the lake. "See the dark point, straight over that way?"

"Dark point? You mean at the top of the cliff I almost crashed into?"

He grunted.

"I see it."

Moving in close, he lowered his head to line up with hers and indicated a high, tree-covered rise. "The rifle shots came from that direction. Just down from my cabin."

"Okay."

"Only way off the cliff is through the woods. It'll take 'em a while." Unless the helicopter managed to get here. Then all bets were off.

She squinted. "Don't see any movement."

"I'd imagine they're heading down now." Something jittery ran through him. "To the lake."

"Those shots came awfully close. They can't be that far behind."

"They'll hit the ice soon. We need to go."

"Are you saying that we got that head start we needed?"

"I'm saying that by the time they get to where we're standing right now, this lake'll be water." He threw a look up at the sky. "If we're lucky." He bent into the wind again, the chill settling hard in his bones. "Better go fast so we don't get caught in our own trap."

That was the problem with nature. You couldn't count on her to be on your side. Even if it was the right one.

She muttered something under her breath and followed in his footsteps.

The air grew noticeably cooler as they crossed, the winds stronger in the middle of the lake. Above them, the sky was as clogged with clouds as ever.

He tried to forge on, but Leo lagged.

He glanced her way, looked down at her boots and back up. Was she hypothermic? She was so little that even with the thick hood on, the top of her head didn't hit his shoulder.

Little, but not weak.

He threw another surreptitious look her way, scanning her figure from top to bottom and back up again. Under those thick outer layers was a strong, agile body. Before she'd added those bulky layers, he'd had an impression of curves. She was narrow, but not frail. Strong, but breakable.

Vulnerable.

And wounded, dammit.

He wanted to pick her up again. Wanted to sprint straight to the other side and not stop until he got her to safety.

But those assholes would be right on their tail. And where the hell was safety anyway? Schink's Station was undoubtedly compromised. Once these guys marked you, you were as good as dead. As far as he knew, he was the only one who'd ever gotten away.

Then again, what did he know? Maybe there was a whole underground network out there, of folks like Leo, who'd gone against the people behind this and survived.

"The people" being the U.S. government sort of complicated things.

A sense of urgency rushed him, adrenaline ridding his body of everything but the need to run. "Come on."

"Are they gaining? You see them?" She turned to look back. "You just said they were a couple hours behind us."

"Hours aren't enough."

Would Leo have a place to hide out in the world? She said she worked with a team. That was good. Safety in numbers and all that.

So, what the hell was she doing out here alone?

They picked up their pace, which wasn't easy given that he needed to test the ice with his pole every couple of feet. Her breath was audibly ragged, even with the racket of wind and rain and the cacophony of crackling ice all around. Her head was bad enough, but God forbid she'd suffered some kind of internal damage in the crash, because that wasn't something he was equipped to deal with.

The thought sent something hot and bloodthirsty running through him, put murder in his veins.

"If only we could crack the ice."

"What?" She squinted up at him, and it was all he could do not to take her shoulders in his hands and pull her into his arms. Which would be weird. "You want to…" She panted. "*Break* the ice?" And then, the woman laughed. "Feel like we kinda did that last night, don't you?"

Something shifted far behind them. It rumbled beneath their feet, like an earthquake. The kind of sound that made every living creature stop and take notice.

"Made you smi—" She slipped and caught herself, legs apart, eyes wide, arms suspended, the stance so Bambi-like that he almost laughed.

"*That* made me smile," he said, more to get a rise out of her than because it was true.

She threw a dirty look his way, snagged his arm, and pulled herself back up to standing.

"You okay?"

"I'm fine. Let's get off this thing." Clenching his sleeve in one hand, the other still up, like an acrobat balancing on a high wire, she asked, "What happens if it breaks now? With us on it?"

"We swim." He turned to continue walking. "And hope we're close enough to shore to survive."

"Great. Just freaking great."

He'd gone maybe a hundred yards in her cautious footsteps before he realized that, for reasons he couldn't begin to explain, he wore a massive grin.

CHAPTER 16

NO MORE GUNSHOTS, NO SIGN OF THEIR PURSUERS. STILL, THEY kept moving at a quick clip. Which wasn't particularly good in this cold. If they weren't careful, they'd sweat and the sweat would freeze. Hypothermia was right around the corner.

Meanwhile, a fog rolled in fast and thick, surprisingly opaque, given the continuing rain. Right. Probably didn't need to worry about sweating when they were already soaked through.

He blinked at the landscape around them. Were they going the right way? The run had disoriented him.

He shifted the bag on his shoulders, cringed, and squinted. There. Was that Dead Tree? No. Just a pine. He turned, stumbled, and just barely managed to stay on his feet.

He shut his eyes for a few seconds, breathed until his pulse slowed, then opened them. *There* was Dead Tree, its branches spread wide, the tallest of the bunch raised up like a spindly middle finger, towering over the trees around it. And, though it wasn't visible right now, beyond it was the first in a long line of peaks. Unlike the mountains they'd just left, they weren't white-capped beasts soaring to blend with the sky. These hunkered low and dark, rooted in the earth, veins of copper and gold, silver and zinc, pulsing straight from her core.

He tripped on a sharp edge, righted himself, and paused, reaching deep inside for the strength he'd need to get through this. This wasn't just about survival anymore. He had to get Leo to safety.

If he could just get her to the river, she could go on alone. That would work.

He glanced down at his body, saw nothing different, and

focused forward again. He'd be fine for now. Just get her that far, that was all.

One plodding step at time.

As she caught up to him, he folded his arms across his front, hunching as if cold. Which, now that he thought of it, he was. Shivering a ton, actually. He shook his head hard to clear it.

"You okay?"

He ignored the question. "Keep walking."

Her eyes, dark and layered as rich, new earth after the thaw, flicked over him, then snapped up to meet his, and he could swear he felt a connection, as if she'd touched him with a bare hand.

Christ, he wanted that. Her hand on him. Just the warmth of her skin would be something.

"What's our objective here?" She had to raise her voice to be heard above the rain's constant patter.

"Look." When he couldn't quite get his right arm up, he used his left to point southwest. "Can't see 'em through the fog right now, but..."

She gave him a strange look. "But?"

"See that tree—dead one?"

Thankfully, she looked up in the direction he pointed, which gave him the space he needed to breathe again.

"The one giving us the bird?"

A laugh burst from him, the pressure on his lungs so harsh he couldn't breathe for a second or two. "Yeah. Always thought that." He snagged her gaze again, got caught in the details of her face, the water dripping from pointy lashes to sluice down her brown skin. If there were time, he'd lean forward and lick it off.

He shook the rain from his eyes. No time. Also, really not the thoughts he should be having.

"Gotta get to the mountains beyond."

She said something that he couldn't quite grasp.

He grunted in response. Grimaced at the pain of heaving the pack up higher on his back.

The ice shifted with a groan.

And even though he'd wished for just this event—exactly what they needed to escape their pursuers once and for all—it was happening too damn soon.

Breakup was starting and they were still smack dab in the middle of the water.

———————

Would this lake never end?

Leo wiped cold water from her eyes and peered ahead at a shore that didn't get any closer, no matter how far they went, how hard they ran.

And all the while, the ice popped and groaned and sagged beneath them. It felt like tiptoeing across a waking monster's back.

Breath coming out in visible puffs, she swiped a hand across her eyes to clear them and stared hard at the landscape—or into it. Was it a landscape if you were part of it? She shook her head, narrowed her eyes, and peered through the falling raindrops to the layered, patchwork scenery with its ever-changing lights and darks and misty reflections. It was beautiful. Awesome, even in the pouring rain. Her next sinus-clearing breath smelled of mineral earth and pine, with something rotting underneath.

She glanced back and came to a sudden stop, blinking at the figure that had grown small in the last few minutes. What was wrong with Elias? He'd stopped and stood sagging against his pole while he drained his canteen. The posture was so different from how he'd been up until now that it set off an alarm bell in her brain.

Stomping back over ice she'd already checked and traversed seemed like tempting fate, but she did it anyway because something was going on with the yeti and it freaked her out.

Maybe she was imagining it, given that she didn't really know him from Adam.

Although, in a weird way she couldn't explain, that felt like a lie. The past twenty-four hours had forged a link between them. An understanding. Hell, maybe more. Maybe even something like attraction, though that was irrelevant in the current situation.

But why was he bent forward like that? Was his pack too heavy? Probably. He'd been hauling it for hours.

Guilt shot through her. After adding her weight to his load for a portion of the trip, the man was probably close to collapsing.

He should rest. They both should. She looked up at the sky. Was it even day still? Impossible to tell with the rain pouring over them. Were their pursuers getting close?

She was sure of very little right now. Could see next to nothing, could barely feel her fingers and toes. And while adrenaline had worked for a while, she was definitely running on empty. There was only so much more her body could handle.

But seeing Elias flagging did more to pierce a hole in her composure than anything that had happened since they'd teamed up.

And it was her fault. He'd taken up her slack. Hardening her resolve, she picked up her pace.

The dog gave a high-pitched whine, ears going straight, head tilting at a cute puppy-dog angle.

A smile pulled at Leo's lips. "What's going—"

The earth growled.

She stopped, mouth open, her last word unspoken.

What the hell was that? She panted, head tilting in unconscious imitation of the dog, who'd adopted a low, tense stance, like she was about to attack, or—

"Run!" Elias's shout hit her a split second before another noise rent the air, so loud she couldn't locate the source, could only feel the rumbling beneath her feet. She'd lived through earthquakes before and this was immeasurably worse. A mix of thunder and heavy artillery and the world ripping open.

The ice boomed beneath her feet and she set off, willing it to stay in one piece.

Please don't break yet.

A series of pops like rapid gunfire sent her skidding to the side, eyes searching wildly for Elias and Bo, who'd been there seconds earlier. In flashes, she took in sky, mist-wrapped trees, Elias's moving silhouette. Her feet slipped out from under her. Water, dark and churning, licked at the ice she'd been standing on seconds before. Faster than she could fathom, her body slithered down what was now a slide. Pure instinct made her dig her boots in and claw hard with numb fingers. With dizzying swiftness, the ice seesawed back, sent her careening up, then down again, tumbling toward the roiling water, at the mercy of the elements and fate, like a die being thrown over and over.

Beyond the terrible grind of ice against ice, she heard one sound, ringing clear as a bell above the hellish din—Elias calling her name. Those two syllables centered Leo, gave her a sense of direction and a goal. One second her muscles loosened, the next they tensed, and using the ice's rhythmic sway to guide her, arms reaching, straining, she pounced. One hand caught the top edge of the piece, her body hitting it with an audible exhale. The other hand found purchase and she heaved up, teetered on the rim, threw her legs over it, and leapt just as it sank.

Stance wide, arms out, she eyed the ice around her. It was a bigger, steadier piece. She hoped.

"Leo, go!"

She didn't wait, just sprinted hard until her lungs hurt, her vision darkened, and the only thing—the *only* thing—was not falling in. Not getting pulled under.

Something appeared in her peripheral vision and Elias was racing beside her. They slipped, jumped, ran so hard one false step could break a limb. It was too treacherous to look anywhere but right in front of her feet. She reached to the side—blind, hopeful, trusting. And he was there. Their hands met, grappled, and finally held on, their fingers entwined like rope.

Nothing existed beyond the two of them, attached like a ship to its moorings, and the ice—the most dangerous moving target she'd ever encountered. She'd seen this lake from the air; she knew its surroundings, its shape and surface. But here, in the midst of breakup, they might as well be in the middle of the ocean, with nothing but each other to count on.

Something marred the surface ahead. A dark, jagged line that reached from one bank to the other. A crack. Was it widening?

Elias's grip tightened. She replied with a squeeze of her own and put on more power, heaved air into her lungs at an unsustainable rate, moved her limbs until every muscle burned.

She blinked in time to see the dog leap over the rip in the ice and land, her feet skidding dangerously on the other side.

The gap grew larger, darker, the noise massive, apocalyptic—the earth ripping open.

Suddenly, they were close enough to see what looked like two tectonic plates, scraping together…apart…together again.

She glanced right, met Elias's eyes, in that split second taking in the world around them—trees and mountains and rain-drenched sky, so close and yet outside this hellish bubble. "On three!" he yelled.

She nodded.

"One!" Her feet pounded the ice. The mist swallowed her every gasp.

"Two!" She could do this. She could do this.

"*Three!*" *They* could do this.

They tightened their hold, squeezed hard enough to break bones. As one, she and Elias jumped.

For a few freeze-frame seconds, they flew through thin, humid air, hands linked, bodies bracing. Above them, a bird cawed, as if life could just go on at this moment.

They landed with a bone-jarring thump, hard enough to knock the air from Leo's lungs and the thoughts from her head. She saw stars and wondered if it was night or day or heaven or hell.

She blinked the falling rain from her eyes, pulled at her hand to wipe it, but couldn't. It was still in his. Or his in hers. Whatever. Still holding on for dear life.

Ears ringing, she concentrated on the first thing she saw—ice. Or snow. Or water. *Focus.*

White, crusted with gray, transparent in places. This close, bubbles were apparent, trapped in the water, swirling. Pretty.

Deadly. Ice scraped behind them. She turned to stare at the opposite bank. It was moving. *They* were moving.

"Elias. Come on. Let's go." Time to get up, away from the edge, off this ice, to solid earth. Bo snuffled at something beside her. Good. The dog had made it.

Head spinning, she strained her eyes in search of the shore. There, straight ahead, were trees, the mountains looming in the distance. Surely that must be less than a mile away? They could do it. No problem.

It took effort to let go of his hand and get herself up on all fours, then finally plant one foot on the treacherous ice. But she could do it. *They'd* do it, together. She and the yeti could do anything.

"Elias." She reached for his hand, ready to help him up to standing, maybe lean on him a little in the process. She was almost smiling when she looked his way. "We're close. We can do this." She grabbed his hand. It was heavy in hers. She squeezed. No response. "Elias." Nothing. His arm was a dead weight, his body unmoving. "Wake up, dammit. Elias, wake up!"

———

Something slapped his face, jarring Elias awake.

He moved his mouth, tested his jaw, opened his eyes and

then immediately shut them. He turned his head and tried again. After a second, things came into focus—water, ice, a dull black that gradually turned to trees as his eyes adjusted to the distance. Everything was gray and brown and black—smears of color slowly taking shape.

"Elias."

He squinted at the silhouette above him and blinked until the face separated itself from the rest of the world.

"Elias. What happened? What's wrong?"

"Fine." He shut his eyes.

"You're bleeding. What the he—"

"Not bleeding." With an effort, he stood.

"That's blood on your coat." Leo's tone brooked no bullshit.

His gaze followed the direction she was pointing. A stain darkened the right side of his coat. "Huh." He met her eyes again. "Must be yours."

She looked down pointedly, where one puddle was darker than the rest—the dirty reddish-brown of rust or winter moss. "You are bleeding," she said.

He looked at her. "Okay. But we don't have time." He swung around, disoriented. "Need to move."

"How can we move if you're injured?"

"Remember which way we were headed?"

"Do *I* remember?" The wide-eyed, brows-raised look of disbelief she threw him actually made him smile. "Did you get shot? Elias, is that what happened?"

"Does it matter?"

"Yes, it freaking matters! If you're hurt, then our chances of getting out of here go way—"

A chunk of ice crashed nearby, startling all three of them.

"You can..." He focused hard on the horizon, finally getting his bearings. "Break my balls about getting shot when we make it to shore. How's that sound?"

"At least you admit that you did get shot."

They were hit by a gust of wind so hard it shifted the ice, slamming and crunching and overlapping the pieces like multicar pile-ups. What he wanted—what they needed in order to get away from their pursuers—was for the glacier along the lake's eastern shore to calve into the lake. Its ripple effect would send waves out across the surface and dump those assholes into the frigid water before they knew what happened.

No, what they *needed* was to make it to shore before the lake chewed them up.

"Let's go." He reached for her hand.

She pulled away. "You won't even tell me where you've been hit?"

"No, Leo." In truth, he wasn't sure. Adrenaline had masked the pain while they ran. If he stayed here much longer, he wasn't sure he'd work up the energy to keep moving. "We don't have time for this."

"Fine." She blew out an impatient sigh. "But trust me, I *will* break your balls about it later." There was just enough snark in her response to put a grin on his face.

He started off, eyeing the crackling expanse between them and the western shore, now blurred by rain. They were lucky the ice in front of them was mostly whole. They were lucky the weather hadn't cleared before this day ended. He turned and eyed the far side of the lake—lost in fog now—and caught sight of the widening gap in the ice. His guts tightened. Holy shit. The rift had to be twelve feet wide, the pieces they'd surfed minutes ago churning up the water like gigantic teeth. They were lucky they weren't dead already.

"Give me your hand again."

He turned to look at her and just kept himself from stumbling to a stop. She shook her hand, waiting for him to take it. A little exasperated maybe, but also solid. Bloodstained, battered, and soaking wet, Leo *should* look like something the cat had dragged in. She didn't.

Her dark eyes met his. She appeared exhausted and possibly feverish, a little angry, and above all, fierce.

A force of nature.

There wasn't time for this now, thinking about how this person who'd been sent to him—who'd literally fallen from the sky—made him strong in a way he'd never felt. Together, he thought, letting his mind take an uncharacteristically fanciful spin, they were more than the sum of their parts.

Her presence, the solidity of her beside him, with her humor and her drive, sent something through him, so unfamiliar he couldn't quite place it. But he knew one thing: for the first time in as long as he could remember, he wasn't alone.

Surfing ice during breakup wasn't nearly as fun as it sounded. In fact, it was more of a *running the gauntlet* type of thing, which consisted of listening to the ice—that was Elias's job—following a seemingly random, invisible maze, led just by sound; sprinting over flat, slippery surfaces; then jumping from one massive hunk to another, in a deadly game of leapfrog that was more exhausting than anything Leo had ever done. The final phase, of course, was the deadliest.

They'd made it far—or so she thought, though it was almost impossible to tell, the way they'd become enveloped in thick, soupy fog. She had no idea how he knew which way to go—or what time of day it was. How long had they been out on this ice? Three hours? Ten hours?

Going any faster than a walk was no longer possible, since they ran the very real risk of falling straight into the water. They slid on, the mist laying a chilly sheen on their coats and gloves and hats and whatever parts of skin it could find. "Better than snow," Leo chanted under her breath, getting a good silver-lining rhythm going. "Better than snow, better than snow, better than—"

He stopped her with a hand on her wrist, tight but not threatening.

"Don't move." He looked one way, then another, and cursed under his breath.

"What?" she whispered. "What is it?" Her voice was swallowed up by the gloom.

He didn't immediately answer, but she heard it then, the gentle lap, lap of water, so close to where they stood that she went absolutely still, forcing herself not to back up.

"This is it. End of the line." He peered forward. "Isn't far, but I'd hoped…"

The water washed suddenly high, over their boots, sending Leo back, while Elias remained frozen.

Then he came out and just said it, though by then he didn't really have to. The hunk of ice was dipping, dipping…

"Nowhere to go…." He looked down. "But in."

He stepped back from the edge, dropped, and started unlacing his boots.

"This why you had all those super-sized baggies in your pack?"

He grunted an assent.

She got to work on her own footwear. "I can't believe I'm doing this."

He shot her a look. "You seem like you were made for this."

"Diving into subzero water?" She stuck her boots and socks into a bag and carefully closed it, then put it into another. "Um. No."

"I don't mean that, but…the rush."

"Adrenaline's definitely my drug." She made a face. "Sort of regretting that now."

"Let me have those."

"I can—"

"I've done this before, Leo."

Her brows flew up to her hairline. "You serious?"

He nodded.

"On purpose?"

His eyes crinkled.

Shit, the dude was some special kind of hardcore. She plucked at her coat. "We do our clothes too?"

Something bumped the ice they sat on, propelling it forward until it crunched into a pile of the stuff. Leo's pulse went wild, which was funny, given that she'd thought it couldn't get any faster.

"No time. It'll crush us if we don't go now." He turned back, dipped his feet into the water, and hissed.

Before he could jump, she grasped his arm, conscious of the risk they were taking. "Thank you, Elias." When he shook his head, she tightened her hold and leaned in, more intense than she'd ever been in her life. "Thank you."

Something crashed behind them.

"Wha—"

"Breathe!" Elias grabbed hold of her by the lapel, just as the ice beneath them shifted into the air.

Together, they dove.

CHAPTER 17

THE SHOCK OF ICE-COLD WATER HIT HIS SYSTEM, SHUTTING it down for the first few seconds.

Without the benefit of oxygen, it was like he just…left his body for a bit.

He'd read about a man who grew accustomed to the cold by immersing himself in frigid water daily. Apparently, this guy trained other people to do it too, heading to polar regions to swim in the water there. He liked the challenge.

Well, he'd read about it and he'd shaken his head and thought, *What a prick*.

And then he'd gone and done it a few times.

What else was there to do around here?

But now? Now he wished he'd practiced every damned day until it had felt like a warm bath. Because swimming—if you could call what he was doing that—in this lake was pure hell.

When he was finally able to move, he spun, looking for Leo. What he saw was a labyrinth of ice chunks—bigger from the water than they'd appeared from above it—floating like icebergs, as far as he could see. From here, the shore looked miles away.

He did another half turn, scanning the surface. They had ten minutes before their muscles gave out. Where was she?

From behind them, Bo barked.

Shit. The dog hadn't followed.

"Leo!" he yelled, kicking in a circle until he caught sight of Bo back on a half-submerged chunk of ice, racing from one side to the other, then hunching before doing the whole thing all over again. She whined and slid a few inches closer to the edge.

Something splashed close by. There. Leo's head, above water. "Elias!"

"Come…on." Every word was an effort to get out. He didn't know if he was calling his dog or Leo or giving himself the world's shittiest pep talk.

Bo let out another high whine.

"Do it! Come on, girl!" Each inhale brought shards of icy air into his body—tiny splinters embedded in his lungs, which he'd then have to somehow exhale again. "Don't…make me…come back there, girl, or I'll—"

She jumped, the splash barely audible. After that, she was quiet, going through that same terrible period of nothing before the pain hit.

By the time he turned around, Leo had disappeared again. Underwater? Or behind a hunk of ice?

"Leo!" The word was a whisper, nearly inaudible against the sound of ice grinding against ice. He pulled in the most painful breath of his life and bellowed, "Leo!"

———————

Down, down, under the surface, blind and frozen and throbbing with a million aching pinpricks of cold water.

Stay still, she remembered from her training. *Go still and wait for the shock to pass.*

It was almost impossible. The cold wasn't like anything she'd experienced. It was like a being dragging her straight to hell.

She kicked, hard, barely budged, and kicked again, only making it out for a single, frantic breath before the ice they'd just been on rushed at another floating chunk, the two bashing together like bumper cars. She was shoved down again, with nothing but the bubble of air she held tight in her lungs.

She spun, looking for a way up. No. No, not like this. Not trapped, drowning, in the freezing cold. In the air, yes, at the controls of anything she could fly, but not like this.

She scrabbled against the underside of what had to be a freaking iceberg. Frantic for a few seconds, before possibly her single working brain cell chimed in with just enough reason to calm her down.

In a helicopter, she would never try to power out of, say, a vortex ring state—she'd establish forward flight and ease out into clean air. *Do it.*

Ease forward.

Pretend it's air.

She put her head down and kicked, easy as pie, in the direction the ice was moving. Another kick got her sliding along beneath it, her lungs full, close to bursting now.

One more kick and something gripped her collar. Not something—someone. Elias. He yanked her to the surface, pulled her to him for a few gasping seconds, during which he said things she couldn't understand. *Thank God. Thank God. Thank God*, it sounded like, though that could've been the beating of her heart.

And then they were moving. Slowly, slogging through the slush to a shore that he swore was there, through the fog, past the next hunk of ice, just there.

Not easy when she didn't have a body. Or a brain. Just breath entering and leaving her…and a strange heat.

Something hit her foot and she stumbled, nearly plunging again until her other numb foot encountered the bottom, and she rose, faced with a mountain of ice chunks.

Her attempt to say Elias's name produced nothing but a hacking cough.

She spun in a full circle. Wait. When had she lost him?

From the center of the lake, ice pushed toward her, rushing her like a logjam. As fast as she could, she hefted her bag, pulled her arm back, and threw it onto the shore with all her might. It slapped down about a foot from where she stood, waterlogged and shivering like a damn jackhammer.

She turned and reached into the water, her hands so numb she wasn't sure she'd even know it if she bumped him.

"Elias!" she called, her voice hoarse, no more than a whisper.

Something appeared from behind a hunk of ice. She squinted, attempting to make it out.

Oh, holy crap.

It was him, forging through the ice-jammed water like something from a postapocalyptic painting, or straight from Norse mythology, something not even human. His pack was on his head and... Jesus, that wasn't the freaking dog under his arm, was it?

He rose, a majestic creature emerging from the deep, a waterfall sluicing off him.

"No!" he bellowed when she struggled to her feet and started toward him. It went against her grain to turn her back on a teammate. *Two* teammates. "To shore! Get dry!"

He was right. With her body's uncontrollable shivering, she'd be no help at all. The best she could do was to get out and get warm. Lead-heavy from her waterlogged clothes, she fought to climb over a pile of geometric ice pieces, then slogged the rest of the way to land as the sun she'd so fervently wished for finally broke through the clouds in a late, flamboyant entrance.

The earth was a soggy, boot-sucking mess. Which didn't stop Leo from dropping to her knees and, from there, her front, finally rolling to her back to stare at the brattily beautiful sunset, shuddering so hard she worried she might knock herself out.

Poof, the storm was gone. Just like that. A disappearing act, complete with fog and a light show, ending with a dark bank of clouds settling to the southwest.

Eyes slamming shut, she breathed through a long, deep convulsion, wondering if she'd ever feel anything again. Or move.

"Got...to..." Elias dragged himself up the bank, slow as a swamp monster, and landed in a soggy heap beside her. Bo followed, low to the ground.

When neither human moved, the dog stood and shook herself, spraying them with water. Not that Leo could feel the difference. Whining now, Bo nudged Elias, who didn't respond.

"Elias."

Nothing. No sound but the frighteningly mechanical shuddering of his body on the beach. Beach, ha! Beaches were hot sand, slowly crashing waves, the easy lap of water on happy toes. Cocktails.

Caught in the fantasy, she rolled right into Elias.

This is where I die.

The dog growled. Leo opened her eyes.

"Elias, up." She could produce the staccato syllables, she just couldn't seem to act on them.

Together, their teeth chattered in a creepy percussion.

How much time did they have? Must have been at least ten minutes since they jumped into the water. Were they screwed? Done for? Hypothermic muscles atrophied?

No. No, forget that.

"No…way." She ground her teeth into silence, planted her hands on the earth, and pushed. "Elias." The word was so slurred it came out sounding like *liar*. She said it again. *Liar. Liar.* "Up. Get up."

No movement. No reaction.

This wasn't happening. It couldn't. They hadn't survived everything—he hadn't been hunted for so long—to end up a shivering pile of meat on the bank of this lake.

As if in response to her thought, another crack resounded from the water's busy surface, immediately followed by the faint echo of a scream. Holy shit, the lake was eating their pursuers. As Elias had predicted, they were stuck. And it sounded as though the ice was grinding them up like hamburger meat.

Too stubborn to give in to the cold's pull, she rolled away from Elias, so hard she wound up with her face in the sludge. From there, getting up was a matter of life and death, since she refused to drown to death—in mud. "Come on. Move it, yeti."

Bo slinked to her and nudged Leo on with her wet nose. She swallowed, planted her hands, and straightened her shaking elbows with a groan.

One stiff leg up and under, then she was standing on her own two feet. Wobbly but alive.

A look at Elias's gray face told her he was too, though barely.

CHAPTER 18

SURVIVAL DEPENDED ON LOTS OF FACTORS. TRAINING PLAYED A part, at least for Leo, and overall fitness—both physical and mental. There was instinct too—that indefinable thing that told people to duck when they hadn't yet heard a weapon being fired. In the air, instinct had saved her ass over and over again.

Led by instinct and hardheadedness, she bent, slid her numb hands under Elias's shoulders, and let herself fall back—his weight working against gravity to keep her up. They went maybe five inches, but even that pulled his feet from the water, bringing the promise of dry ground that much closer.

Her hard exhale blew a cloud of vapor into the air.

Wet fabric clung to their bodies, held them in death's cold grip, seeping through skin into muscles and bones.

The only thing that kept her brain moving and her lungs pumping was her will to survive.

She looked down at the man who'd saved her life, splayed out like an oversized rag doll, and amended that thought. It wasn't just her will that kept her here. It was Elias's.

And now it was payback time.

Another heave back and up, over rocks that dug into his heavy frame, hard enough to bruise. Didn't matter. What mattered was getting him dry and warm. Before his heart stopped.

Talk about a shitty twenty-four hours.

For some reason, that made her laugh. The spasms started low in her belly to mingle with the shivering that still wracked her entire frame, and came out of her mouth in weird bursts, the sound nothing like her usual voice.

Another foot up, closer to the trees now. Close. Close.

Another foot, another.

Was his shivering slowing down? Oh no. That was bad. She leaned forward and grabbed his chin in one hand, said his name loudly. No response. He was cold and wet and pliable as a dead fish.

Had to get him out of those clothes.

Shit. She couldn't do it. Couldn't get them into the shelter of the trees and off this wet, pebbly shore.

His eyes opened. They were green, not the light brown she'd thought. Green and clear as glass in the fading daylight. They met hers, held them for three long seconds, and then rolled into the back of his head.

"Oh, no. No, you don't," she whispered, her voice having let out ages ago. "You stay here, Elias. Stay with me."

Bo let out a low, mournful sound, drawing Leo's attention back to the water's edge. The bag. There'd be something in there she could use.

She raced down as fast as her feet would take her, half crawling and stumbling over the sharp, uneven rocks, and dragged the pack up.

In an offhand way, she noticed something pinging in her knee when she knelt beside him. Other pains popped in and out of her consciousness. Her head thrummed, as if swollen to ten times its size. Didn't matter. Her fingers were red and raw and ached like someone had taken a hammer to them, her feet were bleeding through the cold, wet socks she still wore, leaving dark footprints in their wake. Nothing mattered but getting dry and getting warm.

Even words made a difference, so she used them, out loud. "Dry." She pulled out the first thing she found—a boot enclosed in plastic. No. It dropped to the side. Another boot. Two more.

Something else—soft and rolled up—also in plastic.

"You get Best Prepared in high school, Elias? Huh?" No way could these ice-block fingers open the zip lock, so she brought it to her mouth and bit through it, gnawing like a beaver, then pulled the plastic apart. Sleeping bag.

She spread it out on the rocks, turned to him, hands out, and hesitated.

His clothes.

Something like despair took over when she looked at how big and soaked he was—how many layers he'd put on. How impossible it would be to undress him.

Then she remembered the knife at her waist.

The coat she unzipped. The next layer, too. She did hers, scrambling out of them as fast as she could manage. One layer, another, another, each gripping at her skin like heavy, wet eels.

Next, him. His socks came off, flung aside, his outer pants, then the inner layer—of which, she noticed, there was only one. Bastard made her put on three!

It was his shirt she had to cut off, the thinner one, too, before she stopped dead at the gash in his side, oozing blood, just above his hip.

She sagged, breathed for a second or two, then forced herself back into motion.

From his pack, she grabbed another wet bag, ripped it open, pulled out whatever item of clothing was in it and shoved it against the wound. Damn bullet got his abdomen. How was he not dead?

She swiped at the blood and eyed it again. Not a bullet hole. A graze. Something in her belly released, letting her breathe almost normally again. Blood seeped out, but she'd seen worse.

Time to move him. No, wait. Underwear. As efficiently as she could manage with lead weights for limbs, she slid her blade from his waist down his thigh, slicing the fabric open, without sparing a second's thought to his nudity.

Back to the underarm hold, she hauled him up to the side, away from the remnants of wet clothes and onto the sleeping bag, ignoring his pained moan. Pained moans were good. If he cursed her right now, she'd be ecstatic.

Another scavenging dive into the backpack—more dry clothing that she threw on top of him, stopping when a particularly rough bout of trembling took her over. Shit. Shit, she couldn't see straight. Panic tried to edge in.

She used action to push it back. *Get dry.*

Working hard to stave off exhaustion, she looked at herself, tore the last clinging layers from her body, grabbed the emergency blanket from his bag… Another reach… There. Something bulky and soft. The other sleeping bag, followed by another plastic package. *Oh, hallelujah!* Foot warmers. She knew better than to put those right on his skin, but with a layer or two of insulation, they would help.

She turned on aching knees, caught sight of his massive, shaking form, and stuttered to a stop.

How should she…?

Never mind. There weren't a million choices of how two people could get warm together. There was one. And she set out to do it.

Elias groaned at the painful wrenching of one foot, then the other. *Back off!* he tried to say, though all he produced was a garbled mumbling.

What the hell was pulling at his hands? He shoved at them, hard. Useless. Useless. He didn't have the energy to protest. His eyes closed, darkness beckoning like a bridge to the afterlife.

Someone called his name.

No. No.

A jackhammer to his head—loud and abrasive. He tried to swat it away, but couldn't move. Couldn't lift his arm or his head or make a word with a tongue that was a big, dry slug in his mouth and—

Liquid flowed in and back out, gagging him so he turned and retched. More of it, more.

Over and over. Again. Again. Burning, pain, tingling, moaning. Low, guttural throbbing every time he breathed a fiery path from mouth to lungs. Excruciating agony.

"Come back, Elias."

Come on. Come back. Come back come back come back.

I'm here. Here.

A hand on his shoulder, down his arm, back up. Chaffing. Firm, solid. Real.

Darkness. Warmth. Cocooned.

He shivered again, shaking the body above his. Encased in something soft and warm. Warm.

Forever passed. Years.

"Come on, Elias. Just take this and I'll leave you alone." He listened, tried to move. "We've got to get you warm. Get warm and go. We can't stay here."

He couldn't open his eyes, but let her pry his lips apart, then swallowed the hard little pills, followed by a mouthful of icy water. After sputtering, he tried to settle back and let out an annoyed grunt when she forced more on him. Another swallow. Another.

"Warn me if you need to pee." Her voice vibrated from her chest into his.

An unexpected laugh shook him—a dying donkey sound—and their bodies moved in tandem, hers half covering him, like a blanket.

"Wait…" He raised one arm just enough to slip it up and over her soft back. "*Naked*," he sighed before sinking into dreams of cold, chilly fog and warm, wet female.

Leo cracked her eyes open and immediately shut them again, not ready to face the pounding in her skull or the danger surrounding them or, more than anything, the fact that she was lying on a man she barely knew without a stitch of fabric between them.

A tug of the sleeping bag revealed what appeared to be daylight. Crap. Had they spent the entire night here, out in the open, on the lake's shore?

Somewhere close by, a dog whined.

She swallowed over a thick, swollen throat and the movement pressed parts of her closer to the person she was currently snuggled up to. Naked.

There was no dignified way to get out of this, but maybe if she put out a foot and an arm and inched to one side, taking some of her weight off his…

He groaned, shifted beneath her, and lifted his hips, proving that at least one part of him was awake.

Whoa.

"You conscious? If so, I need you to tell me, 'cause this is kinda…" *Hot* wasn't the right word for the situation, but it was what her brain supplied her with. It took a second before she came up with "Inappropriate."

Another long, low sound emerged from him, this one more of a rough hum. Good. At least he was still alive.

Yeah, well, the hard-on had sort of told her that.

Now time to get off it before this developed into something completely different. Warmth curled in her belly. She ignored it.

"Okay, Elias. Can you open your eyes? You awake?" She craned her head from the sleeping bag, strained to lift up and get a good look at his face, then glanced out at their overbright surroundings before letting the bag fall shut again, careful not to jar his side.

Yep. They'd slept here all night, their naked bodies sandwiched together. It was a terrible spot to have spent the night in, out in the open like this, the sun just coming up in the east, its rays heating the insulated nest she'd created for them.

At least he looked better, though. The parts of his skin she could see were pink instead of gray. That had to be a good sign.

"Can't stay here." Her heavy head dropped back to his chest, in direct opposition to her urging. "Have to move." She didn't want to. She wanted to stay here and sink back into the blissful heat, the musky smell, the languid pleasure of skin against skin.

One arm slid up and over her, not tight, but warm and comfortable. This shouldn't feel as good as it did. Not only was this not the time or the place, it really wasn't the person.

Her libido apparently didn't agree. If it had its way, she'd make her slow way down—

No. She reared back, dislodging that possessive arm and letting in enough cold and sunlight to make him open one of his eyes. The iris lazily focused on her, and the pupil, she was relieved to see, was reactive. It went pinprick small against the glare. "What the hell are you made of, woman?" He grimaced. "Barely human."

"I'm not the one running around carrying me everywhere." She started to lean back and dropped again when the movement put all the focus on her nipples, rasping through chest hair. It made her pulse frantic, her insides heavy with desire.

He coughed out an approximation of a laugh, and she felt a twang of something beyond embarrassment or discomfort or even the attraction simmering in the infinitesimal space between them.

It was warm and squiggly and way more uncomfortable than lust. It contained more *feelings* than she was used to. Like lust squared.

Without another thought to her nudity, she threw off the cover and rolled from him—right back into the sharp, cold, gravelly nightmare of the lake shore. "Shit!"

"You okay?"

"What are these stupid rocks?" she said, much angrier than the pain in her shins warranted.

He grunted. "I'm not sure."

"What kinda tour guide are you?"

He let out another low laugh. "Got an extra toothbrush in my bag. Does that help?"

"Five stars." She didn't watch him stretch and then jolt when the pain hit his side, didn't want to see the thick curves of his chest or the curled hair that had set off that ache in her nipples. "But honestly, look at this place," she blustered, struggling to stand, naked and turned on and really, really unhappy about the situation. "When I asked for rustic," she said, with a good dose of forced humor. "I figured there'd at least be walls, you know?" He smiled, the white of his teeth stark against his dark beard. It sent a liquid rush to her belly—and lower. "The yeti's a nice touch, though." She reached into the pack and pulled out the first item of clothing she found—a long-sleeved thermal T-shirt. "With that pelt, you're like a…hipster Paul Bunyan or something. Hipster barbarian. Barbarians of Instagram." If anything, the cotton highlighted the two sharp points of her breasts. She forged ahead, intent on distracting him—or her, mostly—from this unfortunate want. "You look like Jason Momoa and Tom Hardy had a baby and…" His puzzled expression made her stop. "You don't have any idea what I'm talking about, do you?"

He shook his head, bringing her focus down to his mouth. In the dawn light, with sleep still marking his features, it didn't look hard at all. It looked soft and pliable.

What am I doing getting sidetracked by the sexy yeti? She drove her attention up to his eyes and forced a good dose of iron into her next words. "Can you move?"

He lifted the bag and looked down at himself. "Need a minute."

It took her a beat to understand what he meant. Then, of course, her eyes shot down before her brain had caught up with it. After that, her eyes raced up to meet his—which was another mistake. The man was freaking gorgeous. She knew that, could see it in the perfection of his body parts, the symmetry of his features. The unruly hair and beard barely hid what was underneath. She recalled the pictures of him from before. The ones showing a man being sought for all those murders. His face had seemed too perfect back then, his smile too golden, eyes too limpid. Too good to be true.

This truth, though, of a smooth stone gone rough was so much more appealing. His beauty plucked a chord deep inside her—the answering call of a person who'd become less, not more, polished by life. Sanded down not to a smooth center but a pitted, jagged, broken core that very few people ever saw. If any.

"How old are you?" she asked without realizing she'd even opened her mouth to speak.

"Thirty-nine." He raised his head and lowered it, as if in pain.

"You okay?"

The sound he made wasn't even close to a laugh. "Alive, aren't I?"

"Any frostbite or anything?"

He concentrated for a few seconds—probably wriggling fingers and toes. "Think I'm good." A pause, during which he avoided her gaze. "Thanks to you."

"What kind of man doesn't tell his partner when he gets shot?" She huffed, pulling on a second dry layer from his pack. "You were wounded and you *carried* me." Shaking her head, she threw him a dirty look. "Jackass."

He was so quiet, she almost didn't hear him say, "Partner?"

"*What?*"

Ready for a confrontation, she turned to meet his eyes, only to find that there wasn't an iota of aggression there. "This you breaking my balls, Leo?"

She snorted. "That's right." The fleece she pulled on was too big and it smelled like him. Ignoring the goose bumps, she threw one his way.

"Good." He smiled, catching her in his spell before the shirt landed on his head. When he lifted it off, though, he didn't look quite so happy. In fact, if she had to pinpoint exactly how he looked, she'd say guilty as hell.

Which didn't bode well for this partnership thing.

CHAPTER 19

WINDED, ELIAS LAY BACK WITH A FRUSTRATED SIGH. "COULD you uh…could you help me with this?" He lifted the shirt as far as he could manage. "Can't quite get it up."

"I'd beg to differ." Leo's hand flew to her mouth, cutting off a laugh.

Meanwhile, half the blood in Elias's body flooded his cheeks while the other half returned to the subject of her mirth. Unconsciously, his eyes raked their way up and down her newly clothed body.

Looking awkward, she cleared her throat. "Sorry, that was uncalled for."

"No. No, it was called for." He smiled and watched her. Her skin was a radiant umber in the sunlight, her eyes on him so warm he forgot, for a shell-shocked second or two, how much danger they were in. "Absolutely called for," he repeated roughly, ensnared by the sight of her top teeth biting into her lush lower lip.

Bo came up and nudged him with the top of her head, snapping him out of Leo's spell and reminding him that distractions like this were lethal.

Her eyes narrowed at him. "You're flirting and you can't even stand up."

"Wasn't flirting," he mumbled.

"Right." She rolled her eyes at his efforts to get up. "Stop that. You'll hurt yourself. First…" She grabbed the canteen, then sat behind him and helped him get into a leaning position, right in the V of her legs. "Water."

She put the canteen to his lips and dammit, he tried grabbing the stupid thing, but he would've lost it if she hadn't also been holding on. "Body's not working yet."

"Okay." She leaned, dug around in his damp coat pockets, and pulled out a couple of protein bars. "Eat."

He ate the first in two large bites and scarfed down the second bar.

"All right." She scooted away, taking her heat with her. "I'll be back. Don't go anywhere."

He grunted and tried to put the shirt on again. Though every cell of his being understood the urgent need to get up and out of the bag, he couldn't do it, could barely turn onto his side and watch her head into the sparse pine cover.

He gave up and shut his eyes.

He'd almost died back there. Twice. Hadn't even felt the damn gunshot wound, with all the adrenaline pouring through him. But between that and the shock of the water, he'd be dead if she hadn't gotten him to safety.

With his eyes closed, he listened for signs of pursuit—not that he'd hear with the noise the ice was currently making.

They had to move. If he couldn't, she'd have to go without him.

With a deep inhale, he pushed up to sitting and worked the shirt over his head.

He shoved the sleeping bag aside and took a second to examine the long, ugly gash the bullet had put in his hide. He'd need to disinfect that and bandage it before taking off. Another nudge of the covers revealed his penis, only half-hard now that she'd gone.

"Least *you're* doing okay." He shook his head, disgusted at himself.

"Who?"

Quickly, he covered up again. "Shit, you move quietly."

She smiled vaguely and eyed the tight thermal stretched across his chest. "You got it on."

"Yeah." He lifted his chin. "Think you could, uh, grab me something for the bottom half?"

She got him his things and busied herself putting his pack back together while he struggled into pants.

"Where's your bag?"

"My bag?" She spun in a circle. "Oh, crap."

"Not much in it. See our boots there. Your coat." He lifted his chin toward his bag. "Mine. With my pack, we'll be okay."

"Thanks to your overpreparedness."

"If the…" He supported himself on one hand and made it to standing. "…gear's necessary for survival, then it's not *over*prepared, is it?" He reached for his coat, found it wet, and spread it out onto the stones. "Just prepared."

She snuffled. "Guess you're right."

"I am." He grimaced at the sun peeking over the mountains. "Getting to be that time."

Her eyes flicked up his body before making their way down again—as if seeing him for the very first time. Which, in a way, was the case, now that daylight had chased the shadows away. "To move, you mean?"

At his nod, she cocked her head. "Where are we headed exactly?"

"Where do you want to go?"

"Like I said, I want to talk to Campbell Turner."

That would be a problem. Rather than focus on it, he deflected. "How's your head?"

"Fine."

He didn't believe that for a second. "Figured we'd get you some medical care first."

"I need to see Turner. I need to get to that virus before the Chronos people—" She stopped, mouth still open. "Hear that?"

He shook his head and listened. The most obvious sound was the grind and pop and crash of ice breaking up, running water its undercurrent. He frowned, concentrating hard and then… "Shit."

Something thumped in the distance.

"That's a helo," said Leo, looking truly frightened for the first time since he'd met her. "They're here."

He'd hoped for more time. His eyes flew to Leo. "Go," he said.

The look she gave him was confused. "No."

"Go, Leo. I got this." He bent from his waist but couldn't quite reach his rifle.

"Forget it." She gathered the pack and started stuffing their remaining things into it, haphazardly mixing wet with dry. "I'm not—"

"Come on, Leo. They're close." Another try, and though his side felt like it was tearing open, he managed to grab the weapon, pull back the slide, and focus on the sky. "I'll hold 'em off. You leave. Now."

━━━━━━━━━

"What are you doing?" Leo took another wild look around. Their boots. Shit, his coat.

"I'm staying. You run." The Ruger Guide Gun he held was a bear shooter, best for taking down large beasts at fairly close range. It wouldn't make a dent on their aircraft. They, however, could easily pick him off from the air.

"Like hell." She shook her head, heaving the heavy pack onto her back. "Not leaving you."

"They only want me." He lifted his chin to indicate more items strewn around them on the rocks. "Damn breakup covered up the sound of their approach. Can't..." He grimaced, as if his side hurt. "Go! Now! Take Bo. Get some distance. There's a chance you'll make it out alive."

"And what? You just...go with them? Let them kill you? Torture you till you give them Turner's location?" His lips lifted in the strangest little half smile. "What am I missing, Elias?"

"Get out of here."

"Make me." She moved toward him, snapped up the blanket and bags, and shoved them at him.

The thump of rotors thundered around them, echoing off the peaks across the lake.

He opened his mouth and shut it, staring at her like he didn't get her at all. In the next split second, something vulnerable softened his eyes.

Taking advantage of the hesitation, she shoved the stuff into his open arms. "You don't come now, we're both toast." Her "Come on!" was drowned out by the helicopter, whose shadow now stretched at the edge of her vision.

Bo, who clearly didn't like the sound of the aircraft any more than Leo did, scurried into the woods, hunched close to the ground. She barked once, as if to say, *Come on, you silly bastards! Hide from the big scary thing!*

Whatever he said next couldn't be heard above the sound of the helo, though she assumed it was something like *Whatever, lady,* because he followed her up the rocky lake's edge, toward the woods. It wasn't until they'd made shelter that she spotted her pack. It sat right beside the water, about twenty-five yards from where they stood, disgorging items like some kind of beached monster.

If the team in the helicopter spotted the bag, they were dead.

Without a second thought, she dropped the big pack and sprinted—barefoot and half-dressed—to the bag, which she picked up, shoving the loose items inside and hauling it up onto her shoulder with a cold, wet slap, while she raced back uphill.

The rotors boomed now—above, in front, all around. The once-comforting sound suddenly screamed doom. She trained her eyes on the ground, focused everything she had on keeping upright and on the move.

She barreled under the trees and into Elias, who caught her around the waist, spun her, and pressed her against a trunk, covering her body with his. Throwing her head back, she saw nothing but pine needles and then—shit, that was close—the ship flew directly overhead, close enough to make out the seams in the metal.

Elias bent low, put his mouth against her ear, and yelled. "Almost gave me a heart attack."

The helicopter flew past, over the lake, and away. Still, he didn't move. And she didn't want him to.

As she caught her breath, details emerged—like the hard press of his muscles and the rough scrape of bark, the heat of his deep exhalations. His neck was still bent, she realized, his face still pressed to her cheek. She should move. *They* should move.

But, hell, she didn't want to.

By the time her pulse was back to something approaching normal, the aircraft was probably close to a mile away, hovering over the center of the lake. Running a rescue operation, she'd guess. Though killing the enemy wasn't something she took pleasure in, it was hard to feel regret for the people who'd been caught out there last night.

She turned and rose up on tiptoe, getting her mouth as close to his ear as possible. "Don't do that again, okay, Elias?"

"What?"

"Try to take one for the team. We're in this together now, got it? Survive together, get out together." Her nose grazed his jaw and she pretended not to notice how good he smelled. "Go down together."

He sighed, shifting away. "You're a pain in the ass, Eddowes."

She smirked. "Takes one to know one, Thorne."

CHAPTER 20

HEART THUMPING, LEO PICKED UP THE BACKPACK AND followed Elias into the woods, sticking to what cover there was in the sparse early spring taiga forest. Conscious of the continued risk of being seen from above, they climbed up a steep slope covered with brush that was almost impassible but provided more than adequate cover. Which was a good thing, since the aircraft was clearly searching for them.

After three hours' slow slog, Leo stopped to wipe her dripping forehead and cast a look at the sky, wondering if maybe she should throw up her arms and beg the enemy crew for an emergency evacuation.

Wading through the underbrush had saved their lives, yeah, but as she picked devil's club thorns from her hands and sleeves and gritted her teeth against the ones elsewhere, all she had to give was hate. She'd been through some shit, some long-ass hauls, some pretty gnarly rescues in the world's legitimately deadliest places, but she'd never hated anything more than thick, spiny devil's club.

They'd been at it for three hours and there wasn't an end in sight.

"Shouldn't this stuff be dead? Dormant?"

Elias's back lifted and fell in response. Right. No point arguing with *mothereffing* nature.

"Bitch," she muttered under her breath.

Yeah, she'd lost it.

Hilarious, wasn't it, that after everything, it was the thorns that sent her over the edge?

She narrowed her eyes on the man in front of her. Another Thorne entirely.

All it took to break her spirit was a couple of hours of slogging through swampy, frigid, thorn-studded snowmelt, with those assholes above—searching, with *no* intent to rescue—and the yeti leading the way with absolute stoicism.

Okay. So, maybe she wasn't broken. But she was tired and pissed. Her spirit was angry. It wanted potato chips. And a tall, frosty glass of rosé. A damn bottle. Or one of those boxes so she wouldn't have to leave her place for a while. Her spirit wanted to curl up in front of a nice fire with chips and wine and maybe a taste of that man in front of her.

She came to a dead stop.

Oh crap.

The angry hiking had worked for her for a bit. A decent distraction, especially since she'd spent the last hour or so picking the hellish thorns from her skin. The bastards had pierced her through four layers of clothes—including the damp coat she'd finally thrown back on for protection.

But suddenly she was faced with the truth of what had happened in the last couple of days. She'd developed an unlikely attachment—attraction, lust, whatever the hell you wanted to call it—to the big, messed-up man in front of her.

A crush. Only far more desperate than that.

And the worst part, right now, if she was being terribly honest, was that given the choice between eating chips and drinking wine in a soft bed or having this man on the hard ground, sober and starving, she knew exactly which one she'd go for.

And it wasn't soft or crispy or smooth going down.

Must be the head injury. There was no other explanation. "Hell," she muttered.

"You okay?"

She focused on his drawn brows, the thick beard covering the concern on his sun-gilded face.

A quick nod should have been enough to get him moving again, but something about this guy gave him access to truths others never saw. Leo's secrets were a wide-open book for Elias Thorne.

And that was not okay.

"Turn around," she said grumpily. "Keep walking."

"What's wrong? What do you need?"

"Just go."

"Is it your head?"

Yes. Yes, it's my head…my neck, my back, lick my pu—I've lost it. Singing Khia lyrics in the wilds of Alaska. Totally screwy. "Head's fine." *Aside from the obvious delirium happening here.* "Think we could just…" She put out a stiff hand. "Keep going?"

His eyes did a quick circuit of her body. Must have found nothing out of order, because they then focused in on her face. Which was probably another story. She couldn't get the panic off it fast enough.

"Look. I'm having some…unpleasant thoughts." *Liar.* They were pleasant as all get-out. So pleasant, she'd stopped thinking about the killer prickle bushes and the mud and the enemy for a while.

He was walking back toward her now, and she didn't want that. She wanted him to keep going, to put some actual distance between them and the helicopter search centered above the lake. She wanted to get around this mountain to where the yeti claimed the temperature was higher and actual spring was underway.

If she could thaw out, maybe she could *think*, instead of toiling through this hellish terrain, where cuddling with yetis seemed like a half-decent idea.

"Let's just get around the mountain, yet—Eli—*Thorne*!" She shook her head. "We need to get past this thing, and I'm sure I'll be just fine. Good as new."

His brows rose, lowered, went up, and dropped again, as if he were trying to translate an indecipherable set of hieroglyphics on her face. After a few more seconds, he nodded.

"Whatever you say, boss," he said before taking off again, constant, kind, dependable, easy.

And hell if that didn't mix up one very attractive cocktail.

Mud, cold, injuries, and the constantly sweeping helicopter turned the journey into a slow, ugly grind along the river and up to higher elevations. Well, up a thousand or so feet. They couldn't go above the tree line until the aircraft headed home for the day.

Which was bound to happen soon, given that they'd need to refuel.

The worst part was that he and Leo had probably walked no more than a couple of miles from the lake, and while this hike would usually be a piece of cake for Elias, his backpack weighed him down like it was filled with lead weights and his body was a mess.

He'd carried heavier, gone farther. Normally, he could do this trek in his sleep.

"What's wrong?" Leo had taken the lead a while back, as if she couldn't wait to get this over and done with. Right now, she stopped and narrowed her focus on him. "You look weird."

"Weird? No, I'm—"

He stumbled on a root, the movement pulling at his side, which drew a groan from deep in his chest. He put out a hand, caught himself on a trunk, and waited for the wave of dizziness to pass.

"You're in pain. Why didn't you—"

"I'm fine."

"Let me check your injury, Elias. Just to make sure."

He shook his head. "I'm good. It's just a scra—"

"Don't even try that bullshit. Been through this, remember? I'm not playing with gunshot wounds." Leo went around him and opened his pack without permission, rummaged around in it, and came out with his first aid kit before giving the canvas a firm smack. "Put this thing on the ground. We're doing this right."

Why'd she sound angry? Was she mad at him? "Leo. Leo, you don't have to—"

Her annoyed exhale was so loud, it cut through his actual words—that was the power of this woman's silence.

When he didn't immediately give in, she put her hands on her hips and spoke. "Look, Mr. Big Elias Thorne-in-my-side Yeti Man who's lived on his own for so long he doesn't know how to speak English anymore, I know you hardly *ever* crack a smile, much less express emotions like…oh, extreme pain or whatever. 'Cause you're such a big boy. Real manly. I get that. But I've seen grown Navy SEALs cry, okay? I'm okay with big boy boo-boos. You're allowed to tell me when the boo-boo hurts. 'Cause, frankly, I'm not sure I've got the strength to carry your unconscious, limp—"

"Fine," he grumbled. "Here." He dropped the pack, unzipped his fleece, and grappled with his many shirts to give her access to his side, surprised to find that it really did throb. "Have at it."

The breath she sucked in through her teeth did nothing to appease him.

"That bad?"

"Nah." She threw him a look that he couldn't entirely interpret, then punctuated it with a raised eyebrow. "Just reacting to your insanely sculpted six-pack." She snuffled, leaned closer, and dabbed something to his wound. "Spend a lot of time at the gym, huh? Didn't notice a weight room back at the cabin. Must have been in the…" He swayed, she caught him around the chest and tutted, the sound weirdly reminiscent of something Old Amka would do. "Come on. I need to—"

"It's fine." He shoved his shirt down, shuddered, and got as much distance from her as he could. Her hands on him were too much. Too damn much.

"Did I hurt you? Oh, hey. Look, I'm sorry if I—"

"No." But the concern on her face sure did. The soft, careful path her fingers had trailed along his side. He could still feel the goose bumps, like a brand. They hurt more than the damn injury. And it wasn't blood loss making him woozy; it was Leontyne Eddowes and her knowing eyes.

"Leontyne," he said aloud, enjoying it on his lips. "Pretty."

"Mm-hm. Right. Okay. I need you to lie down."

Jesus, even knowing what she meant, those words made him hard. *Lie down.*

He cleared his throat. "I'll deal with it myself. Just give me the—"

"Lie down, Thorne. Or I swear to God, I'll…"

He held his breath, waiting. What? What would she do? He couldn't begin to imagine—though his brain sure tried.

And then she pulled back, suddenly almost casual, which made him wonder what she had up her sleeve. "Listen. Real talk, okay?"

"Okay." He stared into her deep, dark eyes—huge and serious in that little round face.

"You know this thing going on? It's weird, right?" Though they always spoke quietly, she whispered now, drawing him in closer. "Does it feel weird to you?"

Being chased by an armed militia? Was that what she meant? He glanced at the rugged terrain around them, the wooded slope leading down to the brilliant lake, the rockier ledges above. "It's not… No. I'm used to this place. It's tough, but you'll—"

"Not the place. Not *that*." She moved her hand back and forth from his chest to hers. "I mean *this*. Right here. This *thing* happening. Between us."

He blinked and in the next split second was hit by a sudden realization. None of this was real. Not this woman, with her too-intense gaze that read the secrets of his soul, not the helicopter prowling the skies like some fire-breathing dragon. Even Bo wasn't acting like herself right now, prancing like a pony while their lives were on the line. He must be asleep, dead, or dying.

"You attracted to me?" The question was so light, her voice so casual that the meaning didn't immediately register.

Not real. Not the lake spread out beneath them, shimmering under the noonday sun, not the trees spiking up straight from the soft, slippery ground, not the new smell of melt, and especially not that question.

"That what this is about?" Her index finger seesawed from his middle to hers, the move slow and playful. "The weirdness between us?"

If this was a dream, then he didn't need to answer. And if it was real…he had no idea how to.

"Okay. What I'm trying to say to you, Elias, is…" She bit her lip and he almost lost it. "Are you attracted to me?"

"Yes." She was every one of his fantasies, standing in front of him. Strong and soft, real in a way no woman had been before. What was the point in lying?

She made a silent *oh* with her mouth and then followed it up with a businesslike, "All right then. You know that saying about catching more flies with honey?" She edged closer. "Spoonful of sugar. All that?"

He grunted. It was the closest thing she'd get to a yes. He couldn't for the life of him figure out where this rabbit hole was leading.

"I saw a TED Talk recently," she said. "The speaker said that it's…" At his blank look, she paused. "What?"

"You saw Ted talk?"

"A TED Talk. You don't know what that is?" When did she get so close to him? Her head tilted back, her mouth suddenly so near her breath warmed his neck. It was light and sweet, and now he couldn't stop thinking about honey.

"No," he whispered, though he couldn't remember her question.

"Oh, hm. Okay. Well, research says that the flies and honey

thing is true. You want someone to do something, it's better to sweeten the pot than to punish." Her eyes made a slow circuit of his face. By the time they made it back to his, he was breathing hard and fast, and the want was front and center—bigger than the pain, the exhaustion, his mission. Anything.

"What'd you…" He cleared his desire-clogged throat. "Have in mind?"

"How about a kiss?"

His body leaned in fractionally, but she'd already backed up.

"Is this for real? I'm not sure—"

"A kiss. Yes or no, Elias?"

His "Yeah" was a tight whisper, as if his entire being wasn't screaming for it.

"Get on the ground, then. And let me dress your wound properly."

He was hard as a rock now, his cock throbbing like it hadn't done in ages. And it wasn't just from the promise of a kiss. It was the game he liked—this quid pro quo thing. And maybe also the danger of it all. Like she'd dug into his psyche and pulled out some kinks he didn't even know existed.

"A kiss." He breathed it like a secret password.

She nodded. He couldn't pull his eyes from her lips—the bow-tie curve at the top, the more pronounced pout below. They were pink in the middle, like her tongue. Like maybe other places that he didn't dare think about.

"You'll kiss me." It was incomprehensible. The whole thing.

"Yes." She was all business, her lips tight, her brows up, without a hint of that closeness they'd just had. "Now, come on."

CHAPTER 21

SLOWLY, HE LOWERED HIMSELF TO THE GROUND, FULL OF THE smell of rotting leaves and mud, fresh green growth in there somewhere, poised and ready, though it had yet to pop. She followed him down, pointedly ignoring the way he watched her—like if he blinked, she'd disappear—and got to work.

Instead of shutting his eyes through the painful application of antiseptic, he kept them wide-open, losing focus in the treetops halfway through the bandaging process.

"Lift."

He obeyed, held himself up while she wrapped a bandage around his middle, and settled back down, waiting for her to finish.

Which took forever. Her hands smoothed the tape, her fingers tested the edges, lingered…

When his surprised gaze met hers, there was a challenge in her expression.

Somewhere far away, the helicopter's engine growled, back within earshot. Or maybe it was just that his ears suddenly worked again.

He ignored it. Not blinking, not breathing. Just waiting, watching, his skin prickling, antsy with cold and anticipation.

The air was different, muskier, more alive than it had been in forever—with movement and scents, sounds, and a light, chilly breeze. Birds cawed to the west, just over the crest of this mountain, while the aircraft circled back from the east. They'd have to land on top of him to get him to move right now.

"Do it." His voice was a raw, open thing, more vulnerable than the wound she'd just covered. Want wasn't something he allowed himself. Wasn't much point when everything worth wanting was out of reach.

Only it wasn't right now. It was right here. And he couldn't remember wanting like this—ever.

He put out his hand, let his fingers curl around her perfect ear, let them drag along the soft, brown skin. He gently pinched the lobe, testing its softness, before cupping her ear again, the fleshy part of his palm flush with her jaw.

Her eyelids dropped, opened, stayed at half-mast, and then, like a dream he'd wake up from feeling empty and lost, she pushed back, giving him the weight of her head, the curve of her cheek.

She lowered her head.

"One kiss." The words were a hot breath on his belly, fanning his hair, tightening his abs.

Instead of rising over him and planting those lips on his, she dipped, paused, burned a path over his skin with her eyes, then pressed her mouth right where his pants ended low on his hips.

———————

Leo had had no intention of doing any of this. She'd planned on bussing his cheek, just to tease him, maybe to motivate.

She most definitely hadn't meant to put her mouth in this prematurely intimate place, where his happy trail disappeared, not here against his smooth, fragrant skin. Not in the wild, on the damp ground while the helo swooped toward them like a marauding bird of prey. It was so close now, she felt the thrum through her knees, the ground, his midsection.

Still, she didn't lift her head, couldn't draw away.

It might have been his scent that made her act like an idiot. Or maybe these fascinating muscles—born of the hard labor of a life lived alone. It could have been the sweet, high pink she'd seen in his cheeks before she'd lowered her face, telling her just how much he'd wanted this.

But she knew it wasn't any of those that made her do this stupid,

stupid thing. It wasn't the light, crisp nap of his hair that made her put her tongue to skin and taste. It wasn't the way his rough fingers cradled her ear—gently, like she was something fragile to be cared for and worried about. Taken care of, instead of doing the caring, which had always been her role.

No, she admitted, behind the safe haven of her own closed lids, what had sent her to this unexpected place was the look in his eyes. The man may have been close to forty, with the wear and tear to prove it, but his expression when she'd hovered over him had been so raw, so earnest, the yearning so pure and close to the surface, that she'd have done anything for him in that moment, given him whatever the hell he'd wanted.

The sound of the aircraft above was almost deafening, as if the bastards were homing right in on their perch here. And instead of running, she was tasting him.

What an absolute fool.

The sound grew louder, forcing her to put a hand to the cold, wet ground and press up, half expecting him to urge her back down. Something like disappointment washed through her when he took his touch away. As soon as she gave him space, he rolled to his side and sat, his body moving fast, though his eyes watched her as if they had all the time in the world.

She couldn't seem to move, despite doom's pressing arrival. If she moved, it would be over—the moment gone, blown apart by stark reality.

Once he'd reached standing, he offered his hand, casting his eyes to the sky. He didn't have to tell her they'd be seen under these sparse branches. Christ, this day had taught her exactly how it felt to be the prey on the ground, scurrying like hamsters in a maze. She accepted his firm grip, wishing she could feel something aside from rough gloves, and let him pull her up, almost against him. Another second was wasted while she soaked up his closeness—her chest near enough to his to feel the heat, his height making her feel small, though she wasn't.

Together, they dragged his pack into the shelter of the alder shrubs, sinking into the devil's club's spiny embrace.

They were camouflaged enough. She hoped.

She turned. What was missing? Something was wrong.

"See Bo?" Elias's voice rumbled.

That was it. She shot a quick look around. "No."

"Shit."

With a suddenness that felt almost apocalyptic, the helicopter blotted out the sunlight, its shadow taking over the mountainside like a biblical swarm of insects. She'd never shied away from the end before—always looked it right in the eye—yet something pushed Leo to tuck her head into the crook of Elias's shoulder and close her eyes.

His arm wrapped around her—not tightly, but present, as if he already understood how she worked. She should push him away and stand on her own. She should burst this bubble she'd somehow created between them. It was dangerous to let herself want something this badly.

"Bo!" Elias hissed, bringing her back to reality with a jolt.

———

Where the hell was she?

Elias scanned the woods around them, seeing nothing but snow and mud, tall, straight trunks, a practically sheer rock face to the north, more forest to the west, and—

His eyes skidded, returning to where they'd spotted movement. Oh no.

"What is it?" Leo half yelled through the aircraft's roar.

He glanced down at her, surprised that she'd picked up on his anxiety. Although she could probably feel his heart thumping against her face. He lifted his chin to the ridge opposite. No point trying to talk above the engine noise now.

Slowly, Leo turned, her big, intelligent eyes scanning everything. He felt her jolt the moment she caught sight of their problem—problems, actually.

About thirty yards ahead, through the woods, the ground appeared to slope gently and then rise again. There, just about level with them, a large, white, fluffy horned mountain goat and its kid perched on a ledge.

"Wait here," he hollered, already moving in that direction. He let out a short, low whistle. "*Borealis!*" Maybe she hadn't tried to stalk the goats. Maybe she'd run back into the woods after a squirrel or something. Yeah right. What squirrel?

The helicopter drew closer, so near now he could feel the vibration in his bones. Something moved to his right: Leo, running beside him.

"Don't come," he yelled over the din. "Wait here."

She didn't bother looking at him, just kept pace.

Closer to the promontory, the trees grew sparse, the ground rocky, the slope steep and slippery and—

He threw out an arm just as his boot hit the edge of a massive boulder, cragged and pitted by time. Leo bumped into it and went still. There was no cover here—just air above them. They'd be seen if the helicopter flew this way. "Go back!" he yelled, dropping and crawling to the end. He barely registered the cocktail of fear and adrenaline and anger running through him. Anger at Bo for running after an animal—again. Anger at himself for not training her. Of course, huskies did whatever the hell they wanted anyway, so it hadn't really been an option.

Or the point, really. She wasn't a tool. She was a companion. Just two beings living out here on their own, together.

At the edge, he caught a flash of white and gray, about eight feet down, and the emotions coalesced into relief, so strong he'd probably collapse when this was over. No time to rest now.

She'd obviously picked her way down to a shelf and, being a

dog, not the mountain goat she thought she was, hadn't managed to climb up again. A few precious seconds of intense scrutiny showed him footholds and handholds and a crack he could wedge himself into. Without hesitating, he levered his legs over the side and made the climb—quickly.

Almost to the shelf, he glanced up, unsure if he'd rather see Leo's face looking down at him or not.

She was there, crouched at the edge, eyes on him and then up at the sky. "They're close!"

He shifted his weight. Another couple feet to go. The aircraft seemed headed right their way, the air changing, his eardrums thrumming with the rhythm. A final stretch down and he'd made it to Bo's ledge, which was hopefully sturdy enough to hold both their weights.

A glance up showed that Leo had disappeared. He could only hope she'd found shelter before the chopper reached them.

Bo bumped his leg with her head and probably whined, though he couldn't hear it. Across the chasm, the goat had disappeared in the way of mountain goats in high places. Above, the leaves flapped madly. Close. Too damned close. This was it. There was nowhere to go. No hiding place. Bo's bright fur was sure to be spotted.

The aircraft's shadow seeped into sight and in the next moment, Elias's fear sloughed off like a second skin. His moves were quick and instinctual. Left foot shoved into the crack, weight balanced, he bent and grabbed Bo around the middle. Hauling her up and into his arms, he pressed her to the rock with his body, bent his head, and hoped his coat and dark hair would be camouflage enough. He wouldn't look up, didn't dare move, though he could have sworn he felt the shadow's dark reach.

At some point, he started counting, since his ears could no longer tell the difference between right above and moving away. He made it to ten, fifteen, up to thirty... Each number felt like a step climbed, a level achieved, another year in a decade of being alone.

By the time fifty rolled around, he could hear his breath beating against cold stone, could feel his fingers digging too hard into Bo's ribs, could feel the hard rock like a vise around his foot. Hopefully he hadn't shoved it in there too hard. He'd hate to leave the boot behind. Or his damn toes.

Something like laughter expanded his chest, though he couldn't see the humor in any of this. He did it again, this time apparently waking Bo from her own stupor. She tried wriggling and he tightened his hold, not even wanting to know how far they'd fall if she moved in earnest.

"Holy shit." Leo's voice reached him from above. He couldn't lean back, wouldn't dare to look for fear of dislodging this whole exercise in physics. "What do you need?"

He blinked. Need? A goddamn crane to lift them out.

"Rope? Would that help? I brought your pack."

He blinked, his eyes focusing on the gray and brown and white composite he leaned on. "Can you tie a rope? To a tree, maybe?"

"There's a harness."

A harness. Of course. He nodded, unsure if she could see him. "Okay. Be right back."

For the first time in as long as he could remember, something warm seeped inside—not physically. Hell, suspended up here, he couldn't do much more than follow a vein in the granite with his eyes and hope his body could hold on. Hot and cold meant nothing in this moment. But he felt it nonetheless. A change, solid and reassuring as his mom's hand in his as a child.

"Heads up!" Leo yelled, and by the time he managed to tilt his head back and adjust his vision to something more than an inch away, she'd sent Bo's harness down on a line. It bumped his shoulder and went lower.

Slowly, he bent and whispered a *good girl* into Bo's ear, aware of the thumping of her heart against his arm. Easing his right foot to the side, shifting his weight, and moving his arm away with his torso while keeping her in place were the three hardest things he'd ever done, but he had backup. As long as the helicopter didn't return, he could do this. *They.* They could do this. "Wanna go rock climbing?" he whispered, grasping the thick nylon and quickly slipping the first straps to clip around Bo's head. He pulled her front leg through, then slipped the other straps around her torso. A slight turn, another move, then onto her legs. "Going rock climbing, Borealis. You *love* climbing."

After what felt like a lifetime of threading and tightening straps, choppy breathing, and promises to a god he no longer believed in, he got her in. "She's ready!" he called, still holding the dog's weight.

"Okay. I've got her."

Time to trust.

He shut his eyes, hard, not bothering to pray before sliding to the side and finally letting her go. After an initial drop of maybe half three inches, Bo whined and started rising.

She disappeared above. He pulled his foot from the crack, not allowing the relief to seep in yet, and climbed the few yards to the top.

"Come on." Leo grabbed his hand and helped him to standing. Without waiting, she turned and walked into the shelter of the trees. Bo slunk along beside her, throwing him the same big-eyed look she got when he berated her for rolling in a stinky carcass or animal shit.

He tried to breathe and found his chest too tight, his throat constricted. Was the helicopter coming back? A wild look up showed him nothing but sky.

Gone. For now.

Under the trees, he sucked in deep, the oxygen hit his lungs hard.

Automatically, he slid his fingers into the fur at the nape of Bo's neck, startled to find Leo's hand already there. After a beat, he shifted away.

Though part of him wanted to shut his eyes on this whole damned thing, sink to the ground and hole up in the underbrush forever, he turned, seeking...

Leo's wide-open gaze hit him with a jolt, sucked him in, and held him up like a life raft.

Fear might have drawn them together, but something entirely different sizzled in its aftermath.

The thrill of having a teammate. Of being someone's partner.

And then, because he'd never been a liar—at least not to himself—he admitted to that other thing—the thing that led to kisses from a near stranger, on the belly, lying on the wet, cold ground, ignoring the danger hovering over them like an angel of death.

Was it just adrenaline making them act like horny teenagers who needed to do things *now*? Or was it something else? A need to feel each other's life force, to know they were alive? Maybe some throwback to the cavemen, some now-or-never instinct telling him the beast was gone and this might be his only chance to spread his seed.

Never mind. What was the point in worrying when they truly could be shot down any second? Dragged away? Tortured? He dug his hand deeper into the warm nest of Bo's fur and Leo's skin, reached out to curl his fingers around her slender neck, and pulled her in for a real kiss.

The first touch was surprisingly cool, given how electric their connection was. He pressed harder, crushed those tender lips with his hard ones, and took. Or gave. Shared.

Fuck, he didn't know.

The aircraft went far, farther. Or did it come near? He'd look, but every muscle was straining to get closer to Leo.

Air burst from his lungs when she angled her head and moved her mouth, opened it, licked him, pushed him against the trunk, moaned. Obliterated him with tiny movements.

The tree held him up, and the bark, rough and solid against the back of his head, kept him here, in reality. The rotors somewhere above tore up the air like a storm—the wind and sound and tension a rush like nothing he'd felt in his life.

Or was that the beating of his own damn heart? Were they gone? Did it even matter?

It was unreal how hard he was, how jacked up, how absolutely frenzied. Pain and fear and excitement mixed with adrenaline and craving, the cocktail blasting through him—*them*—pushing him to do things he'd never consider in his real life.

Oh yeah? a voice asked, from deep in his messed-up brain. *Which life is that?* Playing football in college? Throwing his weight around as a federal marshal? Wasting his time loving the ex-fiancé who'd dumped him when things went bad?

Real was *this*. Mud and sky, snow and rotting leaves. Hot, biting kisses against sandpaper bark, danger and lust and something deep and raw and too fresh to look at.

He didn't just throw caution to the wind when he reached for her now; he slung it wide and watched it shatter—the explosion a climax he'd been awaiting for years—decades that felt like centuries. So long he'd become one with his surroundings, died every winter to be reborn in the spring along with the rest of this place.

He hardly registered her hands at his waist, struggling to unbutton his pants. All he felt was the soft, warm give of her mouth as his tongue tasted, teased, fought with hers. Teeth parried, noses sucked each other in.

There was no question of where this would end, no doubt in his mind that he'd be inside her within seconds. How could he not? Everything frantic and needy and animalistic in him wanted this—*now*. And what was he if not an animal?

No.

He wrenched his head away, breathing hard.

"Shouldn't do this."

"I need this." She sounded like she'd just run a marathon. Out of breath and dazed. "Lift me up and I'll—"

He put his hand out, stopping her, and then stared at its placement. Not on her chest exactly, but higher, at the cusp of her neck, the fingers spread wide. If she were an enemy, it would be awfully close to a chokehold, but given that they were on the same side, and that they'd been sucking face seconds before, there was something unbearably intimate in the way he held her at bay.

Her eyes rolled down to his arm and rose again, her expression vague at first, then slowly clearing, like she'd just awakened from a fugue state. Which was how he felt, except he couldn't claim a second of memory loss.

He remembered everything.

"What the hell?" Her whisper came out slurred, almost drunk.

"Don't know."

She blinked, her eyes clearer now that the lust fog had dissipated.

"Better"—he worked to catch his breath—"keep moving."

"Right." She nodded. "We need to warn Campbell Turner and keep the virus out of the wrong hands."

Just hearing the name—Campbell Turner—sent a wave of hopelessness through him. He cleared his throat of the guilt. "Actually, we can't."

"Can't what?" Her gaze sharpened, losing the last vestiges of lust.

No way could he keep the truth from her now—not with what they'd lived through together. Not with the way she made him feel. "Can't see him at all."

"Why not?" Her voice was careful, deceptively calm.

"He's dead." The words didn't feel right on his tongue. Christ, it wasn't easy to admit, even after all this time.

She blinked. "And the virus?"

His mouth opened and shut a couple of times before the truth came out. "There is no virus."

─────────────────

Amka could use a nap. After feeding the dogs, she'd taken Marion and the kids to Ila's cabin on the other side of the lake. She left them with several sat phones and instructions to keep calling Leo's friends until they got through. But there was work to do. Jackasses to destroy.

A town to take back.

A voice crackled unintelligibly in the little communications device she'd stuck in her ear. After cleaning it, obviously. Lord only knew what kind of cooties these people'd brought with 'em from the lower forty-eight.

When the question came again, she figured it was meant for the woman she and Marion had left trussed up in the shed. Knowing their prisoner would freeze to death in there, they'd piled her up with blankets and furs and tied her down so she couldn't move.

Now, back at Marion's place, Amka pushed the little button and replied with a mumble of her own. There. They could have fun trying to understand that.

At the next communication, she did it again and when they replied, sounding annoyed, she pushed the button a couple more times so they'd think their devices weren't working. Then she settled back against the side of the shed to wait.

Sure enough, a few minutes later, an ATV started up.

Grunting with the effort, she heaved herself away from the clapboard siding and went back into the shed.

The ATV drew closer, and she watched through the crack in the open door as two men pulled up in front of the house. They signaled silently to each other before splitting up—one moving to the back and the other to the front. Once they'd gone in, she waddled out into the yard, exaggerating her limp and doing her best to look old and frail—which wasn't in fact all that hard.

By the time she arrived at the porch, one of the men was there to meet her. She smiled and nodded, speaking the few words of Ahtna she remembered from her great-grandma. Didn't even know what it meant, but she thought some of it might be dirty from the way Granny'd laughed when the kids repeated it.

The man remained expressionless, while his eyes swung to the side a few times—looking for help, probably. Backup for an old woman.

She'd have laughed if it weren't so true.

"Could you help me with this, sir? I seem to have lost my—"

Though his gun was out and up, he didn't see the bear spray until it was too damn late. He was down, covering himself and trying to breathe, in too much pain to warn his partner. She fumbled with the tranquilizer gun and almost lost her hold. Her pulse picked up a bit when the sound of heavy boots running reached her, but she kept her cool and just had time to turn the gun before the other one could wrench her arms behind her back.

CHAPTER 22

LEO ADJUSTED HER STANCE, SHIFTING HER HAND CLOSER TO the knife at her waist.

"There's no virus?" She knew that statement for the lie it was. The virus existed. She'd flown a sample of the damn thing out of Antarctica. Her team had it contained in their secret headquarters, where a team of scientists was trying to figure out why it was worth killing for. "Okay." Caution made her voice artificially light. "If you think there's no virus, then where are we headed? Where have you been taking me, Elias?"

She took a quick look around, expecting... Hell, she didn't know. What more could happen at this point?

Don't ask questions like that, dummy.

"*Where?*" Though she had the urge to yell, the word came out low and quiet and gruff.

"I was going to send you to Canada. Like Amka wanted."

"Canada." Her nostrils flared in anger. "And what was your destination?"

"Schink's Station."

"To face the enemy on your own." Not anger, hurt. He didn't trust her. Didn't want her by his side.

"I can't put you in harm's way, Leo. You're injured. I have to get you to safety and then make sure they don't hurt anyone in—"

"When did you plan on mentioning this?"

"Soon." He at least had the good grace to look guilty. "When things were safer."

She nodded slowly, stepping away from the tree where she'd almost done something unforgivably stupid. With the yeti, for

God's sake. The lying liar. That would teach her not to trust so fast. Not to be taken in.

She opened her mouth to give him a piece of her mind and then shut it. Yelling wouldn't solve a thing. She didn't know this guy at all.

Then what the hell am I doing groping him in the woods?

"*Crap!*" She didn't remember ever being so angry with herself. Or so out of control with her body, her emotions. Was this because of the head injury?

"What?" Ever vigilant, he glanced around.

With the helo somewhere to the south, there wasn't much to see. Well, that wasn't true. There was a ton to see—trunks, spiking up from the uneven slope around them, some skinny and white, others dark and wet looking—all of them tall and sturdy as a battalion of soldiers. The ground told its own story, littered with fallen trees and branches, felled by the elements. She didn't want to die in this cold, bitter place, refused to wind up as just more collateral damage in this monstrous business. Which meant no more losing her mind in this place. It was dangerous.

She eyed Elias. *He* was dangerous.

No more her letting her *feelings* guide her actions.

"First." With a head shake, she put her palm out—to keep him away or to steady herself, she wasn't sure. "Let's say that weird post-adrenaline…thing didn't just happen, okay? Never happened. Can we agree on that?"

He didn't answer, and she let her gaze settle on the ground, rather than looking at him. Hell, she'd seen people lose it like this after almost…well, losing their lives. She'd seen colleagues screw complete strangers or—worst yet—people they worked with every day. That didn't end well. Not once had she been tempted. Work and sex never mingled.

Ever.

Resentful now, she looked up at Elias, wanting to blame him

for their frantic makeout session. She couldn't, though, when her skin flushed at just the memory of it. The way her hands had raced to get him out, to put him in her. If he hadn't stopped everything, she'd be having sex with him right now.

"Hey." His voice was soft.

Shaking her head, she shut her mouth tight, folded her lips in on themselves, and waited for this fresh wave of mortification to pass.

"I'm sorry."

About which part? The lying or the almost doing me against the tree?

"I'll take you to Schink's Station and from there, you can get home."

Jaw tight, she glared, shaking her head. "What do you mean there is no virus?"

He threw another look over his shoulder, an unconsciously cautious movement that spoke volumes about his life experience. Then he looked at her and sighed. "Turner didn't have it."

"And you? You don't have the virus either?"

"No." His gaze held hers, firm, honest.

"They must think you have it though. Isn't that what this is all about?"

"I don't have the virus. Never have."

A few feet away, something scurried in the underbrush, reminding her yet again that they weren't alone. The quiet here was deafening for a woman who was happiest listening to an engine's growl, especially when she considered how much movement was happening beneath the surface. Alaska wasn't just a breathtaking landscape, it was billions of living things awakening, stretching, yawning, getting ready to burst forth.

She turned away from the sight of Bo digging at the half-frozen ground and focused on Elias. His expression was wary, his stance tense. "You need to explain."

He swallowed. "The day I took Turner into custody, everything changed."

"How so?"

"He wasn't a criminal. He was a goddamn whistleblower. He knew they'd kill him eventually. Claimed they'd created a false history for him, made him out to look like a bioterrorist when he was just a middle-aged researcher who was thrown into something big." The look in his eyes was chilling. And yeah, she was mad that he'd kept the truth from her, but she believed him right now. Every word. "The work they were doing in that lab…that was some high-level destroy-the-human-race kind of shit."

Leo shivered and glanced up, expecting the aircraft to suddenly appear. It was getting closer, flying over the lake, she assumed. "What happened to him?"

"Campbell?" He scoffed. "He tagged me and then took one for the team."

"What?" Another look at the sky showed nothing—no helo, no clouds.

"Those were his calcified remains found in Mount Pleasant," Elias said, loud enough to be heard above the approaching hum. "Not mine."

"Wait. Are you saying he killed all those people? *He's* the one who carried out the massacre?"

"No." There wasn't an ounce of doubt in his expression. "That was a setup. They'd ruined my life by then, killed my…" A strange low hum left his body—more animal than human and one hundred percent pain. "They slaughtered my parents." His voice broke on the last word. "Made it look like I'd done it. I was on the run, my days were numbered." He was breathing hard, his eyes out of focus, and Leo wanted to hold him, despite the anger still running through her veins. "It was supposed to be me that day in Mount Pleasant. They set up a meet, told me mistakes were made. Said I'd—" Elias's head tilted to listen when the helicopter's hum changed. "They landing?"

Shit.

Someone shouted in the distance, and they both sprang into action, grabbing their supplies, throwing on still-damp coats, scuffing at the signs of their passage.

Before they took off again, though, she stopped him with a quiet, "Wait."

He leaned low, his face beside hers an unwelcome reminder of the havoc he wreaked on her hormones.

"They'll be crawling all over Schink's Station, right? You sure you want to go back there?"

He reached out and pulled her hood over her head, and though brusque, the move was intimate enough to squeeze something in her chest.

"Sure of nothing, Leo. Except we're better off moving." At her quick nod, they set off at a quick pace, side by side. "Got to get to a safe place to hole up. We stay out here, they'll find us eventually."

"If we head there, we fall right into their net. You know that, right?"

"Let me ask you this, Leo. What do you think's happening in Schink's Station right now?"

She'd wondered the same thing, and no matter what angle she considered it from, the answer never looked good. "They're killing people, aren't they?" She huffed out a breath. "Or threatening to."

"It's what they do." He stopped and bent low again, his expression angry enough to border on scary. "My job is to save them."

"Our job, Elias. *Ours.*"

———

"*Stand down, Deegan!*" Ash yelled into the headset to be heard above the din of the helicopter. "Your search is mucking up this operation."

"Mucking it up?" Even at this volume Deegan didn't sound happy. Then again, he wasn't the most expressive bloke. Happy, sad, angry, horny—he probably barked orders in bed the way he did out here in the field. "Far as I can tell, you're the one who hasn't caught up with them yet."

"You've lost half your team *and* the target. If you'd let me do my job the way I requested, we'd be halfway home by now, bonus in hand."

"Halfway home?" Deegan's laugh was forced, his features wooden. "Like hell. The guy's too damn slippery."

"The *guy*," Ash mimicked with a nasal American accent. "What guy do you think we're chasing? Let's start with that, shall we?"

In front, the pilot turned to the side, clearly listening in. Deegan—who looked crap after two long nights spent in the wild—wouldn't like being one-upped in front of his men. Well, fuck him. Ash didn't care for Deegan's feelings. What he cared about was his mission.

"You kiddin' me?" Deegan sighed, shaking his head, and turned to look out the window. "Campbell Turner. Male. Fifty-thr—"

"Wrong. This isn't Turner. We're after someone else."

"The target is here and he's on the run."

He pointed at the lake below. "You truly believe you're chasing an average-size fifty-three-year-old man? Do you? Our bloke's fit as a fiddle. His *feet* are as long as my fucking forearm." An exaggeration, but it got the point across. Besides, the *f*'s crackled nicely in the headset.

Deegan's breathing came through, labored and fast, though his face remained stoic.

"Call off the damned chopper, Deegan, stop the air search, and put me down on the western shore so I can do my job…alone."

"That's not what—"

"Call her." This was a gamble, but Ash trusted nothing if not his own instincts.

"What?"

"You heard me. Call the boss. Tell her you've fucked her

operation. Tell her you lost multiple people, including the one who stepped in a trap and the people you sent into a booby-trapped building. Strange, the bloke in the trap was alive last I saw him. How did he die, Deegan?" The pilot tensed. Poor bastard now knew how likely he was to get out of this alive. Or not. Ash had known the risks when he signed on for this thing. He was quite possibly the only one who understood just how deadly this mission was. That wasn't a problem for him. "The target's gone AWOL because of you. Call off the bloody air search and I'll salvage this mission my way. All right?" He leaned toward the man. "We don't get the man or what he's hiding, we don't get paid."

Breathing slowly and evenly, Ash leaned to look out of the helicopter's window at the scenery below. It was best to give men like Deegan the illusion of power.

"How long you need?"

"Give me five days."

"Four."

Ash shrugged, forcing a serene smile. He'd take the time he needed. "Put me down over there." He pointed toward the bean-shaped lake's western curve, right where it fed into the river that eventually led to Schink's Station.

Minutes later, he alit on the rocky shore, hefted his pack, and let his eyes roam the tree line, surprised when Deegan appeared beside him a moment later, carrying his own rucksack. Doing his best to keep his cool at the man's unexpected presence, Ash cocked a brow.

Deegan smiled, setting off two dimples as out of place on the man's square face as commas at the end of a sentence. "Let's do this." He held out one big, beefy arm. "Lead the way, *tracker*."

He said *tracker* like it was an insult, instead of saying it like a man who, as of the moment the helicopter took off, was entirely dependent on Ash for survival.

Doing his best to ignore Deegan, Ash waited until long after the aircraft's overwhelming hum had disappeared, until its stink and hulking presence were nothing but an oily smudge in an otherwise pristine environment. And only then—once silence descended upon this beautiful, perfect wilderness—did he set off after the mystery woman and her mystery companion.

Unfortunately, Deegan followed.

———

From maybe twelve miles off, Elias watched the helicopter rise into the midday sky and fly west. He swiped at the cold sweat on his forehead and caught Leo's eye. "Need to stop?"

"No." Mouth tight, chin firm, she took the lead. After a few minutes, she glanced his way. "Do you need to stop?"

He half smirked. "Maybe."

She shook her head. "Men. Too macho to admit when they're tired." Her eyes dipped to his side. "Injury bothering you?"

"Little."

"Let me check it."

His breath left him in a whoosh, as if that one experience back there had trained him to think of *checking his wound* as a euphemism for something much more pleasant.

"I'll just check it." Her hands were up in a defensive pose. "None of that other…" She flapped them for a few seconds before they dropped tiredly to her sides.

"Don't wanna kiss it this time?" He meant to smile and make it a joke, but his face wouldn't obey. "Make it better?"

"I've created a monster, I see." He caught just the start of her eye roll as she turned away. "Didn't I tell you not to mention that again?"

"Told me not to mention the, uh…other thing. You kissing me is still on the table." He didn't remind her that he hadn't agreed not to mention the other event either.

He caught just a hint of her whispered "jerk" as she grabbed the pack of wipes and stomped off, toward an area thick with underbrush, her feet slipping and sliding with every step. "I'll be back."

Elias clicked his teeth at Bo, who'd been watching Leo with a bemused gaze that was probably a mirror image of his. "Go on," he said, low enough so only the dog could hear. "Go with her."

With a little *woof* and her happy front-end pony lift, she ran after Leo. Satisfied that they'd keep each other safe—or as safe as they could be out here—he stalked off in the other direction to take care of his own business.

By the time he returned, Leo had set the two rolled-up sleeping bags on one of the Mylar blankets, like logs to sit on, and squatted, rummaging in his pack. He watched as she pulled out the dried fish, made a production of opening and sniffing it, fanning her hand in front of her face—all for Bo's benefit, it appeared, since she hadn't caught sight of him yet. With one of her big knives, she sliced up a chunk and stacked it in a neat pile on the ground. When Bo didn't immediately move, she said, "It's lunchtime. Dig in."

With another pony head shake, Bo pounced.

Leo turned away, grimacing. "Don't know how you eat that stuff." Halfway to sitting on one of the bags, she caught sight of him. "What? Stuff's gross."

"Acquired taste."

"You make it yourself? Catch the salmon, dry it, everything?"

At his nod, she expelled a disbelieving sound, then dove into the pack again. "Protein bar. Protein bar. Freeze-dried meal." She looked around. "Got a camp stove?"

He shook his head and cast a quick look around them. "Need more distance for that." Preferably a hundred miles or so.

"Protein bar it is." He caught the one she threw at him and sat on the second bag. Their knees brushed once, twice. He held his breath, expecting her to move away and, when she didn't, slowly let it out. "Still need to check your injury, Elias."

He sniffed. "Gonna let me see how yours is doing?" Geez, when did talking about their wounds turn into a seduction? Or was that just him?

"Sure." A pause. "Are you?"

His nod couldn't come close to conveying the excitement swirling inside him right now. He swallowed it back with the first bite of food.

While he polished off his bar in three seconds flat, she consumed hers slowly, methodically.

"How's the head?"

Her quick smile was dazzling. "Hurts like hell."

"Still dizzy?"

She considered. "Sometimes. At least my appetite's back."

"Right. The stomach thing." He accepted a second bar from her, though it probably wasn't wise. They should save these for later, when they'd be even more exhausted than they were now. Although, at this point, he could feel the energy seeping from his body.

"Felt like crap. But, hey, I wouldn't be here if I'd felt fine."

"Why not?"

"I was supposed to fly my teammates to Anchorage this...yesterday morning? No. Two days ago. Wow. Anyway, I stayed behind 'cause I was sick."

"Teammates?"

She met his eyes, calculating or maybe debating something internally. Apparently, she decided to share. "Ans and Von are two of the guys I work with. They're friends, too. We were looking for you." She scrunched her lips up into something between a smile and a grimace. Had to tear his eyes away so he could concentrate on eating. "Well, we thought we were looking for Campbell Turner. We'd received intel that you—he—was in this area. A private eye crashed here in the winter and—"

"I saw that plane go down."

Her eyes got huge, but she didn't say anything.

"Seems to be my thing recently. Watching helplessly as planes crash."

"What happened? Why did they crash?"

"Squall hit 'em. You know they call this place the Alaskan Bermuda Triangle, right?" At her nod, he went on. "I was too late."

"Were you going to notify the authorities of their location or..."

"Planned to after the thaw."

She nodded. "I guess we'll figure out a way to deal with that when we get out of here. We need to get those bodies back to their families." She polished off her bar and stared at the ground for a few seconds, then turned to look at him. "I didn't sleep at all my last night in Schink's Station. I felt like absolute crap, but you know, the moment I opened my door to see Old Amka standing there, demanding I fly to you, everything pretty much changed."

"Yeah. For the worse."

When she didn't immediately respond, he glanced up, a little uncomfortable to find her eyes on him, her brow wrinkled. "No. No, Elias, I wouldn't say that."

"Change for the better?"

"In a weird way, yeah." Her hands stayed busy, nimbly folding up the wrapper, sticking it into the trash pocket in his pack—he didn't comment on how she knew which one it was. At this point, it wasn't even his pack anymore. It was theirs.

She checked to see if their coats were dry, sat back, and tapped out a rhythm on her knees. Catching his eyes on her, she stopped abruptly. "Don't do too well with...idleness."

"On the run, stitches in your head, a probable concussion, and you're bored."

"Not bored... Antsy." Her shoulders lifted and fell in a shrug that managed, even in multiple layers of oversized clothing, to look elegant.

A series of images flashed through him rife with desire or yearning. First, her collarbones. Were they gently curved or sharp? Did they protrude or were they camouflaged under a layer of her flesh? Not her breasts or the place between her thighs. A freaking bone. The next image was almost worse—it was her across a table from him, eating a meal. Spaghetti or something. Drinking wine. Smiling, enjoying herself. The need to be there hit him as hard as a blow to the chest, but the last image was the worst. It was the two of them, walking hand in hand. Her fingers entwined with his, warm and strong, his hold on her solid, sure.

Shit, he'd lost it entirely. Not good. He had to keep it together to get them out of this alive.

Clearing his throat, he got up, grabbed the sleeping bag he'd been sitting on, and shoved it into the pack, avoiding her entirely.

"Should split up." He didn't wait for an answer. "Two targets are harder to locate."

"Elias."

"You go southeast, head to Canada, to safety."

"Elias."

"I'll create a diversion so they—"

"Dude! Do I stink or something?"

"No." Most definitely not.

"Why are you trying to get rid of me?"

He didn't respond or look at her. He couldn't. Her company was too much. Too close. Too personal. He was thinking things he had no right to think, fantasizing in a way that he shouldn't. He needed space. "Not trying to—"

"You're not alone anymore, Elias. Don't you get that? I believe you. I know you're not the man the world thinks you are. You can talk to me. You can trust me. If we could just reach out to my team, Ans and Von would turn around and come right back here."

He thought her first touch was an accident—like their knees brushing down below. But when she didn't let go of his arm, he had to admit it was purposeful. He shook it off and turned, only there she was again, looking up at him like she gave a shit. "Elias."

He shut his eyes against that name. Nobody called him that anymore. Nobody called him anything, unless he counted Bo's *feed me* bark.

"How many times do I have to tell you? I'm with you. I won't let you fight this on your own anymore."

She drew close, sending every cell in his body on high alert. Would she kiss him this time? Melt him down until he was just another puddle in this soggy place? He didn't have the courage to turn away. Didn't want to.

"We're on the same team, Elias." One of her arms curved around his back, slowly securing him. The other did the same, drawing him in and down. He was nothing but flesh now, a bundle of nerves and a heavy mass of want, ready for another life-giving shock from her lightning-bolt lips.

Only she didn't do it. She did something so much better. So much worse.

She said his name again, reminding him that it really was *his*. And she hugged him, tighter than he'd have thought possible.

Standing there in the damp, noisy forest, Elias Thorne came closer than he ever had to crumbling.

CHAPTER 23

Aw, hell.

She hadn't meant to hug this guy. Just like with the kiss, she had only intended to bolster him, buck him up with some reassurance that he wasn't alone. A friendly smack on the back. A wink, maybe.

Not this close, warm, solid thing; a connection that was more basic than anything she'd ever felt. Not like that belly nuzzle, with its million complications. This felt like she knew him on a cellular level. Like they'd found each other, two parts of a whole, puzzle pieces coming together when they'd been kept too long apart.

He bent his legs and dipped his head, bringing his mouth to her ear—no, just below it—where he burrowed in, nose pushing aside cloth, breath heating her skin…and held her.

Who's hugging who now?

Who needed it most?

She might have instigated this, but she hadn't bargained on the…power couldn't be the right word, could it? The *power* of holding, being held, hugging, sharing.

"A lot," he whispered, though she wasn't sure she caught the right words.

She opened her mouth, prepared to go, take a step back, give an awkward wave, pack up, leave. Crap, maybe they *should* each go their own way. Whatever was going on here was too complicated. She sucked in a breath to say so, but he broke through it.

"You're a lot."

Was that an insult? "A lot of what?"

His exhale heated her face, sent shivers to nerve endings, made her nipples ache. "A lot for a man who's had nothing for so long."

Oh *hell*.

She should step back and give him room.

Instead, she tightened her hold, gave him her weight, and took as much of his as she could.

"You think *I'm* a lot, Elias Thorne?" Her fingers spread wide, encompassing more of his broad back. He was huge, football-player massive. Rough and weathered and hard as stone.

But hell if she didn't want to hold him tighter, hide him like he was precious, keep him from all the bad stuff the world had thrown his way.

She'd have stayed like that forever if he hadn't finally released a shaky breath and disengaged himself from her embrace. Still close, but not touching.

"Thanks." The word was more growl than language. "Needed that."

"Are you with me, then?" She finally caught his eye. "Promise I won't wake up in the morning to find you gone?"

"I wouldn't do that to you. Wouldn't just disappear."

"But you'd rather be alone."

"Rather be alone? No, Leo. I'd rather save your ass, though."

"How about we save your fine ass, too, while we're at it?" she whispered, her fingers lifting to touch him again, then falling without having dared. Funny, given what a daredevil she usually was.

"Fine?" His eyebrows flew so high, they almost melded with his hair.

Pressing her lips together on a smile, she shook her head. And then, because she'd do something stupid if they didn't leave soon, she took a step back, breathed in something other than him, took another, and another, until finally she tore herself away.

———

The wet, muddy terrain kept them from speaking again, which was good. Better than talking about whatever the hell was happening between them.

Though it didn't stop Elias from thinking about it.

Obsessing, Karen had called it, back when they'd been together. Before she'd turned her back on him, joined in the world's accusations.

Traitor. Murderer. Child killer.

He'd become a pariah once they'd gotten him in their sights. Worse than that—they'd painted him as something evil, turned his life inside out, stripped away his family's privacy, made everything he'd ever accomplished out to be part of some sinister plot.

They'd destroyed his relationships, cut his bonds, worn away any trust he'd managed to forge.

Once they'd done that, really isolated him, without anywhere to turn but home, they'd killed his parents.

And blamed it on him.

His jaw hardened, teeth clamped together, working to maintain his inner calm.

You're obsessing again, E, Karen used to sing. *It's just a case. Can't you leave work at work and hang out with me?*

I am hanging out.

You're at home. I guess I should be grateful for that. She'd turn, miffed, flipping her hair before stomping off to grab her purse. *Too bad you're not spending any time with me.*

Look, I'm almost done.

Right. Uh-huh. She'd slam the door, get in her car, drive off someplace. Even now, he didn't know where she used to go when she was pissed.

"How far is it to Schink's Station?" Leo's voice startled him and his foot skidded off to the side before he righted himself.

"Huh?" His brain was vague and tired of battling memories he'd worked hard to eradicate. He focused on the landscape.

"How far?"

He grimaced at the mountains ahead. "'bout seventy miles, maybe eighty, as the crow flies."

"Okay." Seemingly unfazed, Leo took a long pull at her water, swallowing several times before she came up to breathe. His attention snagged on the beads clinging to her lips. It was a relief when she wiped them away. "How *long*, then, since I'm guessing you've not got a jet pack hidden out here someplace." She threw him a side-eye. "Even if you are Mr. Prepared to within an inch of his life."

"Six days, if we're lucky and the weather holds. Maybe seven."

"Too bad you don't have a phone we can use. We could call my team in. Be out of here in no time."

"I don't."

She narrowed her eyes at him. "How long's it take you on your own?"

"From here?" He shrugged. "Four."

"Then we'll do it in four."

"Ground's tricky right now. Never hiked it this close to breakup. Snowmelt's a mess…" He eyed the earth warily, unhappy with the sign they left behind with every step, then allowed himself another quick glance at Leo. She looked like crap. No, that was a lie. She looked freaking magnificent. Just tired; sunken in or something, like already she'd lost muscle mass from this trek. "*We're* a mess."

"Four to six days, then. A lot can happen in six days."

Another a series of sensory images blasted through him— experiences, feelings, flashes of emotion.

Six days.

It had taken less than six days for them to destroy his life.

Less than six days for his fiancée to leave him.

Six days to become America's most wanted.

Six days for them to kill him off.

Or so they thought.

"Hey. You okay?" He shivered when she touched him, his mind switching to a different kind of countdown, in which six days wasn't nearly enough time. Only six more days with Leo, whose presence had completely upended his existence. He'd found inner calm before she'd arrived. He'd been fine alone. And here she'd come and made it not enough. Made *him* not enough.

"Come on." He trudged on, used a young alder to pull himself up a low rise, turned to offer his hand, but she was already beside him, already pushing forward, leaving him with nothing but a quick flash of her eyes, crinkled at the corners. His gaze dropped to take in the sway of her ass.

Only six days before Leo left and he went back to being alone.

He stumbled, righted himself. Stumbled again. "Dammit!"

"What? What is it?" She was so much smaller than him, but didn't hesitate to come in close, invading his space with her concerned eyes. "Elias, what's…" She looked him up and down, stepped back, and made an angry noise. "You're bleeding again. Why didn't you say something?"

"It's fine."

"It's not fine, dummy."

"It's just a scratch," he tried to say, but it came out as one garbled syllable.

Ignoring him, she drew close, lifted his shirt, bent, and for a few suspended seconds, he waited for her lips, that strange, warm brand that gave him hope he had no right to wish for.

No. No more wishing. No more hoping or daydreaming about possibilities that flat-out didn't exist. They were companions for a few days and then she was gone. He'd leave, too, for some new place where he could settle in and reestablish his inner calm.

"I'm fine. Let's go."

"What? Big man's gonna keep walking until he bleeds out? Big man's gonna fall and break something, get back up, and trudge on." Was she pissed? "I don't need you to save me, big man. What I need is for you to survive this. And while we're at it, how about you stop stalling and start telling me exactly why you're here, on your own in the middle of nowhere. I mean, what the hell's going on, Elias?"

"I tried to—"

"Sit." She put a hand on his shoulder and shoved with surprising strength. No. Not surprising. He knew she was strong.

Suddenly, it was easier to obey than to fight. He wasn't hurting, but maybe that wasn't actually a good thing. He obeyed, blinking when she disappeared for a second. "'s fine, Leo. I...I—"

"Thought you'd power through even though you're leaking blood again like a damn sieve. You know the problem with big men like you? You think you've got all the answers. Think you've got to do it on your own. Won't take help from others, 'cause you have this ridiculous notion that it'll diminish you. Maybe you people think your balls are... *Shit*, Elias." She squatted, bent close to him, and put pressure on his wound.

Ah, there it was. Pain. He could do nothing but grunt.

"You know what you jerks always seem to forget?" She kept one hand on him and tore at the zipper of the bloodstained first aid kit with the other. "The bigger you are..." She was breathing hard, working fast. "The harder you fall."

Jesus, wasn't that the truth.

———————

Turned out, a tranquilizer dart to the nuts was just as effective as a bullet.

The man was in a bad way. Especially after Amka got him with the bear spray too. She almost felt sorry for him.

Or she would have if she hadn't watched through binoculars as they shot someone up at the lodge—Dani Avens, who cleaned and did laundry for the guests. She'd never done anything to anyone.

And now they'd gone and shot her.

As Amka watched the lodge through Ben's binoculars, a wave of panic shook her hands so hard, she couldn't see a thing.

What if she didn't stop them in time? What if this ruckus she was raising was for nothing and everyone she loved got killed?

What if she was making it worse?

No. She refused to think that. These people were merciless. She'd seen what they'd done to Elias, to his parents. She couldn't just go in there guns blazing. They'd shoot her dead on the spot.

They'd demolish this entire town if they thought it would get them what they wanted. Or maybe even to cover up what happened here. Hell, what was a tiny settlement with a population under sixty to people like that?

Nothing was the answer.

And what was happening to Elias? Had they gotten him? Were they flying back right this minute with him and Leo in the chopper? Or a couple of dead bodies?

She sagged against the door of the beat-up Ford F-150 that offered the best view of the lodge.

Then it occurred to her—if they came back soon, maybe she *could* do something.

She scooted to the end of her lookout rock and dropped to the ground, careful not to jar her artificial hip.

Before starting off, she checked her holsters and pockets. Bear spray, tranq gun, skinning knife, pistol. Slung over top were the binoculars and rifle, just in case.

In her ear, the voices weren't speaking anymore, which made her think they were onto her now. Too bad. It'd been fun listening in on their official-sounding jargon.

As she made her slow, careful way down the rocky path from the overlook past Ben's, in the direction of the airfield, she mentally counted out the enemies. Three down. Eleven to go.

She was getting the hang of this.

CHAPTER 24

HE BLINKED UP AT THE TREETOPS SILHOUETTED AGAINST THE pale gray sky, like some intricate lace woven by Mother Nature herself. One of a kind. The wind shifted it, changed the pattern, drew dry sounds from the pine needles, rubbed branches together, scratching and clacking like brittle bones. Winter's wind chimes.

He focused back in on Leo, who shook her head, muttering to herself—maybe to him, though he couldn't quite catch individual words. He smiled. He got the meaning well enough. Whatever she was saying was punctuated by *tsk*ing sounds that he liked. All he could see was the top of her hood. He reached up and pushed it back to get a better look. Or to hear her better. Both.

She went utterly still when his fingers touched her hair, caressed it. He wanted to feel it against his cheek. His lips. His chest.

Though she didn't push his hand off, she cast him an impatient glance and kept working, so pretty and delicate and strong, her features set in concentration. He liked that look—pure, single-minded absorption, focused on him. *Imagine how that would feel under other circumstances.* If they weren't running for their lives, but had united for real. On purpose, instead of randomly thrown together. If that enthralled look were for him, instead of his wound.

Leo pursed her lips. "'Just a scratch,' he said. This is not just a scratch, *Elias Thorne.*"

"Sure it is," he said with a smile.

"If you keep bleeding, you'll need stitches." She turned to rummage in the first aid kit again. "Now, why's this feel like déjà vu?"

"Stitches? Didn't seem that bad to me."

"Of course not." She let out another annoyed series of *tsk*s.

Whatever she did made him groan, the pain shooting out to hit every nerve in his body. The next time he opened his eyes, her face was right above his, hovering.

He blinked. Had it gotten darker out?

No, they needed to get over that rise today, to a semisheltered spot and a defensible position.

He tried to crane his neck toward the west. Where was the damn sun?

"Gotta move." His mouth was cotton, the words barely intelligible, his arms and legs too heavy.

"Drink." She thrust a canteen in his face. "No more walking today, big guy. I used the last of the butterfly bandages, so let's try to keep you in one piece, okay?"

He struggled to sit and took a sip of water, squinting at her. "Should have packed more butterfly bandages."

"Or—bear with me here—we could stop getting hurt." She smirked and stuck out her tongue.

He yawned so wide it cracked his jaw.

When she did the same, he chuckled, which made her laugh and thwack him lightly on the arm. The laugh died, leaving something else between them. Something warm and new.

I like her. The thought was so sudden and out of the blue that he could do nothing but blink dumbly for a while.

She lifted her head, showing him the sharp triangle of her chin, a tiny, warm piece of her throat, and all he could think was that he bet she'd taste good there, in that sweet, private little spot.

And though there was nothing sexual about that place, just the image of touching it with his tongue sent a strange mix of guilt and desire through him, so strong he had to clear his throat and stand.

Maybe he more than liked her.

"So, Mr. Prepared Man. You got another yeti cave close by or are we gonna have to sleep under the stars tonight?"

Sleeping. Beside her. Even with the pain in his side, he looked forward to it.

He shook his head.

She threw him a curious look. "Okay. So, camp outside?"

"Keep going. Next rise is more easily defensible. We can stay there. Take turns keeping watch." Which meant no cozying up together.

She narrowed her eyes. "You sure you can make it any farther today?"

Nope. He wanted to pitch the tent right here, strip off his clothes, and snuggle up inside. Only this time, he didn't want to do it to ward off death. He wanted to do it because it felt good. She felt good. Against him, beside him, talking smack with him. Yelling at him because he'd gotten himself hurt and hadn't told her.

"Let's go, then. Lead the way, you stubborn man."

Man, she was one of a kind, wasn't she? Not only beautiful, but strong, smart, and just grumpy enough to make him want to draw a smile from those lips. He'd always been a sucker for a challenge.

He wanted more than a smile, though. He wanted this to last— past the five or six days it would take to get her to safety.

Dangerous thought for a man who'd lost everything he ever touched. Pointless, too, since this—whatever it was—would be over before it began.

They hiked for another hour or so, their pace slow but constant, the ground drier and higher as they went, until they walked mostly over uneven shale. Each step was an unsteady quicksand dance over the flat, gravel-like rocks.

All the while, Leo kept an eye on Elias. And all the while, she got more anxious—although she couldn't say whether it was his condition or something else about his demeanor that made her so.

She scoffed internally. As if she knew him well enough to gauge his demeanor.

When he finally stopped, she took a quick look around. "This where we're staying?"

They stood at the top edge of the shale field they'd just traversed, high above the lake they'd raced across...was that just yesterday? Between them and the lake, the spikey boreal forest eased down to the water in an uneven carpet, warmed by the setting sun. The incline looked deceptively flat, as if she and Elias and Bo had just meandered up a rolling hill instead of climbing at breakneck speed all day. The trees appeared neatly spaced, too, as if the forest floor were an open, welcoming sort of place. Another of Alaska's evil illusions.

At first glance, it didn't appear to be an ideal location to stop for the night, but when she turned a full circle, she realized it was actually perfect. Walking over those loose stones was loud and slow. They'd hear anyone who approached long before they arrived.

When she turned back to look at Elias, she found him watching her.

"You all right?" he asked.

"Fine."

"Head?"

She blinked for a second before realizing what he'd meant, and touched a tentative hand to the bandage. "Seems okay."

"I'll look at it."

"Sounds good."

They unpacked a few items from the bag—tarps, tent, sleeping bags, blankets—and spread their wet clothes out to dry. After chowing down on the food Elias gave her, Bo sniffed the area with her tail up, amazingly alert for a creature who'd put in as much time walking as they had.

"This is better. You were right." Leo did another three sixty, noting that the flat ground was dry underfoot and the cliff rising above them not only served as protection from the wind, but provided at least one direction in which no one could approach.

She leaned her head back and stared up. Unless they came from the sky. Like a specter, the *thump* of the spinning blades haunted her, and she listened hard before confirming that what she heard was her pulse—not their pursuers.

Not tonight at least.

He grunted a response. Or a nonresponse, as she'd started thinking of them.

"Which way do we go tomorrow?"

He pointed to the side.

"Isn't Schink's Station that way?" She indicated the cliff.

"Yeah. But it's a climb. Goat paths. Not easy. We'll go around." He knocked a tent stake into the ground with quick efficiency. "Tomorrow."

"Right. Tonight, we need rest."

He needed rest, she meant, though she wouldn't say that flatout. She peered at his body and grimaced at his bloodstained clothes. Man, they could use a bath. A laundromat. A bed.

She pictured him, stretched out in rumpled white sheets, his already messy mop of hair standing up from bedhead, a sleepy smile on his wide mouth.

What the hell am I doing? He may not be the killer the entire world thinks he is, but he's still a complete stranger.

She cleared her throat and asked the first question that came to mind. "So, how'd you end up here?"

He gave her a narrow-eyed look over his shoulder, then went back to hammering spikes into the ground.

"Not here *with me*." For some inexplicable reason, her face grew hot at those words. The next ones came out louder. "In Alaska. How'd you go from West Virginia to here?"

"Family lived here."

"Papers never mentioned that."

"My dad got a job managing a mine in West Virginia when I was in high school. I graduated down there, went to college there. Far as anyone knew, we'd cut all ties with Alaska."

"Except Amka."

"Not just her. I mean, she's my godmother, but the whole town's like family." He sniffed. "We never lived in Schink's Station, but I spent every summer there. They're the kind of relationships that don't make it into your background file, you know? And it's not like I ever called her or visited."

"So, what? You picked up the phone and told her you were coming?"

"Hell no."

"You just showed up? Hoping for the best?"

He grunted.

"What if she'd thrown you out? Or turned you in?"

His next grunt edged into snort territory.

"Okay." Getting a response from him was like pulling teeth. "So you hopped a flight and—"

"Hiked."

"You hiked from West Virginia to Alaska?" Now it was her turn to snort. "You're serious?"

"Figured I'd blend in best on the Appalachian Trail, so I took that north. Geared up and started off in West Virginia, got myself a trail name, grew a beard." He ran his fingers over his facial hair, as if remembering life before becoming a yeti. "Far from the most direct route, but most through-hikers have no idea what's happening in the outside world. Nobody recognized me. That got me up to Maine. Crossed into Canada on foot."

"How long did it take you?"

"With some hitchhiking in Canada and some pretty intense wilderness crossings, took me close to a year."

She stayed still for a few long beats, trying to put herself in his shoes, imagining that slow, cold journey overland, with a destination that might be welcoming or—if he'd grossly miscalculated—not. She felt like hell after two days of this shit and he'd done it for months. She'd just opened her mouth to ask what it had been like when he spoke again.

"You shoulda seen her face when I knocked on her door. I was rough, tired, filthy. Like something the cat had maybe thrown up a few times before dragging it in."

A wide grin split Leo's face. "Gross."

His answering grin made him look a decade younger and crushingly handsome. It left her breathless.

"She saw right past the beard, though. Knew who I was in a heartbeat. Everybody said I was dead, but she knew. No fooling Amka. Ever." His smile was bright in the fading light. "Looked me up and down, totally expressionless, and said *Bet you're hungry*, then waddled into her kitchen, like she'd been expecting me. Like she..." He swallowed hard, closed his mouth tight, and breathed audibly. Waiting for the emotion to pass, she guessed. Not surprising given how much his story was affecting her. She could only imagine what these memories dredged up.

The wind whipped around them, chilling her now that they'd stopped.

"What time do you think it is?"

He tilted his head back to take in the sky and her chest went tight. God, he was beautiful, even with the beard and the unruly hair—or was it because of them? Even more handsome now, knowing what he'd gone through to get here, the sacrifices he'd made. Although she still didn't understand quite what had happened. He'd tell her, she figured. For some reason, her need to know wasn't as urgent as it had been.

"Nine? Sun's almost down, so it's at least that. Although the days are getting longer now."

She forced her eyes from his profile and sought a way to occupy her hands. "What's the plan? Are we doing protein bars again?"

"Wanna heat something up?" The question made her stomach growl, and then she salivated at the idea of hot food sliding down. It was all she could do to keep in a moan.

"Love you some MREs, Leo?"

She looked up. "What?"

He shook his head. "You looked sort of…excited."

In a flash, heat burned a path up her skin from her chest to her face. Had he caught her thinking about food? Or about him? Avoiding his gaze, she reached into the bag and pulled out what she'd need to make dinner, relieved when he went back to work, knocking the last peg into the ground with a piece of wood, quiet and efficient.

"We having a fire?" *Please say yes.* "Or…"

Slowly, he stood and turned to look back out the way they'd come. "Best not." His voice was hushed.

"You think there's someone out there?"

He shrugged, though the movement was much too casual for her taste.

"That's not an answer."

"Don't know. There's something…" He glanced her way, the movement just barely visible now. "Yeah. I think there's someone out there."

She repressed the shiver that tried to work its way up her spine. "Camp stove?"

At his nod, she set to work—not as quick or quiet or confident as he was, but she got water heating while he prepared their tent and disappeared for a while. When he returned, he made a sound with his feet and she wondered if he'd done it on purpose—so as not to startle her. As if he was so quiet usually that he walked like a ghost.

"Smells good."

She smiled and held up two bags of hot, rehydrated food. "Think this one says Chili Mac, though it smells almost the same as this lasagna. Got a preference?"

"Eenie meenie?"

"Want to do half and half?"

"Yeah. Variety sounds good."

She shut down the camp stove, leaving them to eat in darkness and silence, the specter of whoever or whatever was out there all around them. Or somewhere below. It was quiet, aside from the wind in the trees, and it was cold, a jittery, bone-jarring cold.

"Fire would be nice."

Without a word, Elias set down his food, went over to the backpack, and pulled some kind of fur from a plastic bag. He rummaged around and returned to lay it over Leo's shoulders. The flashlight went on next, only he turned it on upside down between them, giving them the barest glow to see by.

"Better?"

She smiled and nodded, then went back to her dinner, all the while watching him eat from the corner of her eye.

What would he look like without that beard? Or even just cleaned up? Shampooed and shaved with a fresh set of clothes?

"Hold on. Got something else." He got up and returned with a chocolate bar, broke off a square for each of them, then put it away again. Careful, thoughtful. Competent.

As she scraped the bottom of the chili bag, she pictured him sitting in, or rather overflowing from, one of those old-fashioned barbershop chairs. Suddenly, in her mind, Elias was dressed in hipster regalia—maybe a plaid button-down shirt, rolled up to the elbows. He wouldn't be wearing that fur-lined parka hood and ratty wool beanie that looked like his grandma made it. Instead, he'd have a short back and sides—no hat. Glasses maybe, although those would have to be horn-rimmed, which would distract from his unusual, mottled-green irises and...

What the actual hell am I thinking right now?

She shoved the chocolate in her mouth, shocked at how good it tasted. "This is perfect."

"Yeah? Well, it's no five-star restaurant, but we like our treats, Bo and I." The dog came up and nudged him, expecting cuddles, which he gave with gusto.

"I'd like to speak to the manager, then."

He yawned, covered his mouth, and put his head back to look up at the stars. "Hey, lady, you're the one who asked for the yeti special." He glanced at her, that irresistible smile in his eyes.

She laughed, hard. A belly laugh that she had to quiet quickly or risk giving their location away.

They cleaned up and brushed their teeth in silence, their gazes never quite meeting.

"You're so cute."

That stopped her cold. "*Cute?*"

"Don't like that word?"

She opened her mouth to respond and then hesitated. "It's not a word anybody's used to describe me before." Just him saying it made her feel fragile, which she wasn't prepared to explore.

"Really?"

"Really."

He cocked his head, looked her up and down, and stood. "Just 'cause you're deadly doesn't mean you can't be other things, too. You're…" He opened his mouth and shut it. "Look. I realize you're a complex individual. But let's just say that cute's definitely in there."

He eyed the tent where they'd both sleep for the night.

"Go on in." A shiver ran through her to the tips of her fingers and toes. It was quickly doused when he said, "You sleep. I'll take the first watch."

─────────

Amka sat quietly in a dark corner of the hangar, staring at the helicopter like a cat at a mouse.

The dang thing squatted there, ripe for the picking.

If you knew how to pick that type of fruit.

A yawn cracked her jaw.

How was she supposed to disable a monster like this one? Was there some wire she could cut in the engine? A control she could break off or something?

Carefully, she made her way to the door and pulled it open, surprised to see that it wasn't locked. Then again, who'd they have to lock it against? Wasn't like anyone could steal it.

She stepped up and in, grasping the metal frame for balance while her eyes tried to adjust to the lightless interior.

Finally fumbling out her flashlight, she shone it over the space—which was big and cavernous as a damn bus, with jump seats lining the sides. She turned right to find the cockpit door standing open.

Idiots.

Her smile quickly melted from her face when she took in the instrument panel. Five black screens stared back at her, like mini TVs. More dials and buttons and levers than she knew what to do with—and not a single one of them spoke to her.

Like flying a goddamn spaceship.

She pointed the light at a dial and squinted. Crap. Without her glasses, she couldn't read a solitary thing.

It didn't take her long to realize there was only one solution. It'd be loud and probably get her caught, but it would ensure that those bastards couldn't get off the ground. One less thing to worry about.

First, she needed something big and heavy. A baseball bat would be ideal, but she could make pretty much any tool work. She'd just turned to head back into the hangar in search of something she could use to smash the hell out of this thing when she bumped straight into something.

Someone.

Shit, where'd they come from? She hadn't heard a damned thing.

She backed up a step, heart pumping too fast for someone her age. The silhouette was large, dark. Her mouth opened—to yell? Hell no, she couldn't yell. She didn't have time to get the pistol from her coat pocket before he was on her. Thick arms tightened around her and a hard hand pressed over her mouth.

You were right, Daisy. Shoulda had my ears checked.

CHAPTER 25

THOUGH THE WIND HOWLED AND THINGS CRACKLED IN THE woods below, Elias could hear nothing but Leo tossing and turning in the tent. She'd gone to bed an hour ago and didn't appear to have slept a wink. He could relate. He didn't think he'd be able to sleep either, despite his exhaustion.

It wasn't a surprise when the tent zipper came up and Leo emerged. "Can't sleep." She made her way over to where he sat with Bo splayed out across his feet like a living electric blanket, and settled beside them—close, but not touching. "I'll take this watch. You do the next one."

He nodded but didn't move. "Cold?"

She grimaced.

Rather than go into the tent and suffer through his own insomnia, he sat quietly beside her.

"You like it here?" She broke the silence. "Alaska?"

He blinked. "Um…"

She snuffled, the sound halfway between a laugh and a snort. "You didn't choose this life."

Was this her asking, in an oblique way, what else had happened ten years ago? Maybe. Probably.

"I chose it." He infused as much certainty into the words as he could. Not easy to do while the memories converged—an uncomfortable hodgepodge of images and feelings. He sorted through them, or tried at least. Suddenly, more than anything, he wanted to tell her. Everything.

"It was just a job, you know?" He shook his head. "I could have let it slide, like everybody else did—like we were pressured, and then ordered, to do. Could have toed the line, agreed with my superiors." His eyes flicked her way, though she was just a shadow, any physical responses hidden by the night. "Dr. Campbell Turner was a traitor. That was the message. Plain and simple. He'd stolen something very important from the government. Highly classified. Way beyond my clearance level."

"Why were you involved to begin with?"

"I'm the one who tracked him down. He escaped custody—with the help of a colleague. Who died, too, by the way."

"Everyone dies," she said, quiet and grim.

He wanted to hold her hand. Instead, he nodded, knowing she couldn't even see him. "I'm the one who figured out where Turner had hidden."

"How?"

"Put myself in his shoes."

"And?"

"He'd moved into a house in his old neighborhood." He swallowed. It was painful, tight. "To keep an eye on the wife and kids. It's what I would've done. Anyway, he was holed up in a place that was about to go on the market. I only found that out through a neighbor. On our third interview. Thing was, I expected a dangerous man. What I found was a heavily injured, intelligent guy who didn't want to die but couldn't leave his family behind. He talked right away. Told me about the virus, the research. Let me know he'd tried to reason with his employers. He'd been injured on the run. Never saw a doctor. They'd threatened his family, everyone. Told him they'd take him to a black ops site, where they'd do more than withhold care."

"They planned to torture him?"

"They tortured him." He met her gaze. "They'll do anything to get that virus back."

"I know." She leaned in. "What were they using it for? What's the whole point? We can't figure it out. Are they planning to use it as a bioweapon? Is that it?"

"Sure. You could call it that. But it's not just a bioweapon, Leo. This thing…it's not a subtle killer."

Was Leo holding her breath? He couldn't tell, but he thought so. She was utterly still, as if suspended—waiting for what was next.

"They were testing the novel Frondvirus." He expelled a hard breath and tried not to remember. "There was footage." Memories so raw they hurt. He felt sick, wrong. "Suffering like you wouldn't believe. The damn thing was immediate and unstoppable. It could take out entire populations. In no time at all."

"They were working on a vaccine."

He startled. "How'd you know that?"

"They planned to test it on friends of mine."

The anger swelled again, fresh as the day the curtain had lifted on this whole sick scenario—the pure burn of fury, hot enough to cauterize wounds.

Almost.

"I don't get it. They don't have the virus. How'd they test it?"

"There's another sample."

No. A shock went through him, sizzled at his extremities, set off a buzzing in his head. "Where?"

"Discovered under the ice in Antarctica."

"*Shit.* If they've got the damn thing, then what do they want me for?"

"They *don't* have it." He could hear the smile in her voice. She sounded self-satisfied. He figured she'd probably earned that feeling. "We got to it first. Took it with us."

He blinked. "You have the virus?"

"We do." He didn't need daylight to feel the weight of her gaze. "Just barely got it out before the entire testing facility was razed to the ground. Until that moment, we had no idea how big this was. Thought it was just Chronos, but…" She shook her head, as if in the throes of her own traumatic memories. "Blowing up an Antarctic research station? That's some massive firepower."

That had happened before they'd met, and still the relief he felt was palpable, as if he'd lived through the fear of almost losing her. The feeling was as heady as his first sip of booze after months out here, but deeper, more permanent.

"What are the applications for this...weapon? Did Turner say?"

He shook his head, unwilling to let himself get swamped by it all over again.

"Elias." She set her hand on his arm.

He stared down, though he couldn't see more than the shape of them joined in that place.

"Applications? Kill everyone. Absolute devastation."

"Like, nuclear?"

"Cleaner, was how they put it. No environmental 'side effects.' In fact, they'd apparently sold it to the government higher-ups as the simple, sterile method. No more war. Just nice, neat, blameless slaughter. Population cleansing."

"Did you go to someone with this? Media? Anyone?"

"*Everyone. Dies.*" He said the two words with absolute finality.

"Yeah." She sighed. "Yeah."

"All of them." He thought of the journalist he'd talked to—a woman who worked for the *Post*. Dead. Her editor. Dead. "Everyone this thing touches dies. They all die." He took a breath, let it out. "I killed men, Leo. *I* did it to survive."

"You don't have to tell me."

"No. No, you need to know. I may have been a law-abiding citizen when this started, but I did some of the things they accused me of."

An image pulsed in his mind, as clear as the day it happened. The words came out like pulling shards of glass from his innards, each extraction painful but necessary. "My parents' murderers were still there when I arrived. At their house. No idea if they were government agents or...*consultants.*" He couldn't keep the poison from his voice. "Those bastards are dead. I made sure of it." There'd been nothing noble about slitting the first man's throat. Nothing clean or good or whole. Revenge hadn't been the soul cleanser he'd hoped for. If anything, it had brought him down to their level.

"Elias." His name was a ripple in the cold night air, a dip in pressure.

"It's better for you to know these things."

"Yeah," she said so gently it hurt.

Recently, he'd felt so hollowed out, petrified almost. Only now did he realize his insides were teeming with the things he'd seen. Memories that ate at his soul like gangrene.

He shut his eyes and searched for something else to give her. Anything.

A random picture popped into his mind. "You ever see Chronos Corp headquarters?"

Leo might have shaken her head no. If so, he couldn't make out the movement.

"It's this massive half castle, half bunker, built into a mountain, blended into the boulders and forest. And at the bottom, there's this, I don't know, like big, old-fashioned mansion, commissioned by some guy who wanted to rival the Rockefellers, I heard. Surreal. Anyway, there's a top-secret lab in there. Subbasement level five. Highest security I've ever seen in my life." He coughed out a humorless sound. "Not that there'd have been anything to find when I went there."

"How'd Turner get the virus out? How'd he steal it?"

He smiled. Finally something he could hold on to. "He didn't."

Her exhalation puffed loudly between them. "He destroyed it?"

"All but one sample."

"Why not destroy it all, if it's so devastating?"

He sighed, shut his eyes, and thought of all the people who'd be alive if things had been different. "It's deadly. To everything." He inhaled, let the cold, clean air burn his sinuses and clear out his

lungs. "Including cancer, Leo. Turner showed me photos of doc-
uments. The Frondvirus could literally obliterate cancer from the
surface of the planet."

"Were they doing that?" Her voice was laced with a quiet
excitement. "Working on that?"

"No. They'd just been given the new directive: no more cancer
work."

"So, instead of saving lives, they decided to start taking them."

"Exactly. The virus was too important to the government.
There were threats, insinuations. People started dying."

"People? Were researchers getting contaminated?"

"No. They were dying mysteriously." He couldn't help the raw
edge to his voice. "Dissenters were put down. Like dogs."

"Turner got scared."

"They were all scared. Every person who worked in that facility
was slated to die. *Turner* got angry."

"So what did he do with it?" When he didn't answer, she pushed
harder. "Did he take it or not?"

He puffed out a loud breath, shook his head, and looked at her.
"Shit, Leo… If they find out about this…"

"What? What is it?"

"It's still there."

"There?"

"The virus is in the facility. He never took it out. He hid it. And
I'm the only one who knows where."

"Whoa." After a few quiet seconds, she shifted closer, talking
fast. "It's still there? In that building you described? The Chronos
headquarters in West—"

"They wouldn't be after me if they'd found it, would they?"
He stood abruptly, dislodging Bo and disturbing the quiet around
them. "I'll get the blankets. It's cold out here."

It was colder in the tent. And lonely.

The second he returned to her side, the desolate feeling fell off, despite the gaping dark around them, the endless distance. *This* should be the lonely, echoing place, but it wasn't—not with her pressed against his side and Bo covering their feet.

"Hey. Um." He pulled in a shaky breath. "Should we just set up the…" He swallowed the word *bed* and opted for something less intimate sounding. "Sleeping area out here? Keep each other warm?" He cleared his throat. "The three of us, I mean."

"Good idea." She stood to help him spread out the things, although they did more bumping in the dark than was useful. It lightened the air, though, gave a little levity to an atmosphere that was bound to get heavier before his story ended.

By the time they'd put the covers out and she'd settled under them, he half regretted the suggestion. He'd be warmer, all right, but he didn't trust his body—or his brain—not to do something stupid.

"You staying out there?"

"Oh. Um… No." He crouched, pulled off his boots and slid in under the piled-up bag and fur and blankets she held open. Once in, he settled onto his back and looked straight up at the stars. Beside him, she seemed tense, suspended. Was she even under the covers or had she scooted out to make room for him? "You warm?"

"I'm fine."

He opened his mouth to protest and shut it.

"Oh, wow."

He was on his side before she'd finished. "What? What is it? You okay? Hear something?"

Her barely voiced *ooooh* sounded more amazed than worried, and slowly, his muscles released.

"The stars. There are so many of them."

He lay back again and took in the night sky, trying to see it the way she was. It wasn't the same sky folks saw in the lower forty-eight, or even in Schink's Station. It was bigger, closer, brighter, throbbing with life and mystery. In a place this empty, with no other lights, no neighbors—even distant—the stars and planets were more accessible, somehow, more real, pulsing with warmth and light and possibility. Like looking out your window to see a neighbor's lamp on at three in the morning.

"Incredible, isn't it?" He paused, remembering the way he'd seen the sky after running here. The way he'd looked at everything. "It didn't seem beautiful ten years ago. I mean, I'd seen the sky here before, but never alone, without a light around. Without a soul to share it. On the way here, running for my life."

"Yeah?" The word was gentle. "Kinda like now, then?"

"No." His scalp prickled. "Nothing like now."

"Yeah? What's different?"

Everything. Every single thing. "You."

She caught her breath and rolled toward him. "Me?"

He didn't know what to say now that it was out, but she had to hear the harshness of his breathing. Christ, she had to know he wanted her.

"Come here, Elias."

Shock sparked through him, but he turned toward her. It took them a while to find each other in the dark. Those few fumbling seconds tore at his nerves and ramped up his heartbeat, turned the dull bellyache he hadn't even noticed into something hot and frenzied.

"Come here," she said again, only this time her hand was on his coat and her voice was the low, pained groan of ice scraping ice without finding purchase.

And, dammit, he wanted purchase.

Though their lips barely touched, the sizzle could have lit up the night. None of this made sense—not the current running through them, not the deep, burning need, nor this feeling that he *knew* her. And she knew him.

Her lips moved, enough to make this a kiss instead of an innocent touch, but just that slight friction made him hard as nails. And hungry.

He opened his mouth under hers, sought her soft, silky tongue, breathed, taking in the little things he hadn't had time to notice when they'd lost it against the tree. She wasn't quite familiar, but she was...*right* in a way he couldn't recall feeling before. Her smell, her sounds, the easy way her body moved against his. His hands were already on her, gripping whatever they could find, frustrated by all the clothes.

Her kiss was too gentle to quell the need zapping through him. He grabbed, tugged, until she'd rolled half over him. He tried to pull her all the way, but she stopped, out of breath.

"Wait. Wait." She gasped and leaned back.

"What?"

"I'm sorry. I forgot about your side."

His side? Fuck his side. He tightened his arm and slid a hand to the nape of her neck, urging her closer. "It's fine." The last word was eaten up by the collision of their mouths.

His cock was as hard as granite. And not just hard, but aching with want—mindless with it. He wanted this more than breathing.

Her groan was just as needful, just as low and animal as the stuff flowing through his veins. She bracketed his head with her hands and licked into his mouth, tasting, then biting him, sipping deeper. Her body was the most fantastic thing he'd ever felt. Christ, he was burning up. Didn't need this blanket. Didn't need his clothes either. Couldn't stand wearing gloves when they kept her from his touch.

With a growl, he pulled away enough to shove one gloved hand into his mouth and yank it off with his teeth, then the other. He'd just gone back to the warm, wet haven of her mouth, his skin so close to touching hers, when she shifted fully onto him. Pain shot through his side.

He saw stars, only not good ones this time.

She was off him in a heartbeat—too damn fast.

"Oh no. Did we open up your injury again?"

"No." He wasn't actually sure, but he'd do whatever it took to get her to climb on top again.

"Crap," she said, sounding breathless, her chest pressing his arm with every inhale. "I'm sorry. I lost it for a second. I don't know what's wrong with me."

"Nothing at all," he bit out.

"Yeah, well, then it's us. There's something wrong with us, together."

Wrong? Hell no. Together, they were right. More right than anything he'd experienced in…fuck, well over a decade. He wanted to taste her again, wanted to feel those desperate, panting exhalations, wanted to see what noises she'd make if he managed to slide his hands under all those layers. He'd bet she was soft there. He'd bet she was hot between her legs. And, shit, he wanted her to be wet, to want him like he wanted her, to need him, the way he needed her now—bone deep.

"You okay, Elias?"

He screwed his eyes shut, tried to clear his mind. Not easy, given all the hormones flooding through him. He could almost laugh. "Yeah. Fine. You?"

"Me?"

"I seem to recall that you injured your head a couple days ago. Is it all right?"

"Um, no." Her laugh had a slight edge to it. Was it bitterness? Hysteria? He didn't know her well enough to recognize it. "I'm pretty sure the crash jarred a screw loose or something."

She slid back into her spot—closer than before, but still against him. He liked that. Maybe she didn't regret what they'd just done as much as she thought she did. He didn't regret it at all.

"If you've got one loose, I've got a whole damn box of 'em. But you know what? I don't care." At her happy-sounding sigh, he leaned down and kissed her cheek, full of a tenderness he'd never thought he'd feel again. "*This*," he said against skin that he could have sworn conducted electricity, "is what I've been missing."

───────────────

Getting caught was bad. Amka had expected to have more time. She needed more time. To save her family, her friends. Her wife.

Though her first instinct was to fight, she went completely still, her pulse flickering at the edges of her vision. Shit, she'd never been so scared in her life.

The man—whoever he was—didn't move either. He just stood there in the dark aircraft, holding her so tight she thought he'd cut off her air.

After a good twenty seconds, when he hadn't knocked her out or killed her or even put a gun to her head, she decided that maybe things weren't as bad as they seemed.

"Don't smash my ride," he whispered right in her face.

She swallowed and caught her breath. His ride. Okay. She could do that. She could keep her hands off the helicopter. He hadn't sounded the alarm. This was good.

"Okay." She worked to get more words out. "Don't kill my people."

"Deal."

Her eyes widened.

"If I let you go," he whispered, so close you'd have to be in the helicopter to hear, "you gonna scream?"

She craned her head, trying to get a better view of whoever this was.

"Why the hell would I do something stupid like that?" Her whisper was markedly louder than his. "Last thing I need is the rest of those assholes figuring out where I am."

He let out a puff of air. Maybe a laugh, maybe just a show of surprise. There could also be relief in the way he shook his head. "I don't like what they're doing up there."

"So stop 'em."

"They catch me trying to sabotage this mission, I'm a dead man."

"Think you're *not* a dead man anyway?" He slowly released his hold and stepped back, head cocked, and even in the strange glow from the flashlight she'd dropped, she could read the resignation in the young man's expression. "You think anyone's survived this thing since it started over a decade ago? *Anyone?*"

One survivor. One.

"Shit." He gave her more space, rubbed a hand over short blond hair, and had the good grace to look uncomfortable.

"How many are dead up there?" she asked, figuring it couldn't hurt to get him talking.

"You mean yours? Or ours?"

She blinked. "Some of yours died?"

"Three are missing here. Know anything about that?"

She made her face as blank as possible. "Huh."

"No?" He appeared to consider her and let it go. "Aside from those three, we got a few who didn't come back."

"What do you mean?"

The surfer boy leaned in. "Lost five in the field."

"Five?" Oh, that was good news. Were Leo and Elias making their lives hell? Had they taken down some bad guys? Had they gotten away? She tried her best to keep the glee inside.

"Flew eight out the other day. Only one came back."

Her heartbeat picked up. "One?" Elias was doing it. He was getting away, and in the process, screwing these assholes.

"Two stayed behind. Deegan, our team leader, and the tracker. Scary fucker." He leaned down to look out the open door, jumpy as a jackrabbit. "I have no desire to die here. And I'm not into what they're doing up at the lodge."

"What?" Her body tightened, her old bones ready to pounce if she had to. "What are they doing?"

"Shot three people."

Three! "Who? Who'd they shoot?"

"I don't know."

"Daisy? The owner? Tall woman, long face?"

"I don't..." He closed his mouth and eyed her for a few seconds. "I don't think so."

"Are they dead? The ones they shot?"

"One dead." He wouldn't look at her, and in that moment, she wanted to kill him. "The rest are being held like cattle. Tensions are real high. People are dirty, pissed off, ready to blow." He shook his head. "Something's gotta give."

She considered him. Tall, blond, all-American. Maybe even the kind of guy who'd come here on vacation, head out into the woods to shoot something. Not for the meat or the fur, but just to kill. "You hunt?"

He gave her a *what the hell are you talking about, lady* look. "No."

"Ever kill an animal for sport?"

Something ticked in his jaw. "*No.*"

"Ever kill a human?"

"I'm a pilot. I don't kill. I fly."

Right. The pilot. Of course. He rose in her estimation. "How'd you wind up on this gig?"

"Long story." He shook his head. "Stupidity mostly."

"All right. What's your name?"

"Jack."

"I need you to do three things for me, Jack."

"That it?" he asked, one brow up.

"Are you with me or not, young man?"

"I'm with you."

"First, disable the aircraft."

He walked over and fiddled with something on the console. "Done."

"Can you make a call? To the outside?"

His nod flooded her with relief. Finally, they were getting

somewhere. "Good. Now, you need to get weapons to the people being held in the lodge."

"You nuts?"

"Maybe. But I don't see how that's relevant right now." She pulled out every blade she carried. "Find a way to get them these. Or you die."

"Are you *threatening* me?"

"No, dumbass. I'm telling you what happens when you work for the bad guys."

Though he didn't appear convinced, he looked guilty. That was enough for Amka. He held out his hand. "I'll try."

"What if I distract 'em?"

He considered, a hint of excitement lighting his features. "What are you thinking?"

"I've got a lot up my sleeve." She smiled.

"Such as?"

"Dogs, stunts, maybe an explosion or two. What do you think?"

He squinted at her, head tilted back, as if looking at her in an entirely new light. "I think it's a good thing I'm on your side and not theirs."

"Damn right, son." She snorted. "Damn right."

CHAPTER 26

THROAT TIGHT WITH EMOTION, ELIAS GATHERED LEO CLOSER and stared out into the beautiful night.

She didn't speak for so long, he wondered if she'd fallen asleep. When her voice broke the silence, it was like a caress in the dark.

"We're gonna fix this, Elias. We'll clean it up."

He huffed. "Know how to do that?"

"Yes. I told you. I've got people." He felt her smile against his chest. "My boys. Coop, Ans, Von. We've got others now, too. Couple of scientists, a doc. A chef."

"Strange combination."

"Is it?" She snuggled deeper. "It's a great combination. Angel, Ford Cooper's girlfriend, cooks the most unbelievable meals for us on the platform. Like—"

"Platform?"

"We're based offshore."

"Are you making this up?"

Her laughter bumped her chest against his side. He wanted her to slide back on top. She wouldn't do it. And she'd be right not to. They needed to save their energy for things like, oh, survival. But wouldn't it be nice to forget about survival for a while, to lose himself in Leo?

"It's real. Polaris platform. It's where our operations are based."

"Your operations?"

"We're a security firm."

"Someone hired you to come here?"

She shook her head, each movement nudging that spot right over his heart. "No. This is more of a…personal mission."

"For who?"

"All of us." She lifted her head. "A bunch of us almost died because of Chronos and the Frondvirus. We're not so into that. Decided to make it stop."

He let out a cynical snort. "Good luck."

"Got to you first, didn't we?" There was definite pride when she spoke. "And…" She paused. "We've got some advantages."

"Yeah? Like having the actual virus in your possession?"

"Exactly."

"How'd that happen?"

"Long story."

"They know you have it?"

Her self-satisfied "nope" allowed him to breathe again.

He stared up at the stars for a few seconds, trying to piece it all together. "Why are you here if you already have it?"

"Just because we have a sample doesn't mean there's not more out there. We want to stop *them* from getting their hands on it. To stop the killing."

"It'll never stop." Hollowed out by death, despair, and hopelessness, the words were a sibilant proclamation. No vowels made it through his tight vocal chords.

"I don't belong to that school of thought, Elias."

He grunted a question.

"*Never, can't, won't.* I don't believe in those words." She yawned. Her breath reached him—warm and sweet. He could get addicted to that particular combination. "Even metal melts if you get it hot enough."

He huffed out a laugh. His next inhale expanded his ribs and pressed her closer and maybe drew a little hope into his body. She smelled like hope. Like another chance at life. Like the sweet thrill of possibility.

Resisting fatigue, he opened his eyes wide and shut them for a few seconds before focusing on the sky again. "You should sleep."

Her response was a sigh. At their feet, Bo echoed it.

Time eked slowly by—he couldn't say for how long—when she spoke again, surprising him. "Wish we'd been there for you. When it happened."

"It was a long time ago, Leo."

"Bet it doesn't feel like it."

"Does." He considered. "And it doesn't."

"Tell me."

He opened his mouth to tell her it was late and she should sleep, and then he closed it. She didn't like being told what to do. He couldn't blame her.

"It's like I've been alone forever, like that old life—the one I lost. Job. House. *Family.* Woman who was supposed to…" *Love me.* He couldn't even utter the words. She made a little move but didn't speak, and he kept going. "It's like I only dreamed it. Not even a memory anymore. More vague. Like I saw it on TV." His brain gave him a kaleidoscope of moments from back then—opening mail, paying bills, getting drinks with friends after work. Watching football—*caring* about football. Like it mattered who won the damn Super Bowl.

"So, that's one side. What about the other?"

He scrunched up his face, not really adept at explaining stuff like that. "You ever lose someone special?"

She didn't immediately reply, making him wonder if this would be a one-sided thing. Did Leo take but not give? Would he care if that was her way?

"My mom." She swallowed audibly. "Killed herself when I was little."

All the air left him, like a ball to the gut. There it was. *That* feeling. He wanted to hug her, to tell her he was sorry. But he knew how little good that would do. If he could, though, he'd take the weight of it from her. *That* he would do.

After a bit, he found his voice. "You too young to remember waking up the next morning after it happened?"

"No." Her voice was devoid of emotion. "I remember."

He nodded with understanding. From his outermost layer of skin to his deepest entrails, he knew that feeling. "Every morning's like that for me. Every day, I wake up and..."

After a couple of heartbeats, her hand moved low and found his. Her fingers slid through his and tightened into a fist.

She fell asleep like that, feeding him something he hadn't had in forever.

Eventually, both she and Bo started snoring, the soft, steady sounds stirring up a messed-up mix inside him of equal parts warmth and the unbearable weight of responsibility.

———

Head throbbing, Leo woke in the dark, struggled to get out from under the blankets, and took a quick look around before settling back into her nest—a nest she shared with Elias—and staring up at the sky. It was brighter than before, the inky black from earlier more of a blue, the stars twinkling less, fading. She couldn't see her breath in the dark, but she could feel the cold down to her marrow.

Elias sat quietly beside her.

"How long have you been keeping watch?" she finally asked.

His exhausted shrug gave him away.

"You planning to get any sleep tonight, Elias?"

"Wanted you to rest."

"A lot of good that'll do me if I have to drag your giant carcass back to Schink's Station." She sat up and yanked his arm until he slid into her warm spot with a sigh. "I've been thinking."

"Uh-oh."

She slapped him lightly on the arm and let her hand rest there for a couple of seconds before putting it on the ground and pushing up to sitting. "What will you do? When this is over?"

"Over? What's that look like?"

Good question. "What if I told you there's a place for you? With my team? A place where you'd be safe. People you can work with, for a cause. We can set you up with a new life, a new identity. You'd be—"

"On the run. Still."

She opened her mouth to object and then shut it. "You don't have to be alone, Elias."

He nodded, silent. Her hand went back to his arm and stayed there. "It's my watch. Sleep."

After a while, his breathing evened out and Leo was left alone to think about what lay ahead. Not just the journey they'd have to complete—unless her team somehow tracked them down out here—but what they'd find once they arrived in Schink's Station.

Would it be a massacre like the one he'd been accused of carrying out? Would another innocent person be blamed?

She dropped her face onto her bent knees and let the prospect— just the idea—run through her. For a few tortured minutes, she pictured it—arriving to find the place quiet and smelling of blood, the only sound the buzzing of flies on bodies.

Her eyes shut against the image, then opened to land on Elias's dark form. The man's strength was astounding. She admired it, the way she liked his preparedness and, frankly, his rough good looks. But more than all of it, she liked his heart. He'd lost so much, given so much, lived through hell. He deserved to be taken care of. To be loved.

The idea sent an uncomfortable jolt through her.

Shit. No. Not by me.

She didn't do that nonsense. Didn't know how. Oh, she loved her teammates. Ans and Von and Eric were stone walls she could lean on—men she'd trust with anything, go to the ends of the earth for. Literally.

And yet, in all the years she'd known them, she'd never once mentioned her mom. They hadn't pushed, which she'd always appreciated. And God knew she'd never asked for their darkest secrets.

Now she wondered if maybe that emotional distance had paradoxically allowed her to get close to them.

Even as a kid, she'd never talked to anyone about her mom's death. Not the counselors who'd chipped away at her—using art and music and every therapy available—and certainly not her dad. He'd pretty much sunk everything into music once Mom was gone, which had left Leo to dream, her eyes on the sky.

Shame washed over her. Guilt too. And something more elemental, something she'd never be able to describe. There wasn't a word for this feeling, but she figured Elias knew it well—like she'd been a ghost all these years. Haunted. Doing things, experiencing them, but not really living.

Like she was equal parts flesh and blood and pain.

Bo stirred, pushing her from her morbid line of thought. Thank God, because she'd just about reached her limit of internal philosophizing. And this shit never did her any good.

Was the sky getting lighter?

Good. Though she was still exhausted and every bone and muscle hurt like hell, she couldn't wait to get back on her feet again. To get moving and tackle another leg in this unexpected journey. To face whatever the day would bring.

With Elias by her side, that prospect didn't scare her at all.

———————————

Maybe this sunrise—from the dark blue haze on the horizon to the flames eating up the sky—could cleanse the night's ghosts. Maybe, Leo thought, the new day would bring something good. If nothing else, it would wipe away the vestiges of all that unintended intimacy. Like a bad hangover, the embarrassment of having overshared weighed her down. She could only hope that the light of day would wipe the memories away, rather than shining a spotlight on them.

There was something hopeful about all that beauty, ancient, but fresh. The birth of a new day. Like snowflakes and human faces, no two sunrises were the same, and this one was hers. Just hers.

A cloud skittered across the rising sun, forever changing the view. She swallowed back a wave of premature nostalgia, already missing this bittersweet moment, this time and place, with this man to whom she'd already given too much of herself.

"Oh, shut up," she whispered, rolling her eyes at her excessive sentimentality.

She took a bolstering breath and let herself look down at Elias. And then, it seemed wiser to wake him than to stare at the trail-worn lines of his face. Each one of them hard-earned. Each one deep and beautiful.

"Elias." She spoke louder than she'd meant to, pushing every shred of longing from her voice. Hopefully. "Got to move." The words puffed hot vapor into the cold air, and she shivered at the prospect of moving away from his warm body.

Her words pushed him deeper into sleep, into his firm pillow. Which was actually her lap. He'd wake up if she shook him or rolled out from under him, but that would dump him on the ground.

He made a low, sleepy noise, gripped the blankets, and pulled them up around his head, leaving only his eyes and his thick, wavy hair visible.

She gripped her hands together to stop herself from tunneling her fingers into it.

"Elias." If she made her voice firm, she wouldn't have to touch him…or pull away. "We need to get going."

His eyes opened, focused on her, and then creased at the corners. He was smiling—a sweet, intimate expression—and she almost died from it. It put an actual pain in her chest while she did her best to catch her breath.

Better get some distance. She shifted out of the blankets and got up in a rush, immediately regretting it when dizziness overwhelmed her. With an undignified *oof*, she flopped down again, practically on top of this man she barely knew.

Except she knew him now, didn't she? She knew the smell and the feel of him, the taste of his skin under her tongue, and most importantly, she knew how it hurt to be him.

"Got water?" His eyes narrowed, as if he had seen her thoughts and didn't like them. Or was trying to get a read on her and couldn't. Or maybe he thought she'd—

Shut it down, Eddowes.

"Okay?" The two syllables rumbled from his chest.

For a few seconds, she didn't move, didn't respond, just let herself be close to him.

"Sure."

Slowly, he twisted the top, put the canteen to his mouth, and drank, gasping at the cold. When he returned it, she was disquieted to see that her hand—her whole arm—shook from the weight of the light plastic bottle.

"Feeling okay?"

"Fantastic." She gave him her biggest, smartassiest smile. "You?"

"Million times better now that I slept." He stretched, reminding her of a big, sleepy bear waking up from hibernation. Or of what she imagined a bear to look like, since she'd been lucky enough to avoid them so far.

He eyed her and finally sat up. "Let me look at your head."

With closed eyes, she sat through his examination, half-sad and half-relieved when he patted her shoulder. "Looks good. Let me rebandage it and we can take off."

"Thanks."

"I should…" He pointed awkwardly in the distance. "You know. Take a leak."

"Oh. Right." She shifted away from him, mortified to realize that their legs had been entwined—hers on top. Of course he needed her to move. Otherwise, he'd have been up and moving minutes ago.

He stood and quickly turned his back to her, but not before she got a look at the prominent erection tenting his pants. Her mouth tightened into a perfect, silent O, and her skin went all hot and dry. Much like her mouth, actually.

"Sorry," she whispered, though it wasn't clear if he heard.

When he returned, she considered saying something but then let it go. Morning wood was a thing. She knew that, given that she'd worked alongside men for much of her life, though she'd never experienced it quite so closely before.

"Other side of this mountain, there's a place where we can clean up." He was all business now. "Get a better night's rest before heading into the easy part."

"Oh. The end's the easy part?"

"Well, it's not this crappy broken shale. And we move to lower altitudes, so that's easier. Flatter, too, and hopefully not quite so badly flooded as up here."

"So, better."

"Unless we're being hunted by helicopters, of course."

Her nerves pricked. "Why's that?"

"Well, we've got the mountains here and…more mountains. We can call 'em foothills farther west."

"Right."

"And what's past that? You flew here. Remember?"

She closed her eyes, going back over the area around Schink's Station and her flight here.

"The river feeds into the lake at Schink's Station."

"Exactly." He nodded. "Mountains, mostly bare, and the taiga's a lot sparser there. Just that and the river." His shrug was apologetic. "No place to hide."

"Well, crap."

"That's about right."

It was a long, hard hike west, over treacherous, half-frozen ground. They walked throughout the day without a hitch, which Elias was just paranoid enough to find worrisome.

Where was the search party? The reinforcements? Why weren't they back out, tearing up the sky with their helicopter?

He glanced over his shoulder and forced his gaze past Leo to scour the landscape. Was there someone out there, right now, following in their footsteps?

Something tickled at the nape of his neck and, without hesitation, he pointed to the side, pleased when she continued to follow precisely in his footsteps—using rocks and branches and dry ground whenever available—veering slightly south from their direct westerly path.

Something wasn't right. He had no idea what it was or how he knew it, but one of his senses was sounding the alarm.

When he paused to scope out their surroundings again, Leo watched him closely, eyes wide. She lifted her eyebrows and shoulders in a silent query.

He gave his head a little shake and continued to search.

She drew close and whispered, "Hear something?"

"No."

"See something? What is it?"

"Don't know."

Though her nod looked a little hesitant, she joined in his search. The problem was that, even after five minutes spent in perfect silence and stillness, watching and waiting, there was no physical sign of what he sought.

Dark clouds had gathered in the sky by the time they started moving again, and still he wasn't confident. A good tracker wouldn't show themselves. They could be out there, biding their time, waiting for the opportunity to strike. To come for the virus.

That he and Leo didn't have.

At first, the rain was so gentle it was almost undetectable. A cold mist seeping into hoods and under gloves, covering his beard so subtly he didn't notice until he ran his hand over it and found it dripping water.

He didn't want to stop, couldn't shake the feeling that something was out there, slowly and inexorably tracking them.

Then there was the constant burning in his side and, worst of all, the worry that he'd drawn Leo into something she wouldn't survive.

She whistled low and he turned, adrenaline spiking.

"Can't go much farther with the rain."

"Call this rain?" He leaned his head back and got a frigid face full, then shook himself like a dog, pleased when she smiled in response.

"Even if it's just a drizzle, it's a cold drizzle."

"Yeah." He searched the darkening shadows again, not happy with the roiling clouds or the quickly cooling air and really not happy with the itch at the nape of his neck. "Let's find a place out of the wind to pitch the tent."

"We done for the day?"

Gaze bouncing left to right and back, tension ticking a muscle in his cheek, he replied quietly, "We keep going, we risk exposure." His attention flicked up at the darkening sky. "It's about to come down."

"And if we stay?"

"Don't know, Leo. There's something..." He blew air out his mouth. "There's something."

"Okay," she whispered, her eyes big and skittish. Maybe she felt it, too. "I need a few minutes of privacy."

Stay close, he wanted to say, but she knew what she was doing. Instead, he nodded and forced himself not to watch her walk away, despite an overwhelming desire to stop her.

CHAPTER 27

LEO HAD SPENT ENOUGH TIME IN LIFE-OR-DEATH SITUATIONS to understand a few important things.

Food mattered, though not as much as water. And shelter mattered more than both. In this case, with the two of them in not quite pristine condition and the sky looking like another squall was about to hit, they needed to hunker down and get better.

Turning a three sixty in the quickly fading light, she saw no obvious stopping place.

Oh, they could use the tent, or maybe dig into the underbrush and find some drier layers to call a nest for the night. But it wouldn't offer any help against this freaking wind, especially if the rain got serious. Given the drops falling on her face, she'd take that possibility as a fait accompli.

After peeing, she moved a bit farther into the underbrush, as quietly as she could manage, hoping she'd find the perfect place to ride out the coming weather. The light was seeping out of the sky, though it wasn't yet night. They'd walked maybe eight hours? Ten? Visibility was down to a few feet in any direction, movement just as hampered by the slippery sliminess of mud. If it got any darker, they'd have to search with a flashlight, but that would be pretty much begging someone to see them in this forest. And, though the helicopter hadn't shown up at all today, she had to trust Elias's gut.

You couldn't argue with a man who'd survived such an enemy for this long.

Besides, she felt it too, whatever it was. She couldn't describe the feeling, couldn't quite capture it herself, but it was there—a disquiet that made no sense on its own but couldn't be ignored when coupled with his.

They needed to find a camping spot or they'd be back to hypothermic within hours. Less.

Not here! every one of her instincts screamed. This wide-open location, on the steep slope of the mountain, was too unprotected.

She spun again, seeing nothing—absolutely nothing—to help hide them for the night.

Just a hole was all they needed. Big enough to crawl into, out of the rain.

She blinked into the patchwork of shadows at the base of a tree. Was that a cave?

A raindrop plunked onto her hood with a dull sound, followed by another.

Everything was two-dimensional without light—no difference between logs and shadows. It might not be a good idea to examine dark hollows or caves without any visibility. Time to get back.

A stink hit her, so hard she backed up a step. Good God, what was that? Like the gorilla pen in the zoo or the frat house next door to where she'd lived in college.

Oh, shit.

She went very still, didn't breathe, didn't move a muscle. Not an eyelash or a hair.

Something shifted close by, the sound awkward, heavy. Was that breathing? Snoring?

She pressed her lips together and backed slowly away.

Don't be a bear. Please don't be a bear.

Later, she'd hit herself for thinking she'd been lucky not to run into one. Jinxing herself again.

A quick inventory told her she'd left the rifle with Elias. Because, apparently, she'd lost her will to live since she met the man. Or at least her sense of self-preservation. What kind of a moron walks off on her own without protection?

An exhausted one, sick and wounded and cold and ready to

eat a hot meal. That would be nice. A hot meal. *Truffle fries.* Her mouth literally watered.

Just please don't be a bear.

With mayo. Eurotrash, the guys called her, but she knew they liked it too. She'd seen them sneak fries…

Something snorted.

It is. It's a fucking bear.

Her inner monologue stopped short. It only offered comfort when she could pretend things were fine, but in this case, she'd need something a whole lot more concrete to lean on than mental distraction.

It moved.

And she hadn't even brought the damn bear spray with her. Although the locals scoffed at the idea of that stuff anyway. *Get close enough to spray her*, Daisy had said with a laugh, *better have already put a hole in her hide.*

Or preferably, left it the hell alone.

Well, that was all great advice, really. Useless out here in the real, honest-to-goodness wilderness, without a solitary way to defend herself, but great in theory. *Just great*, she mouthed.

With a slow, careful step away from the fallen log, she took stock—three knives. Waist, pocket, and boot.

A lot of good they would do against claws and jaws that could rip her open and snap her bones.

Another careful step back and another. She'd made it maybe six feet from the den when it chuffed, the noise exactly like a sneeze.

Oddly, that gave her hope. It was sleeping. *Please be sleeping.*

Another step, another prayer that her foot wouldn't break a twig or slide in a fresh vat of mud.

Don't wake up. Don't wake up. Please, please, don't wake up.

Funny how she'd thought the worst had happened today, with the long hike and, oh, being chased by killers over deadly terrain. Just proved, didn't it, that she was right to be superstitious. She was right to think the worst was always to come.

Whenever she thought she could slow down or relax or—hey, stop to maybe kiss a stranger in the woods—it all came crashing down.

Please don't wake up.

The animal shifted and snuffled, the sound so much like a man waking up that she had a quick moment of panic someone else was here after all. But then it emerged fully from the cave. A grizzly, slow and sleepy and probably hungry as hell. Maybe even mad that someone had awakened it this late in the day.

She stopped moving. It was big, but not fat, the way she'd imagined. It was all muscle and bone and sinew, with a thick, wooly coat that hung loose on its frame, its gait slow and rolling. Though she knew for a fact it could run if it wanted. It could chase her down, shove her to the ground and tear her open in the blink of an eye.

She tightened her hand on the knife hilt, keeping it low.

"Hey." Her voice was so reedy she hardly recognized it. No way. If she was gonna die against this animal today, she would at least take a real stand first. She spent a long, slow inhale searching hard for her inner badass.

"How's it going there…bear?"

Its big head turned, shiny eyes finding her in the eerie light.

When it took its first step in her direction, Leo ignored every one of her instincts and held her ground.

Elias smelled it first.

Bear. No doubt about it. A growl just confirmed it. He'd heard that sound more times than he could count, and it was close. Too damn close.

Bo stopped eating, tail down, ears up.

"Stay," he muttered, then hefted the Guide Gun, checked the chamber, and started moving, knees bent, eyes slowly scanning the woods.

He nearly stepped on a branch, held his weight off so it didn't crack, lifted his foot over it, and carried on, afraid of what he'd find.

And hell if it wasn't worse than he'd imagined.

Leo stood utterly still with both hands hanging loose at her sides, one clenching what looked like a KA-BAR knife. Its straight, partially serrated steel blade might as well have been a toothpick for all the good it would do.

He heard something through the rain's light patter and the buzzing in his brain. Leo's voice. Low and melodious.

Wait. Was she singing?

The bear—just a silhouette in the half-light—shifted forward, its body deceptively lumbering and slow. These guys were fast when speed was needed.

His hands tightened on his rifle, his breath left his body, he looked for a clear shot, and—

Leo moved, unintentionally putting herself right in his line of fire. Didn't she realize he was here? *Get down*, he wanted to yell, fear clawing at his throat. *Out of my way.*

She didn't budge, didn't respond at all, just kept up that low, melodious rhythm until the animal settled back on its haunches, cocked its head at a curious angle…and watched her.

All the while, Leo sang.

Elias couldn't feel a thing. Not the wet or the cold or his damp clothes clinging to his skin. Everything he had was geared toward the exchange between the two creatures, every sense focused on keeping the animal in his sights, every muscle there to hold up his rifle, to tighten his finger to fire if need be.

"All right?" Leo asked conversationally. Having a goddamn chat with the beast. Her hands were up, moving slowly, gesticulating as if she were talking to any old person in the world. He was having a heart attack, and she was yammering away like this was a tea party.

She took a step back, slow and careful.

"Don't!" he called, his voice as light as he could make it. "Drop your head but don't back up. Stand your ground, and no more eye contact. Head down." He wasn't even sure the bear could see Leo's eyes in this light. "And keep talking. Keep talking to me."

"I was looking for a place to, uh, camp for the night, Elias. Just wanted to find us a place where we could get warm. Maybe dry off a little."

"You stick your head in this guy's den? Wake him up?" Or gal, if they were really unlucky. Just because the cubs weren't out didn't mean they weren't around.

"Didn't get as far as the den."

The grizzly moved. Elias tensed his finger, squinted through the scope, half-blind from the rain, though he was surprised at how steady his hands were. Firing the weapon would be the worst-case scenario. There was a chance he could take the animal down before it reached Leo, but the sound would blaze a trail straight to them.

The bear shifted, tilted its head at a funny angle, like it was actively listening…and dropped to all fours.

"I don't want to do this, bear," he muttered, loud enough to be heard, but not so loud he'd scare the animal into doing something they'd all regret. "Don't want to have to kill you right now."

Slowly, it turned to the side, took a few rolling steps, its limbs probably stiff from a winter underground, and then stopped to sniff the air again.

Leo said something, calm and quiet, her head down, that knife glinting in her hand.

The air burned as Elias blew it out and blinked past the rain misting everything now, not daring to raise a hand to wipe it from his eyes.

The grizzly walked away a step and paused, one leg still up, suspended, lowered its head toward Leo's toes, and took another slow step away. With each additional foot, Elias found he could breathe a little better, control his muscles with more precision.

Then, as if they'd finished whatever they had to say to each other, the big guy turned fully away, harrumphed over its shoulder, and ambled back into the shadows.

Elias couldn't lower his rifle yet—maybe never would.

The situation was so surreal, reality so suspended, that it was a shock to feel rain falling on his skin when he expected to see the individual drops frozen in the air, like something from the Matrix—time gone still.

When he next focused on Leo, she'd backed up a few feet, put her hands on her knees, and dropped her head. Her deep breathing sounded like an asthma attack.

Bursting into motion, he reached her, grabbed her hand, and yanked her to his side, flooded with relief at just the solid feel of her under his arm.

"Can't sleep here, Leo. Got to move." Better to face the steep higher ground, even in the dark, than to bed down near a grizzly. Add to that God only knew what else was lurking nearby—and not of the animal variety—and they'd be better off taking the risk. "We're climbing the mountain."

"See, there's a *Sound of Music* feel to those words…and yet…" Her eyes got big as they traced the earth's angry silhouette up into the sky. "The view's giving me distinct Mordor vibes," she whispered, before meeting his gaze. "Big time."

For no reason at all, he found that he was suddenly out of breath.

His hold wouldn't loosen when she tried to turn, his arms wouldn't give her an inch of space. His insides felt ragged, innards ripped up like ribbons, as he reached out to wrap one shaking hand behind her nape and pull her closer, forehead to forehead. "Shit, Leo."

"I know." She nodded, ran her hands up his sides to his neck, and watched him with her soulful eyes. "I know."

He bent, she lifted to her toes, and they clashed. Lips crashing, teeth not far behind, tongues twining as if they had to hurry. Which, fuck, they did. The kiss was fast, rough enough to imprint her on his mouth, to seal them together. No way could he feel her through those layers of clothes, but that didn't stop his hands from roving, stroking down to her hips and taking hold the way he wanted to. She leaned in, pressing her bottom half to his, and the groan he made was the stuff of barbarians. He couldn't find words now if his life depended on it.

Not that it mattered. The slide of their tongues was enough—no need for speech between them. Keeping each other alive had given them a language of their own, like they had the key to each other's bodies.

Her gloved hand wrapped around his neck. *More*, the pressure said. *Deeper*.

It told him her hunger matched his. He growled and tilted his head, showed her with his body how essential she was.

Bo yipped and they both went still, their breaths stuttering in time.

She moved away first, the back of her gloved hand pressed to her mouth, looking shell-shocked.

"Christ, I—"

"We—"

Their eyes snagged as they shared a laugh, awkward, but kind of hot in the way it acknowledged the depth of this thing. Her gaze dropped to his mouth and he was three seconds from pouncing when she spoke again. "We should…um…" She swallowed and stared at their surroundings, like she had no idea where she was or how she'd gotten there.

"Go," he managed, ignoring his aching cock, his pounding need.

Without another word, they returned to pick up their things and started walking again. All the while, his heart thumped too hard in his chest, his lungs never expanding quite far enough.

Nerves and happiness mingled to make him smile. Until he remembered that danger was everywhere. He'd been surrounded by it for years. Only now did it terrify him, because now, against all odds, he actually had something to lose.

———————

After an hour, Leo's lips still burned. And not just from the memory of his touch there, but from the intensity of it, the fierceness of him—of *them*, together. For those few seconds he'd crushed her to him, she hadn't felt fragile exactly—the whole thing had been too brusque for that—but she'd felt cherished. Wanted. *Needed* in an elemental way.

The *ferocity* of the man, the power in that one short contact. She'd felt so much. *Too* much. Shit, this couldn't work beyond the here and now, could it? *No. And why am I even thinking about this when we're—*

With a grunt, she lost her footing on the loose rocks and almost went down.

Just as she steadied herself, Elias turned, hand out to help. Heart beating hard with a startled adrenaline rush, she stared at it for a few beats, then looked up at his face.

"Look, we've had a few moments, done things, but this isn't good. It's not me, okay?" The words blew from her mouth. "I work with men. I've worked with literally thousands of men and the last thing I'd let myself do is get involved with one. All this *kissing* is…" She swallowed, frustrated at her inability to communicate what she meant. "I don't sleep with men I work with and—"

He made a noise: half-grunt, half-snort.

"What?"

"I'm not your colleague, Leo."

"No, but we're teammates and—"

"Not officially. Doesn't matter anyway."

She narrowed her eyes at him, not trusting the big, flashy smile on his face. The yeti didn't smile like that. "What? Why are you doing that?"

The man was grinning like the cat that got the canary and maybe pulled down a couple caribou while he was at it. He grasped her hand and leaned in. "'Cause you like me." His smile got impossibly bigger, whiter, more self-satisfied. Devastating.

"What? No. Uh-uh." She took a step back.

His brows rose and what might have been hurt washed across his face. "You saying you *don't* like me?"

"*No.* Oh, gosh no, I'm saying it wouldn't work. It can't work. There's too much…um…"

He cocked his head, along with his right eyebrow. "Too much…?"

"I don't know how to describe it." She threw up her hands. "I just know that it's a bad idea. That's all. End of story."

He mumbled something that she didn't catch.

"What? What's that?"

"Just said maybe this story's got a different ending."

She blinked. "From what?"

"From all your other stories. From the ones you…didn't care about." With a pointed look, he swung away, leaving her no choice but to follow him up. Up the mountain, toward the peak they'd have to crest in order to get where they were going. And to a spot where he'd said they just might have a chance of getting a real night's sleep.

You like me.

Yeah, sure.

As if to punish her for lying—even to herself—the sky chose that moment to open up. It went from a cold mist to a torrent that made them small as ants. Just two tiny people and a dog, as inconsequential as dust against the big picture: mountains and sky, trees, rivers, and rocks, veined with glaciers made of million-year-old ice.

And somehow, that image—or maybe the extra danger or the exhaustion dragging at every cell of her body—pushed her to admit the truth. She did like him. And it made her very, very uncomfortable.

CHAPTER 28

LEO COULDN'T COUNT ALL THE WAYS SHE'D BEEN TIRED. There'd been *studying for college courses* tired and *boot camp* tired, there'd been *survival training, drag your ass through cold rivers just to pass* tired, and the electric exhaustion of a long flight over water, refueling in the air. She couldn't bring herself to dwell on the desolate, lonely, sleepless hours right after Mom died. And the more recent time spent at Dad's bedside. Tired because a few ill-timed seconds of shut-eye could mean never seeing him again.

Then there'd been the hypervigilant exhaustion of almost dying, dodging bullets for hours, doing her damnedest to keep an unseen enemy at bay from the relative safety of her grounded helo. In that case, the only thing between her and death had been her quick reflexes and three Navy SEALs. The bravest men she'd ever met.

And now this unplanned journey. The run over breaking ice, plowing straight into briars, collapsing on the ground with this man... The damn bear. She'd thought that was the worst this would get.

Wrong again, Eddowes.

Visibility was down to nothing, the path they trod so steep, every step was a risk they shouldn't be taking.

But every time she considered yelling up at Elias and demanding they stop for the night, she was met with the sight of his big, broad back, hunched against the winds, soaking from the weather, but still stalking inexorably on. And if he could do it, well then, so could she.

I like him.

With frightening suddenness, her foot slipped out from under her and she was down, her knees and palms and head all ringing from the abrupt contact with solid earth.

She tried to get up and slid, not from the slime, but because she was literally knee deep in a rushing brook. Had this been here a minute ago?

Her eyes couldn't focus on a single part of the slope, but when she leaned her head back and took in their surroundings, it was all rushing brook.

More like waterfall.

Another failed attempt at rising sent her facedown in the stuff. And now she was terrified. There hadn't been a river here seconds ago. Was this runoff from the mountain?

It was pouring down and when she looked ahead, there was nothing to see. Back was the same thing, just a screen of rushing water and night, finally laying its dark curtain upon them.

She pushed up onto all fours, shaking, scrabbled at the slippery stones, and got a handhold on something that didn't roll down the hill.

"Not far," he'd told her a little ways back, and she'd believed him. So, rather than lie there, the way her body demanded, or try to get up again, which was futile at this point, she forged ahead at a crawl, climbing in the steep places, pulling herself up over ledges, helping Elias with the dog when Bo needed a boost.

Not far.

One tiny handhold in the stone, two fingers in, pull up.

For what felt like ages but was likely just a millisecond, she teetered on the edge, her body undecided—could her muscles power her up or would gravity take over?

Her muscles failed; she lost purchase, slithering down those few last hard-won feet. As her body grappled, she stretched, reaching so hard she could have sworn her bones cracked, fingers, toes, elbows, every part of her was in the fight, trying their damnedest to hold on to something—anything.

And then she stopped, with a bone-jarring abruptness, one wrist caught in a viselike grip. The rest of her dangled above nothing but air.

———————

Elias was on the ground, bent over the side of the mountain, holding Leo up with one hand. His feet, which had found a crack in the rock, were his anchor.

Their anchor.

"Other hand, Leo." Frigid water flowed around him, over him, pummeling her, trying its best to end them like everything else in this place.

She threw her head back, took a face full of the stuff, and swung it down again. "Can't."

"Find a foothold. Push up."

He felt more than saw her breathe, as if their joined hands were plugged into each other, bringing their vitals together—pulses and air, shared from contact.

In that place that would decide if she lived or died.

"Find one?"

She didn't have to shake her head for him to feel the answer.

"On the right, put your foot out. Bend your leg."

She did it, her toes reaching for that elusive place, while the deluge tried to drown them.

There was a moment when he thought she'd slip again—was worried she wouldn't make it—and he decided right then he'd rather go with her than be left here alone.

Muttering obscenities, he pulled one foot from its slot to get that extra inch, giving himself to the mountain in a way he'd never dared before. If he could swing her, maybe. Or get her under the arms…

Without both legs mooring him to the top, his body shifted, his efforts more about balance now than security. Stretching his reach with his left hand, he felt the bandages at his side give, the wound open up, the pain providing extra propulsion in a way he couldn't begin to understand.

He dipped lower, slid his hand under her arm, and, with a roar that tore open the night, swung up and back.

There was nothing for a few seconds. No sound, no pummeling waterfall, no death or fear or plummeting to the ground.

And then, with a *whoosh*, he was back in his body, Leo tight in his arms, trembling on the edge of a cliff.

He ripped off his glove and slid a hand around her neck, covering her pulse.

Alive. Cold and hot and whole.

She lifted her head, and though he couldn't make out her features, her breath pelted his throat, the rhythmic press of her breasts to his chest, the wet coil of her arms winding around his neck. He dipped when she tugged, wrapped himself around her sopping body, and held as tight as he could.

They sagged into each other, shiny and wet and shuddering. Vibrating with the thrill of breathing for another short while. He planted one hand on her ass, tight, demanding. The other held her still by the nape.

"I do like you, Elias. I like you a hell of a lot," she whispered, the sound harsher than anything she'd ever let out, like she'd lost her voice on that cliff. "Please kiss me."

He strained up—to hell with the wound and the weather and the world trying to kill them—and drank from her lips. Gulped, consumed. Her mouth was cool against his, her lips demanding, and her tongue when it touched him was a brand.

A tiny, barely cognizant part of his brain knew this wasn't real—this was danger pushing them together. Nature trying to make them mate or some shit like that. Bear attacks as aphrodisiac. Adrenaline like a drug, screaming, *Hell, why not? You're not gonna make it anyway.*

They rolled away from the unsheltered edge, through the actual waterfall, and into the recess behind it. It was suddenly staggeringly quiet and close, the water like a wall separating them from reality, the air in here still except for the cyclone of their mingled breaths. When she wound up on top again, he cupped both ass cheeks in his hands, reveled in the tight squeeze of her thighs around his waist.

This was ridiculous. They couldn't screw here, in what was barely a pocket at the top of the mountain. They'd die if they didn't get dry and warm. *Now*.

Although there was something poetically right about being wet with her again—a strange bookend to the longest few days in history. Completing a cycle.

As if on cue, the wind howled, picking up the snowmelt and blowing it over them with the force of a million little fists, while she straddled him like something from his dreams.

She'd get up now, out of self-preservation. They both would.

He tightened his hold on her butt and then with a strange, belly-deep fear, reached for her wrists, wrapped them with his hands, held them as if her life depended on it. Her curves plastered to his front, her mouth hungry against his, her hands caught in the circle of his.

Alive! He felt the thrill through every pore, every nerve, every cell in his body.

Alive! She responded, her legs and arms and lips an embrace.

Alive! Not so high above them, lightning flashed, and seconds later the ground shook, as if even the sky had to show a sign of agreement.

"This is stupid," he muttered against her.

She nodded, gasped, the sound uncharacteristically shaky, and rubbed her cheek into his.

"Need to get warm."

Her "*yeah*" was a whisper, barely audible with the wind chiming in. "Dry first. Dry. Warm." She ground against him, scalding in that place where their bodies met.

He could only grunt in response, pulling her tight to where he was hard and needy and hot enough to warm them both. "Yeah."

Water dripped from her face onto his, into his mouth and eyes. He closed them and held her for a few terrible moments, where he actually considered being idiots to death.

"This…" He swallowed. "You feel so good." He didn't want her to move, but if she didn't get up, they'd be caught here in this sexy, stupid brush with mortality. "Just want to keep kissing you. Touching you. Can't stop."

"Same. I've known you, what? Four days? Or five?" She rubbed her nose to his. Hers was an ice cube.

"Four."

"Four days." Shuddering hard, she spoke into his ear. "We've got to stop meeting this way, Elias Thorne."

All he could do was laugh.

CHAPTER 29

LEO HAD NEVER BEEN THIS RASH IN HER LIFE. SHE'D TAKEN risks—hell, she lived for them—but a cliff's-edge, soaking-wet make-out session on the brink of hypothermia was just plain idiocy. Yet when Elias barked, "Clothes off," his voice sounding like he'd scraped it up the side of the mountain, her immediate reaction wasn't refusal.

She wanted to get naked, to press her body to his and soak him up.

When he began pulling off his own wet clothes, she realized he wasn't telling her to strip for *him*. He was doing it for survival.

Embarrassment and disappointment wound through her and she tugged off her hoodie, started to wring it out—pointless, given the downpour—and went on to the next layer, and the next, laying them out as flat as she could, until there was nothing left to protect her cold, clammy skin.

The elements raged. Wind, frigid and angry, whipped around them, into the recess and back out, slowed only by the waterfall hemming them in.

Without speaking, he grabbed her hand and led her to the very back of the indentation, lugging his pack behind him.

He threw her a tiny camp towel and wiped himself off with brisk, rough movements. Getting dry seemed impossible with this level of wet and cold. The bastard wind wasn't helping at all, the way it threw water their way, like a cruel practical jokester.

Muttering insults to the elements, she grabbed the tarp Elias shoved her way. Together, they stretched it out, fought to keep it low, and somehow got a sleeping bag spread on top of it. Still too damp to climb in, they anchored the bag with their bodies and pulled out more layers. Another bag, the fur.

"Go ahead!" he yelled. "Be right there."

She opened her mouth to protest and let it drop when he rubbed his towel over Bo. Right. The dog, who looked more like a drowned rat than a canine, didn't protest the treatment for a second.

Teeth chattering, Leo turned to the backpack.

"What you doing?"

"Getting…clothes."

"You sure you need them?" The question whipped through the air between them.

She stilled, stark freaking naked, and stared at him for a good five seconds before dropping the bag, shoving it to the side, and sliding deep into their nest.

Well, I guess that's that. Nerve endings on fire, she drew the covers up and over herself, and watched him work. The blanket did nothing to tamp down her desire when it raked over her tender nipples, drawing them into painfully tight points. Even the hard ground beneath her made her ache in ways she didn't understand. Or maybe that was all him.

It wasn't possible to make out details in the dark, but she got the impression the man wore his nudity the way he'd worn his parka—completely at ease. There was nothing awkward or ridiculous about the sight of him leaning down, scrubbing at the dog, everything out in the open.

Deep inside their shelter, that image flashed back over and over in her mind. Solid and sturdy Elias, wiping down his dog in the nude. That shouldn't be sexy. It shouldn't, but by God, it was. Like made-to-order porn, featuring the world's most efficient, capable, and competent man taking care of another creature.

How on earth would she handle these close quarters with the man after witnessing that? After…everything? Her skin felt stretched and sensitive, like it could barely contain all the want running through her muscles and bones.

And she'd just agreed to sleep naked with him. She shook at the realization. The night before last, getting into the bag *that very second* had saved their lives. He'd been dead to the world when she'd undressed him, after all, and still a stranger. Skin to skin had been a last-ditch bid for survival.

Up here, tonight, with her nipples beaded hard and the heavy weight of want in her belly, things were not the same. At all. She was damp from the rain and soaking wet from wanting him.

She shut her eyes, but still he was there, branded on the backs of her lids, thick muscles bunching and rolling, rain sluicing off him, hair plastered to his head. She couldn't possibly have seen single beads of water, shining like diamonds in his chest hair, but damn if she didn't remember it that way. And his shoulders... She swallowed, thinking of how hefty they were, like his thighs, how strong they'd looked. How strong they *were*. Because the man was a freaking Goliath.

A moan escaped her lips as she shuddered deeper into the still-cold sleeping bag, waiting for him to come and complicate things.

Afraid of what would happen. Wishing he'd hurry.

After feeding Bo, Elias urged her to take up a spot in the blankets at their feet, and slid in before pulling the thick wad over their heads and shutting out the world. The last time they'd done this, Elias had been unconscious.

This time, he was fully aware of every detail, from the clammy press of her skin against his, to the perfect fit of their bodies, to the pain of too-cold blood sluggishly ebbing through half-frozen veins.

Leo's breath heated his chest—the only spot of warmth aside from the dog at their feet. Until the foot warmers he'd thrown inside, wrapped in a few insulating layers of clothes, slowly worked their magic.

Bo shifted, grumbling in the way that meant she was happily settling in.

A shudder at a time, their shivering diminished, Leo's teeth stopped clacking, and even then, she didn't move, didn't give him an inch of space.

Her whispered "Elias" made his hand tighten on her back, his no longer numb fingers sensitive to the point of pain.

"Yeah," he breathed against the top of her head.

"You do that a lot?"

His muscles tightened in preparation for whatever she'd ask. "What?"

"Sucking face right after almost dying? This is, what? Our second or third time?"

His lungs released, his belly jumped with a surprised laugh. If hypothermia had really set in, she could have stopped his heart with that question.

"Just with you, Leo." He listened to her breathe for a few cycles and then, though he was afraid, he asked, "You?"

"Every single ti—" She must've caught the hitch in his chest. Or maybe she felt all his muscles go tight because she got real serious real fast. "Never. I told you that before." Another long, hot exhale, the air between them like a sauna. "You're my first."

And last, he wanted to say, but that seemed way out of bounds given their short acquaintance. Acquaintance. Yeah right. What they had was knowledge of each other—deep and raw and almost painful.

It hurt him right now, in the chest, the throat. Just her presence made his insides dance.

He should let go of her. Should make his limbs obey, slow his pulse to a reasonable rate. He should force his lower half to retreat, given the hardness growing between them.

He'd just opened his mouth to suggest they get dressed after all and eat something, maybe separate their bed in two, when her voice cut through, each word reverberating past his rib cage to thrum at his heart. "I want to do it some more."

He couldn't breathe, couldn't budge, couldn't believe he'd actually heard the right words. One second she was mad that they couldn't keep their hands off each other and the next, this. "Say that again."

"I'm done fighting it. Kiss me, Elias. Heat me up."

Those words burned his skin the way her eyes would if he could see them, searing their way from his scalp to the soles of his feet. His cock was a brand pulsing against their bellies.

There'd never be a better invitation, at least not one he was dying to accept. Before the next heartbeat, he was on her.

CHAPTER 30

Leo had tried just about everything within reason. She'd smoked some things and drunk her fair share. Her thirst for speed made her face incomparable danger—on her bike, in the air, on missions with her teammates by her side. She'd shot at people, taken enemy fire, performed daredevil feats that most wouldn't consider.

Yet somehow, this was the biggest risk of her life.

Not because she'd put her body in peril, but something else. Something she'd never realized hung in the balance. Leo had desires, like everyone. Bodily needs. A thirst for life. Opinions. She sought thrills and experiences. But usually that was it. Emotions weren't involved in any of it. And her heart had certainly never been part of the equation before. This new reality scared the hell out of her.

"Where?" Elias asked, the question blasting through the tight, dark space.

"Where what?"

"Where do you want me to kiss you?"

Ooohhh. He was handing that first belly kiss right back to her. Her skin prickled at the possibilities.

Then she got to thinking… Where had she meant when she'd asked for a kiss? On the lips, obviously. But then the question opened things up until—oh hell, the options seemed endless.

That was the thing with this man—he was one big surprise. Unexpected. Abrupt. Unknown. The world was bigger when he was around.

"Where were you thinking?" she breathed, not flirtatious but curious. *Dying* to know. Out of nowhere, scenarios blasted to life—every inch of her skin screamed to be touched.

One big hand left her back, scattering goose bumps in its wake, and slowly, methodically dragged a fiery path down her spine to the curve of her ass, around to her hip, where it clenched for a split second before moving on. He shifted away just enough to run his fingers between them and down, to stroke the curly hair at her mound.

A startled *oh* left her mouth, more air than voice, and his hand responded as if they weren't two beings but separate parts of a whole—two ends of a taut cord. He dipped a single finger between her legs with the slightest, quickest of touches, barely skimming her lips, though it set her off like a tuning fork, its echo shimmering in the dark night.

By the time she caught her breath, his hand had left her soft center to travel up over the round rise of her belly, sinking into her bellybutton—just a swirl—then to her rib cage, where it took in the rise and fall of her breathing. Not breathing, gasps. She was panting and moaning, and when his callused skin reached the underside of her breast—the soft part that had never had this many nerve endings—she grunted. Like an animal.

He cupped her there, held her, as if this spot, this body, this exhausted shell were somehow precious.

She wasn't precious or fragile, not the way this massive hand made her feel in this tight, warm space. She was tough, hard as nails, fast, furious, and ready to face anything.

It didn't make sense when his fingers drew a sob from her lips. And they hadn't even reached her nipple yet, so she couldn't blame it on hormones or lust or the magic of that hypersensitive place. It was the spot between her breasts that he'd claimed now—a place no one ever noticed during sex. A place that had no nerve endings as far as she knew. And yet, his sandpaper hands showed her otherwise.

I'll kiss you here, they said. *And here.* The promise grazed her nipple, drawing a whimper, the sound like nothing she'd uttered before, and then coasted up, up to her collarbone, which he learned as if he'd been meaning to for a while.

A while, she almost laughed at that idea. As if they'd known each other for longer than the time it had taken to get here.

But then that thought deserted her, flew away like a balloon in the air when he cupped her chin, his hand so large it cradled her jaw and her ear and made her feel tiny before his beard brushed her face, and then his mouth did the same, and she was gone.

Drawn into this kiss as quickly as the others, scorched by his intent, consumed by his want—and hers, if she was honest. She'd never wanted a person like this, never craved these sweet, tiny touches.

And he'd barely touched her, barely moved, just brushed those dry lips to hers, giving her the time to move, to take over like she usually did.

But she didn't. Why would she when giving herself to this man's slow, tender mastery was every bit as dangerous as jumping off this cliff?

Without consummating the damn kiss, he pulled back, making her grasp at his shoulders like someone dying of thirst, scrabbling for purchase, power, a drop of control. Then he was back. Just his nose, skimming hers, pulling in her scent as surely as she was his, lips following in its path, up, to kiss her eye, then back down, with the slow, calm patience of a man who'd lived alone for a decade. A man with no expectations.

But she wasn't like that. She craved million-mile-an-hour winds, sought adrenaline like a drug, and jumped from airplanes, all while wishing for more, more, more. Nothing had ever been enough.

He backed up, forcing a muted scream from her throat until his hand wrapped around it, loose but secure, and—oh no, oh no, this was it, what she'd needed all these years. Her sex went heavy, flooded with warmth and wetness, and she wanted to scream at him to move.

This glacier-slow control was the steady bass to her wild treble. It should have been discordant, but it only grounded her, kept her in her body when she'd always sped her way to completion.

"Slow down, Leo. Let me do this my way," he rumbled, like something older than the earth's crust.

When she shivered this time, it wasn't from the cold or even from stimulation, but with recognition. This...him...together. The primitive rightness of this man's touch was like hydrogen and oxygen coming together to make water. More than the sum of their parts.

———

In this world, there was nothing as soft as Leo Eddowes, nothing half as sweet. The most fearless woman he'd ever met, who faced her own death with humor, whose spine was strong as diamonds, while her brain was just as sharp, had somehow opened up, giving him her soft, tender core.

And he was in absolute awe.

With reverence, he took her mouth, her heat, this emotion filling the air between them and gave her everything he had.

Though, really it wasn't much. Rough hands, tired muscles, bones that felt worn down to nothing.

With chapped lips, he explored her soft cheek, the straight line of her jaw, the tender skin beneath her ear. The noises she made were incredible. Low and sexy, breathless with wanting.

Wanting him.

And fuck if he wasn't hard enough to plow through the damn bedrock beneath them.

"Do it, Elias. *Kiss* me for God's sake."

Her words surprised a laugh from him, along with something else—something not quite so bright and sweet. Something feral and animalistic. A bestial desire to make her do things his way.

He threw a leg over hers—startled to realize in an offhand way that Bo had left their nest a while ago—and pinned Leo to the hard ground.

"No," he whispered right into her ear.

When she tried to move her hands only to find her wrists trapped, her surprise was palpable, vibrating through his chest as surely as her long, thready moan. She reached with her hips, her breasts, tried to bite him with that mouth, and for a few, drawn-out seconds, he could do nothing but shut his eyes and breathe. That or he'd embarrass himself all over her belly.

Which was probably the way this would end anyway, given how long it had been. And how badly he wanted her.

Once he'd gotten as much control as he could on the situation, he let his hungry inner beast take over, let his blood thicken and his pulse slow.

With the speed of lava easing from the earth, her wrists tight in one of his fists, he lowered himself back on top of her, let her feel his heavy erection, and then rose when she tried to kiss him again.

He could get addicted to this power—the power of a strong woman wanting him, showing him, and fighting him just enough to prove it.

"More," she demanded. "Come on, Elias. Let me feel you… Give me a…"

She opened her legs wide and his body reacted like he'd been electrocuted.

He was the one who grunted this time, the sound punctuated with a quiet "*damn*" when he encountered all that wetness. The very real possibility of slipping inside her made him go very, very still.

Not because he didn't want it, but because he needed it so bad.

If he didn't kiss her again, didn't get his fill of her taste, then he'd do something irrevocable.

He bent, put his mouth to hers, and lost his ever-loving mind.

CHAPTER 31

FOR THE FIRST TIME, LEO GOT IT—WHAT IT MEANT TO WANT
something more than life. To crave to the point of endangering
herself. It was how she'd felt just now, as Elias withheld himself.
She'd thought that it would go away when he kissed her.

Silly woman.

Just a kiss. Lips, teeth, tongue. It wasn't so much to ask, no big
deal. Where was the danger in that?

Here was the answer. *Right here.* Because kisses weren't supposed to be all-consuming, but this one was. It tore her open,
made her feel things she'd never acknowledged. Or even understood were there.

They were pressed together, writhing, the sleeping bags and
blankets in serious danger of taking off in the wind, but she
wasn't cold. At all. She was nothing but a ball of hot, searing
sensation.

And now she wanted more. Him, inside her. Her body bucked,
reaching for him. And like before, he lifted up, pulling out of the
way.

"I want you, Elias," she muttered against his lips. "Want you so
bad."

His "Yeah?" was a deep bass. "Want you, too." He took a long,
slow breath and nuzzled the side of her face like he had all the time
in the world, like he could do this for hours, days, years. "But we
need a condom."

"In your pack."

"You found those, huh?" He made another low, happy sound,
close and intimate. "I'm too happy to move."

She inhaled his warm breath, listened to the wind, which hadn't been there a second ago, had it? And homed in on the scattered rap of rain on the top layer of fur.

Okay, so maybe he was right. They needed a break.

Her next breath in was full of musky man scent. She should hate it, be disgusted by the smoky sweat smell of him, but instead, she wanted to lick him everywhere. The idea drove her wild, made her squirm and reach for his erection. "Can I touch you?" At his nod, she went on. "Let me make you come."

"I don't need to..." He grunted when she ran her hand up his shaft to cup the thick crown. "Fine. Together. Let me do the same for you." He nudged her. "On your side."

Leo hadn't left the armed forces to take orders from men, and yet those three words worked in ways she wasn't prepared to examine. Her breasts went tight, her hips flexed of their own accord, and before she knew it, she'd slid off him and done as he instructed.

"Here." He curled up behind her, did something down low, and urged her to lift her top leg. For a breathless second, she wondered what she'd just agreed to.

"I didn't think we were..."

"I'm not gonna fuck you, Leo," he said, spooning her close from behind. "I mean, I *will*, when the time's right. If you want that. But not without a condom." He paused, and even his breathing went silent for a second. "Are you on the pill?"

She shook her head, so pissed at her past self for going off it, even though the hormones made her miserable.

"Better like this." All business, he tapped her thigh and she closed it, ensnaring his erection, hot and hard and right against her wet lips, snug between them.

He wrapped his arm around her and put one rough hand to her belly—not a place she usually liked being touched. From there, though, he could guide her or hold her still while he moved. And she liked that very, very much. "And I want to fuck you when I'm not bone tired. When we do it"—he slid forward, the tip of him hitting one pleasure point after another, turning her mindless— "we'll do it right."

She had no doubt of that. Given how just this friction felt, sex with him would be mind-blowing.

He came and went between her legs, in slow, long slides, each move calibrated to give her pleasure—and to take his own—in a way she found refreshing. He was unabashed, forthright, and sexy as hell.

"That's good, Leo. So good." He pulled her hip back until she was flush to him, reached up to use her belly as leverage, and quickly plucked at one nipple—the whole thing an easy, expert dance.

And all the while, she couldn't possibly breathe a word, didn't want to stanch the masterful ebb and flow of his body, playing hers like a maestro—like a man who loved women.

A jolt of something ugly reared up, and she shut it right down. No point in being jealous of whoever came before. She wasn't the jealous type.

Or she hadn't been—until right this moment.

"I'm close. You?"

She could be.

"Can you…touch me there?" Her voice was a meek echo of its usual self. Where was regular Leo? The one who told dudes what to do, was happy to let them get her off, and even happier if she never had to see them again. Men were complicated, annoying, filthy, and…

He didn't have to do much to play her like his own personal instrument. He cupped her between the legs and let a finger dip down, quick to give her the pleasure she sought. Panting, control gone, she shifted back and forth, seeking nothing but fulfillment.

"Yeah," he whispered hotly in her ear and she wished she could see him, see the yeti out of breath and almost out of words. "That's it." He thrust again between her slick inner thighs and this time took a break from touching her to grab the head of his own erection, the move so unconsciously hot, so base, so *in his body* that she couldn't have kept herself from coming if she'd tried.

She sucked in air—what felt like every drop of it present in this tight space—and held it high in her lungs while the rest of her exploded. He worked her hard with his cock, giving her enough friction to draw it out…and out… And still she couldn't breathe.

His hand was frantic now, his breathing in her ear a shaky, messy chorus of sounds that she'd never imagined someone like this making. Finally, just as she reached the highest peak of her climax, he let go with his own.

Somehow her hand was there. Had she been touching him this whole time? When he came, she rubbed him, loving the quick, angry jerks of his body, and once he was spent—in a move she'd later have to deny—she slicked it up, over her belly to the nipple he still pinched between his fingers.

For a few long, languid, out-of-body seconds, they rubbed him into her skin together, the act so lurid, so intimate, so different from anything she'd ever done that something inside her blew. Tears pushed at her eyes. Every muscle tightened in her effort to hold back the emotion.

"Hey." He let go of her hand, nudged her shoulder until she flopped to her back, and leaned over her. "Hey, Leo. Sweetie. Leo. Leo."

Okay, so maybe the yeti didn't have the magic words to fix this—whatever the hell she thought needed fixing—but the kiss he put on her lips went miles toward setting her insides straight. And his little noises did that too. Soft, sweet sounds, so different from the way he'd literally growled through his orgasm.

But, crap, she refused to cry. She wouldn't. Swallowing back the burn, she forced a touch of humor into her voice. "I may have lost my mind." Or at least a few brain cells.

He sighed, the sound shaky, and put his forehead against hers.

"Not the only one." His body scooted to one side, where he leaned on an elbow, giving her space—but not too much. She liked that—being boxed in with him, with the option to escape. "You okay?"

She opened her mouth, an easy yeah on the tip of her tongue, and then closed it. Was she? This wasn't her, getting emotional for no reason. This *feeling* things. Overwhelmed by sensations she'd never experienced before. "I don't know."

He seemed to be holding himself very still. "You regret it?"

Her muscles jolted like she'd been shocked. "No! Oh, God no." She wrapped her arms around his neck, pulled him close so she could whisper. "It was good. This is good."

"Yeah?" He drew back and though she couldn't see his smile, she could hear it. "On a scale of one to—"

"Stop it." She bopped his shoulder and let out a shaky breath. "Hey. Where's Bo?"

"Must've taken off for calmer climes."

"It's storming outside." A light laugh tumbled up and out.

"Yeah, well. Got pretty rowdy in here."

"It was…"

"Unbelievable." He shifted. "What about for you?"

"Honestly? That was the best orgasm I've ever had. Colossal. Like…I don't know… The one orgasm to rule them all."

He barked a laugh. "And in the darkness bind them?"

She snickered. "Bind us."

Their laughter petered off. Uh-oh. Why did that seem so real? A bond more inexorable than rings on fingers.

For a few careful seconds, she held her breath. She couldn't see his eyes, but she could feel the humor in them, could sense the affection there. Could picture the lines splaying out at the sun-creased corners. And hell, there it was again—that outpouring of emotion that she had no freaking idea what to do with. It wasn't easy, but she held it back and concentrated on him instead, letting her hand explore his mysterious face, learning it in the dark.

While she was running her fingers over his lips he yawned, ended on a chuckle, and pulled her in to give her the sleepy, slow, content kind of kiss she remembered her parents having. When she pulled back, he nudged her over, half on top of his splayed-out limbs, the position a perfect yin and yang.

Every muscle in her body hurt, her skin chafed, and her belly rumbled with hunger, but it was nothing compared to this thing blooming inside her. What was it? Was it *happiness*? Possibly. Probably. But good God did it scare her. More than crashes and enemy fire and running for her life across a frozen lake. Shit, it turned out, had just gotten real, in a no-going-back kind of way. And she had no idea how to handle it.

CHAPTER 32

Elias couldn't recall waking up this sore before...or this satisfied. He stretched, popping joints and easing muscles, tightened his arm around the woman who lay against him, and shifted lazily, enjoying the feel of female flesh against his morning erection.

And then remembered just where he was.

At the top of a mountain, in what could barely be called a cave.

He eased an arm out from under their piled-up covers and brought it quickly back into the heat.

Cold as hell out there. And he didn't hear rain anymore—or the constant thrum of the waterfall. Bad news. He'd be surprised if the rain hadn't turned into something worse in the night.

And here they were, outside and buck naked.

He pulled in a deep breath and let out a sigh, unable to stop the smile from splitting his face.

Best wake-up. Ever.

His eyes cracked open, just enough to watch her.

On a wave of heat, everything they'd done came rushing back. Not just the kissing and touching, but the bone-deep emotions. The stuff that he couldn't begin to explain—the stuff that had plumbed his soul.

Though he didn't think the sun was all the way up, there was enough light that they needed to get moving again. How good would it be to stay here, instead? Perched in the clouds, where no one could see them? They could—

With a light humming sound, she stirred, her body going through the early phases of wakefulness the way his had.

In a moment of certainty, he opted to play it casual. No

morning-after weirdness, no pressure to make this something—even though he knew that what had happened between them was cataclysmic. Leo, he surmised, wouldn't appreciate pushiness at this point. She didn't like having her mind made up for her.

He rolled out from their nest, giving her space to wake up and time to adjust to this new reality.

The cold slammed him like a fist, and for a few seconds, he wanted nothing more than to crawl back in there with her. His penis, thick and languid a moment before, begged him to, but he ignored it.

The sky was lighter than he'd realized.

He threw on a shirt and long underwear, went around the bend to answer nature's call, and returned quickly.

"It's cold and it's late, Leo. Better get going."

"Yep. Yep. Sounds good," she said, voice thick with sleep, as she emerged, wrapped in blankets. Though her sleepy eyes lingered on his body, it didn't take long for them to skid past him to where what had been a waterfall last night was now a massive icicle. Beyond it, so big it took his breath away, was the wilderness they'd spent the last few days crossing. The entire vista glittered in the sunlight, crystallized like the breath in his lungs.

Growing up, his mom had put figurines on the mantel around the holidays every year—a Christmas village. He'd loved those things as a kid—the warm glow of the lights in each little window, the sparkle of the snow-crusted roofs and trees. Not once in the last decade had he felt cozy looking out at this place. Not once had his cabin seemed as warm as this overlook today, a snug haven in a land frozen solid.

"How on earth did we climb up here?" Leo's question was light, but there was a definite thread of *holy shit* in there. Like she'd had no idea how far they'd come.

Careful not to meet her eye and show her what she'd done to his world, he responded with a nonchalant, "Good question."

She crawled forward, almost to the edge. "Nothing but a goat path."

"Sure is."

While he pulled out dry clothes and threw her items that would, again, be way too big, she turned to take in the shallow shelter they'd spent the night in.

"And today…"

Halfway dressed, he sat beside her to pull on socks and, finally, his boots—which were miserably wet.

"Today, we do the summit. Hopefully before the helicopter arrives." He pointed straight up. "Hope not to break our necks in the process."

She shut her eyes. "I was afraid you'd say that."

"Yeah, but once we get over the top, it's all downhill." He stood and then, because he couldn't deny this thing—didn't want to—he squatted beside her, wrapped a hand around the back of her neck, and leaned in for a quick, clean kiss.

It was nothing of the sort. The moment they touched, it turned dirty and deep, vocal and more complex than most of the relationships he'd had, including the one with the woman he'd almost married.

When he finally pulled away, he imagined his expression was something like hers—shell-shocked and exhausted and hungry for more.

"We've got to go," he said, letting her hear the regret in his voice.

"You sure?" She grinned and bit her lip, drawing his eye to that lush, sexy mouth.

"Hell no, I'm not. But on the other side of this mountain, there's something I want you to see." Feeling boyish and excited, he leaned down and kissed her forehead. "You're gonna like it."

He handed her one last layer and went to feed his dog.

Downhill wasn't all that easy—especially with the ice coating the rocks for most of the morning—but it was a cakewalk compared to last night's climb.

And, Leo had to admit, it could've been a million times harder and she'd still be smiling like an idiot.

They paused rarely throughout the day, but each and every time, he gave her looks that sped her pulse up, sent warmth to her belly, and had the two of them grinning like kids.

As she took the lead after lunch, she had to consciously relax her mouth, purposely turn those lips down. And maybe, just maybe, she put a little extra sway in her step.

When he let out a low, quiet wolf whistle, she knew she'd been caught out. "What?" She squinted at him over her shoulder. "You think you're the only one with swagger?"

He shook his head with a grin. "No. No way, Leo Eddowes. You've got swagger for days."

She gave in and let the smile reemerge, a little flirty, a little prim. "Why, thank you, sir."

She'd walked another few steps when he caught up and passed her. "That what it's about?" He turned and walked backwards. "Swagger?" His expression changed, became challenging, as if he knew that under all her bravado she was a vulnerable ball of nerves and emotion—an open, beating heart, ripe for destruction.

She didn't like the shift. What was it with this guy getting serious all the time? What was it with her falling into his traps?

Right. A trap, Eddowes?

"Might be." She meant to turn it into a joke, to say something, but she couldn't. Not with him.

Who's the one making things serious here, huh?

"Sometimes, when you're neck deep in the mud, eighty guys all trying to get the same thing you want…where you're a woman, weighed down by literal boobs and centuries of misogyny…and oh, hey…you're Black, to boot?" She threw a hand up into the air.

"Well, sometimes, you pull yourself out of the shit with nothing but swagger."

"Swagger didn't get you here." He sounded so certain, as if he knew her inside and out.

That certainty put her back up. "Think you know me?" She kept her voice light. "What do you reckon got me where I am?"

"Intelligence. Mostly. Good instincts too. I...*reckon*"—he underscored the word more than she had, leaned a little too close when he did it—"there's a decent dose of talent in the mix. I've seen your reflexes. I'd bet they've been honed, but I wouldn't be surprised if you were born with some...connection with the sky. An ingrown understanding of gravity or mechanics or things that go vroom."

A shiver went through her, starting high and shimmering through her quads and kneecaps on its way down, into the earth. She was like a lightning rod, only instead of electricity from the sky, she drew it from him. Or him from her. Something like that. And it freaked her the hell out.

"Am I right?"

Right on target. She opened her mouth to make some jackass comment and stopped when he put up his hand.

"I won't tell you you're special, 'cause we both already know that's true—and I wouldn't want to embarrass you. But what you've accomplished? Most people couldn't do even a fraction of that. Beat out thousands to become an elite pilot. What were you? Firehawks? I'll bet you were." When she didn't deny it, he went on. "And unlike me, you're not a big, strong white man, so that makes you at least a hundred times more qualified than I could ever be. But that's not even it. Not the..." He snapped his fingers lightly, his eyes looking everywhere for some elusive word. "There's something deeper than all of that. Something solid, at your core. It's the thing that I get. The place where we inters—"

She snorted to cut him off, to keep him from saying the big stuff. The dangerous stuff.

Not at all fazed, he cocked his head and watched her closely. "You believe in doing what's good, what's right."

"Right? You mean like good versus evil?" A sigh drained slowly from her lungs. "You saying it's all black and white, Elias? It's not. I do what I can to help, but..." She narrowed her eyes at him. "Wait. This is pretty rich coming from the king of sacrifice himself."

He stopped his slow, backward walking and stared at her, incredulous. "You think I gave up my life on purpose?"

She waited.

"You think I'd have done this if I had known the consequences? You think I'd do it again?" He looked older than before, his face lined, shoulders heavy.

"Yes." More intense than she intended, she stepped close and tilted her head way back to look him in the eye. "Yeah. You'd do it all over again."

He swallowed, his Adam's apple bobbing. It was all she could do not to kiss it.

"Am I right?" Suddenly, unexpectedly, she wanted to take back the question. What if he said no? What if he preferred his old life to this one? Seriously, who could blame him? There'd been loss and death—so many prices to pay for doing the right thing.

The problem was, if that was his wish—to go back and get a second chance—then he'd wish her away, wish all of *this* gone, never to have happened at all. And she couldn't bear the idea of never meeting the man.

In a way, she already felt bereft, as if knowing him had carved a hole inside her. But not knowing him would be a million times worse.

Breathing too hard, she moved past him. "How much farther?"

He didn't answer right away. After another few steps, she looked up and realized that he didn't have to.

"Where the *fuck* are they?" Deegan barked, clearly not bothered about being overheard.

Standing ankle deep in half-frozen mud, Ash searched the forest below and the cloud-tipped mountains above. They'd both fallen this morning—Deegan twice and Ash once, bruising his hip so badly he'd thought it was broken. Once he'd started walking, it only ached when he slowed.

"I don't know."

"What do you mean, you don't fucking know? They're out here, aren't they, *mate*? You're the *shit-hot tracker*, right, *mate*?"

Ash didn't glance at the other man, whose attempt at imitation was Dick Van Dyke–level absurd. He kept his eyes on the ground, scanning, slowly, carefully. Quietly.

Or at least, that's what he'd have liked.

"Are you sure they're even out there?"

Rolling his eyes internally, Ash turned. "They are." He squinted up at the mountain, then down again. *Maybe if you'd shut up, I could think.*

Deegan apparently expected more from him. When he didn't get it, he made a disgusted sound, reached for his sat phone, and headed into the woods, dialing.

Ash turned a full circle, ignoring the man. He loved this place. The harsh, ever-changing weather made it all the more beautiful, as far as he was concerned. What was more enchanting than going to sleep at night and waking to find everything frozen in place? He'd have enjoyed it a lot more if this arsehole hadn't been with him.

He tilted his head, listening to the low drone of the man's voice. He couldn't make out the words, but the tone was not happy. At all.

If only he could leave Deegan behind.

He shut his eyes for a moment, picturing taking it one step further. It would be so easy to end the fool—a clean slice to the throat. Yes, well, though the idea of cold-blooded murder had its appeal, it was not the mission.

He must focus on the mission.

Deegan stomped and slid back up the slope, clearly angry. "Chopper's down."

Ash's brows rose. "Down?"

"Out of commission. Pilot's working on it, with some geezer from town. Shit." He sighed, his little eyes flicking around. Deegan had one of those square-jawed American faces so often immortalized in comic books and action films. He was big and blond and strong looking, as far from Ash's physique as a person could get. And yet, even with his wonky hip, Ash could best this man in a confrontation. The trick with Ash was that he was unobtrusive. Nobody saw him and thought, operative! Nobody assumed that he was the hunter. "Look, you got a bead on them yet?"

Rather than respond, Ash uncapped his water, leaned back, and let his gaze go soft.

The air was cold and crisp, the wind so sharp it pushed the clouds along like recalcitrant sheep. One minute, the peaks were visible, the next, they appeared to be topped with cotton, spun from sugar. Something the other children's parents would have got for them at the carnival. Something Emma would have begged for.

Had she lived.

He pulled in a breath, let the oxygen brighten his vision and stir up his senses, and tucked his canteen away before setting off again, ignoring Deegan's muttered obscenities, his thoughts full of the past that never was.

"They can't have got far," he said over his shoulder. "Not with the wounded woman, not with last night's weather and this morning's deep freeze." He allowed himself an evil smirk. "Think you can pick up the pace?"

It had been shit luck that the downpour to end all downpours had come through and cleared all trace. There wasn't an identifiable track to be found. The rain, the freeze, the wind, they'd all come together to obliterate any signs of passage.

After a long day's slog, they'd come to a crossroads. Three possible paths toward Schink's Station, none of them direct. None of them the obvious choice.

A sign would be nice right now. Not that he believed in divine intervention. There'd been times when his life had depended on some kind of goodwill—whether Ganesh's, God's, or Mother Nature's, he frankly hadn't cared. Of course, the last time he'd looked to the heavens for help, he'd lost everything that mattered. But then, he had more faith in nature than in any god. In his mind, the two were intertwined, he supposed.

Maybe he should have brought Emma here, when all was lost. Maybe this place would have healed her when the medicine hadn't.

Shaking that silly notion from his head, he let the past wash out of him and focused on today. At this moment, he wished for a sign—not to save face in front of Deegan, but to finish this thing once and for all.

The clouds parted and he spotted it then—high in the sky: a bald eagle, the bird slow, wide winged and graceful. Its lazy, circular descent brought it to alight at the very top of the mountain before him, where it perched proudly, framed by clouds on other side, like a painting, or a dream.

Or the very sign he'd been seeking.

"Up it is," Ash said with a smile, feeling lighter than he had all day.

Muttering curses behind him, Deegan scrambled to keep up.

CHAPTER 33

HOLY CRAP. LEO COULDN'T BELIEVE WHAT SHE WAS SEEING. This was a hallucination. It had to be.

Her eyes flicked back to where Elias waited, watching as she climbed over the last rocky rise. From below, he was a bulwark—a silhouette flattened by the dark and outlined by the sunset, which would have been breathtaking enough on its own. But what lay just beyond him made everything all the more surreal.

He stepped over the stream and reached for her hand.

"Come on." His grip tightened, he moved forward and she let him pull her up beside him. For a breathless handful of seconds, she took in the sight of the iron-red structure, built into a shallow dip in the mountain. Not once had she spotted this place from the air, which wasn't surprising, given how the trees had grown around and even inside it.

"Parts of the roof look intact," she said, trying not to sound too hopeful.

"Yep."

"There a fireplace in there?"

"No." He shook his head. "Too risky anyway."

Her excitement ebbed, leaving her feeling dull and deflated. "You really think someone's close?"

"Not close," he said, his voice rising on the end. That inflection told her he had his doubts.

"But you feel safe here."

"Can't be seen from the sky, only one way in, so it's easy to keep watch." He eyed the path they'd taken to get up here. Not that *path* was the right word for it. Incline might work, although devil stairs was closer. The path was there; it was just so well-hidden among the sheer rocks that it was almost impossible to spot. "And those traps I set will help. For now, we rest." He looked up at the sky. "And wait out the weather."

Her heart sank. "Again?"

He turned back to eye her with a smile and a wink. "Yeah. But I bet you won't mind it so much here."

After placing that mystery at her feet with as much pride as a cat with a kill, he continued up into the tight little valley.

The structure—rambling and rickety looking—was pure Alaska. Hopes and dreams beaten, time and again, by nature. It climbed up along what looked like a crack in the mountain, which revealed itself to be a river, loud in its bubbling, frenzied rush to the bottom. She couldn't tell if the place was a house or a factory or a mine, but the multiple levels and sloping metal roof made her think the latter.

Bo followed Elias at a run, yipping with excitement, while Leo went more slowly, caution making her careful—although she wasn't sure what she was most worried about: her bones or her heart.

At the bottom, water flowed from an unseen source and gathered in small, strange-colored pools. "What's that smell?" She squinted. Was the water steaming?

"Sulfur."

She turned just in time to see Elias drop the pack and start stripping like his clothes were on fire.

"Hey, what are you..." Understanding set in—a little late, granted, but it wasn't like she'd ever seen anything like this before. "They're hot springs?"

"Yep." His grin was enormous, his eyes so bright, she knew exactly what he'd looked like as a child. "Come on."

Without waiting for a second invitation, she got undressed and followed him into the water.

"I'm never leaving," Leo groaned in a voice that Elias felt to the tip of his cock.

This place was pure magic. Oh, it might stink of sulfur, but everyone knew that was good for your skin. Being warm and clean now that they'd soaped up, soaking aching muscles, reclining beside the most beautiful woman he'd ever known... He'd take a little sulfur smell in exchange for those things any day.

She shifted, her leg brushed his, and he got impossibly harder, painfully so, though the pain was all relative, given that it felt good at the same time. So good to sit beside her, to watch her truly relax, easing lower and lower until her breasts no longer bobbed at the surface.

Which was a shame.

She moved again subtly, her hip connecting with his and staying there. He couldn't complain. Could only luxuriate.

"Still hungry?" he finally worked up the energy to ask.

When she didn't respond, he slitted his eyes and watched her turn, bringing their faces close enough to almost touch. Her sigh enveloped him like a siren's call—beautiful, all-consuming, and impossible to deny.

And, hell, why should he?

With a slow inhale, he leaned in, put his nose to hers, and drank in that sigh, made it his like something he could take inside and hold forever.

"Thank you," she whispered.

"Don't thank me, thank..."

She pulled back to give him her *shut up* look and he amended his statement. "You're welcome." He turned forward, set his head back on the rock ledge, and smiled lazily up at the sky, uncaring as rain pelted his face.

"Ever see passenger jets fly over here?"

"Sometimes. Rarely, but sometimes." He shut his eyes. "More often bush planes."

"Not the same feeling."

He glanced at her and then watched, transfixed. Her rain-slick face glowed from the barest of lights from above. It limned her elegant forehead, highlighted those cheekbones, already more sharply cut than when he'd first seen her, shone bright on the sweet curves of eyelids. She looked, in this liminal place, like something otherworldly, straight from his dreams. But the feel of her was pure, solid earth. Reality and fantasy in one.

Strange to see her still for once.

"What feeling?" he murmured, wishing he could touch her without breaking the spell.

"Of everything out there. Everything to see. All the people going places, traveling, cities, worlds… Other places to be." She inhaled audibly, the exhale shaky. "Always wanted to be someplace else. Go farther, higher, faster, you know? Just *go*."

Which made this stillness all the more unexpected.

He met her eye and gave a tiny nod, though he didn't truly understand. He didn't thirst for the same things she did.

She snuffled out a laugh. "Always heard the story, growing up, about going to day care and watching the planes fly by. Apparently, the personnel carried me all the time." She glanced his way, one side of her mouth lifted in a smile. "I was pretty darned cute."

He pictured a tiny Leo, round-headed, with fat cheeks and those chubby baby thighs, big brown eyes playful and soulful in equal measures. Of course they carried her everywhere. He'd bet baby Leo'd had every adult she ever met wrapped around her fat little finger. "Sounds familiar."

"That's right. You think I'm cute."

"You are. You're also…" He couldn't say it. Couldn't open himself to her like that. "I meant the carrying you everywhere part."

She made a wry noise and elbowed him gently.

"As I was saying…" She pointed up at the sky. "Planes would fly by and I'd point at 'em before I could even talk. I'd look at the women, all excited, eyes wide, like, *Hey! D'you see that? See!?* They'd nod. *Okay, Leo.* As soon as the plane disappeared, I'd give them the baby sign for more." She tapped the gathered tips of her fingers together like two beaks pecking. "More! More!"

He laughed, the feeling lazy and warm in his gut, so easy he almost didn't notice how rare it was. "You were addicted to planes even then."

She nodded. "Yeah. Always wanted to fly." Another sigh and she laid her head on his shoulder. He didn't dare move. "After Mom…died, Dad was convinced I'd be an opera singer, like her."

"Wait, what?" he asked, careful not to dislodge her. "Your mom was a singer?"

"Yeah. Pretty well-known too."

The weight of her loss settled on him with devastating familiarity. "I'm sorry, Leo."

He reached for her hand, landed on her slick, naked thigh instead, and moved away. A second later, she delved into the water and found him, threaded her fingers through his in that way that felt perfect, and let him hold her—or held him. He couldn't tell. Wasn't sure he even cared.

That was the way with her, wasn't it? Sharing, trusting.

"What about you?" She shifted closer, pressed their sides together.

His first attempted *What?* didn't clear his vocal cords, so he tried again. "What about me what?"

"Did you know who you were? What you were? When you were a kid."

A fugitive from the law? An accused murderer? A recluse roughing it solo in the wild? He didn't say the words. It wasn't what she'd meant and he refused to drag the moment down. Instead, he considered, long and hard.

"I wasn't anything special. You know, my dad worked for the oil company and Mom stayed home with me. I didn't go to school till I was in first grade, I think. Childhood was just this. Being outside."

Her little noise of acknowledgment wasn't quite a laugh, but it was close.

"Right? Got recruited to play ball in high school, 'cause I was big and fast. In shape from…just *being*, I guess." He wrinkled his brow in thought. "Dependable? Is that too boring? Is that sad? Even as a kid, I was big and dependable."

"You're not boring." Her sniff made him think she was crying, but it was impossible to tell with the rain in the mix. And what was there to cry about anyway? "You're so fucking beautiful, Elias."

In the next split second, he was on her, tasting her, drinking up her… Damn, this couldn't be love, could it? Already? It felt like it, though. It felt warm and real and urgent in a way he couldn't ignore. Didn't freaking want to.

He gripped her waist with one hand and cupped her far hip with the other, pulled her onto his lap, and used every bit of will-power to keep himself from sliding right inside this body that had, in such a short time, become the absolute center of his existence.

Though he wanted that. More than anything right now. More than life, probably, and that was big coming from a guy who had nothing to his name but a brain and a beating heart.

———

"Okay, Jack," Amka muttered to herself. "You better be ready, boy-o."

She pulled a helmet over her head and squinted through the dark plastic as dogs barked everywhere, so loud and hungry that you'd think there were fifty of 'em instead of the couple dozen she'd released from the kennels. She couldn't help a little chuckle at that. Poor dogs. Those bastards better not hurt a hair on the dogs' hides.

She wouldn't give them the chance to anyway.

"Here I come, Daisy," she muttered under her breath as she turned the key and revved the engine. "Coming to get you, baby." She exhaled. "Sorry about the window." A laugh escaped her, half-hysterical.

"Sorry, Ben." Though it was about time he replaced this piece of shit truck.

With that, she took her foot off the brake and let the old Explorer roll down the hill toward the lodge.

She took another slow, deep breath in and let it out. Nope. Not gonna be nervous about this. Not gonna let it scare her. If this was it, this was it. Hell, she'd always liked the idea of going out in a blaze of glory.

One of the dogs howled, then more joined in and it turned into a frenzy. She accelerated.

Too bad Daisy wasn't here beside her. It'd be one hell of a Thelma and Louise moment. Except in their story, they'd survive and raise hell together for the rest of their days.

The old Explorer picked up speed, bouncing over rocks and ruts on its way downhill.

She gripped the wheel tighter, fighting hard to keep the vehicle in line. Wouldn't do them a lick of good if she wound up in the lake, would it?

Somewhere not too far off, one of her makeshift bombs exploded, making her jump. Her breath came in nervous, excited little gasps. Hell, if it startled her, the baddies at the lodge must be jumping out of their skins by now, right?

Did they see her yet? Were those dicks aiming at her? Or would they be caught with their pants down when she plowed through the lodge's back window?

Please God, let Jack the pilot have done his job. Please, God, please. If he'd done it right, then her people would be armed and ready for Amka's arrival. She'd distract the guards and they'd have their chance at an uprising. *Away from the window*, she'd told Surfer Jack, like twelve times. Dear God, please let them be away from the window.

Whoo, she felt good now, alive and awake and over-the-top excited—like electricity ran through her veins.

The urge to duck and wrap her arms around her head grew stronger the closer she got. A hundred feet, fifty… She forced her gloved hands to stay on that wheel, kept her eyes on the lodge's big, well-lit bay window, not daring to blink or look away. At maybe thirty feet she saw movement inside, heard what might have been a shot.

Was that one of them? Shit. *Shit!* She ducked just as the guy standing inside lifted his rifle and shot at her. Instead of braking, as she'd planned—cause Lord knew, Daisy really would kill her if she destroyed the whole damn lodge—she shoved her foot back on the accelerator and went for him, hell-for-leather.

The crash was deafening—glass shattering, wood splintering, people screaming.

Shaken, but conscious, Amka came to a breathless stop, then sat there for a good ten seconds before she remembered to slide the gearshift into park, trembling so hard she couldn't hit the seat-belt button on the first couple of tries.

By the time she'd gotten it off and laid her hands on her rifle, the place had settled a bit. She lifted the weapon and pointed at the first thing that moved, though she couldn't see a damn thing. "Take a step and you're bear meat."

"It's me—Daisy."

Amka squinted, unsure. Were they being coerced? Daisy sounded weird. "Must've got glass in my eyes. Can't see a god—"

Someone grabbed the helmet and pulled it off her head, giving her back the gifts of sight and sound and oxygen.

She squinted at the people around her—Daisy and Ben, Cane and the rest of the crew. None of the asshole bad guys were visible.

"Shit. I could have sworn it was one of those pricks aiming at me. Did you already subdue 'em?" Her heart dropped into her stomach. "Don't tell me that was you I just tried to run over, Daisy?"

"No, honey. No, you got the last one." Daisy wrapped one strong arm around Amka's shoulder and hugged her tight.

"Damn, lady." Jack's grin was wide and white and bloodthirsty as hell. "That was one hell of a stunt."

"You get through to Leo's friends?" Amka peered at him through the dust. "Don't know if Marion and the kids have had any luck."

"No, ma'am." He lifted a sat phone. "Workin' on it."

With an impatient sound, Daisy put one hand on Amka's cheek and nudged her face in her direction. "You did it all, honey. And just in time."

"Good." Amka kissed Daisy long and hard, finally admitting how scared she'd been, then stepped back to take in the wreckage. "Guess we better start cleaning this shit up."

CHAPTER 34

THE BLOOD RUSHING THROUGH LEO'S VEINS SHOULD HAVE been slow and sleepy from the heat of the water, but instead, it raced through her, burning a hot path from her heart to her limbs and back.

The second Elias pulled her onto him, they kissed, and it was nothing like the kisses they'd shared thus far. There was no exploration, no seeking, nothing sweet or new. It was all need and crushing hunger, gnashing teeth and battling tongues. Before she knew it, she was writhing on his lap, desperate for him, starving for this fire they'd lit together.

His big hands—so *capable,* so steady and strong—were now demanding and rough. There was nothing steady about the way he handled her, like he couldn't get enough, like he didn't just want her, he *needed* her.

"Elias," she said into his mouth, her body moving, out of control. She couldn't stay still, couldn't get her muscles to do what she wanted. These urges were as uncontrollable as hunger, as unconscious as breathing. He made her feel *fevered.* She let out a little scream and he ate it right from her mouth, consumed it the way she pictured him consuming the rest of her. And she itched, my God, why was she burning like this—not from the hot springs, but from a desire to get inside this man. To do things, to be *done* by him.

"Hell yes. Yeah, do that again."

She blinked, tried to look at him, though it was too hard to see and she had no idea what she'd just done. All she knew was that her breasts needed contact, her nipples needed his hands, his cock, his mouth. She was burning with it, not just hungry, but different...

rearranged by him, by their raging connection. Like she'd changed for him, somehow, created a space for him. And now he needed to fill it.

This isn't okay, a little voice of reason intoned. She didn't change for a man, she'd never make a space in her life for someone else. That wasn't who she was at all.

He bit her neck, pulled her away from her nagging fear, her worry that if she let him in, she'd never be enough on her own.

"Hey."

She dove in, bit his lip, worked her hips in a tight circle.

"Hey, Leo. *Leo.*"

His hands moved from her waist, grabbed her wrists, and held her still. Or at least tried to. She wasn't having any of this thinking business, not letting the doubts wiggle in and poison what was just a moment of enjoyment. Pure pleasure, no emotions, nothing that could hurt her.

She wouldn't let him inside her that way. Would never put her heart on the line.

"Leo, sweetheart. *Leo.*" He let her wrists go and cradled her face with such sweetness, such care, she knew what a liar she was. She was already lost. "Leo, sweetheart, you're crying."

She nodded, tried to smile, and gave up on that, like she'd just given up on guarding her heart and soul and body from this man. It was probably too fast and too urgent and too early for love, but it was there. As undeniable as the solid body beneath hers, the rock supporting them both.

Rather than use words she could never take back, she leaned in and told him how she felt with her lips and her eyes and the tears streaming down her face.

By the time she realized what she'd done, it was too late to take back the kiss and the message behind it. With a sigh, she kissed him harder, gave him more, and committed herself without an ounce of regret.

"Sweetheart. Leo. God, Leo, let me get a condom. Don't…" She lifted up, suspended above his cock, and for a few seconds, he was so ready to do it like this and all the consequences be damned.

Hell, who knows? his reckless side chimed in. *We could die tomorrow, right?*

"I'll get it." She stretched, giving him the perfect opportunity to explore her shoulder, her side, her shoulder blade—all the hidden secrets—and yanked at the pouch he'd left by the side of the pool. Hopeful, assuming too much maybe. Whatever. Right now, all he could do was thank God he'd saved these last few condoms after his brief foray into town last year.

"I love how prepared you are," she said as she ripped open the package.

"Always buy a pack in town." He shrugged. "Actually forgot that was in my bag, but I'd rather be prepared than left in the cold, you know?"

Biting her lip, she put the condom on the tip of his cock and looked up at him. "You have any idea how sexy that is? A man who's ready for anything?"

"Uh…" He shook his head and stared down at her hands working the rubber over his stiff dick. "Hm?"

"It's the hottest thing I've ever seen." She ran one hand down his shaft, then the other, squeezing him tightly. "Wow, Elias."

With a last look and a shaky breath, she met his gaze again, head-on. "Ready?"

"I'm…*very* excited right now." He laughed and blew out a hard breath. "Never been readier."

"Same, Elias."

"You want this."

"Oh yes. I want this. I want *you*."

Everything inside him went warm and liquid.

All he could do was hold her, eyes focused on the top of her head and the soaked, fresh bandage he'd applied, her square shoulders, her smooth arms, those lush hips, straddling him, lined with light, shiny stretch marks that were absolutely perfect, like every other part of her. Flesh and blood, muscle and bone, strong though too vulnerable for his taste. If she were his, he'd encase her in armor, Kevlar, steel, and cushion her with cotton, or silk or whatever was the softest thing in the world.

They breathed for a bit in unison, now that the initial frenzy had died down, and he could've sworn he felt the beating of her heart.

Strong and steady and sure. And the longer he looked at her arms, the more details came out—like the pores and tiny hairs. The power in those thighs, the resilience of a woman who'd almost died more than once these last few days. A couple of scars here and there, in varying shades of silver and brown and tan. He wanted the story behind every scar, wanted to *know* her—from that little girl who'd wanted more airplanes to the woman she'd become, he wanted to know every little piece of her.

He focused on the bandage on her head again—thought of the scar that would one day be another mark to add to her story. It was healing so fast, she almost didn't need it wrapped anymore.

She almost didn't need him.

"Now who's in his head?" That thin, tensile hand gripped his beard and pulled up—not hard, but enough to sting, to bring him back. "Who's thinking instead of enjoying this moment? Hm?"

"It's hard, Leo."

"No." She sniffled and gave him a smile. "*You* are hard. And you've got a condom on. And I really, really want to know how you'll feel inside me." She arched up, her breasts taunting his chest, her mouth close enough to kiss, though she didn't. Breathless, he waited. "Can I come on your cock, Elias?"

More blood rushed south, making his erection almost too hard, too hot to touch. "Probably not if you keep talking like that."

She smiled and kissed him, took her soft heat away long enough to fist his erection, and pressed him to that place where he so desperately needed to be.

He watched, transfixed, as the tip disappeared. And then she stopped.

His gaze rose to meet hers.

"I'm sorry." She sniffled.

"What?" Shit, she was crying again. "Oh, sweetheart." His chest tightened and he tried to back away, to give her space. "We don't have to do this if you're not sure."

"No. No." Slowly, so slowly, she sank another inch, taking him inside her body. "I'm just scared of…how I *feel*, Elias. Why do I feel like this with you?"

How? How did she feel?

His body wanted to thrust and his brain wanted to comfort, but somehow he held himself perfectly still, listening and watching and waiting for what came next.

"I want you to feel…" He grunted when she backed up and worked her way down him again. "Good. Leo, I want to make you feel *good*."

This was heaven. Her lush heat, the slow give and take of her body—their bodies together. He just wished he knew how to wipe that tragic expression from her face.

"Me, too, but I…" She swallowed and leaned into his chest. Was she hiding? "Never mind." She arched her back again, turned to the side, her face tight, and took him in so deep and fast, he had to shut his eyes so he wouldn't explode right there.

Which would be a terrible idea given…everything. And there was a lot here. A lot going on—some that he got, some that he didn't. He'd never been the most astute when it came to women.

He put his hands on her waist, moved them down to her hips and squeezed, getting enough purchase to lift her slowly before she slid back down on her own. They built something, one unhurried thrust at a time, each leisurely penetration kindling their passion, their connection.

And while their bodies worked seamlessly together, he recognized that he hadn't imagined what was happening under the surface. He felt rearranged by this woman. His insides would never be the same again.

Another languid up, a slow, sweet down. Another and another, the water lapping at them, the sky pouring down. Together, they were fire and water and earth and air. Together, they were *everything*.

She gave him more, pressed harder; he went faster, groaned with every slick slide of her, every tight embrace, every glance from those big, intense eyes.

And then he couldn't keep the words in anymore. "You're *mine*, Leo." She tightened around him. "Mine." He lifted a hand to weigh her soft breast, to flick her nipple, then up to caress those voluptuous lips. "I can't..."

"Can't what?"

"Let you go. I can't."

Her movements stuttered, the rhythm fell apart, and she released a wounded little noise, ending on a rough, "*Kiss me.*"

He leaned forward and gave her what she wanted, though he couldn't stop at that. He stood and turned so she could put her feet on the edge, and he took her, hard and fast.

"I'm coming."

"Yeah." She wrapped herself around him, put her cheek to the top of his head and let out a low, constant groan. It sounded almost like pain. And maybe it was. Tearing them apart after this would be like ripping off a bandage. Worse: like losing a piece of himself.

"Me too."

"What do you need?"

"Just this. Just you, Elias."

It was coming. He was coming. Hard. Harder maybe than

he'd ever come in his life. And now, past the point of no return, he couldn't have held it back if someone came over the hill shooting.

How could he, when she was moaning his name like she loved him?

———————

It took a while to come down. Once she'd caught her breath and disentangled herself from his body, Leo moved to get out of the water, bracing herself for the tight-bellied regret that almost always came after sex.

Only it didn't this time. Not when he joined her in the cold, wet rain, wrapped her in a blanket, and picked her up. Not when she giggled all the way to the old cabin, let him dry her and dried him in return, before snuggling into the bed they'd set up earlier. Not when he made his slow way down from her mouth, over her body, giving every pore, every hair the kind of attention it had never received, winding up between her legs, where he made slow, sweet love with his mouth.

And tongue.

And teeth and nose and beard.

Good Lord, he was good at this.

She didn't scream when she orgasmed—they'd been quietly cautious even in their wildest moments—but she felt it in the deep, dark reaches of her core.

In the aftermath, she looked down at his silhouette in the dark and knew that this was it.

They'd probably have nothing in common outside this place, probably wouldn't even get along, but she didn't *care*.

Getting along was overrated after all.

He moved slowly back up, kissed her taste into her mouth, and flopped to his side with a happy groan.

"My turn." She started to move, but he stopped her with his hand on her shoulder.

"No…I…" He snorted, giving her a sheepish smile. "I want to see your face. The first time we…you…go down there."

Oh boy. Something twisted in her chest. "Okay."

"I want to be inside you again." Another smile. "But we've got to eat first."

"Keep up our strength." Their shared smile tapered off.

"You want this, Leo? What we're doing? You like it?"

A funny sound escaped her. "Like it?" She started to shake her head and stopped when it occurred to her that it might send the wrong signals. "'Like' is too weak a word for this. Whatever it is."

He didn't move. Not an eyelash stirred, not a muscle twitched, but something changed in the way he watched her. "What do you think it is, Leo?"

"Do I think this would have happened in the outside world? Is that what you're asking?"

"Maybe."

The question fluttered in her throat. If she stood up now, her knees might not hold her. "This is where it happened. Where this"—she flapped her hand between them—"was made."

He blinked, narrowed his eyes and waited.

"My parents used to tell the story of how they fell in love. People went wild. *So romantic*, they'd say. Now that I think about it, though, it wasn't really their story. It was my dad's."

Elias's brows rose, but he didn't otherwise move.

"Saw her in London. 1975. Starring in *Aida*." She huffed out a little breath and threw him a smiling glance. "Mama was known for her charisma."

"Bet she could sing, too."

She laughed. "That's putting it mildly. Growing up, there were a ton of framed reviews on the music room wall. They called her the Ethiopian Queen."

"That where she was from?"

She nodded. "In one of them, the critic said that she had the voice that launched a thousand ships."

"Whoa."

"Yeah. The story goes that Dad fell in love with her the second she opened her mouth. By intermission, he was fried. Had the conductor—a colleague—introduce them after the show. Two days later, they were planning her move to the U.S."

"That's…fast."

"Right? Mama said she'd never met someone who got her like Dad did. Who knew her inside out. So, maybe it's…" She huffed out a strangled sound, so out of her element here, with this opening up her soul thing. At the same time, she felt compelled to tell him. "My point is…who's to say how these things are supposed to happen? Is *this* less legitimate than if we'd met in a bar or in some college class?"

"*No.*" The word dropped into the quiet room between them, solid as the rock floor they stood on.

"I doubted their love for a long time, you know? Doubted everything pretty much, after she died." Unconsciously, Leo's eyes rose to the dark ceiling. "After she *killed* herself." The tears were back, only this time, they weren't the clean, flowing kind. These were sharp, stagnant things that had sat too long inside her.

"Why?"

"Yeah, that's not something I'll ever know."

"Your dad…"

"Destroyed." She half shrugged. "I figured it was my fault?"

"Oh, sweetheart." She let him move close, didn't stop him when he put a big arm around her. "Still think that?"

Shaking her head put her face right against his chest, where he smelled good—like smoke and mountains, with a hint of sulfur. "Depression and some of the meds she was on were probably at least partly to blame. My dad pushed her, too, you know? To be this big diva when she'd been talking about retiring for a while. Maybe teaching. Spending time with me. It wasn't his fault either."

"Where is your dad? Now, I mean."

She sighed. "He's alone. In a…place. A home, I mean. For people with Alzheimer's."

"Shit. I'm sorry."

"She's still alive as far as he knows, so…silver lining, right?" Elias's arms went tighter, drew her in until there was no space between them. No chance she could fall. "I'm sorry," she managed to gulp between sobs.

"Stop it."

"I…I…can't."

"Not crying. I mean apologizing. Don't apologize for what you feel, Leo."

"I don't cry. I never cry." The next sob was laced with humor. "God, you'll never believe that."

"Sure I do."

"Seriously." She was giggling now, though the tears and laughter were indistinguishable. A little levity to lighten the pain. "I didn't cry when she died. Didn't cry at her funeral or when I…" She gulped back her next words.

"When you what?"

"How about I save some of my"—*hiccup*—"stories for another day?"

"I want it when you're ready. All of it. Everything you've got to give—good or bad. The hard shit. The sad. I want every little bit of you." He leaned down, put his lips to the side of her head, and whispered, "You don't scare me, Leo Eddowes."

"No?" She sniffled, her voice thick with emotion. "Well, you scare the living hell out of me."

———

They ate quietly, side by side, bodies touching, feelings too close to the surface to disguise and too new to talk about. Leo was wrung out, shaken, but not weak. Like a person after major surgery, everything ached—including her soul—but under that was a better life, a strength she'd never felt.

After years of shoving the truth deep down, she'd ripped herself open, exposed her innards to the light of day, and now needed to heal.

The scarring process, she figured, would hurt like hell, but this newfound fragility felt precious.

After dinner, she went off to clean herself up, stumbling in the dark as she went.

"You okay?" Elias called from inside the dilapidated cabin.

"Yep."

"Need help?"

She opened her mouth to say no and changed her mind. "Not right now."

By the time she returned, he'd cleaned up their dinner stuff and set the bedding up again. Without lifting her head from the floor, a sated Bo woofed a gentle greeting that made Leo smile.

Without discussion, they settled under the covers, and though they'd been here before, Leo couldn't help a nervous thrill at his nearness.

"Something I've been thinking about, Leo." Elias's voice rumbled through his big chest.

She snuggled closer. "What's that?"

"How long's your dad been sick?"

"Got bad about five years ago." She swallowed down the bitter taste of guilt. "Noticeable to me, I mean."

"Is that when you left the military?"

She released a long, slow breath. "Yeah."

"Your team know your dad? Von and Ant or—"

"Ans. Short for Anselm." She smiled. "Can't believe you

remember their names. We call Von the Grim Reaper and Ans is Ladykiller."

His brows lifted. "What about you?"

"I'm Terminator. Or, if they're being really annoying, Arnie."

"Oooooh. That's rough."

"Right."

"Eric Cooper. He's kind of the leader, right? And Ford's his brother. The scientist who's with the chef."

She paused. "When did I even tell you this?"

"I listen. I take an interest."

"Apparently so. I feel…" *Seen.*

"Remember what you told me, Leo? That I wasn't alone anymore?"

"Yeah."

"I know you've got your crew, but…guess I wanted to say that you're not either. Alone, I mean."

Fresh emotion prickled through her. "Don't."

"Don't what?"

"Make me cry again."

"Okay," he whispered, stroking her back, her side, her back again. "Okay, sweetheart." The long, slow sweeps of his hand over her thin base layer put her to sleep like a lullaby.

At some point in the night, the touches changed, his or hers, she couldn't say, but caresses turned to nudges, sighs turned to pants, laziness to intent. She was on her side, with Elias behind her, one hand working her breast, sensual and slow.

The touch lacked the urgency of their previous encounters but had another element she couldn't quite put her finger on. It was dreamy, comforting.

She arched her back, pushing her hips toward him, and felt him, hard. Another shift brought them closer. He grunted when she ground against him and—there—a taste of their earlier frenzy.

"I want…" She reached back and found his erection, hot and hard and ready.

"Yeah…"

"Can you…"

"Yeah." He yanked at her pants, pulled them down so her ass was bare, and let her feel how badly he wanted this. "*Yeah.*"

"Elias." It was all she could say. One word, though it felt like she'd offered up her heart.

"Hang on." He disappeared for a few moments, taking his firm, heady heat. She barely heard the sounds of him rummaging in his coat pocket, followed by crinkling foil and snapping rubber through the quick beating of her heart. His return was preceded by the acrid scent of latex. "Let's get this off." He yanked the pants the rest of the way off her body—without much help from her—slid in behind her again, and nudged her top leg until she lifted it. At the feel of his blunt, heavy tip against her, she tilted until he lined up and slid slowly in.

They shared a sigh as his body filled hers, the sensation still not entirely comfortable, although she was wet.

Yeah, well, if this adventure had taught her one thing, it was that comfort was overrated.

After a minute or two of just being together, he moved and she responded, each taking turns leading their bodies in this magical, electrifying dance. Only this time, orgasm didn't seem to be his goal, any more than it was hers. It was togetherness they sought.

Every slow slide brought more heaviness, more heat, more sighs of contentment, desire. She had no idea how long he stayed in her like that, how long the ascent lasted. But at some point— could have been hours later—he tightened his full-body hug, deepened the penetration, and came hard, with a low noise that she felt to her marrow.

After recovering, he reached down—still inside her—and

rubbed tight circles over her clit. Panting, she came, not even a little surprised when she started leaking tears again.

This must be the new normal. The feelings right there on the surface, instead of suppressed.

He pulled out, arms around her, and lay still for a bit before getting up—probably to deal with the condom, maybe to get away from the soupy swamp of emotion she couldn't seem to contain around him. When he didn't immediately return, she rolled into a ball under the blankets, trying to prepare herself for the possibility that she'd cried one too many times with the guy.

The scuff of his returning feet told her she'd underestimated him.

Without a word, he climbed in and eased his big body in front of hers, then sort of under her until her head was on his chest.

She rubbed her face into him, breathed him in, and let herself be happy. So she'd cried a few more tears. Maybe what she felt for him was too big to be contained. Trusting him and winning his trust had opened her up to the possibility of something deeper. It felt good to let him in—cathartic actually.

His hand rubbed circles on her back with a familiarity that spoke of years together, not days. Years of this closeness. What would that be like?

She stretched and made a low, happy sound, fully coming to when his voice rumbled gently in her ear.

"Mom and Dad fell in love at first sight."

The words sent a shiver down her back. When he didn't go on, she prompted him. "Seriously? Yours, too?"

"Mom's blind date never showed. And this guy sitting beside her at the lunch counter bought her a milkshake. Said something cheesy about pretty girls looking sad. Way he told it, she rolled her eyes and turned away, telling him that she wasn't interested in smiling for any man."

Leo chuckled. "Sounds about right."

"Said he was done right there. Kaput. Like lock, stock, and whatever. Told me never to settle for a woman who didn't challenge me. Said I'd hate my life if I chose easy instead of interesting." His breathing was too measured, as if he were holding it in, doing his best to control it. "Karen—my ex. The one I was supposed to marry. She was nice. I mean a really good person."

Leo snorted. "She left you."

"Can you blame her?"

"Yes. *Yes*, I blame her." Leo would never do that. Never. "I won't get mad about it. Her loss and all that." She settled back into his warmth, a little surprised at how worked up she'd gotten. "My gain."

He gathered her close and sighed against the top of her head. "I'm wild about you, Leo. No matter what happens, I'll never regret a moment of this. Not one single second."

"And if we wake up surrounded by bad guys tomorrow?"

"Not gonna happen."

She stiffened. "How do you know?"

"While you were heating up dinner, I set my traps."

She settled back down. "Any chance of Bo stepping in them?"

"She knows better." He nudged her, as if to remind her that she'd almost stepped in one herself. "We've been practicing this shit for ages."

Sadness welled up at that thought—at a life spent preparing for the worst.

"Don't."

"What?"

"Don't get maudlin about me again, Leo."

"I'm not."

"Good." He tightened his arm and kissed her head. "'Cause I don't think I've ever been happier than I am right now."

CHAPTER 35

Elias couldn't sleep, despite his exhaustion and the relative safety of their surroundings. It wasn't just the unfamiliarity of holding Leo in his arms, it was the fear of losing her. What if this was it? This one night, his only chance at being with her.

He couldn't relax, couldn't lay his mind to rest. If this was it, he wanted to be awake for every single second.

So, rather than fight wakefulness, he embraced it and let himself be. With her, let her smell comfort and stir him, let her low, cute snore reassure him, let the feel of her body restore him.

He must have fallen asleep for a while, because maybe half an hour before sunrise, he came to and found her awake.

"You okay?" he asked, his voice rough and groggy.

She nodded.

"Sleep any?"

"Yeah. Really well, actually."

A predawn light shone through the room's single window, glowing blueish. "Want to see something?" he asked, though really, they should try to sleep a bit more.

"You know it."

Fuck, he loved her. And not in the sweet, comfortable way he'd loved Karen, but so deeply, the feeling so raw and harsh and new it hurt. He didn't love her with his heart, he loved her with his skin and bones and guts. Or maybe his heart, but not one of those pretty ones that people drew with their fingers in the air. No, his love was coarse and earthy and real, pumped full of blood and its own electric current.

"Come on," he said, as gruff and unpolished as the yeti she'd called him. "Boot up."

Without a word, they dressed. He grabbed his rifle and led the way out the door and up a set of rickety wooden stairs. Around the corner, through a wooden structure, out the door, and up more steps, then more. The river rushed alongside them, washing ice and snow and debris from the top of the mountain to the lake, accelerating breakup.

His lungs puffed faster as they rose to the top of the peak. Though subtle, there was a change in the air after yesterday's storm. It didn't smell like winter anymore. It was full of rotting grass, fermented berries, and decomposing remains, newly unearthed and cloying. Death giving way to the fresh flush of life. Seedlings and buds popping out with their own sharp perfumes. Sulfur from the springs wafted on the air, weighted by what smelled like mushrooms but was actually mud, thawing after months beneath the snow. It wasn't good or bad as far as scents went. It was just... Alaska. Just life.

Bo trotted up beside him and stopped, one paw raised, ears pricked. Out of habit, he stopped with her, chuffing out a lungful of air when Leo bumped into him. She put her arms around him to steady herself, silent and no doubt ready to roll in case of trouble. He pressed his hand to hers and squeezed once, not as a sign of intrusion but of affection. He turned and smiled and held back the desire to pick her up just to hold her. "Almost there," he whispered, his eyes scanning the east for that first glow. "Better hurry."

Faster now, he climbed, the half-rotted, creaking steps warning him to tread carefully. About twenty yards from the top, the sun pierced through and he knew it would be worth the extra trip.

At the top, he waited, grabbed Leo's hand, and held her still. "Close your eyes."

She did without hesitation.

"Here." He sat on a rock and pulled her onto his lap, enjoying her weight on him. "Okay, open."

He craned his neck to watch her face instead of the view and for a second, there was no reaction, nothing. Then he felt her indrawn breath.

He tore his eyes from her and looked, making himself see it as if for the first time. Funny how his lungs did that same capture and release hers just had, his mouth dropped open like hers, his eyes wide and avid, taking in the scene like they were hungry for beauty.

"I've never…" Another shaky breath from Leo, this one deep and slow. "This is astonishing."

He nodded, rubbing the side of his face against her shoulder.

"There's a name for this, right?"

"Alpenglow."

"I thought it was a sunset thing."

"Happens when the sun's just below the horizon." He shrugged, feeling like a dog offering up a bone.

"Hugging the horizon." She lifted her shoulders and settled back into him with a sigh.

Content and calm, he put his cheek to the side of her head and took it all in—the star-dusted sky, still flirting with night, the jagged edges of the mountains, carved sharply in the east and opposite, washed with the sun's nascent glow. None of it looked real, though he knew from experience that it didn't get more solid than this. Society's constructs, now that was a load of bullshit. But this, right here—this was the real stuff.

"You'll miss this." Her voice touched that deep, aching place inside him.

Everything he'd been feeling wadded up in his throat, knotting hard and implacable.

He tightened his arms and forced words past the obstruction. "You're talking like you know what's next."

When she shifted, he didn't expect her to twist and lean back to get her leg over, squirming until she straddled him. His arms loosened but stayed around her to keep her from falling backwards, and something about the trust in that one move hollowed him out and somehow made him whole again.

"We're next," she whispered as she wrapped her cold hands around his hot neck. "You. Me." She glanced to where the dog sat, tongue lolling, ears half-perked, content to enjoy the scenery alongside her people. "Borealis Thorne."

He'd already started shaking his head when she moved her hands up and into his hair, catching it in her fingers and tugging. The sting tingled from his head to the bottom of his feet, pooling warm between his legs.

"Us" was all she said before she put her lips to his to prove it.

Christ, he could die right here, in this sun-washed place, with the scents of newborn life all around him. He could die and he'd be fine. More than fine. He'd be in heaven.

———

Pleasure hummed through Leo's nerves, buzzing over her skin and loosening her bones, even through the coat and the layers of clothes. She'd forgotten her gloves in her haste, which would be a problem if her fingers weren't warm against Elias's face and in his hair and raking through his backwoods beard. His mouth—so grim when she'd first seen him—was nothing but heat and lush pleasure. And hunger. Mostly that, which she couldn't help but echo.

Her hips moved of their own volition, circling slow and hard against his erection. It made her want him all the more. His desire—so obvious it was almost innocent—was as appealing as his hard exterior and molten center. Earning this man's trust was the best thing she'd ever done.

Because together, they were more than the sum of their parts.

He groaned and tightened his hold, lifting his hips to get more, harder, closer. Fuck, she loved this—him. The way their brains worked and their bodies played and everything they did made sense. Together.

His mouth opened and she slid her tongue alongside his, his taste and smell as perfect as any part of the landscape. The thought made her eyes open and land on his. His opened a second later, the sun refracting through the green like through a glass bottle, his pale tan skin washed in pink and orange, the half-night sky still above him.

She went still, framing his face with her hands, and leaned back. "What?"

She chuffed out a nervous laugh and shook her head. "Nothing."

"You look spooked."

She opened her mouth and shut it, fell forward, and put her head on his shoulder. "Thank you," she whispered in his ear.

"For what?"

"Showing me this."

"Figured you'd like it."

Humming her assent, Leo closed the gap with his neck and kissed it, letting her tongue slide over his skin, under his chin, and up, rubbing her face to his soft beard and then putting her nose to his. "You smell good."

He gave her a disbelieving smile.

"You do. Like a safe, warm place. It's sexy." She grinned, a little abashed. "I'm know. I'm ridiculous."

"You're beautiful."

Something shifted—a bank of clouds scuttling across to block the sun's rays, stealing dawn's heat and light and with it the feeling that they could stay here forever. They turned, as one, cheeks pressed together. "Show's over."

She nodded, breathing him in, along with the bittersweet cocktail of Alaska coming to life after a long winter. With one last look at the blue and white and pink of the world waking up, Leo pressed her lips to his, and rose. "I'm starving."

He stood and looked down at her, his expression peaceful and happy, smile almost young. "Then let's get you fed."

―――――――――――

Ash almost stumbled when he caught sight of the building. It was hard to see in the early light, but he didn't need details to know. They were here. If not now, then recently. He could feel it, could taste their presence on the air. There was nothing magic about it either. All signs pointed here. And who wouldn't prefer a roof over their heads, given the chance?

"Shit." Deegan came up beside him. "What the hell is that?"

"Old copper mine, I reckon." He glanced around at the thick forest and the racing river and amended that. "Or gold. Probably gold."

"Think they're in there?"

After a long, slow inhale, Ash nodded. "Yes. I do."

Deegan didn't wait before trundling off up the path like a fucking bulldozer set on devastation.

Rather than yell or call him, which would surely let anyone know they were here, he hung back and peered through the morning's tepid light.

He'd gone about twenty meters when the scent of sulfur hit him and another few steps more when the bell started ringing.

CHAPTER 36

A BELL RANG JUST AS THEY FINISHED BREAKFAST.

The sound was a light, musical tinkling, alien to this place. Leo's eyes flew up to meet Elias's before the ringing cut off abruptly. "Is that your trap?"

"One of 'em."

"Animal?"

He let out a light snort. "Could be."

"And if it's not?"

"Better haul ass either way."

In the murky interior, she couldn't see his face as he rose and put their breakfast things back into the bag. They were fully dressed and already packed, which made for a speedy exit.

"How long do we have?"

"Five minutes. Ten at most."

Quickly, with a strange calm, they put their things together and got them on their backs. Elias made his way to the door they'd taken this morning, instead of the one leading back the way they'd arrived the night before.

"Wait." She stayed in place. "You said there's only one way out."

"Only one way *in*. There's another way out. Up past the overlook from this morning. It's dangerous."

"I'd be disappointed if it weren't."

With a gruff chuckle, he leaned down and gave her a quick peck on the lips. "And that's one of the things I love so much about you." Another peck. "Because I do." His voice went lower, rougher— half-whisper, half-tearing out his insides. "I fucking love you so hard, Leo Eddowes."

Emotion ballooned inside her, but she would *not* freaking cry today. And then, because she'd already shown him her soft under-belly ten times over at least, and, frankly, nothing had felt better in her life, she let herself say it. Let herself feel how real it was. "I love you too, Elias Thorne."

"Let's go, then." He smiled—damn, he was gorgeous—and led the way, jogging back up the steep steps, through the thick undergrowth lining the valley. They hit the peak, breathing harder than the last time they'd done this. She turned to take it in again—just a glance at the orange-washed, snow-covered peaks, the lake, the deceptively smooth-looking slopes, so much beauty, so much danger—and memorized the sight for another day, another time.

They worked their way down, their feet crunching in slippery patches of snow. She lost her footing, caught herself on a boulder, and almost lost her mind when Elias went down on a slick spot. "Never tried this after a big rain," he muttered with a smirk as he fought his way back to standing. "Snowmelt."

"Your side okay?"

"Yes," he said, grabbing her hand and kissing her hard before forging straight back down the narrow, sheer path.

Finally, Leo's shoulders loosened as the ground flattened out. The tree cover thickened. The sound of rushing water over-whelmed the heavy rasping of her breath. Spine tingling, she glanced over her shoulder, her pulse still going hard after the climb and the descent and the threat of close pursuit. Bo raced ahead and came running back, dancing like she'd found something familiar.

Her footsteps followed Elias's, bringing them so close to the river that her own sounds were entirely drowned out. He stopped a few feet from the bank. She stared, her brain not comprehending for a few seconds.

The river was narrow here, but wild and high and brown, topped with foamy whitecaps and littered with glacier runoff debris. A tree had fallen across it, creating a natural bridge.

"Uh. No." She stepped away from the edge, afraid of heights for the first time in her life.

It wasn't the fifteen-foot drop that scared her. It was the rapids, frothing and roiling, racing around boulders on their way into the valley. Leo took risks all the time, but they were calculated. She liked adrenaline, not actual death.

"I don't—" She bit back a gasp as Bo traipsed over the log spanning the waterway. It was so perfectly placed she wondered if it had been dropped there by humans. She glanced at Elias. Had he somehow put it there?

Back to Bo, whose tiny dog feet couldn't keep from slipping over the slick surface. She slowed toward the end, looking less confident as she reached the thinner part of the log.

"You got it, girl. Go on. Jump."

For possibly the first time in her life, Leo shut her eyes from fear. By the time she opened them again, Bo was safe on the other side and Leo went weak in the knees. Was she having a heart attack? Oh crap, she couldn't watch Elias cross. She couldn't take it. "Look, maybe…is there another…"

"This is it, Leo. We do this, and we're golden." He shook his head and threw her a side-eye. "Ish. Okay?"

"I'm not…"

"Will you trust me on this? I'll get you over. But you've got to trust me."

"I trust you, Elias." She couldn't control the sob welling up inside her. "I just cannot…" *Lose you.* "I can't take it if you fall in."

"I won't. I won't, sweetheart. I've done this a million times." He grabbed her hand. "Come on." The closer they got to the very edge, the louder the river roared until it overwhelmed her with sound and motion, the wind whipping her hair, the meltwater spraying up to lash them.

"Remember the ice cave?" he whispered in her ear. "Remember sitting there laughing? You were so cute. I hadn't laughed in years."

She tried to turn back, but he faced her forward again. "Sit down and scoot across. It's that easy. Scoot and you'll be fine."

"You'll scoot too? No standing up?"

"I'll scoot." His eyes did a quick circuit of their surroundings. "Got to do this now."

She knew he was right. She didn't have to be a daredevil here. So, she sat and pulled herself forward a few inches at a time. At one point, she turned back and he waved, his big hand so steady, his teeth flashing in a confident smile. She moved forward again just as Elias got down to slide on.

Then everything blew apart.

The first gunshot hit the log right next to her fingers, so close she was showered with tiny splinters. She lifted her hand with a yelp.

Oh God. She had another five feet to traverse—at least.

She crab-crawled as fast as she could and then threw herself forward, suddenly more afraid of the gunfire than the crossing.

The next shot tore up the wood she'd just occupied.

In a heartbeat, she went from frantic to wired—adrenaline hitting her in the usual places, lighting her up like a runway, making her sharp and ready in ways she could never explain.

She crouched behind a tree wishing she could return fire when two men appeared on the other side, high on the slope heading down to the river.

One of the men lifted his rifle again to fire—at her or Elias, she wasn't sure. In the next heartbeat, something gave.

The saturated earth that held the piece of waterlogged wood currently straining under Elias's weight just collapsed. Bo barked wildly and leapt back as the bridge went down, the whole thing much too silent for something so terrible.

"Elias!"

The mud slid, painfully slow but too fast. He was there, hanging by one arm, knuckles white where they grasped a branch. Leo screamed when the whole thing sank another few feet, propelling him inexorably toward the rushing water. It was so loud, her scream probably didn't even reach his ears, but he craned up, the movement awkward and painful looking, and met her eyes.

She stopped breathing, stopped thinking entirely. For a handful of seconds, she was nothing more than blinking eyes and beating heart, pumping blood.

Nothing.

She glanced up for a split second to see the shooter draw closer. He'd kill Elias, kill her. She shifted as close to the edge as she could get without getting sucked in.

"Go! Run!" he gasped, the words barely audible against the racing rapids. "Go, Leo!" He strained to get footing on the side of the river, but his feet slid and the log shifted again.

"No!" Her yell echoed off the opposite bank just as the killer slid to a stop. The second approached slower. No time to think. No time to decide. Only time to do. "Do or die!" she shouted, repeating something Elias had said days ago.

It felt like a lifetime ago.

It felt like the end.

At her words, Elias nodded once. He opened his hand and was gone.

All she could do was jump in after him.

"Fucking bastards!" Deegan was irate, his pig eyes frantic and full of rage. Ash wanted to throttle him. Or laugh.

This was a mess. A lovely, odd, interesting mess. If he was smart, he'd turn around and head back to the place they'd just left. There'd been a hot spring there—no doubt exactly what had drawn the fleeing couple to begin with. He could rest his aching muscles for a spell and get the hell out of here.

Then, he'd watched Deegan shoot at them—the idiot—instead of slowly, skillfully reeling them in.

Deegan clearly couldn't believe his eyes. Even after a minute passed, he was still blinking at the place where their quarry had been. Across the river, the dog barked madly.

"Shut up!" the man yelled and the animal immediately stopped.

"Good dog," said Ash with a smile. He could have sworn the dog understood him.

It let out another bark—purely to annoy Deegan, who raised his rifle as if to shoot it—and took off into the woods opposite as if pursued by the hounds of hell.

Ash sighed, taking a look around. "Well, now. You must have a plan, correct?" *Or not.* "Shooting at them was just the first step, I imagine."

"Fuck you."

"Look mate, you've got us in a right mess, it's only fair that you shou—"

"*Shu' up, mate.* I'm thinking."

Good luck with that. Ash eyed his surroundings speculatively. Upriver, the canyon was so steep, they'd need rappelling gear to climb. As well as hours they didn't have, thanks to Deegan's stupid stunt.

"The big guy." Deegan was out of breath, his pacing bringing him awfully close to the river's edge. "That wasn't Campbell Turner."

You twat.

"What's the plan now?"

"*You* shot at them. You tell me." Aside from the path they'd come in on—which was treacherous enough—there was no way out but the river. Ash lifted his chin toward the rapids. "Only one way forward as far as I can see. Shall we?"

"What? Fuck off." Deegan looked more disgusted than anything else. "They won't survive anyway."

"Won't they?" he asked lightly. *Possibly not*, he reasoned with himself. But then again, those two had led them on quite a merry chase. They were resilient. No, he couldn't accept that this was the end of them. After a few silent breaths, he gave in to what his insides demanded—*pursuit*. An answer. And maybe somewhere at the end of this long and terrible road, retribution.

He set his rucksack down and unzipped it. Yes, the couple were likely dead. The job was no doubt over, the trail cold. But…what if they weren't?

He hadn't come this far to give up his mission now.

He pulled out what he sought and shot a glance at Deegan, who paced and cursed by the water's edge, more savage than the dog who'd just taken off.

If there were any chance the other two had survived, Ash wanted to be there. He wanted to *know*.

"I'm not jumping in there." Deegan turned from the water and caught sight of the pack raft.

"I am," Ash replied with a smirk. He held up his oar. "Coming?"

Deegan threw him a dirty look and muttered, "Crazy fucker," before following him down the steep side to the roiling water's edge.

CHAPTER 37

Elias knew how to handle rapids. He just couldn't get into the right position.

For long minutes, he worked hard not to suck in water while he was thrown around like a rag doll. Once he got through the first phase of breathless shock, he struggled to get his legs out in front—took another frigid face full of water and went under, pulled by something heavy.

It took three forceful dips for him to realize his pack was dragging him down, but when he yanked at the straps, he couldn't work it off his body and—*shit*—he just missed getting brained by a rock. The water was shooting him from one side to the other like a damn pinball, his feet hitting boulder after boulder until he couldn't feel them anymore.

Water in his mouth, his head submerged.

He fought hard—too hard probably—and couldn't move. Couldn't push. He was caught on something.

Didn't feel the cold, just the drag of the water, trying to wrestle him off whatever held him here. Fast as he could, he toed off his boots and undid his belt. Still, he was trapped, anchored in place. He pushed his pants down in hopes it would help. Still caught, he blinked, stared at the thing hanging in front of him, reached for it.

His rifle, the strap snagged on a branch. He managed to grab it and yanked, hard. It wouldn't budge.

His lungs burned, his eyes were close to exploding.

Leo'd never truly prayed before. Oh, she'd wished and she'd begged, but she'd never asked for anything.

But something divine happened in that monster of a current. It turned her upside down and tried to shove her under, but instead of fighting, she let it take her.

What did she care if the damn thing killed her? It had Elias and that was all that mattered. It took the man she'd *just* gotten—the only person she'd ever wanted like this—and…and *hell* if it didn't piss her off.

Do or die, she'd told him. Not die or die.

With explosive suddenness, the anger sparked, lit her up, gave her fire to fight the water and from one second to the next she turned from cold, clammy flotsam into something unbearably hot.

With precision and patience in total opposition to the river's entropic chaos, she kicked and straightened out, looked ahead… and lost it.

Less than fifty yards ahead, the river just…disappeared.

Even through her struggles, she knew what that meant: *waterfall*.

Her body had already started a frantic scramble for the side when something punched the air from her belly and stopped her midstream. She grabbed on to it, expecting hard, wet bark, instead scraping canvas. Elias's pack, floating, caught.

Working on pure animal instinct, Leo forced her head under and searched the impenetrable depths. Pointless. She got her head up, wound a strap around her wrist, gasped, and dove under again.

That was when she found him, snagged, as if in a net. Which had saved him, probably. Saved both of them. But now she had to get him out of the water and to safety, without letting the current drag them to the falls.

Her prayers ramped up, changing from a vague, frantic scream to a looped, never-ending *no*. No. No freaking way. She pulled hard at Elias's arm. No response. She wouldn't have it. *Yank*. Wouldn't allow it. *Tear*. Wouldn't even consider the possibility.

Quick as a flash, she changed tack, grasped the backpack, gulped more air, dove back for him. Better to go down the waterfall than leave him here to drown, trapped in the water, alone. Blinded by the churning water, she didn't see the gun strap until it caught her around the throat, like a tentacle pulling her down.

On instinct, one hand reached for her knife, working hard not to struggle against the leather restraint and lose her air, finally got a hold of the handle, and nearly died of fright when something grasped her other wrist. Blade freed, she spun, ready to lash out—

Elias watched her, eyes blinking, straining to get out. Shit. Shit, she couldn't hold her breath much longer. How was he surviving this?

She thrust her knife into his outstretched hand and kicked up for the surface, gasping when she got there, lungs on fire, head about to explode. Without hesitation, she shook off her boot and yanked at the knife strapped to her ankle. Breath in, back down to where he sawed at the leather, his movements slow and awkward.

Together, they sliced through the strap in seconds and exploded up, hands clasped. Gasping, sputtering.

The current pulled, harder than before, trying to separate them, sink them, drag them down and then out, straight into the abyss beyond.

"Waterfa—" Retching, gasping for air, she dug her hand into his arm, lost her hold, slid, too fast—

He caught her, twisted his fingers around hers, and held on.

"Tree!" Elias choked on water, spat, and tried again. "Your right!"

She kicked up as high as she could, caught sight of a dark blur, approaching way too fast. Beyond it was maybe twenty feet to the drop and then nothing but sky.

One hand in his, she reached out with the other.

Three… The water pulled her left and down.

Two… She kicked, hard.

One… Strained so hard she pictured popping vertebrae.

The tree skimmed fast, too quick and too far to grab.

With a roar to rival the rapids', Elias dove in front of her, long body blocking her movement, shoving her to the right; her arm stretched, caught a branch…and held. She came to a brutal stop, thwacked into Elias, and waited for her body to break into pieces.

A second later, she opened her eyes to find him firmly lodged in the branches, eyes burning and fierce. Safe.

Okay, maybe not quite. With their combined weights, the tree could come loose from the bank and they'd be screwed, but they were *here*, not out there, hurtling toward whatever lay at the bottom of the waterfall.

She got her head up, hacked out the water she'd swallowed, and kept going. Against the elements and all odds, she plowed on, Elias beside her. Kicking, pulling at brittle, wet pine that could crumble at any moment, struggling, until her bare toes bashed into solid stone. It would've hurt if she hadn't been numb.

She found footing, slogged out, one slow step at a time, climbed up onto the ledge, with Elias right beside her, and finally crawled until she was free of the water's pull. Sucking in a scorching breath, she flopped onto a flat, wide boulder, boneless.

She moved her toes, did the same with her fingers and found her left hand caught. Her eyes rolled to the side, where her fingers were still entwined with Elias's, knotted like two ropes.

It would take more than a river to pry them apart. More than snowmelt and bullets. More than all of Alaska with its crumbling ice and raging waterfalls and fickle skies.

More than men with guns. More than bullets. More than death.

She squeezed, turned to look at him, and blinked.

He blinked back and she actually fucking smiled, the taste of blood in her mouth like victory.

They were together now, as solid as the rock beneath them, and nothing in the world would change that.

"Leo." With a lopsided grin, he dropped and rolled toward her, so close she felt the cold coming off him. "Made it."

With a weak laugh, she strained up and pressed her lips to his, surprised to find heat beyond the first wet touch. "Where'd you lose your pants?"

"Well, shit" came a voice from above. "Look at this."

———

Finally, Ash got a good look at his quarry.

While Deegan dropped to the wide rock on which the two lay beached, Ash stayed out of sight and watched from above, fascinated. And not the least bit disappointed.

They were wonderful, poignant in a way he couldn't explain. First of all, they'd been kissing when Deegan had so rudely interrupted. A true couple, then. Together. That twisted Ash's stomach up into knots. The nice-looking Black woman—the pilot, he surmised—lay half on her side, one hand entirely hidden within the huge bloke's grip. And blimey, what a specimen *he* was. Big-boned, muscular, raw in a wild sort of way.

"Hands up." Deegan stood a few feet from the couple, his rifle trained on one or the other, blustering blindingly ahead yet again. "Where's Campbell Turner?" Ash backed up another step. Could the man truly be so stupid? "Where's Turner? We want Turner."

Do we, though? Leaving Deegan to it, Ash went to his raft and rummaged amongst his things for fire-making supplies. The water was too loud to hear the exchange between the three of them, though he couldn't imagine they were making any headway. Loaded down with his things, he returned to the ledge. "Shall I light a fire?"

They looked at him, the man's brow tight with distrust, the woman obviously calculating, and then Deegan, wide-eyed and clueless. Where on earth did they find this man? "One of them is bleeding, Deegan." He eyed them and pointed his chin at a stain on the rocks. "Appears they both are."

The woman put a hand on the rocky incline and pushed, only to collapse onto her arse, shaking and oozing blood all over the place. From her head, her mouth. The man was doing more of the same. They were a mess.

And yet, still alive.

He breathed deep. "They can hardly move. They'll die of exposure. How does that help us? Hm? Ever questioned someone as they freeze to death?" Unsurprisingly, Deegan didn't reply. With a sigh, Ash piled his supplies within view of the couple: a Mylar blanket, his sleeping bag, some clothing. He smiled, shaking his head. "Shoot either one and you lose your edge." A glance at Deegan showed irritation on the man's face. Of course he'd be annoyed by Ash showing him up in front of the enemy. But it was time to stop blundering around and finish this job. Even if their goals were wildly different. "Have you called in your team for an extraction?" When Deegan shook his head, Ash cast his eyes to the sky. "If they've repaired the helicopter, of course." He suppressed his smile and turned to the couple. His eyes flicked between them. "You." He lowered his head to the woman. "Are one hell of a pilot."

Deegan turned to look at her as if he hadn't understood this.

"Aside from that, I know nothing about you. And you…" He gave the giant an eager smile. "Where on earth did you come from?"

Neither answered.

"Well, the good thing is that we've got time. Haven't we, Deegan?" Arms full of life-saving supplies, Ash jumped down to their level with a smile. "Not sure the same can be said for you two unless we get you warm."

Leo met Elias's eye. He didn't blink or nod, didn't do a damn thing but look at her. It was all she needed. They'd have one chance to get out of this.

She reached for the knife strapped at her ankle. Elias pushed up to all fours with a growl.

The big blond man approached, leading with his rifle.

Her knife wasn't there. Shit. Shit! It was lost at the bottom of the river.

She arched, straining behind her for her last remaining blade, and leapt. While she sprang, she heard a scuffle, felt the air change as the big blond man fell. Deegan, the other one had called him. That one—the one whose black hair and tawny skin spoke of South Asian descent and whose accent sounded British—hadn't shared his own name. Her body slithered forward, right arm whipping out, aiming for his Achilles tendon. And then stopped dead, smashed flat to the stone under his heel. Her numb hand pinned, fingers useless, and before she could do a thing, he was on her, his weight on her back, knee digging into her spine.

He planted a hand on her neck, leaned his weight forward, snatched up her blade, and held it to the side of her head at the opening to her ear. She went dead still. No breathing, no movement whatsoever but the tightly controlled clacking of her teeth.

"I don't want to kill you. Please don't leave me without a choice," he said just loud enough to be heard over the rushing river's roar. "Now put the rifle down, all right, mate?" He was talking to Elias, she realized. "Throw it in the river. We're better off without it."

Elias's eyes were trained on her attacker with a deadly watchfulness. She'd bet, judging from his expression, that if she didn't have a knife point literally inside her ear, the man would be dead.

Or maybe not. He was dangerous.

He sighed and leaned down to speak close to her face. "Tell him. Tell him to do what I ask."

Leo wanted to tell Elias not to give in, to yell at him to fight until the very last minute, not to give up, not to worry about her—she probably wouldn't feel a thing—but she was afraid to move her mouth. And God, though it was tough to admit, she really didn't *want* to be stabbed in the ear.

"Good," the man said before Elias had even begun to move. As if he'd read his opponent and already knew it was a done deal. "Good lad," he said with a breathless half laugh that made her sick to her stomach. "You two…" Another chuckle, this one weirdly affectionate. Like they were all friends here. Like they were just a few pals meeting up for a pint after a rough rugby match. "You two have run Deegan's entire team ragged. Right, Deegan?"

She opened her eyes and focused through the animal fear on Elias tossing the rifle into the water, his hands going up just before the blond man rose and shoved him to his knees. "You're dead," he snarled, one hand on Elias's collar, the other gearing up to punch him.

"Deegan," the dark-haired one warned. "The client won't be happy." The weight on her back shifted and Leo shut her eyes hard. *No, please.* Something rustled—possibly from his pocket—he jostled her and yanked first one arm, then the other behind her back, put something around her wrists, and pulled tight. Though she felt nothing, she could only assume it was plastic cuffs. "Here. Restrain the giant."

He threw one at the other man, Deegan, who sucked in an angry-sounding breath, shaking his head, then grabbed the handcuffs and roughly put them on Elias.

"Wasn't hard, now, was it?" The man with the British accent was all friendly bonhomie. Leo'd never heard anything creepier in her life. He backed off of her entirely and stood up. "Now let's get you warmed up. We've got lots to talk about."

He smiled at Leo. Her teeth chattered loudly in response.

Behind his back, the other man hauled off and punched Elias in the face.

Which was the wrong thing to do.

Every cell in Elias's body was throbbing—from pain, cold, fear. He couldn't tell anymore. Didn't fucking matter anyway.

The guy's punch snapped him out of his stupor and made him mad—as hell.

These were bad men. The shit they'd do to them—to Leo—didn't bear thinking about.

Elias would do anything to get her away. He'd take twelve more hits to the head, he'd jump into the falls, cut off his own fucking hand. Head roaring with the sound of rage and rushing water, he bent and used it like a battering ram, head-butting the big blond asshole in the solar plexus with every ounce of strength he had. The guy fell and Elias kicked. Again. Again, his body heating with the movement, nothing in his brain but pain—his, the other guy's. It didn't fucking matter. Nothing mattered but getting out.

Survival.

The man rolled, and Elias went after him. Kicked. Another kick. He needed to get these cuffs off. Needed to pummel him with his bare hands.

"Elias!" Leo screamed. "Behind you!"

Halfway through his turn, he dipped, got slammed with what felt like a sledgehammer to the head, and went down.

"Idiots!" Ash was angry. He'd had enough of Deegan's stupidity. The big mystery man hadn't listened either. He'd thought, after all the giant's careful planning, that he at least would see reason. But no. Not a bit of it. And now there was blood everywhere, the men acting like beasts instead of civilized human beings.

He turned to find the woman on her knees, watching him, her stare the most threatening thing he'd seen in his life. Unease snaked down his spine. "I want to talk!" he bellowed at her. Hand shaking, he swiped his hair from his face and threw an arm behind him. "How is *that* talking?"

"Your friend…" She put one foot on the ground. "Hit…" With obvious difficulty, she pushed up to standing. "Him."

He could have knocked her over with a feather. And yet she wouldn't stop. Like the bloody Terminator, she kept coming.

"He did." Ash glanced at Deegan. "But he's not my friend."

Clearly unhappy with that response, she rushed him—no doubt slowed down by her dip in the frigid river. He sidestepped, slipped in behind her, wrapped his forearm around her neck, and pulled tight. "I don't want to kill you. Understand? It's not my objective. I want Turner. And I want what he has."

She shook with something that couldn't possibly be laughter. Cold, probably. "It's…not…here." Her teeth rattled. "Never… fucking…was." Another bout of shaking, so hard he felt it to his core. "No Turner. No virus."

He went still. "No virus?"

"It's not here."

"Where is it?" he asked, keeping his voice as level as possible.

This time, there was no doubt that she laughed. The sound was so incongruous, given the situation, that his unease turned into something else—something far deeper, more disquieting. Like fear, only colder. Had the virus been destroyed?

On the ground, one of the men moaned. He had no idea which of the two. He wasn't sure he cared. "Stop laughing," he said.

The shaking only got worse. He loosened his hold and let her drop to her arse. Shit. This was out of control.

He looked around, spotted his things, and went to get them. When he turned back, she was on her side, shuddering. No surprise. He was wet just from holding her, the cold already seeping through his clothes. She was soaked through.

"Deegan!" No response. No movement. All right. Well, that

simplified things. At least he wouldn't have to argue with the man. He felt for Deegan's pulse. It was there.

Sucking in a breath, he stood and reached for his bundle of zip ties. He'd need to do their legs. And then he'd make sure Deegan couldn't move either.

After that, he'd build a fire, find out the truth, and if needed, call for an evacuation. It was up to him now to end this.

Leo wasn't faking the cold. But she also wasn't lost to it yet.

When the man drew close, she'd prepared to kick him, but he was smart. He stayed to the side, behind her back.

The moment she realized what he intended to do, she writhed, frantic, but it was too late. He'd already cuffed her ankles together.

Something landed softly over her, making everything dark. A Mylar blanket. It rustled when she trembled. The creepiest thing, though—the part she'd never ever forget—was when he put his hand on her arm and patted her. *There, there*, the move said. *Stay calm. It'll all be fine.*

But it wasn't. Because this man, whoever the hell he was, wasn't keeping her warm because he cared about her. He was doing it because they couldn't question a corpse. Or torture one.

She listened for some sign of what was happening, but the roar of the falls overwhelmed every sound.

Swept up by urgency and something too close to hopelessness, she didn't wait another second. She half rolled, got the blanket off her face, and took a quick look around. No sign of the Brit. She strained and saw Elias on the ground, bleeding from his head, a couple feet from the man called Deegan.

A low, grim, animal sound burned its way from her guts, up and out, to be lost when it hit the air.

"Please, don't be dead. Better not be."

Or what?

She had no idea who she was muttering to. The Brit or Elias or God above. Didn't matter. She wouldn't accept it.

Like she wouldn't accept these fucking cuffs.

Pain shot through her as she crunched into a ball, bringing her legs to her chest.

"Leo!"

Breathing hard, she looked up and caught Elias's eye, flooded with relief.

"Go. Get loose and go."

Struggling hard to loop her arms over her bottom half, she shook her head, mouth tight, eyes wide open.

Something scuffed close by and she scrambled to cover her arms with the Mylar blanket as the man dropped back down to the rock beside them.

"You take your blanket off, love? Won't last long without heat." He'd just squatted beside her when Elias started thrashing, in the throes of what looked like a seizure.

"Elias," she yelled.

The man stood, eyes narrowed.

"Help him, for God's sake! Help him! Something's wrong!" Her chest felt close to exploding as she watched the man dip and examine Elias from a distance, caution no doubt keeping him from getting too close. Her rib cage couldn't possibly contain her breaths and screams and the wild beating of her heart. "Goddamn it… *Please*." The hysteria in her voice was real, though the man wouldn't care about that. She needed leverage. It came to her a split second later. "Help him. He's the only one who knows where the virus is."

With a grunt, the man dragged Elias to the ledge—no easy feat given how much bigger he was. Leo strained to watch as he wedged him against the rise, hopped easily up and then hauled from above, no doubt scraping him in the process. It wasn't until Elias was up and facing the river, that she caught sight of his face.

Though he shook hard, his eyes were clear and cognizant and staring straight at her. Holy shit, he was faking it.

He closed his eyes once, and with that move gave her all the assurance she needed. *I love you*, the look said. *Get us out of here.* And, finally—the biggie: *I trust you.*

Straining, she shoved hard and forced her hands past her ass to her legs before the men disappeared from view. She couldn't get her feet through with her ankles cuffed.

Where was the man taking Elias? He'd said something about a fire, which made sense, if he planned to question them. Couldn't build a fire down here, so he'd gone up, away from the wind and water, she guessed.

She craned her neck, giving her eyes a split second to take it all in—the twenty-foot slab of rock she was stranded on, with an unconscious Deegan. It was stained dark with blood in some places and slanted down to the river that danced on as if nothing had changed when really the world hung in the balance. *There.* Her eyes narrowed in on something. A bump in the rock face that rose up from where they lay—not sharp as a knife, but certainly caveman worthy. A tool was a tool. Inchworming the few feet to it took much too long. By the time she'd made it, she smelled smoke.

Already? The Brit would come back any second. Shit, shit, shit. Frantic, she lay flat on the rock, lifted her legs toward the protrusion in the rock face, and used it to saw at her bonds. A dozen times was all it took and her feet were free. Quickly, she drew one foot through her looped arms, then the other. Now the rock served to saw her hands. Done. Hands loose, she remained in a squat, spun in a circle, hoping that the man had left a weapon—her knife at the very least? Nothing.

Something moved in her peripheral vision. Deegan? She stared for a few seconds, braced herself, and moved slowly in his direction, pausing for a stunned second.

He, too, had been cuffed. She blinked in confusion. By his own teammate.

What the hell? Was there infighting on the other side? Different groups banding together?

It didn't matter. She had to get to Elias, get him loose, and get the hell out of here. Now.

But, first, she had to search Deegan.

Hesitating for no more than a second, she steeled herself and patted him down, starting high. On her second pass, she rolled him over, ran frozen fingers up under his thick parka, grossed out by the contact but still enjoying the body heat, and encountered something blocky and hard. A whimper escaped her—a sound of sublime relief or deepest despair. Not daring to hope, she grasped, fumbled, and pulled, blinking for a few shocked seconds before recognizing it for what it was: a satellite phone. The holy grail.

Call. Call now.

No, run first, hide, gather weapons, then come back for Elias. She glanced up at the sky.

Before reinforcements arrived.

CHAPTER 38

THE GIANT WAS STILL SHAKING, THOUGH HIS SKIN HAD LOST its blue tinge. Ash piled another sleeping bag on him and stood, casting a quick look round before stalking back toward the river's edge. He needed to get these two away before the evac team descended upon them. Not easily done with an unconscious eighteen-stone man in tow.

He was tired suddenly. To his very bones, in his marrow. Tired. So tired.

This had to end. He needed answers. He needed to get back to Chronos. He pushed himself to pick up the pace as he neared the big slab of rock.

Empty.

The woman was gone. And so was Deegan.

Shit. He wasn't even surprised. This whole thing was a mess. Every bit of the mission, every move out here. If they'd only let him come in alone. My God, all the lives that could have been saved.

Too late now.

Quickly, he pulled out the bloody Glock he'd found at the crash site, eyeing the rocks for a few quick seconds before following the two wet pairs of footprints south, toward the waterfall.

———

Leo picked her way along the river's edge for fifty yards, the phone gripped tightly in one hand. Unsteadily, she climbed over soggy logs, trudged around rocks and branches and other debris, getting as far as she could from those two men. But also from Elias.

Stumbling on the uneven shore, she slowed and took in her surroundings, already trying to figure out how she'd get to him. She'd work her way down along the water, then head back up into the woods and circle around to where that fire threw out smoke like a beacon. If she worked fast enough, she might even keep the element of surprise.

She struggled on for another twenty yards or so. Here, the riverbank steepened and she had no choice but to go up higher into the rocks, closer to the sound of rushing water. The falls were right here.

She'd left wet tracks on the stone surface behind her. If either of those men followed her, she'd be toast. Time to call. This was it—her one chance.

She shimmied around the last outcropping of boulders and leaned back, shocked by the water's spray from below, hitting her right in the face. In front of her was nothing but a twelve-foot slab of rock and then air. The waterfall they'd fought so hard to avoid.

A dead end.

My God. She'd jammed herself into a corner here. Craning her neck, she saw nothing but a sharp rock face above.

"This is fine," she muttered under her breath. "Everything's fine." Denial was the only thing keeping her upright.

She focused in on the phone, stared hard. She needed a number. Any number. Her finger hit 9 and stopped. No. Not 911. Who knew who they'd send? She didn't trust them. Anyone.

Eric Cooper. Friend, teammate. One of the guys she'd trusted with her life. She dialed his number, her fingers like ten thumbs, and waited. Nothing happened. Again. She tried again. Still nothing.

In the distance, something reverberated and though it was too far to hear, she knew with blood-curdling certainty that the helicopter was headed their way.

The phone dropped to the ground, too heavy for her numb hand.

Shit! She glanced around, then up at the smoke. It seemed thicker. A look back. No pursuit. Yet.

She fumbled the phone up, tried again…nothing. Okay. Another number. Von's. Her numb, trembling fingers hit the wrong number twice before she slowed.

Voicemail. The generic kind because Von would never leave a physical record of himself. Anywhere.

Shit, shit. Ans would be in Colorado by now, out of range, probably. She tried anyway. Nothing; more *fucking* voicemail.

She sobbed. Her people, her team—always there for each other—and she couldn't even get through.

Concentrate. Who else? Who could she trust?

The helo was louder, flying toward the river maybe? Or along it? The men must have locator beacons for reinforcements to be so near. When she tried to picture Elias and what was happening with him, desperation tried to hem her in. She shoved it back.

Call. Now. Then get Elias. No more messing around.

In that moment, unbidden, almost like a mirage in the desert, an image came to mind—her friend Angel, Ford's girlfriend, who'd recently opened a nonprofit. A kitchen where low-income families learned to cook together. Familia was the name of it.

Familia… The last six digits of the number spelled *Family*. She dialed, wincing at the helo's approach. It was loud enough now that she didn't just feel it in her bones, she actually heard it above the roar of the waterfall. Quite a feat, considering that the damn falls were *right there*. She pressed the phone tight enough to meld it to her ear, blocked her other ear, and listened. Was that ringing? No. Nothing. The line was dead.

With a growl, she pressed the buttons again.

"Familia, this is Abby."

"Ang—Sorry, Abby." She couldn't call her Angel. It was dangerous. Angel Smith had died as far as the world was concerned.

"Uh…you must have the wrong—"

"It's Leo! Listen…" God, where to begin? Angel was too far to help, but at least she could get a message out. "I can't get through to anyone else and…" Shit, would Angel even hear her over the thunderous racket? "They're closing in fast, but…" All she could do was give the information. Pass on what she knew. About Elias and the virus and… Crap, she couldn't think! Couldn't hear her own thoughts through the dull thud of pain and that *sound*!

What did she need to tell her? If they died here. Right now, what did Eric and Ford and the others need to know? "It's the virus." She sucked in a breath. Her head pounded from the noise and her own yelling. "Shit! They're coming. Listen, tell Eric. And Ford. Tell them all. There's something about the virus you need to know."

Boom!

A gunshot ripped through the air, the bullet shocking her with how near it was. What the hell? Where was that? She craned her neck to look up at the boulders behind her. Who was that?

Phone tight in her shoulder, she yelled, "Ford was right about the virus. It's deadly. But it can also cure cancer. The world needs it. It's a miracle cure, but they want to use it to kill people and… They have it, Angel. They just don't know it. It's in the company's… Angel? Angel?"

Another crack, closer this time, startled her into dropping the phone. She reached for it and stopped halfway.

"Who were you talking to, *matey*?" the big blond guy asked in a terrible Cockney accent, one hand on the phone, the other a rifle to his shoulder. "Never mind. I'll just call back."

She reached for the phone, but it was too late. The rifle was already swinging for her head.

Not again was her last cognizant thought before the lights went out.

Ash got off a shot just as Deegan disappeared around a group of rocks. By his estimation he had two shots left. But it didn't matter. He was too late, with the evac team rushing in to the rescue and now this. Deegan had the rifle. And wasn't one to ask questions first. He was the *take no prisoners* type. The bloke who'd follow a mission to the letter, never thinking that maybe they'd been after the wrong man all along, working for the wrong people, selling their souls for the wrong reasons. He had to stop him. Had to stop the mayhem.

Just as he set off again, something shifted behind him.

He turned and came face-to-face with the giant.

Just wonderful.

———————

Exploding into motion, Elias dropped to the river's rocky edge.

Anger made him rabid, more beast than man, his conscious mind gone, devoured by the need to kill. He didn't feel a damn thing—not the pull in his side or the throbbing in his head, not the cold or the rocks under his feet. He couldn't feel where the cuffs' plastic had melted against his wrists from the heat of the fire. He didn't let fear touch him either, though it had been there seconds earlier, as he'd watched the dark-haired man shoot at Leo.

All he knew as he attacked was rage. Sharp, piercing, hot enough to burn it all down.

He punched the asshole's face, crunching bone, but that wasn't enough. He wanted to grind it to a powder. Killing the man wouldn't suffice. He needed to obliterate him, dismantle him into his smallest possible pieces, until there was nothing left but a smudge.

"Stop!" the man yelled, backing up a step, Glock up, arms steady. "I'm on your team, I'm with you."

Was that Leo's gun? "Nobody's with me."

The man's eyes flicked to the side. "The woman appears to be."

"She's it." His nostrils flared with emotion. "If you've killed her, then I'll—"

"Who are you?"

"Who the fuck wants to know?" Elias circled left, the gun trained on him every second of the way.

"An interested party."

Elias narrowed his eyes. "Interested?"

"I'm not with them."

"Bullshit."

"Look, mate, I'm not with Chronos. I'm intelligence. I know about the virus. I know what it can do. I've been after this thing for—"

Fury bubbled up.

"You shot her."

"I didn't. No. No, I shot at Deegan, not your..." The man held the weapon to the side, loose in one hand. "I didn't aim for her. I swear on my...my daughter's—"

Elias pounced.

The guy was quick. Without hesitation, he kicked low, just missed Elias's knee, and shot back up, delivering a quick uppercut to his chin. Strong, too.

Elias's head snapped back, he saw stars...and, above, the helicopter.

Fucking helicopter.

Another shot rang out—not from the man this time. From above?

Elias shook his head to clear it, noting in a distant sort of way that they'd moved downriver, toward the falls' endless bellowing. They weren't yards away from the fucking thing—they were almost *on* it. Leo had disappeared. Where? Around the next bend? She couldn't have fallen in. She couldn't be dead.

Head down, eyes steady, he eased to one side, circling the man, spinning on his own axis, putting his back downstream.

"I'm not with them," the man said. "Let me help you." The man's eyes shifted. "He's still there. Deegan. We need to take him down, together."

Elias was slow, exhausted, and hurt, waterlogged, cold. His eyes couldn't seem to focus on the guy, but he could damage him. He could tear him apart, maybe throw him in the river. And then he'd move on to the next obstacle between him and Leo. That was it. All that mattered. One down. Another to go.

He attacked. The man swung wide, and Elias dipped, sunk his fist into hard solar plexus. His knuckles hurt almost pleasurably.

This time when the man kicked, he was ready. He blocked it with his own leg, the pain of connecting shinbones electrifying. The shock resonated on the other man's face, there and gone. Instantly replaced with grim determination.

The man wasn't big, but he was fast. And he could take a hit. Ulnas collided, arms swung. Fists missed...and then got their targets with bone-crunching pain.

Elias couldn't feel it, wouldn't give himself the luxury. Quick swing, dip, lunge to the side. The man grabbed his hand and twisted. Elias wrenched away and sent an elbow up, curled, came back with a roundhouse to the side of his head. The man lunged to one side, Elias to the other, out of breath, his throat raw, chest heavy and tight, but driven by this hunger to hurt. This rage.

A thrust, a parry, and they'd rounded the last outcropping of rocks before the falls hit them with spray and sound.

"Elias!"

Where was that coming from? He shook his head to clear it. That definitely wasn't Leo's voice. He twisted. She was on the ground in a crumpled heap, just a few feet from the edge. Deegan stood over her.

"Give us a shot!" the voice yelled again from above.

A shot?

He wanted to glance up but didn't dare look away from the two men, one to his left and slightly behind, the other upriver, on his right. Both were armed. He didn't stand a chance.

"They yours?" the smaller, dark-haired man with the English accent yelled above the din, his eyes flicking up at the aircraft, then back down again.

"Aren't they yours?" His head swam, his vision dark at the edges.

"No." The man looked at something over Elias's shoulder. "Behind you."

Before he even turned, he knew it was too late.

The other guy—the big blond one—kicked his feet out from under him, sending him down, knees connecting hard, then palms sliding on wet stone, legs dangling in thin air, hands grasping at the slippery rock. He slid slowly, then fast, his feet finding no purchase, the water splashing him from below.

His fingers dug in hard. His body stopped moving. He looked up.

The blond man swung a rifle up over his shoulder like a baseball bat.

On the downswing, Elias tightened every muscle in his body, preparing for the end.

———

Ash shot Deegan through the head, then lowered the gun and double-tapped him in the heart. The man's body took a slow tumble into the falls. His biggest regret, now that his hand had been forced, was that he hadn't killed the idiot days ago. He didn't bother asking any of those fickle gods why they'd save this man's life and take his little girl's. Questions like that led to nothing but pain. No such thing as fairness in this world.

Someone shot at him from the helicopter. Wonderful. That would complicate things.

Without waiting for the body to topple, he ducked, rushed

to the edge and dropped to his knees, reaching with both hands. "You've got a foothold on the left. It's a reach," he yelled. But if anyone could make it, it was this man.

Pulse hammering, he watched as the giant swung just a bit left… His bare foot caught the ledge, slipped, and then held.

Ash let out a long, slow breath.

"Come on. You've got it." He didn't look at the aircraft, though he wondered why its occupants had stopped shooting. The man's foot found purchase and he was up, one hand in Ash's, climbing fast and hard until he stood, towering over him.

"Told you I'm not your enemy."

"Who are you?"

"Can't tell you that, mate."

The man moved aside and another shot cracked a bloody centimeter from Ash's foot. Ducking, he spun, sought cover, and eyed the aircraft. They weren't shooting at the giant, he realized, but him.

He crouched behind the outcropping of rock, hoping his proximity to the woman would keep them from firing at him again.

"I'd better be going," he said, leaning to the side with a quick look down. Ignoring his distaste at the idea of following Deegan's corpse, he noted the pool at the base of the falls, white with froth. Possibly deep, then again, maybe not. If he jumped far enough out, he'd just make it. "That's your team up there. Not mine," he called, watching the giant's face go through a series of expressions—from that adrenaline-crazed look to indecision and finally some kind of understanding. "Tell them to stop."

After a moment, the man waved his arms at the helicopter.

Just the distraction Ash needed. He stood and moved a few meters back, peripherally noting that the woman on the ground was moving again. A tiny spark of that old, untrustworthy hope returned. "You're Elias?" he yelled, to which the giant finally nodded.

"I'm Ash."

"Okay."

Before the man finished the word, Ash was off, bypassing him with a grin. "See you around, mate!" he bellowed as he threw himself off the cliff and into the water's roaring embrace.

———————

For two seconds, Elias stared, stunned, as the man disappeared into the waterfall.

A moment later, his instincts kicked in. Not trusting that the people in the aircraft were his, he turned and raced back for Leo; diving, he wrapped her up in his body and rolled against the ledge—the only cover he could find—expecting to be riddled with bullets in the process.

Nothing. No shots fired. No sound but the never-ending pounding of water to stone. In his brain echoed the man's last words—*See you around, mate*—said like some fucking James Bond.

"Elias!"

Who the hell was that, calling from above as if he knew him? He ignored the voice, wrapped his arms around Leo as carefully as he could and put his lips to her ear. "Leo," he whispered through his raw throat. "Sweetheart. I'm here. I'm here." She stirred, though her eyes didn't open. Both of them shook from the wet and the cold.

The helo hovered low, its shadow darkening the entire slab of rock. The shadow chilled him almost as much as the wind from the rotors.

There was no way out. Well, they could take to the water like the Bond dude, but at this point, neither would survive.

He was flat out of energy.

"Elias. Elias Thorne." A man dressed in khaki tactical gear rappelled to the ground above him, then jumped from the ledge to land a few feet away. "I'm Von Krainik. Leo's teammate," he yelled. "Come on, man. Let's get you guys to a doc."

Elias shook his head and refused to move. They'd have to get through him to touch Leo.

"Elias. Amka sent me."

"How'd you find us?"

The man nodded his head to where the two men had fallen a few minutes earlier—one a dead body, the other a freaking stuntman. "One of those guys activated a personal locator beacon a couple hours ago."

"There are more."

"They've been contained."

"How?"

Though he didn't actually smile, the glee on Krainik's deeply scarred face was the creepiest thing Elias had ever seen. Well, the second creepiest, after the British guy's maneuvers. "Your godmother led a rebellion. From what I heard, the old lady tore their shit up. Contained 'em before we ever arrived on the scene."

That would have made Elias happy if Leo weren't lying limp in his arms.

"There'll be more."

"We've been informed the team expected no backup. This was a one-and-done operation."

Do or die. Jesus.

And what the hell was all of this for? Money?

He didn't think that Ash guy had done it for the money. Whoever he was, there'd been a zealousness to him that didn't speak of profit and loss. "What about the one who just jumped? Said he's not with them."

"We'll go after him once we—"

Something occurred him and he strained to get up with Leo in his arms. "My dog! Someone needs to find my dog."

"Whoa, whoa, stand down, Thorne. We'll come back. We'll find him once we get you some medical care."

"No hospitals," Elias said, that old fear of being found still at the forefront. Worse, now, with Leo to take care of.

"No hospitals," the man repeated as his hands reached for Leo.

Elias ignored them, let desperation push him the rest of the way to standing, his limbs so heavy he could do nothing but brace and hold her. "I go where she goes."

"Understood. But you've got to let me send her up there. Come on, man. We'll get her help."

He couldn't release his hands, couldn't stop touching her, couldn't trust anyone. Not even one of her teammates.

And then his brain clicked back into place. "Von Krainik," he said, remembering what she'd said about this man with the scarred face and the dark, empty eyes. He looked like a psychopath. "What's your call sign?"

The man gave a short, approving nod. "Reaper."

Elias looked at Leo. "And hers?"

Von's jaw hardened. "Terminator." His eyes crinkled, turning his marred face into something from a nightmare. "Arnie when she's being a pain in the ass."

"Elias?" Leo croaked, squinting up at him.

Shocked at the sound of her voice, he looked down. "Leo. Sweetheart." He curled forward. "I'm here."

"Hey, Arnie." Von's voice was a deep, resonant bass, his accent pure Texas.

She turned to stare blearily up at the other man. "Von? That you?"

"Affirmative." Krainik's eyes met Elias's as he held out his arms. "May I?"

Something twisted in Elias's chest when he released her to Von's care, his gaze glued to Leo's the whole time.

"Hey, Elias?" What might have been a smile ghosted over her lips.

He leaned in. "Yeah, sweetheart?"

"Might wanna get some pants on." She broke out into a full-on grin as Von carried her away.

CHAPTER 39

THE SECOND THEY TOUCHED DOWN IN SCHINK'S STATION, LEO was surrounded by people.

Elias fought the hands touching him, tried to shove them aside when they wouldn't let him stay with her. He was too weak to fight them—and once he'd passed her off to the doctor, the Von guy stuck to him like a damn burr.

Which was good, if he truly was a grim reaper. Elias would rather he do his thing here than on Leo. Leo needed to make it out. He turned, swung his gaze in search of Bo, before remembering that she was still out there somewhere.

The pain of loss made him stumble. "Reaper," he called as the man forced him onto some kind of gurney.

Krainik waited, expressionless.

"Don't let her die."

"Won't." Von put his hand on Elias's shoulder. "And I'm headin' back out for your dog."

Elias gave a single nod, lay back on the gurney where they poked something into his vein, and passed out.

Amka didn't usually like strangers in her town, but these guys were okay. She was the one who'd called them after all.

They'd come in with their own damn medical team, which she sure appreciated. An attractive, fiftysomething ER doc and her big, hairy sidekick, who claimed to be a nurse but seemed more caveman than anything.

What followed was twenty-four hours of comings and goings,

blurred medical procedures—on her godson and Leo. New faces, old faces, and scenes of Schink's Station like something from a war zone.

Amka smiled as she hauled her ass up onto the cabin porch. Given that she was responsible for the worst destruction of property here, she couldn't be too pissed about it. Well, she could, but she could also enjoy the memory of smashing through the lodge's window. That would be a highlight she'd look back on fondly for the rest of her life.

A guy stepped out of the shadows at the door to the cabin. Tall, reddish hair, kinda looked like that *Outlander* guy, though without the pretty accent, and held a rifle in his hands like he knew how to use it. "Help you?" the man asked in a voice that had been run through a meat grinder. This guy had come in just a few hours ago. One of three groups to descend upon Schink's Station in the past few days.

She cocked her head. "What's wrong with your throat?"

His eyes widened before narrowing again. "Uh, people don't usually ask me that the first time we meet."

"I'm old. I'm allowed to ask nosy questions."

One side of his mouth kicked up. "You're Old Amka."

"And you are?"

He smiled full-on now and she almost had to step back at the movie-star wattage of the thing. "Dr. Ford Cooper."

"Doctor? Why aren't you in there with my godson, then?"

"Not that kind of doctor. I'm a glaciologist."

"Huh." Useless, then. She lifted her chin. "I wanna see him."

"He's asleep, but…"

"You keeping me out?"

The handsome man lifted his hands and stepped away from the door. "Nope."

She put her hand on the doorknob and turned. "What are you doing out here, exactly, Dr. Ford Cooper?"

"Guarding the cabin, ma'am."

"Worried about the guy who got away?"

He shrugged. "We prefer to err on the side of caution."

She lifted a brow and opened the door, then turned back. "Never told me what's wrong with your voice."

"Took some shrapnel in Afghanistan."

She shook her head and snuffled out a laugh. "Glaciologist my ass." She shut the door, turned to look at Elias, and let the tiniest bit of regret seep into her heart.

She hadn't done right by the boy. Hadn't gotten him out in time. He looked like hell. A black eye, cuts on his face, his cheeks sunken. From what that creepy-ass Von had told her—and Jack, her second-favorite pilot after Leo Eddowes—he and Leo had survived just about every possible danger this place could throw at them. And come out on top.

She smiled.

"Just gonna stand there staring?"

Elias's voice startled her.

"Shit, boy, don't sneak up on me like that."

"Sneak up?" He let out a pained-sounding laugh. "I'm stuck in bed. Pretty sure you were the one doing the sneaking, Amka."

She glanced around the cabin, exactly like the one she'd gone in just over a week ago to convince Leo to go look for him.

Her feet hurt now when she shuffled over to the chair and sank into it. Funny how she'd barely felt the pain in battle mode, but now her arthritis was back with a vengeance.

"How is she?" Elias asked, and for some reason, she knew exactly who he meant.

"In pain. Doc thinks it's a concussion. Too many hits to the head. She's observing her."

He nodded. "That's what they told me too."

Her eyes narrowed on his face. "You two…"

"What?"

"I don't know. You do more than run for your lives?"

"Yeah, Amka." He shut his eyes and sighed, deep and mournful. "We did a lot more than that."

"Pam the hot doc seems to think Leo'll pull through." She struggled out of the chair. Thing was too damn soft. "Think Dolores is salvageable?"

Elias cringed.

"Went out in a blaze of glory, huh?" She couldn't help a wave of pride at what her old plane had managed to do on her last flight.

"Yeah." He got a far-off look in his eye. "Should have seen her."

She cocked her head, wondering if he was thinking of the plane or the woman flying it. Little of both, she figured. For that one flight, they'd been one and the same.

She cleared the emotion from her throat. "So, remember the blond guy? One they called Deegan?"

He went stiff. "Yeah."

"Found his body washed up a few miles downriver from your... altercation. Smashed up good. Three bullets in him."

Elias paled and his face went blank, reminding her yet again that her godson hadn't signed up for this bullshit. He'd always been one of the good guys, not the bad.

"That other man killed him. Not you."

He opened his mouth and shut it again. "Any sign of him?"

"The spook? Vanished." She bent forward. "You think he's undercover MI6?"

"Hell if I know." He stared off at something. "Maybe he was one of the good ones. He saved my life after all."

She nodded in return and bent low. "*You're* the good guy here, Elias. Always have been. Always will be." Giving in to a rare urge to show physical affection, she kissed his cheek and whispered, "Proud of you, boy. Like your mom and dad always were. So damn proud."

He replied, tight-lipped, "Thanks, Amka."

"I love you, Elias." She nodded once, holding back the wave of emotion that tried to seep out, and left without looking at him again.

Outside, she turned to Dr. Ford Cooper. "He'll be going with you when this is done, I figure."

The fake *Outlander* guy made an *is that so* face and waited.

"Finally got something to live for."

CHAPTER 40

Elias spent all of his time in Leo's cabin, sitting in the big armchair by her bed, waiting for her to wake up.

The few times she woke, she called his name and he was there to hold her hand, to touch her, even if she was so out of it on pain-killers that she probably wouldn't remember the next time she awakened.

People came and went on a regular basis and it became quickly apparent that her teammates really did care about her. Seeing that level of support and trust made his heart hurt in a way he couldn't really explain.

They'd been back for close to forty-eight hours when Von knocked on the door. "Having a meeting. Hoped you'd join us."

Elias didn't move. "Not leaving her."

"I get that." Von gave a slow nod. "Pretty sure we need you there."

"What about her? Shouldn't she be there?"

"It's why we need you." Von stared him down with those near-black eyes. "Come on. Pam says you need some air."

After a long look at Leo, Elias finally shoved out of the chair.

The lodge was crowded. Filled with Leo's teammates and the folks of Schink's Station, with the exception of the wounded. A sheet of plastic closed off the back half of the space, where Amka had driven through the window apparently. He could almost laugh at that image.

Almost.

He liked what he'd seen so far of these men and women. He liked the hyperserious glaciologist who'd recently flown in, and his girlfriend who made food, apparently 24/7. Her name was

Angel, which seemed unbelievably fitting. He liked the dude's older brother—Eric Cooper, the leader of the group. He liked Pam, the doc, and the doc's boyfriend, Jameson, who was even bigger and hairier than Elias. A redheaded Santa Claus with a laugh like a bulldozer.

And, weirdest of all, he liked Von the Reaper, who despite his grim name had probably done more saving of lives than taking. Ans, the missing team member, had left the morning this whole thing started, headed for an abandoned mine in Colorado.

Then there was the pilot, Jack, a guy who'd come in with the other group but turned on them and, with Amka, had taken the town back and called in Leo's team.

In all this mess, the only people he couldn't stand were the ones who'd tried to kill Leo and him.

And there was only a handful left of those.

The issue now was what to do with them.

"Take 'em out back and shoot 'em," Amka yelled.

"Okay, hon. We're not doing that." Daisy put her hand over Amka's.

"They're a menace."

"They are, but we can't."

Amka grumbled but didn't disagree.

Elias watched the interaction between the Schink's Station people who'd chosen to attend this strange town hall and the outsiders who'd somehow seamlessly taken control of the place.

It was odd being in a room with so many people, voices, and opinions but all of them aware. In on it. On his side.

And they all knew his name.

"Elias." Eric Cooper broke through the chatter, quiet but sure. Everyone stopped speaking. "You're the expert here. What do you think?"

Expert? On what? The virus? Or running for his life?

He opened his mouth and shut it. "I'm no expert."

These guys were the experts on black ops and cover-ups. Less than ten hours after Von had led them back to Schink's Station, the rest of Leo's team had swooped in here, taken control, and made it look smooth and easy. Eric cocked his head. "What's next for you, then?"

That wasn't a question he could answer in front of this crowd, with all these eyes on him. Especially when the one face he most wanted to see—the one he cared about—wasn't here.

And that, right there, was his answer. "I make decisions with Leo."

A few brows rose, one head nodded. That was Von, who'd seen them on that riverbank. He more than anyone knew what Elias felt for Leo.

"Okay." Eric—the team leader—and his brother, Ford, exchanged a look and smiled. "We hold the prisoners, keep this here, in town. And wait for Leo to wake up." He looked around the room. "That work for everybody? You guys okay with keeping the town contained for a while?"

"Depends." Amka snorted. "Y'all gonna sit around or help us rebuild?"

"Now you're talking my language." Jameson, the big Santa Claus guy stood. "Where're the tools at?"

———

In less than a day, Von and Elias developed a weird sort of partnership—the kind that neither of them was used to. Von had his team and that was it. And Elias, well, he'd had himself. Until recently.

Which was why it surprised the hell out of him when Von volunteered to head out into the mountains with him that afternoon in search of Bo. Initially, Elias figured Von was there to babysit—either they didn't trust him not to take off, or they thought he physically couldn't handle it after the last week's adventures.

Adventures. Funny way to think about the lifetime he and Leo had spent running for their lives.

For five hours, they searched for Bo, taking breaks only so Elias could catch his breath—he'd broken a couple ribs after all, gotten shot, and had his head bashed in—and drink water.

But his legs still worked and his feet, though a mess, could handle the terrain now that he'd managed to borrow boots in his size from Jameson.

Shoulders bowed, back hurting, he trudged back into Schink's Station, Von at his side, straight into a rebuilding scene like he'd never imagined.

Leo's team was efficient, that was for sure. As they neared the lodge, a couple guys stopped cutting and hauling and hammering long enough to nod hello. Their eyes skipped quickly to Von and back before returning to work. Nobody mentioned the missing dog, which he appreciated. He'd find Bo. He wouldn't give up.

He focused on the work the people had done in the past few hours. Amazingly, they'd almost finished repairing the lodge's structure. All that was missing was the massive window, which they'd had to special order from Anchorage.

On the lodge's front porch, Von stalked to a cooler and grabbed a couple beers, throwing Elias one.

Just the sound of the tab popping did things to his insides. The smell reached his nose and his mouth watered. His first slug drained half the can. When he looked up, Von's cynical nonsmile cut into his deeply scarred face. For a second, Elias wondered if the man could smile at all with those injuries.

Von lifted his brows and grabbed a couple more beers, which he brought to a picnic table before sitting down.

"Doing okay?"

Elias had a feeling he wasn't talking about his physical injuries.

"Fine."

"You sure? You seem…" He tightened his lips. "Not fine."

Oh, good. Another guy who matched him in eloquence.

He opened his mouth to reply and then paused, let the air puff from his mouth, shut his eyes, listened to the sounds, took in the smell of fresh-cut wood, the bitter taste of beer on his tongue.

Slowly, he shook his head. "No, man. I'm…lost." His eyes opened and met Von's black ones. "What if she doesn't come out of it?"

"She will."

The other man's confidence did nothing to boost his own.

"What if she…" He swallowed and let the thing he'd been denying swim to the top. "What we went through?" He tried to smile, but it was pointless. "It was just five days, man. Five days. She might not even remember me when she gets up." He thumped his fist to chest. "People don't just…" *Find their soul mate in five days.* He couldn't say it out loud. This guy wouldn't get it. And, frankly, just thinking the words made him feel ridiculous.

"People?" Von took a swig and squinted out at the lake, the mountains, birds soaring above as if everything were perfectly normal. "Not sure you and Leo count as regular old…people." He shrugged. "Anything can happen if it's meant to be."

That sentiment shocked him, especially coming from a man who looked like emotion wasn't in his wheelhouse at all.

"I, uh, could use your help." Von cleared his throat, shifted, and leaned in. "Need you to tell me more about the virus. Exactly where it is. How we can get it."

Elias nodded, took a breath, and let it out, eyes hard on Von's. The man's gaze didn't waver.

"Turner destroyed every sample but one. That one, he hid in an old locked storage unit." Saying the words was liberating and guilt inducing. "Labeled XR-54. It's supposed to be cold viruses or something. Archived research and stuff. But that tube, the one he hid, is labeled as a variola sample." He grimaced. "Hidden way back in a freezer."

"That's smallpox."

"Yeah. Chronos isn't supposed to have smallpox at their facility. It's only housed in two places in the world. But there've been cases of it showing up randomly in labs. He said if they found this one, they'd treat it as a highly infectious pathogen." Elias swallowed and forced the words out, which was hard after keeping them in for so long. "He refused to destroy it. Said it held too much potential—on the cancer front. Had to keep one sample. He planned to go back one day and…"

Von watched him closely, intensely, as if memorizing every word.

"That's where I came in. He passed me the baton." He shut his eyes, remembering. "Passed it to others, too, but they're all dead. Every last one of them."

"You survived."

Elias opened his eyes and stared out, not seeing the water or the mountains or the lodge in the foreground. "Yeah. Yeah, I did."

Someone shouted and both he and Von turned. "There." Von lifted his chin to where Pam stood on the porch of Leo's cabin, waving her arms, with a huge grin. "Looks like Leo's awake."

―――――――――――――

Again Leo tried to get out of bed, and again Pam stopped her with a firm hand and a firmer smile.

"Just wait," the woman said. "He's coming."

A second later, the door flew open and a massive, handsome, bare-faced white man blew in. She looked past him for Elias.

When he didn't show up, she shot the doc an accusatory glare. "What kind of—"

"Leo."

She turned and stared. He was a massive monster of a man, the kind she'd definitely have looked at twice, with his sharply cut jaw—those squared-off indents bracketing his mouth—and freckles scattered over his nose.

She opened her mouth to ask him to clear the doorway for Elias when he said her name again and her heart stopped beating.

"Elias?" she croaked.

Her eyes took in the rest of him—a nose that looked carved from bedrock, hair with those sun-tinted curls that salons could never properly emulate. There was gray in there, too. Just enough to match those two sunburst sprays of creases around evergreen eyes.

There was love in those eyes right now. Tenderness. So much tenderness that she almost lost her shit right there and started crying.

"Yeah, Leo." He was at her side, reaching for her hands and then backing up, as if afraid he'd hurt her.

"You're fine," Pam said, which didn't make sense until Leo realized there were tubes hanging out of one of her arms. And her nose.

"Leo." He knelt by the bed, brought her hand to his mouth, and warmed it with his breath. "Leo."

It was apparently all he could say, which was fine, because every time was a new iteration, full of emotion, full of love.

"Yeah." She turned her hand, cupped his naked chin, caressed his beautiful bare skin, and nudged him up. "Hi."

"You weren't waking up and…I thought…" He dropped his face into his hands, shoulders heaving. When he lifted it up again, there were honest-to-God tear tracks on his cheeks. "I can't lose you."

"You won't lose me, Elias." Full of tenderness for this man, she leaned in. "And I can't lose you, either. I love you." She breathed in the wood and smoke of his hair. "I wouldn't trade those days with you for anything in the world."

He huffed out a disbelieving sound. "Right."

"I mean it."

"Good times, right?" he said, one brow up, a grin curving his ridiculously beautiful lips, a sparkle in those deep green eyes.

"The best." A laugh burst from her, quickly turning into a pained groan. "Crap, my head."

"Ah hell, sweetheart. I'm sorry."

"No. No, it feels good to laugh." She smiled and lost her breath when she met his gaze and got caught up in it. "It was worth it."

"Yeah." He nodded. "It was. Every second. I'd live through those five days again for you, Leo. Hell, I'd live it on a loop for the rest of my life if it was the only way I could be with you."

Emotion swelled up, filling her, warming her. "Same." She squeezed his hand and nodded. "Good thing we don't have to."

———————

"Where's Bo?" Leo asked over breakfast the next morning.

Elias met her eyes and looked away, feeling crushed yet again at the loss. "Haven't seen her."

"Since when?"

"Since I fell in the river."

She threw down her napkin, shoved her tray out of the way, and moved to get out of bed.

"Leo! You've had a concussion, you can't—"

"Can't?" She stopped him midsentence, her eyes huge and direct in that way she had. It pummeled him right in the solar plexus. "I *can*, Elias. You know that."

He shook his head and felt the beginnings of a smile on his lips. "You can. I just want you better."

"I'm better." She walked to her closet and pulled it open. "Let's go." Reaching in, she grabbed some clothes and started throwing them on.

He wasn't exactly sure how to handle her right now. On the one hand, she needed to get back in bed. On the other, this was Leo. The woman he loved. And he loved her because she wouldn't give up. Ever.

"Listen." He stood and walked over to where she was struggling into a pair of jeans, clearly not in any shape to go tromping through the woods. "Von's helping me. We're heading out there every day, looking for her."

"Well, I want to go."

He opened his mouth to tell her that she needed to stay in bed and then shut it. After a second, he asked, "I'm not gonna change your mind, am I?"

"No."

He nodded, watching as she started to throw more shit into a bag. "What are you doing now?"

"Packing."

"For what?"

"In case!" She backed up and looked around the room, wide-eyed. "Who are you and what have you done with Elias?"

"What are you talk—"

"The man I know and grew to love in an absurdly short time would never leave home unprepared." She stepped toward him, dropped the bag, and put a hand on his chest. "It's one of the things that attracted me to him."

"Preparedness?"

"Yeah. And competence." She smiled. "It's kinda my thing."

"Competence." He couldn't keep a disbelieving note from his voice.

Biting her lip, she nodded, and with a rush it occurred to him that this was Leo flirting under pretty normal circumstances. No running for their lives, no hanging from cliffs, no getting naked for body warmth. This, right here, was Leo being Leo. And he liked her.

A lot.

"Okay," he said, letting his own smile take over his face. The woman had managed to get his mind off his lost dog for a minute—while talking about his lost dog. She was a freaking miracle. "Tell me more."

"I have a better idea." She folded her arms over her chest and tilted her head, and he could feel the challenge coming off her. He couldn't wait to hear what she'd say next. "Take me out in the woods, Elias. We'll find your dog and then…" She leaned in and whispered in his ear. "I'll show you how much I love your competence."

———————

After two days of searching for Bo, Leo's head wasn't so bad and her body wasn't so rough, but her desire for Elias was off the charts. She'd never seen a man do things with such fluid ease.

They kept their searches close to home—his requirement—but they walked for hours—hers. She could tell he mostly avoided ridges and more dangerous areas, but at one point, they arrived at a stream and he wouldn't let her cross it.

"No jumping," he insisted. "Pam's rule."

She turned and gave him a look.

"You jump that, Leo, and I'm going home."

"Home?"

"To your cabin."

"Fine." She smiled. "We need a bridge."

"Fine." He smiled. And went and built her one.

The pile of sticks and branches looked wonky at first, but within fifteen minutes, he'd made something solid and wide enough to cross without any risk of falling in.

She fell a bit more in love with him right there. "That's the sexiest thing I've ever seen."

"Yeah?" He shook his head with a smile. "Taking you to Pam to get your head checked again."

Holding hands, they started up the slope on the other side at more of a meander than the speed-hiking they'd done out in the wild, calling for Bo every minute or so. They'd made it almost to the top when Leo heard something.

"What's that?"

Elias shook his head, sniffing for bears or any other creatures that could turn this into an unhappy adventure.

"There. That's a dog. That's barking." She was sure of it. She turned, faced west, so excited she stomped off in that direction.

And then came to a dead stop.

There was Bo, running towards them, a white streak in the late-afternoon light. Elias squatted just as the dog jumped into his arms and they both went rolling on the ground.

But Leo didn't take part in the festivities. She stared, instead, at the silhouette on the next ridge over. It was the time of day when the snow-covered ridges shone with sunlight, while the shadows moved up from the ground like ink seeping through paper. The figure stood where the two met—neither shadow nor light. She might have thought him a tree if he didn't lift his hand in a long, deliberate wave before turning away.

"Elias," Leo said, her low voice somehow cutting through the dog's happy whines.

He got up without hesitation and came to stand beside her. "That's him." They watched the figure get smaller. "Leaving."

She nodded and drew a shaky breath, then reached for Elias's hand, laughing when Bo nudged her instead with her wet nose. "Yeah, baby, we're here. You're back. We found each other." She hugged the dog and could have sworn the animal hugged her back. "We brought your stinky food. Yeah. Who wants some stinky food?"

When she rose, Elias looked at her, then squinted back out at the setting sun. "Got a feeling we'll be seeing him again."

"Great." Her eyes followed his progress as the last bit of silhouette melted into the horizon. "A wild card."

"I thought I was your wild card," he said, low and rough.

"You're my wild man." She leaned in, put one hand on his chest, the other on Bo's head, and tilted her head back for a kiss. "My highly competent wilderness man."

"I'll take it." He kissed her—not a light, happy thing, but a claiming, out here in his domain. When he drew back, she was light-headed and hot and ready for frankly anything. And what a miracle it was that she had this man by her side.

EPILOGUE

"WHAT ARE YOU NOT TELLING ME?" SHE SAT IN AN ARMCHAIR by the lodge's big fireplace with her guys and a few of the people from Schink's Station in a circle around her.

Eric and Ford exchanged looks. Von remained expressionless. When she craned her neck to look at Elias, at least he met her eye.

"Come on." Her eyes darted around. "What the hell?"

"First." Eric sat up straight. "We're working on next steps."

"Okay."

"We can't keep the prisoners here indefinitely."

"Sure we can," muttered Amka, earning a couple of smirks, a laugh, and one head shake from the rest of the room. Oh, Leo had heard about the old lady's exploits. Hell, if there was one thing she'd learned from this entire business, it was not to underestimate the elderly. In fact—she grinned at the woman with deep appreciation—quite the opposite. She knew exactly who she wanted to be when she grew up.

"What are your thoughts?" Leo asked.

"We've got—" Eric's eyes shifted to Elias, then back to her. "We want to hear yours first."

Her brows rose as she watched the byplay. Well, this was fun.

"Okay." She started to nod and stopped when she remembered how much that hurt. "My thoughts: enough secrets. I want to blow this thing wide-open." Elias's hand tightened on hers. "I know it's been done before, but there are more of us now. Hell, we've got a whole town. We call the media, call every freaking government agency. Hand the prisoners over in the most public way possible. So they can't just…disappear like everyone else. At worst, we're considered oddballs. This is viewed as some conspiracy theory. At best, we break it wide-open and people finally get the truth."

Eric nodded, clearly in agreement or at least satisfied with that response.

"First, though, we get the virus out."

"Right," said Eric. "It's hidden at Chronos headquarters."

"Do we need to get it out, though?" Jameson asked. "Can't we report that too?"

When Elias leaned in and spoke in his deep, slow way, everyone stopped to listen. "I could see them blowing the place up. Self-destructing to get rid of the evidence. Or taking it out first. We need someone there. In place."

"That's absurd." Daisy stood, shaking her head. "Is the CEO really that unbalanced? Does she have that much power?"

"That kind of order might not come from her," said Elias.

"This thing is huge," Leo agreed.

"And I don't care how much media you talk to, they'd kill us all," Elias responded.

Ford Cooper nodded in agreement. "They didn't hesitate to blow up an entire Antarctic research station. They'd make this look like an accident. Whole town destroyed by a gas leak."

"Don't got gas here," said Amka.

"Doesn't matter," Ford said. "They'll invent a goddamn pipeline."

"He's right." Elias sighed. "I don't know of every death, but there have been dozens at least. Law enforcement, the press..." He cleared his throat. "My family."

Leo squeezed his hand, showing him the fierceness of her love. "We'll do this right."

"Good." Ford exchanged a satisfied look with Angel.

Leo took in the circle of faces, grim determination on every one. Until she got to Eric—Ford's big brother, the team leader. Her friend.

"I think we've got an in," he said.

"An in?" Elias asked.

"Von's flying out tomorrow to accept a security job at Chronos Headquarters."

"Holy shit," breathed Leo. She looked at Von. "Are you—"

"In and out. That's it." One hundred percent Von. Expressionless, deeply certain. Willing to put his life on the line. Maybe because he didn't actually value it all that much.

"That leads me to the next order of business," Eric said.

Her eyes shot back to him, since his tone had changed. She waited, breath held.

"It's Ans."

She took in every face in the room and realized she was the only one waiting. This was what they weren't saying. "What? He's in Colorado, right? A dig at a mine? Another stupid Chronos project?"

"There was a cave-in." Von delivered the news. Fitting, given that he was the Reaper. "Ans is gone."

"No way." Leo rose from her chair with difficulty. "I'll get him out."

Beside her, Elias stood too.

"Don't try to stop me." She flashed a look his way, all bravado, since a breeze could knock her down right now.

"Hell no." He gave her one of his heart-crushing smiles. "I'm going with you."

Eric stood, as did Ford and Pam. "We all are."

"We're in this together, Leo." Elias dropped his smile, leaned in, and spoke for her ears only. "No matter what, we're in it together."

She squeezed his hand and nodded, knowing that nothing on earth could stop her with Elias Thorne by her side.

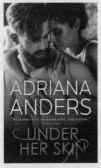
Old hag in need of live-in helper to abuse.
Nothing kinky.

UMA READ THE AD AGAIN.

Jesus. Was she really going to do this?

Yes. Yes, she was. She'd come all the way back to Virginia for the hope its free clinic offered, and if this was the only job she could get while she was in town, she should consider herself lucky to have found it. *Especially*, she thought with a wry smile, *since it's one for which I'm so qualified.*

The smile fell almost immediately. Everything was moving so fast. Not even in town for a day, and here she was, standing on a stranger's front porch. The house, thankfully, wasn't even close to the haunted manor she'd imagined. Then again, who knew what waited behind that chipped red door?

Taking a big, bolstering breath, Uma slipped the newspaper clipping back into her pocket and knocked.

There was a light *thunk* on the other side, followed by what sounded like footsteps, a scuffling, and then nothing. She waited, trying to hear more over the drone of a nearby lawn mower, and thought of all the reasons this was a horrible idea.

Abuse? *Abuse?* How could she possibly take this job in the shape she was in?

But as usual, the desperate reality of her situation pushed all arguments aside. Food, shelter, money. There was no arguing with necessity, even if this place felt off.

And the situation was perfect. No one could find her here. In theory. She was pretty sure her new employer wouldn't be phoning up any references or doing a background check. The woman must be desperate too. She'd practically hired Uma over the phone, for goodness' sake.

Someone should have answered by now.

Uma knocked again. Hard, her hand starting to tremble.

Something moved in her peripheral vision, startling Uma into a gasp. The curtain in the front window?

The cloth twitched a second time. The woman was watching. Making Uma wait out here, overdressed in the unseasonable heat, sweat gathering along her hairline. Okay, fine. She could see how it made sense to check out a stranger before letting her in. She'd give the lady a few more minutes to finish her perusal. If only she could get some air. Just a little air in this stifling heat.

When there was no response to her third knock, Uma panicked. According to the oversize watch on her arm, three minutes had passed. Three minutes spent standing on a porch, enduring the scrutiny of a self-proclaimed *abuser* who represented her only chance at a job. Not the auspicious beginning she had hoped for.

It was all so familiar too. Maybe not the exact circumstances, but the feelings she lived with on a daily basis—insecurity, worry, fear clawing at her chest, crowding her throat so each inhale was a struggle. Before they could overwhelm her, she shoved them away and walked down the rickety porch stairs and around to the side of the house, where she could gather herself unseen beneath the first-floor windows. She needed to *breathe*.

Uma took a shaky breath in, then out, another in, before biting into the meaty pad of her thumb. The ritual was safe, easy to sink back into, the shape of her teeth already worn into her hand. *Just a little while*, she thought. *Until I sort myself out, and then…* Then she had no idea what. She had nowhere to go, nothing left to aspire to.

One step at a time. That was her life now. No planning, no future.

She was vaguely aware that the lawn mower drew near, no longer background noise, buzzing close and echoing the beat of her heart. She'd have to push off this wall sooner or later, but the warm clapboard was solid against her back, and along with the sharp smell of freshly clipped grass, it kept her right here, present, in her body. A few more breaths and she'd move. Time to decide whether she'd head up to the house to give it another try or cut her losses and take off, find something else.

Yeah, right.

The problem was she wouldn't be cutting her losses by leaving—she'd be compounding them. How on earth could she go back on the road with the gas gauge on *E* and ten bucks to her name?

Strike that. After this morning's breakfast, she had only $6.54.

Uma sank down onto her haunches, the ground squelching under her heels, and squeezed her eyes shut so hard that black dots floated behind the lids.

She had nothing left—no home, no job, no way of making money, no skills but one…and Joey had destroyed any chance of pursuing her true livelihood when he'd smashed her cameras. Doing that, he'd destroyed *her*. Six months later, she was still trapped.

If she let herself feel it, there'd be no shortage of pain, inside and out. As usual, her wrist under the watch was raw, and her skin itched everywhere. It must be psychosomatic. It couldn't still itch after all this time, could it?

Visualizing his marks on her skin was enough to make her hyperventilate again. And the tightness was there, that constriction that had left her constantly out of breath these past several months. She'd thought the miles would clear the airways, but they hadn't.

And now she was back. Back in Virginia. Shallow breaths succeeded one another, pinching her nostrils and rasping noisily through her throat. Joey was close. Two hours away by car. Way too close for comfort. She swore she could feel him looking for her, closing in on her.

Something cold and wet swiped Uma's hand, snapping her back to the present. She opened her eyes with a start, only to come face-to-face with a *dog*. A black one with a tan face, floppy ears, and pretty brown eyes rimmed in black, like eyeliner. It smiled at her.

It was something else, that dog, with that sweet look on its face. Like it gave a crap. Weird. The expression was so basically human, it pulled back the tunnel vision and let some light seep in. The dog nudged her chest, hard, and pushed its way into her arms in a big, warm tackle-hug. Uma had no choice but to hug back.

Its cold nose against her neck shocked a giggle out of her. "Oh, all right. You got moves, dog."

"She does," said a deep voice from above.

Uma's head snapped back in surprise, sounding a dull *thunk* against the clapboard. Oh God. Where had *he* come from?

"She's a barnacle."

Uma nodded dully, throat clogged with fear. *Stop it*, she berated herself. *You've got to stop freaking out at every guy who says two words to you.* She tried for a friendly smile. It felt like a grimace.

The man just stood there, a few feet away, looking at her. She waited. He waited. He looked like a big, creepy yard worker or something. Tall. Really, *really* tall.

"Gorilla," he said.

"What?"

"My dog, Squeak. She's a guerrilla fighter. Thought about callin' her Shock 'n' Awe."

"Squeak?" She stared up at him, craning her neck with the effort. She was wrong before. To say he was tall was an understatement. The man blocked out the sun. With the light behind him, it was hard to see much, aside from the big, black beard covering half his face and the shaggy mane around it. His voice was deep, gravelly. *Burly.* It went with the hair and the lumberjack shirt. You didn't see guys like him where she came from.

"Wasn't her name originally. She earned it." When he talked, the words emerged as if they hurt, purling out one slow syllable at a time. As if being sociable was an effort. Yet, for some reason—for her—he was trying.

He waited, probably for her to say something in response, but she'd been running too long to be any good at repartee. She'd turned into more of a watch-and-wait kind of girl.

The man finally continued, tilting his chin toward the house she was leaning on. "You her next victim?"

Uma winced, embarrassed. "Guess so."

He lifted his brows in semi-surprise before turning to the side and stuffing his hands deep into the pockets of jeans that had seen better days. They were stained and ratty and littered with what looked like burn holes.

Backlit by the sun, his profile was interesting, despite the bushy lower half of his face. Or maybe because of it. He looked like something you'd see stamped into an ancient coin—hard and noble. The scene came easily into focus: clad in something stained and torn, wading into the thick of battle with his men, sword in hand, face smeared with enemy blood, and teeth bared in a primal war cry. Her hands came to life, itching for a camera.

She blinked and emerged to see him as he was: a filthy redneck with a rug on his face. He was intimidating, to say the least. Not the kind of guy she'd choose to work in *her* yard—not looking all roughed up like he did.

But this new phase of life was about taking back what Joey had stolen. It was about *courage*, and because this guy was so intimidating, Uma decided to face him head-on. Show no fear. Another rule for this new self that she was constantly reinventing: no more letting men intimidate her.

"Help me up?" she asked.

After a brief hesitation, he complied. His grasp was rough and solid, ridged with calluses in places and polished smooth in others. For a moment, after pulling her up to stand, he didn't let go of her hand. Instead, he turned it over and eyed the crescent her teeth had left behind.

She fought the urge to snatch it away.

He raised his brows but finally let her go without a word. Burning with the need to put some distance between them, she took a hurried step back.

"Thanks," she said as he squatted down to scratch Squeak roughly under the chin. The dog's eyes closed in ecstasy.

Forcing herself to steady her nerves, Uma caught his gaze and held it. He was even scarier without the sun behind him, skin marred by a shiny, white scar along his hairline and a dark bruise on a cheek already peppered with errant beard hairs. His nose was crooked and thick, no doubt broken in a barroom brawl or something equally disreputable. She envisioned him in a smoky basement, duking it out for some seedy underground boxing title. Carved squint lines surrounded eyes that were a cool blue.

Or…*oh*. No. She realized with a start that his left eye was blue and the right was dark gold. She was instantly thrown off-kilter. Which one was she supposed to focus on? She blinked and turned aside, uncomfortable with the way he so effortlessly unsettled her.

"I've…" he rumbled, coming up out of the squat to tower over her again. She waited for him to continue.

"You've...?" she finally asked after the silence had stretched too long. She wondered if she was as off-putting to him as he was to her.

"Ive. It's my name. Short for Ivan."

"Oh. I'm Uma." She gave him her real name without thinking. "You mow the lawn here?"

"You could say that." His eyes crinkled. What little she could see of his mouth turned up into a surprisingly warm smile. "Figure I might as well mow her lawn while I'm doin' mine."

She looked at the house behind him. "*That's* your place?"

Her surprise must have been obvious, but he didn't react, just gave a single, brief nod.

"Wow. Nice." The house was nice. *Really nice.* Incongruously... civilized. He looked like the kind of guy you'd find chopping wood by his cabin in the boondocks, not maintaining the lawn of his lovely old farmhouse.

It was straight out of *Southern Living*, nicer than some of the places she'd photographed.

The caricature she'd formed in her head of this man melted partially away to reveal something a little softer, less defined. It didn't jibe inside of her, but she'd been running on stereotypes and first impressions and messed-up *wrong* impressions for so long that her instincts clearly needed a reset. Another thing to add to the growing list of upgrades for Uma 2.0.

He nodded, face serious, but she thought she could detect pride beneath the gruff exterior.

She caught sight of a bright-red tricycle in the drive beside a clunky Ford pickup. Kids. Probably a wife. Her perception shifted yet again, and he didn't seem half as scary as he had a moment before. Wow, she couldn't straighten her life out at all, and *this guy* seemed to have his shit together. So much for first impressions.

Uma briefly wondered what he'd look like without all that fur on his face.

She took in the house, the trike, the coziness of this sweet mountain town. A town so small that elderly ladies hired you right over the phone without even asking for references.

That reminded her of why she was here: the ad. *Maybe not such a sweet town after all.*

"Well, I'd better get to it." She kept her hands in her pockets, not wanting to risk another touch of his rough skin.

"Yeah. Don't wanna piss her off." Was that a joke?

She gave Squeak a quick pat on the head and turned away from man and dog. His voice stopped her after a couple of steps.

"Hey, Uma." It came out rough, and he cleared his throat. "You ever need a break, come on over and see us. Have a beer."

"Oh. Sure. Thanks." *Us*, he'd said. Yep, married.

She shot a last look at the house over his shoulder, thinking she might even be willing to marry a guy like that for such a great house. Oh well. Maybe she and his wife would become friends.

A friend. That might be nice.

When she got back to the porch, something had changed. Was the gap in the curtains a little wider? Was it possible the woman had witnessed her panic attack? Strike one against Uma if she had.

The lawn mower started up again somewhere behind the house.

Uma took a deep breath in, blew it out hard, made a fist, and pounded.

ACKNOWLEDGMENTS

Thank you to my family for bearing with me through the writing of this book—it's been a long, arduous journey. To Mary Altman, editor extraordinaire, thank you for taking these words and polishing them to a shine. You are the best. To Christa Soulé Désir, thank you for your thoughtful edits. It was a pleasure working with you. To the wonderful Sourcebooks copy editors and proofreaders and cover designers who have come together to make *Uncharted* into a beautiful, finished book, I am so grateful for all the work you do. It's a labor of love and I'm so lucky to be a part of this team.

To Kasey Lane, Alleyne Dickens, Amanda Bouchet, Tracey Livesay, Alexis Day, and Andie J. Christopher: I'm pretty sure I couldn't have written this book without you guys telling me to just keep going, push ahead, forge on… Kinda like Leo and Elias, right? I love my writer clan.

Arnaud, you're my real-life yeti. Je t'aime.

And thank you to my readers: This has been one hell of a journey. Glad you came along for the ride.

ABOUT THE AUTHOR

Adriana Anders is the award-winning author of romantic suspense and contemporary romance. Her debut, *Under Her Skin*, was a *Publishers Weekly* Best Book of 2017 and double recipient of the HOLT Medallion award. *Whiteout* was named a *BookPage* Best Book of the Year, an *Entertainment Weekly* Top 10 Romance, and an *OprahMag* Best Romance of 2020. Her books have received critical acclaim from *Booklist, Bustle, USA Today Happy Ever After, Book Riot, Romantic Times, Publishers Weekly,* and *Kirkus Reviews,* amongst other publications. Today, she resides with her husband and two children on the coast of France.